THE
PSALMIST

Also by James Lilliefors

The Leviathan Effect
Viral

JAMES LILLIEFORS

THE

PSALMIST

A BOWERS AND HUNTER MYSTERY

WITNESS
IMPULSE

An Imprint of HarperCollinsPublishers

THE PSALMIST. Copyright © 2014 by James Lilliefors. All rights reserved under International and Pan-American Copyright Conventions. By payment of the required fees, you have been granted the nonexclusive, nontransferable right to access and read the text of this e-book on screen. No part of this text may be reproduced, transmitted, downloaded, decompiled, reverse-engineered, or stored in or introduced into any information storage and retrieval system, in any form or by any means, whether electronic or mechanical, now known or hereinafter invented, without the express written permission of HarperCollins e-books.

EPub Edition July 2014 ISBN: 9780062349682
Print Edition ISBN: 9780062349699

10 9 8 7 6 5 4

To J, T & C

"I will turn the darkness before them into light, the rough places into level ground. These are the things I do."

—Isaiah 42:16

"There are some trees, Watson, which grow to a certain height and then suddenly develop some unsightly eccentricity. You will see it often in humans."

—Sherlock Holmes, "The Case of the Empty House," by Arthur Conan Doyle

Prologue

THEY SAY THAT nothing happens in Tidewater County during winter, besides the weather. Sometimes they're wrong. March 14, a Tuesday, was one of those times.

Luke Bowers opened his eyes to the sound of wind whistling through the bare trees and the soft pelt of icy rain on the bedroom windows. He blinked at the dull light in the gauzelike bedroom curtains and knew what people were thinking as they woke across Tidewater County that morning.

Bowers pulled on his robe and stepped into slippers, careful not to wake his wife Charlotte. He stopped at the rest room in the hall and then padded to the small space off the entryway, which they called the sitting room.

Within two minutes he heard a familiar clicking on the hardwood floorboards. The door squeaked open and the leathery snout of Sneakers, their mixed Lab, appeared—tentatively at first, as if he wasn't sure he was welcome. Then Luke said his name and Sneakers hurried in for a vigorous neck and head rub. Sated, the dog stretched out beside the antique rocker and lowered his chin to the floor, as if he, too, had come here for prayer and reflection. The two of them were silent for several minutes, although it wasn't a morning conducive to meditation. Gusts of wind rattled the shutters and windows, causing Sneakers to periodically lift his head and frown up at Luke. Once, when a particularly strong blast shook the house, the dog tilted his head and went into his drawn-out growl, a menacing sound that temporarily seemed to still the wind.

"Let's go see what we can do about that," Luke said.

Sneakers sat up alertly, his tail sliding back and forth across the wood as Luke shrugged on his overcoat. He opened the front door into a burst of freezing air, and the dog galloped out in the icy drizzle, then stepped gingerly into the yard. As he relieved himself, he watched Luke intently with his sad, pathetic eyes.

"I know," Luke told him. "You just can't take it personal." Sneakers was a rescue dog who'd come with his name but no explanation for it. Luke, too, had been adopted at an early age and never knew his real parents or the story behind his name; he felt a certain kinship with Sneakers.

Walking to the end of the driveway to retrieve the *Tidewater Times*, Luke realized that the pavement was a sheet of ice. Like a vaudevillian on banana peels, he lost traction under his right foot, then under his left, then his right again, nearly going down each time. He slid involuntarily along the slight incline before regaining his footing. "Jeez!" he muttered. He took tiny steps the rest of the way to the newspaper and then shuffled back to the house, as Sneakers watched from the porch.

The cold was on people's minds that morning in Tidewater County, as it had been for weeks. It was the greeting topic at the Main Street luncheon grills, at the post office, the harbor store, the pharmacy, the grocery: "Where's spring?" "Is this ever going to end?"

But it wasn't the cold that people would remember about March 14. It was something else. Something that had happened overnight.

AFTER BREWING A pot of coffee in the kitchen, Luke poured himself a cup, sat at the butcher block table and paged through the *Tidewater Times*, front to back, then folded it closed. Nothing to read, as usual. He poured himself a second cup, gazed out across the breezy grasslands behind their house as he sipped, watching the sunlight trying to emerge through clouds above the bay.

He had woken overnight again with an unsettled feeling—as if things in his life were out of order, although he couldn't put a finger on what exactly those things might be. In fact, all evidence pointed to the contrary: he was in fine health, happy in his marriage and in his work. But the feeling drifted in early in the morning sometimes and seemed to linger like an ache in his soul, a debilitating yearning with no clear object or origin, the sort of ailment that occasionally prompted congregants to come to *him* for advice, not imagining that he, too, might suffer from it. He could only counsel himself as he counseled them: accept the gifts of grace, have faith and patience, seek guidance in Scripture. On mornings that began this way, Luke often drove to the office early and worked on his sermon alone for an hour or so; by the time Aggie, his office manager and receptionist, arrived at nine-thirty, he was fine.

He washed out his coffee cup and loaded a new pot for Charlotte, who would be up at eight-thirty. His wife was a historian who worked at home, in an office nook beside the kitchen, which was only slightly larger than the sitting room. Two days a week she volunteered at the Humane Society, which was where she'd discovered and rescued Sneakers. Their house was an old captain's cottage, on the edge of a marshlands preserve, with a distant, windy view of the Chesapeake. It was too small for both of them to have offices, but they made room for each other.

Before leaving, Luke glanced in the bedroom and saw that Sneakers, whom he'd toweled down and given treats, was now asleep on the bed, the dog's chin resting contentedly on his pillow. Charlotte was turned away from the dull light slanting through the curtains. Luke admired her profile for a few seconds; she was the only woman he'd known who always looked elegant while sleeping.

As he stepped backward, a floorboard squeaked.

"Be productive," she whispered, without opening her eyes.

Luke smiled. He hadn't always made the best decisions in his life, but marrying Charlotte was one that he never regretted.

HE FOLLOWED BAY Drive past the American Legion hall and Tommy's Marina, where a corner of the parking lot was piled with crab traps. Summer afternoons this two-lane was bumper-to-bumper, tourists cruising the produce and fruit stands and the open-air seafood markets. But it all looked pretty desolate right now, the wind gusting sheets of dried snow across the fallow corn and soybean fields.

At the intersection of Bayfront Drive and Highway 22, he turned right toward the water, steering into a blast of wind that nearly blew his Ford Fusion into a gully. Then, ahead, through the leafless birch trees, he began to see the whitecaps of the Chesapeake and the great twin bridges in a suddenly brilliant glare of sunlight. Bayfront Drive dipped, cleared a small rise, and the old cedar-shingled church building and its giant majestic cross came into view—the building angled haphazardly, it always seemed, on a bluff above the bay as if it had fallen there from the sky.

Luke parked in the gravel lot beside the offices and ran to the door, ducking into the wind as he fumbled for his keys. It was always colder here on the bluff, without a tree break, the air stinging his lungs and watering his eyes.

He clicked the lights on and breathed the warmer air inside—an old, reassuring smell. No matter how many layers of clothing he wore, though, the cold seemed to get inside of him and stay in his lungs. He adjusted the thermostat, listening for a moment to the strange chorus of creaks the wind made on the wooden building. "If these walls could talk," people said. These walls *did* talk, every time the wind kicked up, although no one could understand what they were saying.

It had taken the congregation fifty-four years to outgrow this old building. But come next winter, a larger, more modern church would be constructed in its place. There were fervent disagreements about that, still—over size, cost, and location—although most congregants had finally agreed that a new church was needed.

The thermostat clicked and heat breathed through the vents. Luke opened the door to his office, set his knapsack on the desk. He walked down the long unlit corridor that connected the offices to the sanctuary, still feeling some of his early morning apprehension. He opened the choir door and peered in on the sanctuary: sunlight streamed through the second-story rear windows and lit the tall, east-facing stained glass, the dust motes resembling colored snowflakes. All places of worship were bridges to the eternal, he thought, and there was a stark, simple beauty to this place, particularly in the mornings, that could be awe-inspiring and rejuvenating.

He stood at the front of the sanctuary and looked up at the rafters and the second-story seating, where sunlight glazed the polished wood banisters. Then he let his eyes roam the rows of empty pews on the ground level.

That was when he saw her.

She was seated alone in a slant of sunlight toward the back of the sanctuary, off to the left in the next-to-last row—dark-haired, hunched forward, her elbows extended over the pew back. Her chin was lowered into her joined hands, as if she were praying; her eyes, it seemed, lifted to the altar cross.

"Hello?" Luke walked several steps toward her. She couldn't have come in to worship, he thought. He'd locked all the doors himself the night before. Or had he missed one? He felt his heart accelerating.

For a brief moment the sunlight seemed to form a wreath around the woman's face, an accidental magnificence. But as he drew closer, Luke realized that something was off, the woman's pose seemed theatrical, not how someone would actually pray in church. He even wondered for a moment if she might be a mannequin, something kids had left as a prank. Stuff like that happened here in the long off-season.

"Hello?" he said again, and stopped, seeing more clearly now.

The woman was real, certainly, but her eyes weren't right. From the front of the sanctuary she'd seemed to be worshiping, looking reverentially toward the altar cross. From here, he saw that her eyes, although open, were blanks, the corneas coated with film. They were eyes that couldn't see, that wouldn't see again.

IN TIDEWATER COUNTY, the Emergency Operations Center was based in the new Public Safety Complex, a huge block-shaped building of concrete, brick, and glass just inside the Tidewater city limits, which consolidated municipal, county, and state police departments, fire companies, EMS, district and circuit courts.

As a member of the county's Public Safety Advisory Committee, Luke had been among those who'd pushed for a centralized twenty-four-hour call center, now standard throughout the state. But this was the first time he'd actually had to use it himself.

"Nine-one-one, what's your emergency?"

"This is Luke Bowers," he said, seated now at his desk, his eyes absently scanning the parking lot and the distant whitecaps on the bay. "I've just found a woman in our church. She's not breathing."

He instantly recognized the throat-clearing sound on the other end.

"Pastor Bowers?"

"Hello, Mary."

"Hi, Pastor Bowers. Are you all right?"

"I'm fine."

It was Mary Escher, a single mother of three who still chided herself for thinking she had any business singing in choir two years ago.

"What is your location?"

"I'm at the church, Mary. Seven Bayfront."

He heard her typing. Then clearing her throat again.

"Does she appear to be visibly injured or impaired?"

"No, she appears to be dead."

He listened to her type some more, waiting, taking in his own sparsely furnished office—the pictures with Charlotte in Rome, in Kenya, and here, on the deck of a sailboat last summer, the evening sky the color of cotton candy.

Before going out to wait for the sheriff and state police investigators, Luke called Charlotte. It was eight-forty now and she was up, fixing breakfast, her classical music playing in the kitchen.

By the time Luke returned to the sanctuary to have another look, the light had changed a little, brightening the back of the room, and he saw things that he hadn't noticed at first.

The woman was older than he'd thought, probably in her thirties, and there was an exotic, slightly Asian or Hispanic cast to her features. She wore a dark leather jacket, buttoned against the cold.

Then he noticed her legs, which were splayed grotesquely out to the sides, dressed in dark stockings and expensive-looking black shoes.

Luke Bowers closed his eyes and prayed, for the woman and for the community. Then he went outside to wait for the police.

STANDING UNDER THE cedar-shingle overhang out of the wind, Luke studied the two entrances to the parking lot—one from the east, the other more or less from the north. Raising his collar, he began to walk in a wide arc around the offices, the parlor, and the church itself, looking for anything out of order or left behind, for shoe prints, signs of a struggle.

Deputy Sheriff Barry Stilfork arrived as Luke was returning to the front of the building, patrol lights spinning blue in the raw morning light.

Stilfork's breath frosted the air as he walked over, his legs stiff as stilts.

"Pastor."

"Barry."

Stilfork had irregular features—a very long nose, dark close-set eyes, a wide, slotlike mouth. Some of the locals affectionately—and some not so affectionately—called him "Beak."

As Luke was explaining what he'd found inside, Sheriff Calvert pulled up, skidding his Jeep at a hard angle in front of Stilfork's car, as if there was any cause for urgency. Before becoming a seminarian, Luke had worked as an EMT and as a paramedic; he'd been to plenty of scenes like this where there was nothing anyone could do.

The men greeted each other by title rather than name, the sheriff dressed in jeans and a flannel coat.

"Pastor."

"Sheriff."

"What've we got?"

"Nothing good, I'm afraid."

"Let's have a look."

Inside, the light had changed again. The woman cast a longer shadow across the pews, which resembled an arrow now, pointing, it seemed, to the altar.

"Who is she?" the sheriff asked.

"No idea. First I've seen her."

Calvert squinted at Bowers for a moment as if he wasn't sure whether to believe him. The three of them walked to the end of the pew and the sheriff nodded to Barry Stilfork. Stilfork left a trail of wet and muddy shoeprints across the wooden floor before placing his right hand on the woman's neck.

When the paramedics and crime scene techs arrived, Calvert gave instructions—although for the first time in years, this would not be the sheriff's case. Last spring, in a move many locals thought overdue, Tidewater County commissioners had voted to change the policy on homicides, making the Maryland State Police homicide unit the lead investigators. Calvert, a proud, thick-chested man who'd served as sheriff for seventeen years, had not responded well to the change.

Luke watched as the evidence techs photographed the church sanctuary and then began on the victim, the sheriff hovering and pointing. Calvert's face was like an optical illusion, Luke sometimes thought: at certain angles, it appeared rough and pock-marked, but when he turned slightly it seemed to smooth out and assume a distinguished veneer.

"Anything unusual happen here the last couple of days?" he asked as the two men stood out front.

"Not really. What did you have in mind?" Luke said.

"Haven't had any dealings with Robby Fallow or his boy lately, have you?"

"Pardon?"

He said it again, louder this time. Robby Fallow was a strange little man who owned the Ebb Tide Inn up on the highway—an old 1950, 1960s era motel closed more often these days than it was open. Fallow's grown son lived in one of the motel rooms. They'd both had minor run-ins with the law, but that'd been years ago.

"No," Luke said. "Why?"

The sheriff spat on the gravel, turned and looked out at the bare trees, shaking his head. Most investigators collected evidence and molded it into a theory, making sure they didn't focus on one suspect at the expense of others; Calvert's strategy often was to go at it the other way. It was the main reason commissioners had changed his status in county homicide cases.

Barry Stilfork took Bowers's statement in his patrol car, coughing incessantly as Luke talked, working phlegm from his throat.

Driving away, back up Bayfront toward his home and his wife, Luke Bowers passed an unmarked white Camry going the opposite way, and suspected that it was Amy Hunter, of the Maryland State Police homicide unit. He felt a small sense of relief that it was Hunter who would be running this investigation, not Sheriff Calvert.

Stilfork had asked most of the questions that Luke expected. But he'd left out a few as well. Luke thought about them as he drove home over a gentle roll of countryside, the rising sun glittering on patches of frozen snow out in the fields and in the white birch woods. One in particular. Something Beak had seen, and no doubt the sheriff had seen by now as well: what appeared to be a series of bloody numbers in the woman's cupped right hand, cut into her flesh like carvings on a pumpkin.

PART 1

A Certain Kind of Evil

"I am gone, like a shadow at evening."

—Psalm 109:23

Chapter 1

WHEN THE NEWS circulated Tuesday that something had happened overnight at Tidewater Methodist Church, curious citizens began making pilgrimages to see for themselves. All day, cars inched along the entrance drive and people stared at the strange old steepled building above the bay. Children rode their bicycles to the church after school, parking behind the crime tape, and imagined what might have happened inside.

There was nothing to see, of course—at least not after the body was wheeled away by the medical examiner shortly before 10:00 A.M.—but that didn't matter. Something sinister had infiltrated Tidewater County, and the people who lived here wanted to understand what it was.

For Luke Bowers, the police tape was a reminder that evil, too, worked in mysterious ways. Pastor Luke was in the good and evil business. His job was to help people find greater meaning in the ordinary march of their days. But his work had also taken him to some of the darker corners of the human soul. This, he sensed, would be one of them.

Because Luke had discovered the body, townspeople looked at him a little bit differently all of a sudden—as if he knew things they didn't, and could answer questions they couldn't. The sheriff, in particular, regarded him with a more suspicious eye. Luke had been responsible for bringing new things into Tidewater County—AA meetings and NA meetings, prison ministry; things not universally welcomed. A woman turning up dead in his church seemed, in the sheriff's estimation, simply a further extension of that trajectory.

On Tuesday the church offices had been meticulously combed for evidence and finally cleared early in the evening, although there was still black fingerprint powder on some of the surfaces. The sanctuary, parlor, and main entrance remained closed.

As Wednesday dawned in Tidewater, the yellow crime scene tape was still there, stretched among the trees and wooden barricades and across the front doors to the church, its stark message flapping in the wind: POLICE LINE DO NOT CROSS.

The tape seemed to divide the county into two places—one familiar, the other unknown, but both occupying the same space. It would stay divided, Luke suspected, until this seemingly inexplicable crime had been explained.

"PASTOR BOWERS?"

"Yes, Ag."

"Amy Hunter is here to see you?" Agnes Collins—Aggie—stood in his doorway, slender, prim, wearing a charcoal gray business suit, frowning at her schedule book. Only the hesitant cast of her pale eyes hinted at how brittle she was. "I don't see that she has an appointment. Would you like me to tell her you're on a conference call?"

Despite Pastor Bowers's open-door policy, Aggie felt it was her duty to be his buffer to the public, a holdover from her years as executive assistant to a D.C. attorney.

"No, that's all right." Luke rose behind his desk, banging his knee. "Ow!"

"Are you all right?"

"I'm okay," he said.

He smiled, recovering, as Amy Hunter walked in.

"Good morning, sir," she said. Aggie gently closed the door behind her. "Hope you don't mind."

"No. Please, have a seat."

Amy Hunter was young, though not quite as young as she looked. Her plain clothes—rumpled work shirt and khakis under a bulky green army jacket—were a contrast to those of Aggie Collins. Her dark, medium-length hair was wildly mussed from the wind, her cheeks pink with the cold.

Like many people in Tidewater County, Luke knew *about* Amy Hunter without actually knowing her. He'd heard the stories— that she had trained at the FBI Academy and worked her way up to sergeant with the state police homicide unit while in her mid- twenties; that she was able to look at a crime scene and see things other people didn't see—what was there, what was missing, what shouldn't be there. Over the winter, she'd solved a four-year-old cold case, earning regional attention and the contempt of the local Sheriff's Department.

"So, how are we doing, sir?"

"Other than the fact that our church has become a murder scene? Can't complain."

She showed a hint of smile, opening a manila folder on his desk. She was attractive, in a wholesome way, with attentive light brown eyes that seemed to Luke slightly too large for her face.

"I heard your sermon a few weeks ago. It was inspiring."

"Thanks," he said.

"I confess I don't go to church all that often. I'm a devout secularist. But I had family visiting."

"Ah." Amy Hunter made eye contact quickly. Luke sensed she wasn't comfortable with small talk. "Which sermon was it?"

"The crab chowder one?"

"Oh, yes. Matthew 5:13. Salt of the earth. Well," he said, "we'd love to have you again sometime."

Her eyes were back on the papers in her folder. "I have the transcript of your statement from yesterday," she said, "with Deputy Stilfork? I just have a couple of follow-ups."

"Sure."

"You said you checked the church doors and they were all locked at eight o'clock on Monday night. Is that correct? Five doors?"

"That's right. Two to the church, two to the offices, one to the parlor. Though they all use the same key."

"And how many people have keys? Other than yourself." A question the deputy had missed.

"Well, let's see, at least five," he said. And counted again. "Or six. The assistant pastor, financial secretary, office manager, director of music, youth director, and the sexton."

A single line creased her forehead.

"Custodian. Martha Cummings. We call her the sexton."

He waited as she jotted their names, her head tilted intently. "I might add," he said, "that this is an old building and I don't think anyone has a clue the last time the locks were changed. So there may be a few other keys floating around."

"They wouldn't have been turned in?"

"Not necessarily. We don't keep any gold bars or ancient relics here. It's a place of worship. It's possible someone made copies that were never collected."

She glanced back at her notes. "How about windows?"

Also something Stilfork hadn't asked.

"No. Martha said she checked them when she cleaned on Monday afternoon," he said—although, knowing Martha, he suspected she hadn't actually done so.

"She was here until what time?"

"She would've been finished by five."

"But there was a meeting in the parlor after five, wasn't there? An AA meeting?"

"That's correct. At six."

Hunter's gaze held, as if she expected him to say more. "Not everyone likes the idea of AA meetings at the church, I understand. Which is something you initiated?"

"Yes. NA meetings even less."

"And how do you feel about that?"

"Feel about it?" He saw that her steady eyes were waiting, alert like the cold morning. "I try not to. I was brought here to broaden the ministry, which we're doing. But I'm also respectful of tradition. I think we've struck a pretty good balance."

Hunter shuffled a sheet of paper to the top of the pile. "Agnes Collins supplied a list of church members yesterday. Two hundred and twenty-seven names. Is this a complete list?"

"Probably not," Luke said. "I mean, it's everyone who wants to be on it, I suppose."

"Some don't."

"No. Some people aren't joiners." He shrugged. "I guess they don't want to be part of any club that would have someone like them for a member."

"Right." Hunter showed her version of a smile again; two tiny brackets on either side of her mouth. "How about Robby Fallow?"

"Ah, Robby Fallow." Her eyebrows lifted curiously. "The sheriff asked me that, too," Luke explained. "He wanted to know if I'd had any dealings with Robby lately."

"Have you?"

"'Dealings'? No, not that I know of."

"Any reason to think he might've had anything to do with what happened?"

"No."

She nodded, wrote two words in the margin and underlined them. Luke squinted, trying to read what they were, but couldn't. The sheriff didn't like Fallow and was probably going to try to push the case in that direction.

"Now, you came in the church yesterday through the office entrance back here, and walked down the connecting hallway to the front of the sanctuary, as I understand it—entering through the choir door."

"Correct."

"And you found the woman at approximately seven forty-five." Luke nodded. "At first you thought she might be praying. You said she looked 'tranquil.'"

"No, I think the word I used was serene."

She frowned at her transcript. Beak evidently had written the wrong word. After the fact, probably, Luke suspected, as he was typing out the interview, unable to read his own writing. "Okay, similar idea," she said. "First impressions can be deceptive, though."

"Yes. They can." The image of the dead woman returned to him—although he realized after a moment that he wasn't recalling her face as he'd actually seen it, but her face from the dream that had awakened him that morning. "Close-up, it was different," he said. "I saw that her legs weren't right. They both looked broken."

"They were," Hunter said. "Left arm and several ribs, too."

"Really."

She nodded, her eyes steady—and, it seemed, suddenly much older than the rest of her. "That's not for public consumption yet," she said. "Someone did a real number on her. Beat her repeatedly. Postmortem. A lot of anger there. Do you know anyone who might've done something like that?"

"I don't."

"Anyone ever broken into the church before?"

"No. Other than some kids, a couple of summers ago."

"Ever had an issue with transients?"

"Transients. No." They shared a brief smile. On the ten o'clock news the night before, Sheriff Calvert had said the woman "might be a transient, we just don't know." Luke didn't think so; not unless transients had begun wearing Louis Vuitton and Ferragamo.

"Any idea what might've happened? Who might've been involved? Why she was brought here to the church?"

"No," he said, "on the last two."

"And on the first?"

"Well." Luke decided to tell her what he'd been thinking. "Whoever it was, he must've parked in front at the main entrance. Walked back around the offices and climbed in through the parlor window, which was probably left unlocked. Then he came back through the corridor to the entrance doors, unlocked them, and carried her into the sanctuary."

She nodded almost imperceptibly. "And why do you say that?"

"It's the only explanation that makes sense. I noticed there were shoe prints outside the parlor window. And what looked like three sets of the same, or similar, shoe prints in the hallway. But they were heavier going toward the sanctuary than going the other way, so he must've been carrying her."

"Yes. Very good," she said, casting her eyes back to her questions; Luke wondered if she had already figured this out or if he was telling her something.

"There aren't any security cameras or alarms in the sanctuary, or the entrance lobby?"

"No, just in the offices here." He pointed to the single camera mounted in a corner of the ceiling; he smiled at it, and waved. "Where the safe is, and where we keep our financial records. We've talked about getting them for the sanctuary and the parlor, but somehow it always ends up becoming a political issue."

"There's some disagreement within the congregation on the subject of growth, I understand," she said.

"Some, yes." She was waiting for him to say more. "There are those who don't want it. Some of the traditionalists are afraid that if we're not careful, we'll become a megachurch. And in a few years Joel Osteen will be hired as our pastor. It was a challenge just to get the video screens approved for the sanctuary."

"What happened yesterday wouldn't be related to that."

"To?"

"The disagreement over growth."

"No. I don't see how it could be."

"Okay." She looked back at her notes, about to wrap up, he could see. But then she surprised him. "The victim had several numbers cut into her right hand," she said. "You noticed that, correct?"

Luke blinked affirmatively.

"And I see here that Deputy Stilfork contacted you again late yesterday afternoon, at the instigation of the sheriff, and asked you about those numbers."

"He asked me about *numbers*. He didn't say anything about them being cut into her hand. He showed me three numbers written on note paper—three numbers and one letter, actually—and asked if I had any idea what they meant."

"And you said . . ."

"I said no."

"Do you remember what they were?"

"Sure. Five, one, i, and eight. I told him I had no idea."

She glanced back at the transcript. Luke liked the intensity in her eyes, the glints of what seemed like submerged wisdom. "But he asked you to speculate."

"Yeah, he asked me to tell him anything that came to mind. I told him maybe 'fifty-one I ate'?"

"Fifty-one I ate."

"Yeah. He asked me what that meant and I told him about the hot dog eating contest at Coney Island. Fifty-one, I told him, I think that's about how many hot dogs the winner used to eat each year."

"Okay."

"He asked me if I thought I was being funny. I said, no, evidently not."

"Actually, I think it's possible the third digit wasn't an i," Hunter said. She surprised him again, pulling an eight-by-ten photo from her folder and sliding it across the desk. It was an image of the dead woman's right hand, from the medical examiner's office in Baltimore. Cleaned, blown up. The flesh cut, the wounds like rivulets in the earth carved by ancient rivers.

"Want to give it some more thought?"

"Okay, I will." She pulled the photo back and closed her folder. Bowers scooted his chair, ready to stand, surprised that she had given him so many details; a trade-off of some kind, maybe.

"Oh, one other thing," she said. "Several fingerprints were found on the body. Did you touch her at all?"

"I felt for a pulse, yeah," he said. "On her neck."

"Anywhere else?"

"No. I mean, I may have touched her hand. I tried to read the numbers."

"But you couldn't."

"No."

Hunter nodded and stood. "All right. Thank you, sir," she said, and extended her hand. Her shake was what he expected: firm, though not aggressively so.

They said their goodbyes standing by the front door to the church offices. Aggie kept her head down, pretending not to listen. Hunter pulled a business card from a pocket of her army jacket and handed it to him.

"I know this is difficult and I appreciate your cooperation, Pastor Bowers. If you think of anything else, please call me."

"I will."

"We're going to solve this."

Luke nodded. It was a strange remark, although he liked how it sounded; and, for some reason, he believed her. For just a second before she left, her eyes looked like those of a young girl, full of the untested promises of life. That she could seem so wise and look so young was both engaging and a little mystifying.

Chapter 2

Minutes after the door to the church offices closed, Aggie Collins came in carrying a fresh cup of coffee for Luke in both hands. She swapped the new cup with the old, straightening his stapler and turning a page on his desk calendar.

"Thank you, Ag."

"My pleasure."

Luke was making notes for his Sunday sermon—starting again from scratch, exploring the idea that evil can find us anywhere, even in a church sanctuary; and when it does, how should we respond?—when he realized that Aggie was standing in the doorway with her steno pad.

"Come on in, if you'd like, Ag."

"Oh, thank you." She sighed and then quickly took a seat. "I just thought you'd like to go over your telephone messages."

"Sure." Luke closed his notebook.

"Was it a good meeting with Miss Hunter?"

He nodded, and then answered her real questions—What did she say? and, Do they know anything? Despite her proper appearance and presentation, Aggie was an avid and accomplished gossip.

"She didn't really say much," he said. "They don't know a lot at this point. No good leads yet."

"Mmm hmm." She lifted her chin. Aggie had been model-beautiful as a young woman, and now habitually raised a hand to cover her neck or jutted her chin at odd intervals, as if to hide the physical changes age had sculpted onto her face. She had been a full-time volunteer at the church for years before Luke hired her for a paid position.

What do *they know*? her silence seemed to ask.

"The perpetrator probably parked in front of the church, they're thinking," Luke explained. "He walked around to the parlor and entered through a window, walked back to the church entrance and opened the front door."

"Oh. And *carried* her in?"

"That's what it looks like."

"Hmm." She smoothed her skirt under her and then lowered her voice conspiratorially. "I know I shouldn't say this—but she seems awful young to be heading up the investigation."

"Yes, although I wouldn't let appearances fool you. She's quite sharp, actually."

"Oh, I'm sure. I just know the sheriff has some issues with her."

"Well," Luke said. "His real issue should be with the county, I would think. They're the ones who stripped him of his power."

Aggie nodded once. "I hear it's more than just that, though."

Luke tried to make his face blank, hoping the topic would go away.

"I was told he made a very inappropriate comment to her," Aggie said. "This was a couple of months ago. I can't repeat what it was."

"No, please don't."

"But she supposedly came right back and cut him off at the knees." Her face and ears reddened as his eyes met hers. "Or at least that's how it was described to me. Supposedly, he hasn't spoken to her since."

"Well, I imagine he'll have to now," Luke said. "Since she's heading the investigation."

Aggie responded by straightening her posture even more, which he hadn't thought possible. He did the opposite; he slumped back in his chair, getting comfortable, trying to imagine what Amy Hunter could have said to the sheriff that would have "cut him off at the knees."

"But anyway." Luke glanced at his sermon notebook. "Enough whisperings."

"Yes. I'm sorry." Aggie cleared her throat. Her veneer of efficiency had hardened since her husband's death some four years ago. Nearly everyone in Tidewater County knew he'd taken his life, but it was a subject no one mentioned. "You had eleven telephonic messages while you were in conference with Miss Hunter."

"Okay."

She went through them in order. Seven of the calls were congregation members, sending thoughts and prayers. Three were media.

"The television reporter from Channel 14 wanted to interview you on-camera this morning. Knowing how you feel about that, I informed him that you had several meetings and unfortunately would be unable to participate."

"Thanks."

"Also, the *Tidewater Times* called again. The reporter Nancy Bunting asked if you could comment on what the deceased woman looked like. Then the other reporter, Sandy Bunting, called and asked the same thing."

The local paper, the *Tidewater Times*, had been owned for several generations by the Bunting family. Nearly all of the staff members were Buntings or married to a Bunting.

"Sandy Bunting said she had heard reports the woman was unclothed at the time you discovered her."

"Reports?"

"Yes. I referred her to the police."

"Good, thank you."

"My pleasure," Aggie said. "I know you don't like being bothered by the media."

Luke smiled; he didn't mind talking to the media, but he often preferred not to talk on the record. Someday, he'd have to tell Aggie about that.

"And finally, Mr. Frank Nayak, Sr. called, from the Nayak Company? He just said to tell you that he thought you and he ought to have a chat."

"Really." Luke chuckled. "Since when?"

Agnes frowned at her notes. "Since nine forty-three, I guess. That was when he called."

He smiled. Sometimes, Aggie took his questions too literally.

"You know what, Ag?" he said. "I'll return the calls later. I think right now I'm going to go out and try to do something worthwhile with my day. How does that sound?"

"Oh," she said, squaring her shoulders. "That sounds just fine."

JACKSON PYNNE TOOK a long drink of carry-out coffee, then studied the headline on his screen, as if somehow it might have changed over the past forty-five seconds:

WOMAN'S BODY FOUND IN CHURCH.

Pynne gazed up at the traffic. He took another sip and looked again. Finally, he clicked the link.

His thoughts ricocheted wildly as he read and reread the brief news account that appeared.

Police are asking for the public's help to identify a woman whose body was found yesterday morning at Tidewater Methodist Church, 7 Bayfront Drive.

The Sheriff's Department reports that the church's head pastor discovered the woman when he arrived at work shortly after 7:30 A.M. The woman was reportedly seated in a pew inside the church sanctuary and looked at first to be praying. Police believe she had been dead for several hours.

Sheriff's Department spokeswoman Kirsten Sparks described the woman as Caucasian, between 30 and 40 years of age, with dark brown hair, brown eyes, 5' 6" inches tall, weighing 115 pounds. The woman had a small tattoo of a serpent on her left ankle.

Officials did not release the cause of death and would not speculate on why she was in the church. Sheriff Clay Calvert declined to discuss specific details of the case but said, "This is an active investigation and we're looking at several leads." Pastor Luke Bowers, who discovered the woman, was unavailable for comment.

The case is being investigated by the county's new Homicide Task Force, which includes members of the Sheriff's Department, Tidewater Police Department, and Maryland State Police. The task force is under the direction of State Police Sgt. Amy Hunter.

*Hunter yesterday referred all media inquiries to Sheriff's
Department spokeswoman Kirsten Sparks.*

Each time Pynne read the story, he got stuck in the same place:
"Caucasian"

But, of course, that might've just been a mistake.

He looked out at the highway and reached for his pack of Chesterfields. Either way, he knew that he had to go back. He could think of no other option at this point. He tapped out a cigarette and pushed it between his lips, struck a match and inhaled. And then, just briefly, he felt better.

Chapter 3

THE EBB TIDE Inn had the faded look of an earlier time. Once, Amy Hunter imagined, it had been an inviting oasis beside the highway. Twelve clean rooms, affordable family rates, chairs beside each door, a small aqua-colored swimming pool. Picnic table out back, a shady oak tree, horseshoe court, grills, hammock. A short drive downhill to a hard sand beach and a boat launch.

But independent highway motels, and the type of family vacations that supported them, had become relics of an earlier time. And lazy, whimsical names like Ebb Tide had been abandoned in the rush for service and connectivity.

Robby Fallow, too, seemed left over from another era—a small, gritty man with brooding features who lived alone in a small wood-frame cabin at the highway end of the motel. Anytime she passed the place at night, Hunter would see the light of his television flickering on the walls. Fallow worked the grounds during the day, although the motel's appearance never seemed to improve; its name was fitting, Hunter thought, as she pulled into the entrance drive—the tide going out, not coming in.

She'd been thinking about Pastor Bowers on the drive over. Hunter had a good feeling about him. She liked the matter-of-fact way he'd told her about the shoe prints—heavier coming in than going out. And she liked the knowing, slightly wry look in his eyes. He was someone who might be able to help her. Hunter was a meticulous but quirky investigator; at times she sought counsel from unlikely allies. Pastor Bowers seemed like he might be one of those. It was just a feeling she had. In theory, the county's new Homicide Task Force, which she headed, was a seasoned team with a broad set of skills and experiences. But in fact it was two teams, the old guard and the new; the sheriff was captain of one side, Hunter of the other. Wendell Stamps, the large, even-tempered state's attorney, although always at pains to appear neutral, was clearly on the sheriff's side. It would make for some interesting problems.

Robby Fallow was bent over the engine of a huge Oldsmobile 88 at a clearing among the birch trees, wearing an old knit watch cap, layers of flannel, oil-stained jeans. He'd inherited the motel from his father in the early nineties when it was still frequented by families. The clientele now were mostly drifters or else freelance watermen, working a few weeks during the winter oyster season or the summer blue crab season. Developers had tried for years to buy the property from Fallow, in particular the Nayak family, the largest landowners in Tidewater County. But Robby Fallow wouldn't even talk with them. The motel—never an "inn," despite its name—was Fallow's pride, and his source of identity; it was all he had, really.

Fallow's son, the only other permanent resident at the Ebb Tide, lived on the wooded end, the last of the motel rooms. He worked there tending the property, and was known to have an affinity for marijuana. In summer, when highway traffic was heavy, Junior Fallow, as he was called, sometimes sat for hours in a lawn chair beside the highway, waving at passing motorists. Some travelers referred to him as the "Waving Man." Junior's mother had died years earlier, in an alcohol-related drowning in the motel pool.

Hunter had spoken with both Fallows during a cold case investigation she was assigned over the winter, but without much success. The victim was a twenty-four-year-old unemployed woman named Andrea Dressler, who'd stayed at the motel with her boyfriend thirteen days before she was found in a Delaware cornfield, strangled to death. For weeks the Sheriff's Department had treated Junior Fallow as the primary suspect. Later they named the boyfriend a "person of interest." But they never collected enough evidence to bring charges. Months after the sheriff had given up on the case, Hunter learned that a Delaware middle school custodian had been stalking the woman off and on for weeks. DNA tests eventually proved that he had raped and killed her.

Robby walked out to greet her now, as if he didn't want her getting too close to his business.

"Help you?"

"Good morning, Mr. Fallow. Amy Hunter. How are you today?"

"We're all closed up right now, ma'am," he said, wiping his hands on a rag that seemed greasier than his hands.

"Yes, I'm aware of that." Hunter held out her ID. He nodded, but didn't look. "I wonder if I could ask you a few questions?"

"No, ma'am," he said, cordially. "Not today."

"Not today."

"No, ma'am."

"Can I ask why not?"

"Well, that would be a question, ma'am," he said. An unexpected twinkle came into his small, sunken eyes. "Any questions, you'd have to talk to my attorney."

"Okay."

Hunter looked away. The door to a rusty shed was open in the birch woods behind his car. It was like peeking at another time: a 1960s Evinrude on a block, a couple of Johnson Sea Horse outboards, banged-up water skis, discolored yellow vinyl tow ropes.

"So you know why I'm here?"

"No, ma'am."

"I'm investigating the death of a woman who was found in the Methodist church yesterday morning. Some people have said you may know something about it."

"No, ma'am."

"You spoke with the sheriff about it, though, didn't you?"

He looked down, rubbing his hands more earnestly in the rag.

"I'm the lead investigator in the case, sir," she said. "I have no reason to think you were involved. I'd just like to eliminate you as a suspect. Which we can do very quickly."

"Uh-huh," he said. "Any questions, you'd need to talk to my attorney."

"Yes, you mentioned that."

Hunter took a breath and looked down the highway at an uprooted stretch of forest and the sign: FUTURE HOME OF WAL-MART.

"Okay. And who is your attorney?"

"Mr. Louis Gunther."

"Okay." Gunther was a Tidewater native who represented mostly DWI and "personal injury" cases. He was well-known locally for his fifteen-second summertime TV commercials. "If you should change your mind, please give me a call," she said.

Hunter took a business card from a pocket of her army jacket and held it out, but Robby Fallow made no motion to take it.

"Thank you, ma'am," he said.

He turned and walked back toward the Oldsmobile.

Hunter put the card away and returned to her car. She knew that she was being played, but not by Robby Fallow. She wondered what the sheriff might've said to Fallow that would have spooked him this way.

Chapter 4

ALL MORNING THE dream that had awakened Luke overnight kept replaying in his head, its details so vivid that he seemed to be remembering an actual event.

He enters the church sanctuary through the choir door, exactly as he had done on Tuesday morning. He watches the play of stained-glass light across the pews and eventually notices a woman, seated in the next-to-last row, just as on Tuesday. As he approaches, she lifts her head and seems to recognize him. Her expression changes several times before he reaches her—surprise, pleasure, sadness, and finally several degrees of pain.

The woman tries to stand but can't, her eyes indicating that her legs are broken. Luke nods, but urges her to try again anyway. On her second attempt she manages to hoist herself up unsteadily and begins to walk toward him, her legs jerking and buckling. For just a moment she stops and her eyes seem very happy; her arms begin to flap and Luke wonders if she's trying to dance. Then she loses her balance and he rushes forward to steady her. They hold each other, her face braced in his hands. Her skin is damp, as if she's just come in from a drizzle. When he pulls his hands away, he sees that pieces of her are sticking to him.

That was when he woke and saw Charlotte sleeping beside him. He looked past her at the clock on the bed-stand: *3:17.* He closed his eyes and listened for a while to the deep breathing of Charlotte and Sneakers, in alternating rhythms, as if they were nocturnal jazz musicians riffing off of one another other as they slept.

SOME RUMORS TAKE their time; in Tidewater most travel quickly, especially during the off-season. Only the sparest details about the "church killing"—as people were calling it—made the *Tidewater Times* or the local TV news. But several versions of what had happened were circulating through the gathering spots on Main Street. As people came and went, they exchanged the currencies of what they had "heard": that the victim, an Asian woman, was most likely a high-priced escort, possibly from Baltimore, who'd advertised her services on Craigslist; that the sheriff and homicide detectives had "been out to talk with Robby" two or three times already; and that the pastor "knows something." This last rumor, based on nothing, had caused people to look at Luke a little funny ever since Tuesday morning.

Tidewater County was a sprawling, largely undeveloped place with three thriving industries—fishing, farming, and tourism—and two incorporated towns—Tidewater and the simply named, more traditional old town of Bay. In summer, tourists packed the quaint streets of Tidewater, once a fishing village, now an enclave of Victorian-style homes, souvenir and curiosity shops, dockside crab and oyster restaurants, and seafood packing plants.

Luke's parents first brought him to Tidewater as an impressionable eight-year-old, and he had been instantly charmed: the

breezy bay views and seafood smells, the wood-planked water-
front, the working harbor, and, especially, the generosity and
fetching backwoods accents of the locals—which he'd later determined were a blend of Old South and English brogue. He and
his parents had taken a skipjack ride into the windy Chesapeake
that morning, then wandered Main Street much of the afternoon,
exploring the shops and sampling the seafood. Finally they'd
discovered the commercial docks, where crabs and oysters were
picked and packed, and watched as a crew unloaded fifteen bush-
els of oysters onto giant stainless-steel pans.

Luke's parents were travelers who'd nurtured in him a capacity for wonder and a healthy sense of curiosity. When he was a
boy, they'd taken him to remarkable places—Grand Canyon, Yel-
lowstone, Niagara Falls, Mt. Rushmore—as if wanting to impress
upon him how large and enchanting the country really was. As
an adolescent, though, he often turned his curiosity inward, and
pondered his own heritage.

He'd always been told that his father's family was Irish and
French, his mother's Eastern European. But he didn't look much
like either parent, or, for that matter, their relatives or ancestors.
His mother and father were both short, with strong features and
darkish skin. When Luke was fifteen, lean and still growing, he
stood two inches taller than his father, three and half inches taller
than his mother. Eventually he'd tower over his mother by nearly
a foot. Both parents were brown-eyed, although there had been
blue eyes on his mother's side, they told him. "That's where *your*
blue eyes come from," she used to say. But since the photographs
she showed him were always black and white, it was hard to tell.
Luke's father had begun to lose his hair in his early twenties,
whereas Luke had thick hair—"unruly," a barber once called it—

and it was an odd color, a dark and light-blond mixture; "surfer hair," according to Charlotte.

By the time he entered high school, Luke was all but certain that his parents' stories about where he came from had been no more genuine than their tales about Santa Claus or the Tooth Fairy. Coincidentally, it seemed, when he was sixteen his parents called him to the family room on a Saturday morning and confessed the truth, with lowered eyes and a tone of gravity. His father began with an oddly constructed sentence that Luke still remembered with great affection: "As you may have guessed by now, Luke, we have something to tell you." The fact that he'd been adopted didn't cause him to love his parents any less; it was the opposite— recognizing how much they had *wanted* to be his real parents and, in their way, how much they *had* been, he loved them more. The fact that his parents had brought him, as a wide-eyed eight-year-old, to these briny, seafood-scented streets of Tidewater County made it feel like home to him years later when he returned with Charlotte.

At the Gas 'N Bait in town—which sold everything from apples to ammunition to hangover remedies—Billy Banfield, a genial, obese man, came lumbering out as soon as Luke pulled in.

"Hey there, Pastor, what d'you say?" He pretended to be checking a pump on the next island. "Terrible thing down to the church. They know anything yet?"

"Not that they've shared with me, no."

He stepped closer, moving side to side.

"Is it true what I heard—the gal was naked when you found her?"

"No." Luke watched the numbers whirl. "Not true."

"No?"

"Nope, sorry."

Billy moved a step and a half closer, trying not to seem eager, but his eyes belied his interest, as if he were entitled. "Hearing a lot of rumors, anyway."

"Oh, I'm sure." Luke smiled. He pulled the nozzle out and inserted it in the pump, walking tenderly from having banged his knee earlier. "Probably best not to pay a lot of attention to that sort of thing, Bill."

"No. Wouldn't mention it, 'cept when you hear one that you know ain't true—*can't* be true—when it's about someone you know *couldn't* be involved . . ."

Luke realized from the way Billy's eyes had narrowed that he was talking about him. He smiled again and decided to let it go. "Anyway, take care, Bill."

On the little "strip mall" along east Main Street, he stopped at Palmer's Florist, where a reedy, silver-haired man he didn't recognize was selling a bouquet of tulips to a young blond woman.

"Pastor Luke?" the man said, once he completed the transaction. "That you?"

Luke lifted his eyebrows.

"George," he said.

"Oh." Luke realized, shaking hands, that this must be the owner, George Palmer. Like a lot of people in Tidewater County, George was only there occasionally during off-season.

"Sorry, didn't recognize you," Luke said. "I'm used to always seeing attractive young women working here."

George Palmer smiled and looked down, as if embarrassed. "Had to return for some family business. Hoping I'd find warmer weather. What happened, anyway?"

"Wish I could say."

"We're hearing all kinds of stories."

"People do like to tell stories, don't they?"

"Yes, they do."

Luke bought two roses and continued his drive east. One of the roses he would leave at Tidewater Hospice with Millicent Blanchard, a church member who was living out her last days there. The other he'd take home to Charlotte.

Visiting the hospice always grounded Luke and seemed to comfort the patients. Today it also took his mind off of what had happened at the church—and what the people of Tidewater County imagined he knew about it. He stopped to visit with each of the patients briefly before going to Millicent's corner room. At least *she* wouldn't ask him what had happened.

"How are *you* today, Millie?" he said. He lifted the blinds to let sunlight in. "You *look* good. Here, I brought you a rose."

He held the flower out and Millie took it, although her watery gray eyes didn't seem at first to register what it was or who he was. Then she finally looked up at Luke and smiled broadly, like a child.

"So, you're feeling comfortable? Good. Yes, I know, gorgeous day, isn't it? Just look at those clouds. Aren't they beautiful? You know what they say: there's a lot more going on in the sky than there ever is on television. I'm glad you agree. We've always seen eye-to-eye on things like that, haven't we?"

Luke had to provide both sides of the conversation now with Millie, an oysterman's widow in her late sixties who had collapsed in her backyard five months ago, a few nights after sitting with Luke at an all-you-can-eat church crab feast, bragging on her great-grandkids. At first doctors thought she'd suffered a stroke, but it turned out to be a rare, degenerative brain disease.

Millie wasn't expected to last more than a couple weeks longer—although if anyone could defy expectations, it was her.

Luke felt a clutch of emotions, as he always did, holding her fragile hand, praying for Millie and her family, thanking God for Millie's life, for her work with the church and in the community. As he walked away from her room, into the corridor, he felt weighted down with sadness, knowing that these visits with her were numbered.

He took the northern route back, through farmland that seemed to stretch without end in all directions. The morning haze had burned away and noontime light cast a stark clarity on the farm fields, the grain silos and wooden barns. Some places were zoned to become bigger, to attract industry and promote growth, but most of Tidewater County—other than a few stretches on the waterfront—was zoned to never become anything other than what it was. It's what he loved about the place.

He pushed in one of Charlotte's CDs. Chopin, *Fantasie Impromptu*, the console read. Charlotte, at his request, had begun teaching him a little about classical music, with mixed results. So far he'd learned that he liked Mahler and Tchaikovsky, although he sometimes couldn't tell the difference. This one he liked; the music quickly drew him in, lending a subtle grandeur to the countryside as he drove back toward the coast on a shoulderless two-lane road, trying out anecdotes in his head for Sunday's sermon.

Distances became a little tricky in this open country—so that you might see a truck across the fields and not know how far away it was or which direction it was going. He was absently tracking a pickup now as Chopin's piano melody took a mysterious turn—a big silver truck, moving parallel to him, maybe half a mile away, but traveling faster than he was. Route 11, probably. Going west by southwest.

It must've turned left then, because when he noticed it again, the truck was coming directly toward him, perpendicularly. And then it was right there: Luke was stopped at the two-way at Goose Creek Crossing and the truck whooshed by, shaking his car. A new-looking double cab Ram pickup with a prominent dent on the right front fender.

More surprising than the vehicle—it was rare to see anything but old pickups out here—was the man driving it. As the truck passed, the driver turned his eyes to look squarely at him.

Jackson Pynne.

He recognized him. Except why would Jackson Pynne be driving through Tidewater County?

It had been months since Luke had even thought of Jackson Pynne—and much longer since he'd actually seen him. But seeing him now gave him a bad feeling. Jackson was a hotel and condominium developer who'd come here six or seven years ago with deep pockets and plans to build a high-end hotel-marina project. *The Baltimore Sun* had called him a "maverick, larger-than-life businessman" back then—which Jackson liked, although that article may have also begun his unraveling. Tidewater County rarely made room for people who were "larger than life," particularly when they were what locals called "come heres" rather than "from heres."

In some ways, though, Jackson *was* larger than life. Tall, long-legged, with a self-assured step and cool, craggy features, he always reminded Luke of a 1950s film actor, in the Robert Mitchum, William Holden mold. There was an inherent drama in his face that often made him seem to be saying more than he actually was. People would sometimes do a double take when they spotted Jackson walking the streets of Tidewater, thinking he might be someone famous. And, for a while, Jackson Pynne *had* been a player in the business of Tidewater County, albeit a controversial one, convincing some of the newer commissioners and zoning board members that his hotel-marina would transform the water-front, attracting a "new caliber" of tourist to Tidewater.

But the old guard had been quietly wary of him from the start and never made life easy for him. There were invisible layers of tradition in this county, Luke had discovered, as mysterious at times as the ways of a religious sect. Each of the three bayfront projects that Pynne tried to build had failed, costing him huge losses of money and prestige. Each time Pynne went before the county zoning boards—boards that routinely approved Nayak projects—he was asked to scale back his plans or to make numer-ous changes. In the last case—a boutique luxury condo/hotel with a restaurant he wanted to call "Jackson's"—the delays ultimately led the state to file fraud charges against him after Pynne accepted deposits for units that were never built. He eventually repaid the deposits, but by then he'd worn out his welcome.

Toward the end of his years in Tidewater, Jackson Pynne had, improbably, adopted Luke as a friend. By then his frustrations with the zoning process and the "old boy" network had made him an angry man, cutting him off from nearly everyone else in the county. Sometimes he'd show up at the church unannounced and rant to Luke about the people who had "screwed" him, using his colorful nicknames for zoning board members—Baby Huey, Mr. Magoo, and the kraut, among them. Charlotte claimed Luke had a weakness for underdogs, and by then Pynne's whole life seemed to have become a long shot. Luke tried to find the good in people, and there was a lot of good in Jackson Pynne, even a sense of nobility at times. There was also a deep yearning for something more meaningful in his life, which was probably what had drawn him to Luke. Jackson was a strange amalgamation of traits, which didn't seem to mesh well.

People used to say, "Something strange happens every time Jackson Pynne comes to town."

Remembering the sentiment, Luke felt a chill race through him.

Chapter 5

THE DEBRIEFING MEETING of the Homicide Task Force was scheduled for eleven-thirty at the Public Safety Complex. It left Amy Hunter time to drive into town and talk with Louis Gunther, Robby Fallow's attorney. But she called ahead, and was told that Gunther wasn't in the office on Wednesdays this time of year.

Just as well, Hunter thought.

This case wasn't about Robby Fallow, she was certain of that. The Tidewater killing was sophisticated and remarkably clean, in a way that didn't yet make sense, but that almost certainly eliminated the Fallows as suspects.

Investigators talked about a forty-eight-hour rule on homicides. Forty-eight hours after the victim was discovered, detectives should know what kind of case they had. But Hunter didn't believe in those kinds of rules. In a case like this, without witnesses, the circumstances of the crime were like a heavy fog that had drifted in from the bay. You worked in the fog until it began to clear, however long that took. The idea that it should happen in forty-eight hours was just an excuse for lazy cops. On Wednesday morning the fog in the church killing was still impenetrable. There were no good leads on the victim's identity, or on the killer's. And the way the woman had been left, posed in a rear pew as if praying, felt not only like a challenge, but a taunt. A puzzle left for Hunter to solve.

Also, the case had tabloid potential, she knew, because of the numbers carved into Jane Doe's right hand, which was why Hunter wanted to make sure that this detail was kept from the media for as long as possible.

Complicating the case was the unspoken conflict with Sheriff Calvert. This was the first Tidewater County homicide since commissioners had taken away his authority. Hunter would have to work around that.

She was thinking about Jane Doe's eyes as she walked down the bright corridor to the conference room, wind driving dried snow against the ceiling-tall parking lot windows. Hunter had stood directly in front of the woman and stared into her film-coated eyes, wondering where she'd come from and why someone had done this to her. In every case, Hunter kept an image of the victim on her desk and also in her head, a reminder of who she was really working for. Years earlier she had herself been the victim of a violent crime, in a leafy suburban neighborhood where violations of that kind didn't happen. It was something she didn't talk about. But the way the case was mishandled had shaken her priorities and given Hunter her interest in law enforcement. She'd begun her career in Pennsylvania, working CID for the state police before Maryland hired her on an investigative track five years ago. The MSP had one of the most successful homicide units in the country, with a closure rate of ninety-two percent and a conviction rate over ninety-nine percent. But some cases defied percentages; some went cold for weeks and months, and a few never warmed up at all. This was beginning to feel like it could become one of those.

"All right," she began at the task force meeting. "Let's just summarize what we've got, where we need to go. Bottom line, somewhere, probably in this county, someone knows something about what happened. We need to find them."

Nine others had gathered around the conference table, showing various levels of interest: state homicide investigators Sonny Fischer and Ben Shipman, Hunter's partners—sometimes called "Fisch and Ship," an endearment neither of them cared for; State's Attorney Wendell Stamps, a large, shrewd man with a perpetually impassive expression; the state's attorney's lead investigator Clinton Fogg, a thirty-year veteran who still had a hard time looking Hunter in the eye—as if he couldn't accept that she was really in charge of the Homicide Task Force; sheriff's deputies Barry Stilfork and Susan Jones, whose allegiance was to the county sheriff; John Jay Blount, a captain with the Tidewater municipal police, who often gave Hunter the creeps, the way he stared at her; and the county's public information officer, Kirsten Sparks, who vigorously chewed gum with an exaggerated motion of her jaw and neck as Hunter spoke. Hunter's boss Henry Moore, the case officer with the state police homicide unit, was also in the room. He'd given her latitude in this case, like a coach allowing his quarterback to read the defense and respond accordingly. There were eighteen men and women in the state police homicide unit, and seven of them were now assigned to this case.

The sheriff, although part of the task force, had skipped the meeting, which was his way of making a statement. His loss, Hunter thought.

She glanced at her notes and continued: "Jane Doe arrived at the M.E.'s Office on Penn Street yesterday morning shortly before noon with Ben Shipman accompanying to maintain chain of custody. Preliminary autopsy and forensics reports from the state CSI are now back. Toxicology pending. Trace and biological analysis still under way in Pikesville."

She then shared details from the M.E.'s report: "The victim was five foot five and a half inches tall, weight one hundred sixteen. Estimated thirty to thirty-five years old. Asian or Hispanic heritage. I want to make sure we get that out to the press today," she said, making eye contact with Kirsten Sparks, the public information officer. "The paper used the word Caucasian. Which, as you know, is a word we don't even use anymore."

Sparks stopped chewing; her pale skin colored. "I've already spoken with them," she said defensively. "Obviously, I wouldn't have used the word Caucasian. I don't know where they got that from."

"I'm not saying you did. I'm just saying let's make sure they have it right in future references."

Hunter looked back at the report as Kirsten Sparks resumed her gum-chomping at a faster pace.

"So far, dental, fingerprints, and DNA have not resulted in an ID. Yesterday, two photos of Jane Doe and one of the tattoo on her ankle were sent electronically to law enforcement agencies throughout Delaware, Virginia, Pennsylvania, New Jersey, New York, and D.C. A physical description and sketch to area media. We've contacted every police department in the state for missing persons reports. With no match so far."

Hunter turned another page. "Okay," she said. "This next part isn't for the media yet, or for public consumption." She glanced quickly at Sparks. "Preliminary autopsy shows four broken bones in her legs, two broken ribs, and a broken bone in her left arm. All of those wounds appear to be postmortem. The cause of death is two .22 caliber gunshot wounds to the chest."

Kirsten Sparks stopped chewing. For a moment even Clinton Fogg's eyes rose to look at her. "Wow," Sparks said.

"Lividity of the body indicates she had been moved, probably twice, before the perpetrator carried her into the church and left her in the pew. The M.E. found signs of ligature on her wrists. Nowhere else.

"Yesterday, investigators went house-to-house interviewing residents along Bayfront. We've got four people who say they saw vehicles near the church overnight or early Tuesday. Two say they saw a white or tan SUV driving along the church road. One put it at around one-thirty, the other at one forty-five or one-fifty. Then we've got two reports of a silver pickup on Bayfront just after sunrise Tuesday. No plate numbers on either vehicle, unfortunately.

"State police have talked with church employees, including the six people who had keys to the building, and most or all of the AA members who attended a meeting in the parlor Monday night. It's likely the parlor window had been left unlocked and the perpetrator entered through that window." She turned a page in her notes. "Three stores in Tidewater County were open all night and we're still reviewing the tapes. There are several cameras up on the highway and at the Bay Bridge, so we're in the process of checking everything coming and going." She nodded to Henry Moore, who had moved three state police homicide investigators to Tidewater County just to help sift through surveillance tapes.

Hunter didn't bring up the numbers that had been carved into the Jane Doe's right hand. She also didn't mention that sheriff's deputies, in particular Barry Stilfork, had compromised much of the crime scene and probably contaminated evidence. Nor did she speculate on the possibility that this crime might be connected to others, which Hunter was beginning to think possible. She thought it would help explain why the local case had such big problems.

"Questions?"

No one spoke. John Jay Blount, she noticed, was staring at her, a cryptic, lopsided smile on his face.

"Captain Blount, how's your day going so far?" Hunter said, and he immediately lowered his eyes.

Then Kirsten Sparks, talking and chewing at the same time, said, "I'm getting inquiries about whether this was a homicide. Can we at least tell the media it was a homicide?"

Hunter nodded. "I don't see any reason not to. Unless there are any objections."

State's attorney investigator Clinton Fogg made a snorting sound.

"Mr. Fogg?"

He shook his head and closed his eyes. He was a peculiar man, who barely acknowledged some people and was overly friendly with others. Often he acted as if he was hard of hearing, though he wasn't. Fogg was thorough and highly competent as a detective, but loyal to no one but the state's attorney, Wendell Stamps.

"Okay," Hunter said. "Anything else, then? If not, let's get back out there and solve this thing."

Hunter took her time pushing papers together as the others rose and filed from the room. She knew that she sounded more like a football coach than a homicide investigator, but that was how she approached her job; so far it'd served her well. Sometimes she caught herself saying a phrase that reminded her of her father, who'd coached high school ball most of his adult life, and who had drilled in her simple lessons about winning and losing, pumping her with sayings from people like Vince Lombardi and John Wooden.

State's Attorney Wendell Stamps waited until the others had all left.

"How do *you* feel about this?" he asked Henry Moore, the case officer with the state police homicide unit, who was still seated. "Just curious."

But Moore wouldn't bite.

"It's Hunter's investigation," he said, looking at the state's attorney. Moore was a deliberative man in his late fifties with a ruddy, wind-burned face. "I won't comment beyond what she told you."

Hunter tried not to smile. The state's attorney nodded to her politely, said, "Sergeant Hunter," and left the room.

Chapter 6

"PICK UP SOME lunch?"

Ben Shipman was standing in Hunter's doorway, wearing his old red lumberjack coat and worn, bleach-spotted jeans.

He twirled his keys once around his index finger. "I'll drive."

Ship was a stocky man with rusty, wool-like hair and earnest blue eyes. He was in his mid-forties, divorced four or five years, with a teenage daughter. But he could be like an adolescent himself at times; this morning, Hunter had noticed, his socks weren't matched—almost the same color, but one thick wool, the other nylon—and he'd missed two belt loops on his jeans. Also, he looked tired; the day before, Ship had driven to Baltimore and back, to witness the preliminary forensics on Jane Doe.

When Shipman asked if she wanted to "pick up" lunch, it meant McDonald's, one of the two fast food restaurants in Tidewater County. Usually, it also meant he wanted to talk.

The Beatles' "Strawberry Fields Forever" blasted from the car's speakers as Shipman started the engine. "Whoops," he said, punching it off. He kept two CDs in his car, *The Beatles 1962-1966* and *The Beatles 1967-1970.* It was, as far as Hunter knew, the only music he listened to.

"You know what's going on, don't you?" he asked as they cruised onto Main Street.

"No, what's going on?"

"G.J. city, here we come."

"What's G.J. city?"

"Grand jury."

"For whom?"

"Fallow."

"But Robby Fallow didn't do this."

"I know, I'm just saying."

Shipman went silent after that, hunched over the steering wheel. The homicide unit was assigned unmarked cars, none of them too obvious, like a Crown Vic. If Ship's Mazda had been a suit of clothes, it would've been two sizes too small. Shipman had grown up here in Tidewater County and his speech was rich with Eastern Shore inflections—*water* was "wu-ter," *about* was "a-boat." He'd worked for the sheriff's office for three or four years before earning his stripes as a state police investigator, and was still friendly with some of the deputies. He was Hunter's liaison to what the "other side" was thinking.

"Tell me about that," she said as they came to the first of Tidewater's three traffic signals.

"Well, I mean—another week goes by, right? We don't have any more than we have this morning? They're going to convene the grand jury. Guarantee."

"Based on what?"

Shipman shrugged and, as he sometimes did, answered a different question: "I'm telling you, this thing is freaking them.

'Course, being an election year, it wouldn't hurt any if they can show that *they* were the ones who solved it, not us."

"Guess not." Hunter waited, knowing he'd say more. Ship tended to open up around her more than he did with anyone else. Early on there'd been a few awkward moments when he'd suggested that they should go "*out* out" sometime. But they were long past that now, and Hunter thought of Ben Shipman as an older brother.

"If they can't have a real solution," he said, "they'll settle for the appearance of a solution. A 'necessary outcome.'"

"I don't like the sound of that."

"I know. I'm just saying. It is what it is."

Yes, it is, Hunter thought, feeling her face flush with anger. They rode in silence again past the Blue Crab Diner, Holland's Family Restaurant, and the white frame Baptist church at the other end of Main Street, then over the northern trickle of Jimmy Creek toward the highway and the county's small commercial strip. As with most of her cases, Hunter had already raised the stakes of this one, figuring there was more involved than just finding a criminal; there was also a darker riddle of human motivation to be answered. She had heard the term "God's work" used to describe homicide investigations years before she understood what it meant. Now she understood, but tried not to think about it.

"What are they saying about the numbers in her hand?"

"Not much," Ship said. "The state's attorney evidently thinks it's irrelevant. A red heron."

"Herring."

"Herring."

"But for what purpose?"

"Just Robby, trying to divert attention."

No, Hunter thought. Not possible. Robby Fallow doesn't think that way. The number in her hand is something else. The number in her hand has to mean something. It's probably the key to understanding this.

"There's another reason, too, you know." Ship was grinning slightly as he switched lanes.

"Which is?"

"A lot of people don't like Robby Fallow. People respected his daddy, but not him. Lot of people'd be glad to see him gone. They just don't want to go to war with him. Robby can be a stubborn guy."

"Yeah, I know." Hunter recalled the hand-painted plywood sign he'd nailed to a tree last winter reading, Private Property. Keep Out. This Means You.

"So this would be a way of forcing him out?" she said. "That seems a stretch."

"Don't underestimate what the sheriff's capable of when he gets a bee in his bonnet. I can see it going there—I mean, say they end up working out a plea deal, he agrees to leave Tidewater. The case is quietly dropped. Maybe Robby sells the property, gets enough to buy a nice little retirement place down in Florida or the Carolinas, for him and his son. Everyone lives happily ever after."

"And a murderer goes free?"

"Well," Shipman said. "There's that."

SHIP PLACED THEIR orders without asking Hunter: Oriental salad and small fries for her, Big Mac and large fries for himself. Otherwise a healthy eater, Hunter harbored a weakness for McDonald's french fries.

They were driving back when Sonny Fischer, the other local member of the homicide unit, called. Fisch was Ship's antithesis in many ways, a heath and exercise nut who could literally become ill in the presence of fast food. He was also highly antisocial. Both, though, in their own ways, were exceptional investigators.

"Going or coming?"

"Coming," Hunter said. "Why?"

Ship reached for a handful of fries.

"Might have something. Pickup truck ID'd from description."

"Video?"

"Partial plate. Checking."

"Okay."

Fischer often spoke in a peculiar verbal shorthand, which Hunter was able to decipher.

"Anything?" Ship asked, glancing over.

"Don't know yet. Maybe."

Maybe it's the break we're looking for, Hunter thought. But probably not. At least ninety-five percent of her work on homicide cases ended up as wasted time. But she had to go through it to get to the five percent that wasn't. Meaning none of it was really wasted, just incredibly tedious.

Chapter 7

THE BIG MAN had been eating pancakes alone at two-twenty in the morning, the only customer seated at the counter, when the phone vibrated in his trousers pocket; it was the one call he had to take.

"Gil Rankin."

"He needs to see you," the familiar voice said.

"I thought we were finished."

"No. One more."

So Rankin, his muscles still tingling from pumping iron, had no choice but to follow instructions. He flew that morning to New York City, where a driver met him at LaGuardia and took him to meet the Client. This time the man was sitting in the back of a delicatessen in midtown, eating a pastrami on rye and drinking coffee, the *Daily News* open in front of him to the sports pages. A slight, otherwise plain-looking man, with silvery hair and dark, disturbing eyes.

"I wish it hadn't come to this, Gilbert," he told Rankin, taking his time folding the paper closed. "It isn't a result any of us wanted.

But it has to be done. This sort of betrayal—it's like fruit that has gone bad. Have you ever seen spoiled fruit made good again?"

"No," Rankin said, trying, with mixed success, not to look at his client's eyes. It was like looking at the sun, something you shouldn't do.

"No, that's right," his Client said. "It doesn't happen."

How did things get to this point, anyway? Rankin asked himself on the limo ride back to LaGuardia, watching the city through a driving, icy rain. It was hard to say. He had worked for lots of high-end clients over the years, all sorts of characters. But a decade ago his list had shrunk to one, and stayed that way ever since. His assignments now were infrequent but always lucrative. And the rest of his time was his, to do whatever he wanted. For a man who liked to work after dark, Rankin had made a good life for himself in the Sunshine State. He was married to a beautiful, intelligent, Puerto Rican–born woman who was also his best friend. They lived in a 17,000-square-foot Spanish-style place on the water, paid for, fully staffed. They had one boy in elementary school, one in middle school. Sometimes, Rankin and his family took his boat into the Gulf of Mexico, far from everything, for days at a time. Nothing made him happier.

The only thing he didn't have anymore was the luxury of saying no. That was their arrangement: you take the assignments you're given, you know the pay will be enormous, you don't ask questions. And Rankin did a good job. It was the only reason he'd gotten to where he was today.

This deal, from the beginning, had been the Client's strangest assignment. But it came with the sweetest incentive: this job could be his last, if that's what Gil Rankin really wanted. Meaning, he could walk away, if he wanted, millions of dollars richer, and never have to go back. There was an adage he'd heard all of this life—that eventually, everybody gets caught. It wasn't strictly true, but close enough. Rankin had known hugely successful people who now resided in nine-by-nine-foot prison cells because they'd played too long and gotten sloppy, or made deals with clients who were wearing wires. He had always wanted to get out undefeated, the way Rocky Marciano had.

So now he was driving back to Maryland to complete the last part of the Client's deal. It meant returning to the little town of Tidewater, to a rented house the Client was providing for him. The rest would be up to him. The final part of it was simply to take out Jackson Pynne before he talked. According to the Client, Pynne would probably make it easy for him. Fact was, Pynne might be on his way back there now, right back to the scene of the crime.

Chapter 8

"How DOES SHE-CRAB soup and homemade cornbread sound?" Charlotte asked.

"Mmm."

"Good. Because it's the only item on the menu today."

Sneakers raised his head and thumped his tail twice as Luke pulled the rose from behind his back and handed it to Charlotte. Kissing her, he breathed a nice blend of body lotions, spices, and corn bread. Classical piano music played in her study.

Luke fetched a bottle of water from the fridge and leaned on the kitchen counter, admiring Charlotte. Their cottage was officially a parish house, owned by the church, but she had converted it into something quite different, finding it too musty and rustic. It now resembled a quaint Queen Anne–style New England bed and breakfast, decorated with an assortment of antiques and nautical knickknacks.

Charlotte turned down the music.

"If I had to guess, I'd say one of Beethoven's late quartets," Luke said. He took a drink of water.

"Good thing you don't have to guess," Charlotte said.

"Brahms?"

"Ravel."

"Well. I was close, anyway."

She just gave him a look, and began to ladle the soup. Although she worked at home as a writer and historian, Charlotte dressed smartly each morning, as if she were going into an office full of people rather than just one largely indifferent mixed Labrador retriever—except on those days when she volunteered at the Humane Society. Today she wore charcoal gray slacks and a tan wool pullover. Her ash blond hair was up in a claw clasp.

"So, what have you been doing?" she asked.

"Just trying to pretend it's a normal day," he said.

"Any luck?"

"Not yet."

"Your public has been calling."

"I was afraid of that."

"Don't worry. I turned off the ringer."

Charlotte watched him as he walked to the table.

"Are you limping?" she said.

"No, I'm okay. I just banged my knee earlier, at the office."

"Oh." She brought their lunch to the table and Sneakers resettled beside her chair. For most of the day, the dog stayed in close proximity to Charlotte. Luke, despite his deep affection for Sneakers, would always be his auxiliary master.

"How was your meeting with the investigator?" she asked, looking at Luke with her intelligent, pale blue eyes. "Learn anything new?"

"A little." He told her about the morning meeting with Amy Hunter as they ate. Luke shared everything with Charlotte. The night before, they had sat in these same places and mulled over possible explanations for what had happened at the church Monday night. Today none of them sounded right. Nothing did.

"This is delicious," he said. Charlotte smiled appropriately, although he could tell she was waiting for him to say more. They'd always been good counterweights—Charlotte the product of a wealthy and privileged D.C. upbringing, Luke raised middle-class in towns all over the States. But Charlotte had a rebellious side; she'd apparently crossed swords often with her famous father on political issues before the two of them settled into an awkward truce some years ago. Her only sibling, a younger brother named Nelson, had died when she was ten, and it remained an uncomfortable topic between Charlotte and her parents. She had an inwardness that still intrigued Luke, an ability to be sociable when she wanted and also to spend long periods of time in silence.

"You know what's funny?" he said, noticing that she was still looking at him. "I think I saw Jackson Pynne today, on my way home."

"Really."

"Yeah, way out in the country. Passed right by me in a silver pickup."

Charlotte tilted her head, interested. "Are you sure it was him?"

"Not entirely. Except we looked at each other as he passed and there seemed to be a moment of recognition."

"You should tell the inspector."

"Yeah, I know." He smiled, not sure if her word choice was making fun of Amy Hunter or not. "I will."

Her eyes stayed with him as she went back to her soup. "He used to really think the world of you, you know."

"Jackson did?"

"Of course. He thought you could fix his life."

"People overestimate me sometimes."

"I don't." She gave him a smart, mischievous look. "And *you* don't. That's what matters."

Sneakers suddenly raised his head as if remembering something he needed from the store. After a moment he settled back to sleep.

"Darlene from the college called," Charlotte said.

"Your occasional friend."

"Yeah."

"This must qualify as an occasion."

"She heard that the killing had to do with the vote on the new church. And with the Nayaks. Someone in the office told her that. She wanted to know if it was true."

"To which you replied . . ."

"I laughed. I couldn't help it."

"Good. An appropriate response," Luke said.

Amy Hunter had asked about this, too: if the debate over church growth might've had anything to do with the killing. The congregation was split on whether to build a new church on the existing site or sell the land and relocate. Frank Nayak, Jr., or Little Frank, as the old-timers called him, had offered to purchase the church and donate a large parcel of inland property for the relocation. The church, Little Frank liked to say, was "a nonrevenue producer, not the proper use of that land."

"You know how when the mafia wants to deliver a warning, they leave a dead fish on the front porch?" Charlotte said. "Maybe this was a variation of that."

"Leaving a dead woman?"

"Maybe."

"Who would they be warning?"

She widened her eyes, giving him her *Who do you think?* look. "It's not like I own the church."

"No. But you have an opinion. And you're the face of the church, aren't you?"

"Only the mouth."

"So to speak."

"But my opinion is in line with what the majority of the congregation thinks—that we keep the property. Though, of course, it isn't up to me. The district superintendent, the bishop, and the staff/parish committee make those decisions."

"You don't have to convince me, counselor."

Luke smiled. He let his thoughts roam a little as he finished the soup. Back to the dream. Back to Millie at the hospice with her child's smile. Back to the meeting with Hunter. *We're going to solve this thing.*

When he finished, Luke was surprised to see Charlotte studying him.

"Let me guess," she said. "You're not thinking about those numbers again."

"I was, yeah."

More than that, he suddenly had a pretty good idea what the numbers in Jane Doe's right hand meant.

Chapter 9

BEN SHIPMAN PARKED in one of the nine spaces assigned for state police alongside the Public Safety Complex, where Hunter, Fisch, and Ship worked in small adjoining offices.

They dropped their bags on Hunter's desk.

"Ready?" she asked, outside Shipman's door.

He was rubbing his hands together.

"Let's do it," he said.

Ship went first, with his distinctive, somewhat clunky walk, as if his shoes were an inch too long, wiping his hands again on his red lumberjack coat.

Fisch was in the office, seated in front of twin monitors, perfectly postured in a black T-shirt and dark pressed jeans. He turned and his nose immediately wrinkled; the fast food aroma evidently still clung to the two of them.

"Sorry," Hunter said, looking self-consciously at her hands. Shipman, she saw, had hidden his behind his back.

Fischer was a tall, elegant-looking man, half Cuban, half African-American, originally from Miami. He ate no processed food and kept vitamins, fruit, and protein bars on his desk. He was an anomaly among cops, certainly among homicide investigators. But he was also one of the most disciplined and diligent detectives Hunter had ever worked with. She liked him a great deal even though he seemed unknowable in some ways. Ship had told her more than once that Fischer was gay, but she sensed he was just speculating.

"What've you got?" Hunter asked.

"Pickup. Matches ID."

Fischer called up the digital file on his screen and tapped some keys, Hunter watching how the sinewy muscles in his arms worked.

"Low res," he said. "Texaco, Highway 50. 8:37 A.M., Tuesday."

About an hour after Pastor Bowers found the body.

Hunter and Shipman watched the brief sequence, keeping a respectable distance. A silver double-cab Dodge Ram pickup stopping beside a gas pump. The driver's door opening. A tall man in an overcoat and baseball cap getting out, reaching for the gas nozzle. Seeming to duck his head away, as if to avoid standing in range of the camera.

"May be something, maybe not," Fischer said. They all watched again. This time Hunter noticed the top of the license tag.

"Can you freeze that? Is it Delaware?"

"Already have. Blown it up several ways. Last number's cut off. It's Delaware."

"What did our witness say?"

"Mr. Charles? Thinks so, can't be sure."

"We ought to release it, then," Hunter said. "Did you e-mail it to me?"

"You have it."

"Good. Good work."

Hunter and Shipman walked back to her office next door. They ate their lunches together, mostly in silence, Hunter at her desk, Shipman at her worktable. Ship ate fast, as if racing to finish first, talking inconsequentially about the case. Hunter savored her food, particularly the fries.

"You know, you shouldn't eat so fast," she said.

"Uh-huh."

"Seriously."

"Yeah. You're probably right." Which came out as "Pwafly wut."

He ate the rest the same way, though; there was no slowing Ship down once he got going. After he returned to his office, Hunter ran the gas pump sequence again on her own computer screen, this time in slow motion as she poked at the rest of her salad. There was something familiar about how this man carried himself. He reminded her of an actor, someone well known. But she couldn't quite place who. She ran it again.

Hunter caught a whiff of Polo cologne then and looked up.

STATE'S ATTORNEY WENDELL Stamps was in her doorway, looking on with his wide, expressionless face. Dressed, as always, in a tailored suit, this one navy with pinstripes.

"What've you got?"

"Oriental salad," Hunter said. "Want a fry?"

He flattened his lips as if she were asking him to play dolls.

"What've you got on the case? Anything?"

"Not much." Hunter nodded at the screen. "Image of a pickup that matches description of a vehicle seen parked outside the church yesterday, about an hour before the pastor showed up."

She wiped the grease off her hands and turned the monitor screen, showing him the digital footage. The state's attorney temporarily parked himself on a corner of her work station, breathing audibly as he looked on impassively. Stamps was a large, square-shouldered man with pale skin. The whole Stamps family was tall and fair. His two girls were sports stars at Tidewater High.

"Huh," he said afterward. He stood. "Kind of weak, isn't it?"

"Well, we don't know yet."

"Tell me about it again."

"Which part?"

He nodded once at her computer monitor. Often, Stamps's eyes glazed over as people explained things, but he registered the general topic so he could circle back if necessary and ask them to tell him "again."

Together, they watched the man pulling out the nozzle and ducking his head away.

"He looks familiar, somehow," Hunter said.

"He does." Stamps sighed ambiguously. At the door, he turned. "Oh, and say, have you done anything with those numbers yet? The numbers on her hand?"

"Not yet." She raised her eyes to his. The sheriff, no doubt, had briefed him on it. "We may send them to other agencies this afternoon or tomorrow."

"Think it could wait another day or two?" He moved a step closer and assumed a hushed tone: "The only reason I mention it, there's something brewing that the sheriff wanted to talk with us about. He's the one requesting it."

"He hasn't requested it to me."

"No, I know."

Hunter felt the back of her neck bristle. She'd left four messages now for Sheriff Calvert and twice driven to his office downtown, only to be told he wasn't in. But she didn't want to show her anger or frustration to the state's attorney, so she pretended to smile.

"I don't know the details," Stamps said. "Apparently, someone saw something, but won't talk to anyone other than the sheriff." His sentence ended with the inflection of a question mark.

"Having to do with Robby Fallow, by any chance?"

"It may be. I really don't know."

"I'll talk with the sheriff," Hunter said. "If there's some new information he has, it would need to come through this office, of course."

The state's attorney held up his hands in a surrender position.

Hunter's phone began to ring.

"We'll talk," Stamps said.

She nodded, took a deliberate breath and answered the phone: "Hunter."

"This is Luke Bowers."

"Oh. Yes, hello."

"I think I've figured it out."

"Sir?"

"The numbers. I think I know what those numbers mean."

"Oh," she said, looking at where the state's attorney had just been standing. "Excellent."

Chapter 10

Amy Hunter's office was near the end of a long, wide, shiny-floored corridor. Night and day from the dingy brick police building on Main Street, now set for demolition, where anyone could walk in and wander the halls: citizens, criminals, crazies; all had done so at one time or another. Here, you entered through an X-ray scanner into a glass atrium with four security cameras; a guard called ahead for authorization, issued a visitor badge, and you waited for your escort. Everything smelled of plastic and plaster and new construction.

Hunter welcomed Luke with her professional handshake and led him down the long hallway. In her office, she motioned for him to sit. Luke set his old Bible on her desk. The room had an odd smell, he thought, like french fries.

He took a quick inventory: charts and laser print photos on a corkboard, a timeline with tiny print handwriting. Three computer terminals set up on the desk. He liked the austere aura of efficiency here, which seemed to fit with the directness of her eyes. The only personal photos were of a black and white tuxedo cat and one that seemed to be her parents, standing stiffly beside a waterfall, taken some years earlier. Luke wondered if they were still alive, and if she had time for much of a personal life; probably not, he guessed.

A typed quote, maybe twenty point, was tacked to the bottom of the corkboard: *If you do what you've always done, You'll get what you've always gotten.*

"I like that quote." He nodded at it. "Sophocles?"

Her eyes turned and her face colored slightly.

"Tony Robbins."

"That would have been my second guess. Sorry." He *was*, actually, and summoned his best contrite expression. It was, in fact, the sort of quote Luke liked to slip into his sermons occasionally; unfortunately, people tended to respond more to inspirational wordplay than they did to scriptural passages.

"So." She frowned, getting to it. "You think you know what the numbers mean."

"I have an idea, yeah. The details about her arms and legs helped. Being broken, I mean."

"Although that was on the QT."

"Right."

"Okay." She leaned forward and clasped her hands on the desk. "So what is five one eight?"

"A Bible verse."

She glanced at the old Bible he'd set on her desk.

"In the Old Testament, there are only three books with fifty-one chapters. Psalms, Isaiah, and Jeremiah. None of the books of the New Testament would qualify, the longest being Matthew and Acts, which each have twenty-eight."

"Okay." Her eyes shone with interest.

"So, that narrowed it down. I looked up each, and one seemed to fit—Psalm 51, verse 8. If we assume the *i* was actually a colon, that is."

He opened the Bible to the page he had bookmarked, rotated it and slid it across the desk to her. Hunter leaned forward, setting her elbows on either side of the Bible. Her eyes found Psalm 51, then the eighth line.

She read silently at first, then aloud.

"Make me hear joy and gladness
That the bones you have broken may rejoice."

She looked up. "Okay," she said, her tone neutral. "Tell me about that. What's Psalm 51?"

"It's a prayer of repentance," Luke said. "One of the better-known Psalms, actually. It was King David's expression of remorse over his affair with Bathsheba and the fate of her husband, Uriah, whom he sent to war to be killed. He's saying, basically, I was wrong, I sinned, forgive me."

"King David."

"Yeah."

Hunter's eyes went back to the Bible. "This is the same David from David and Goliath, right?"

"Same fellow. Goliath was back in his teen years. Before he went off into the wilderness. More than half of the hundred fifty Psalms were supposedly written by David. Although some scholars question that."

"Okay." Her eyes stayed with his. "So, if this was a message, or a calling card of some kind, the message would have to do with repentance, you're saying?"

"Well, that's one interpretation. Of course, it might be something else entirely."

She read it again, and finally pushed the book back to him. Not quite convinced, Luke could see. "Any idea why someone might've carved the number of a Psalm verse into this woman's hand?"

"No."

"Okay," she said. Clasping her hands again. "Well. Thank you for that information, then, Pastor. I'll certainly let you know if we have further questions."

Luke was mindful not to smile at her sudden formality. "Sure," he said. "And if I could change the subject for a second?" Hunter nodded. "I do have one other bit of information that I wanted to share. It probably doesn't mean anything, but I assured my wife I'd mention it."

"Please."

"I was driving out in the country around lunchtime today, coming back from hospice. And when I got to the stop sign at Goose Creek Crossing, I happened to see someone from my past, driving south. The county's past, actually. Jackson Pynne. Do you know who he is?"

Her eyes filled with a sudden interest. "Yes. He was the developer behind a couple of big projects that were never built. Tidewater Landing? Jackson's restaurant?"

"That's right."

"And why would that be of interest to us?"

"Well, I don't know exactly. I just remember there was a saying people used to have around here: 'Something strange happens every time Jackson Pynne comes to town.' And, of course, something strange did happen this week."

Hunter held her frown.

"It just seemed odd. As far as I know, he hasn't been here for several years. I think he may still have a few enemies in the county, I don't know." Luke could see things clicking and whirring behind her eyes. This, for some reason, interested her more than Psalms. More than he'd imagined.

"What kind of vehicle was he driving?"

"Pickup. A Dodge Ram, I believe."

"Silver?"

"Silver, yes. How do you know?"

She reached for a manila folder, and handed him a computer printout image of a pickup parked by a gas pump. "This look like it?"

"Yeah, actually," Luke said. "I think so. Where is this from?"

She showed him another, of a man wearing a dark overcoat, pumping gas, a baseball cap jammed down over his face.

"Is that Jackson Pynne?"

"Actually, I think— It's hard to tell, but, yeah, it looks like him."

"Any idea why he might've been here? Or how we might reach him?"

"No, not really. To both questions." Thinking about it some more. "Why? Where did this come from?"

"Between us? This matches the description of a pickup truck that was seen idling on the church road early Tuesday morning. About an hour before you found Jane Doe."

"Oh."

"Yeah."

She called up a map on one of her monitors and asked Luke to pinpoint where he'd been driving and which direction in which Jackson Pynne was going when they intersected. Luke felt numb, knowing where this was heading. His instincts told him Pynne couldn't have been involved in the church killing, although Jackson's life had a been a mystery for the past several years.

Afterward, they walked in silence to the lobby, as if traveling in separate dimensions. Standing in the atrium, realizing it was time to say goodbye, Luke said, "Still no lead on who the woman is, I guess."

"Not yet."

"I guess sometimes bodies are never ID'd."

"Thousands a year, unfortunately."

"Could I share one other thought?" Luke asked.

"Please."

"I just have a funny feeling," he said, "that if the carving in her hand was a message of some kind, it might not be the only one. There might be a larger context to this, in other words." Hearing his own voice say it, though, he realized he was just trying to convince himself that Jackson Pynne couldn't have done this.

Watching her watching him, Luke again had the impression that there was someone much older inside the physical shell Amy Hunter inhabited.

"Why do you say that?" she asked.

"Well, it's just a feeling."

"Okay." Hunter nodded. He felt sure that she was about to say something else, but she just thanked him again.

AMY HUNTER RAN Jackson Pynne's name through the motor vehicle data bases. Two minutes later she had a registration ID on the truck. She spent the next thirty minutes running public records and motor vehicle searches on Pynne, finding a Delaware driver's license, an address listed in Newark, and companies he owned, or co-owned, in Delaware, Florida, and Maryland. There was another vehicle registered under his name, a 2009 white Audi, and three cars registered to his company, Bay Forest Development, which owned property in several states, including a town house in Tidewater County.

She saw that Jackson Pynne had been charged with a DWI in Rehoboth Beach, Delaware, seven years earlier, and with a domestic assault in Boca Raton in 2006. The assault charge was dropped in a plea deal.

She skimmed through the transcripts of the house-to-house interviews conducted on Tuesday by sheriff's deputies and found the two descriptions of a silver pickup. *That has to be it.* Hunter called in an alert on Pynne's license tag. State police cruisers were equipped now with trunk-mounted license plate scanners that automatically photographed the plates of passing cars. The plate-readers were capable of scanning 1,800 license plates a minute and checking them against registration records, fugitive warrants, and criminal data bases.

Jackson Pynne.

Pynne with two n's. What kind of name was that, anyway?

Hunter went through the FBI data base and then ran Internet searches on Pynne. There was a sister in Anne Arundel County, or had been, but she couldn't find a current phone number. And there were no active phone listings anywhere in the country for Jackson Pynne. It was as if he had gone out of his way to keep a low profile.

Hunter glanced out at the parking lot, feeling a kick of adrenaline. Ever since she'd been called to the church on Tuesday morning—*after* the sheriff was called—she'd felt obsessed with this case. In the middle of the night she opened her eyes and her mind immediately went to work. For the two years that she'd been assigned to Tidewater County, her job was to sift through cold cases and assist on hot cases elsewhere in the state. This was the first homicide in her own backyard. She wasn't going to let it get away from her.

It might not be the only one.

A larger context, in other words.

Hunter had been thinking the same thing, ever since she'd witnessed the crime scene. This was a case with big problems. And maybe the biggest problem was that it wasn't what they thought it was. Everyone was treating this like a local case. *What if it wasn't?*

Chapter 11

THERE HAD BEEN seven Jane Doe/John Doe cases in a six-state region over the past month. Printouts from all seven were in a folder on Hunter's desk. Fisch had made contact with detectives in three of the jurisdictions but hadn't yet turned up anything useful.

Fischer was on board with the idea that the Tidewater killer might have also killed elsewhere. Shipman wasn't, although he was too good-natured to say so. Ship seemed to have bought into the sheriff's theory that Jane Doe had been a paid escort, probably from the Baltimore or Washington area. Someone had hired her, maybe through Craigslist, transported her to Tidewater County, and dumped her body in the church. The only thing that seemed to give this theory any credibility, Hunter observed, was its repeated retelling.

But Fisch had been unable to find any evidence of escorts who'd gone missing anywhere in the region, and no one who advertised on Craigslist matched her description; also, it seemed unlikely to Hunter that an escort would have ended up in Tidewater County, let alone in a pew at the Methodist church.

Four of the John Doe/Jane Doe cases were fairly routine—a man and a woman pulled from rivers; two women, one young, one old, sexually assaulted, their bodies dumped in remote wooded areas. But the other three contained odd details, not typical in these sorts of cases. Those were the ones Hunter wanted to look at more closely.

In a small Delaware municipality an hour and a half to the north, an arson fire had destroyed a storefront wax museum four days before Tidewater's Jane Doe was discovered. A woman believed to be in her forties died in the fire, among melted figures of George Washington, Abraham Lincoln, Batman, Wonder Woman, and Elvis Presley.

In West Virginia, a woman in her late thirties was discovered at the bottom of a 4,000-foot waste pit four days before that, wrapped in a sheet and bound with duct tape.

And in central Virginia, the body of a man was left in the woods beside a rural highway. He'd been shot once in the chest, but his body had also been mutilated. After he was killed, his lips were surgically sliced off and his tongue cut out.

Hunter saw from Fischer's task force log that Detective Michael Gale headed up the case in Delaware. Fischer had obtained a copy of the case file, then played telephone tag with Gale for two days, getting only his voice mail. Hunter decided she'd try again herself.

FORTY-SEVEN MILES FROM the Tidewater County line, Gil Rankin placed a call to Kirby Moss in Massachusetts. He would need Moss for the last part of this assignment, the details of which he was still working through in his head.

"I need you to come back here," he said.

"What are you talking about, I thought we were done."

Rankin said nothing at first. Then, "I know you thought that. But we're not. I need you back here."

"Jesus."

"You have a problem with that?"

"No, of course not. You need me back there, I'll be there."

"Right. Very good."

Moss had been with Gil Rankin Monday. He'd returned to New England thinking he wouldn't hear from Rankin again for months. Maybe never. But Moss had a talent that Rankin needed. And he could help make this happen quickly.

Rankin's arrangement with Moss was similar to his own deal with the Client. When you were called, you made yourself available. You carried out your assignment. You received substantial compensation. You went your way and never talked about it again.

The difference was, Rankin couldn't cast a spell over people the way his client did. Nobody could. Sometimes, in idle moments, Rankin still wondered how that worked. How the Client pulled it off. But trying to figure it out was like going into a maze full of dead ends.

Rankin knew that idle time could be the worst part of his job— thinking too much, and sometimes thinking in the wrong ways. It made him miss his boys and his wife and the good things he had down in Florida. Things he had to leave behind every time the Client called.

One hour after hanging up with Kirby Moss, Rankin was lifting weights at a storefront gym near Cambridge, Maryland. Bench-pressing 250 pounds, a dozen reps. Going to the edge, using up all the reserves of strength he could summon. Lifting was Gil Rankin's self-medication when he was on an assignment. He thrived on the process of tearing down muscles and building them up again. The feeling of new strength growing inside him.

He felt good walking out into the cold Maryland afternoon, the fresh air in his lungs, his muscles tingling again. The sky was gray and cloudy over the cornfields, a taste of snow in the breeze. But as he drove away, he heard the Client's voice in his head, as clearly as if he were sitting right there in the Jeep beside him.

Fear has a smell, Gilbert. So does betrayal. A different smell. Two very distinctive smells. You understand that now, don't you? We help these people because no one else will. They're considered malcontents and we make them soldiers. But when they turn onto those crooked paths, they become something else. We smell that betrayal, we have no choice. I wish they hadn't made us do this.

Chapter 12

"WHAT DO I think?" Charlotte asked, gazing at Luke over her wineglass. "I think we ought get away for a couple of days."

"It's not a good time for that, is it?"

"Why? Couldn't Mel fill in if anything happens?"

Actually it *wasn't* such a bad time. He had no appointments, and Melissa Walker—"Mel," the assistant pastor—was in town, so there would always be a pastor on call, as the church promised.

"It'd be good for you, anyway," she said. "We'll escape for two nights, just the three of us."

Luke glanced at Sneakers, who was lying on his left side, his legs fully extended, sound asleep by the heat vent with his favorite toy, a slobber-stained tiny reindeer. He offered no opinion.

"I've checked on reservations," Charlotte added. "We could be gone Thursday and Friday nights, be back in plenty of time Saturday for you to prepare."

"And where would we escape to?"

"The mountains. Me-ville," she said.

Meaning Charlottesville. Other people called Thomas Jefferson's old haunt "C-ville," but Charlotte liked to call it "Me-ville." Being Charlotte and all. Fortunately, Luke was the only one who ever got to hear her say this. He suspected that if she tried it on anyone else, it might sound pretentious; to him, it was like hearing his favorite song from high school.

"I could do some research at Monticello," she said. "You could hike the mountains with Sneakers and polish your sermon. Or else drive down to the university and ogle the coeds."

"Hard to resist that."

"Yes, I know."

"Actually, I think I've forgotten how to ogle."

"Of course you have."

She went into the kitchen for more wine, comfortable in her Maine moose pj's and slipper socks. Sneakers lifted his head, a vacant look on his face; he lowered it only when Charlotte had returned.

"So you want to squire me away from all this for a couple days," he said.

"Squire?"

"*Take* me away."

"I'd gladly squire, if you insist."

"Maybe later."

"It'll be good for us," she said. "Good for the soul."

"Yes." It was a pet phrase of Charlotte's, and one that Luke liked, although he had once made the mistake of asking where it came from and she'd told him it was a line from a Bob Seger song—which spoiled it just a bit.

"Anyway, if I didn't try *some*thing, I'd be an enabler," she said. "And then how would I live with myself?"

"What would you be enabling?"

"You're a smart man, but you have a rare obsessive disorder, you know. And I can see that it's starting to flare up."

"How can you tell?"

"Well—those 'Do Not Disturb' signs in your eyes. That's one clue."

"Ah."

"It'll be good to get away. For all three of us."

He looked at Sneakers. She was right, of course. People were still eyeing him a little too long when they saw him at the grocery or the pharmacy. Something had gotten into Tidewater County, it seemed, a certain kind of evil, and with it a sense of suspicion and distrust that Luke hadn't seen here before.

He looked out toward the bay. A high moon glazed the marshlands.

"Just let the investigators handle things for a while," Charlotte said, in a gentle, chiding tone, pulling her legs up onto the sofa. "I'm sure Tidewater County will be okay for two days without you."

"You really think so?"

"I do. Plus, getting away would give us a chance to talk about *things*," she added, and her blue eyes seemed to soften, becoming a place and a promise; it was the same look that had inadvertently seduced him the first time he'd met her nine years earlier.

"Ah yes," he said. "Things."

She raised her wineglass and they toasted. Moments later Charlotte looked out the window, and he noticed that her eyes had moistened, as if her mood had been momentarily subverted into some troubled private harbor. She'd been doing that on occasion lately. But each time he asked if anything was wrong, her face brightened quickly and she changed the subject.

It often struck Luke how easily Charlotte had been able to adapt to the role of a pastor's wife—at Sunday services and at congregation gatherings. But, in fact, Charlotte's spiritual passions were rooted less in religion than in music and literature and out there, in nature; it was part of her reason for wanting to visit the mountains. Her family's religious background had been weirdly eclectic: her dad was raised Unitarian, her mother Jewish, and the two somehow seemed to cancel each other out; when he met her, she'd been reading the texts of medieval mystics. But it was the silence and subtlety of changing seasons, of the landscape, the sky, the wind and water, that quietly lit her eyes and seemed to give her clarity, as if she had found her own way of measuring grace.

"I'll check with Mel tomorrow," Luke said. "If she's okay, let's do it."

"Good."

She smiled warmly and they touched glasses again.

"You've already booked us, haven't you?"

She shrugged, turning her eyes evasively to the television.

THE LEAD STORY on the ten o'clock news was, again, the weather.

"Snow Way!" Mindi Bunting, the energetic local anchor, proclaimed. "That's right, get out your snow shovels one more time, people! More of the white stuff is headed to Tidewater County this weekend! All of which is leading county residents to wonder if winter will ever end!"

A brief report about the "church killing" followed, beginning with video of Sheriff's Deputy "Beak" Stilfork ducking under the crime tape, moving with a stiff, jerky motion as if he were in a silent movie, then turning and staring disapprovingly at the camera.

"*Police continue to follow leads, but still have not identified the 'mystery woman' who was found dead in the Tidewater Methodist Church early Tuesday morning.*

"*The Sheriff's Department today confirmed that the woman was the victim of foul play but released no new details on the case.*"

"'Mystery woman," Charlotte said.

"Yes, I know."

The scene shifted to State's Attorney Wendell Stamps, walking out of the press conference at the Public Safety Complex, looking cool as can be.

"*State's Attorney Wendell Stamps, seen here at the Public Safety Complex today, and Maryland State Police homicide investigator Amy Hunter, say they are following several leads, but declined to elaborate. One source told* Eyewitness News at Ten *that the woman died of a .22 caliber gunshot wound to the chest. However, we are unable to provide independent confirmation.*"

The camera zoomed in on Hunter, wearing her army jacket, carrying a thick binder under her right arm as she rushed from the conference room into the corridor, eyes downcast. Then they repeated the clip twice.

"Is that her?" Charlotte asked. "The head investigator?"

"That's her."

"She looks like she's seventeen."

"She's fourteen," Luke said. "But mature for her age."

"Ha ha."

The segment ended with the clip of Deputy Stilfork again, his odd-featured face turning toward the camera and beginning to scowl.

Charlotte muted the sound as the news went to commercial. "So what *aren't* they saying?"

"Pretty much everything. But that's only because they still don't know anything. Although Sergeant Hunter seemed very interested today when I told her about Jackson Pynne."

"*Really.*"

"What?"

"You call her *Ser*geant Hunter?"

"Well. I don't know that I do. I guess I just did."

Charlotte got up to wash out her wineglass, an action meant to change the subject. Sneakers lifted his head and groggily followed her, in case she needed any help, although his tail hung listlessly. Charlotte was funny about women becoming too friendly with him, sometimes displaying what seemed a preemptive jealousy.

When Charlotte and Sneakers returned to the living room, Luke said, "Where was Frederick Douglass, by the way, on the day Thomas Jefferson died?"

She tucked her legs up on the sofa, gazed out toward the still-darkening bay. The book she was currently researching was on Douglass and Jefferson. Sneakers turned in two circles on the throw rug before settling. After a moment, Charlotte gave him her sweet smile.

"Douglass was living in Baltimore when Jefferson died," she said. "He was only six years old."

"I bet I can tell you where Douglass was on the day John Adams died."

She laughed. "Funny man."

Every once in a while Luke felt an urge to demonstrate that he had some sense of American history, too. That the second and third presidents of the United States had both died on July 4, 1826, within a few hours of one another, was a detail that he found endlessly interesting. Coincidences fascinated him.

Charlotte clicked off the television. She was frowning at him strangely.

"What is it?" A look of deep concern seemed to consume her face. "No, tell me. What is it? What's wrong?"

"You're not looking so well," she said. "I think you may need an emergency therapy session."

"Oh," he said. "Really?"

"Yes." She had become Dr. Nicely again, Luke's expensive sex therapist, who made house calls, one of their favorite recurring role plays. "I won't know for certain until we have a look, but I'm getting a little concerned," she said.

Luke smiled, but Charlotte, fully in character now, would not smile back.

"Maybe you're right," he said. "Maybe I do need a session."

"Yes." Charlotte stood and her eyes nodded toward the bedroom. "Let's go into the examining room and have a look. I'm getting very worried."

"SHIT!" AMY HUNTER said, gesturing emphatically at the television. "What 'sources' told you about the caliber?"

Hunter's long-haired tuxedo cat Winston watched alertly from his perch atop the bookcase. They were alone in her apartment above the marina, case files and crime photos stacked neatly on the coffee table. A small empty pizza box from Domino's was on the stove, and the last two inches of a bottle of red wine on the table.

Hunter knew that the church case was about to turn a corner. She wasn't sold on the Psalms verse, but she had a gut feeling about Jackson Pynne. She didn't like it, though, that someone was leaking information to the media. Was this the sheriff, she wondered, trying to keep her off-balance? Who else could it be?

"What do you think, Winnie, should I try to extend an olive branch to him in the morning?" Winston sashayed through her legs, swishing his tail against her. "Of course, it's not so easy when he won't return my calls, is it?"

Winston made his favorite comment, a superior-sounding *ellll!* that often sounded to her like "Hell!" He trotted importantly back to the bedroom, tail pointed straight up, as if he didn't have time for such concerns.

Hunter drank the rest of the red wine straight from the bottle. She sat for a long time that evening on her porch in the dark, watching the marina and the stars. How much longer would it take to wrap this case? To find what was behind the numbers? In three weeks she would celebrate her thirty-first birthday—although *celebrate* was not the right word. She wasn't big on birthdays, or any holidays, for that matter. Holidays made her uneasy, particularly the Thanksgiving and Christmas dinners in Pennsylvania, where her brother's wife and children always became the center of attention. Last year, Ship had suggested the two of them go out for dinner on Thanksgiving and then catch a movie. She'd almost agreed. Maybe this year. Her mother would send her a Hallmark card for her birthday, with a check inside for $150. It would arrive one day before her birthday. Her cousin Richard from California, who still wasn't sure of the date of her birthday, had already sent this year's card. It normally arrived three to five weeks early. The only other card would be from Ben Shipman, a novelty card that would inevitably make her laugh.

Hunter had a hard time sleeping that night. She couldn't turn off her thoughts—wondering if the sheriff or someone from his office was slipping details of the case to the media. Several times she was awakened by the wind, gusting rain against her windows.

Once, she was jolted out of sleep by her telephone, which rang once and stopped. "Unknown Caller." Was it a wrong number or someone trying to rattle her? *Don't be paranoid*, she told herself.

Wide-awake now, she looked out at the darkened marina through the rain-beaded windows of her living room, the boat masts tilting from side to side. For a few minutes the raw sweep of nature conjured in her the happy energies of childhood—before what her mother referred to as the "unfortunate incident." Hunter's thoughts drifted back to their single-family brick house, the hopscotch sidewalks and afternoon lawn mowers of suburban Pennsylvania. She still drew strength from those memories. But her ambitious personality always seemed to propel her forward to whatever was at hand.

She padded to her study and checked e-mails, saw one from Shipman. Sent at 10:32 P.M. It was just a subject line: *Meet for breakfast?*

Hunter debated calling him then; but no, not at three-fourteen in the morning.

She lay awake in bed awhile longer, her eyes open, her thoughts shuffling restlessly. Finally she closed her eyes and waited for sleep.

TWELVE MILES AWAY, Gil Rankin walked on a gravel driveway alongside Jimmy Creek. He noticed lights in distant farmhouse windows, the way the ice in the wind made a glassy rattle through the marsh grasses, the long casts of moonlight on the creek water, the stealthy movement of predators, and potential routes of escape. Rankin was in his element at night, moving, hearing everything clearly, breathing the cold, bracing air, figuring out exactly what he had to do here in Tidewater County.

Chapter 13

In the morning, newly minted icicles hung from the wooden awnings and drain spout just outside the bedroom window. Luke pulled on his robe and stepped into his slippers. He savored the quiet of early morning, the chance to spend time in prayer, to be thankful. After thirty minutes in the sitting room, he walked down the hall and glanced out at the front lawn.

Sneakers was thumping his tail in anticipation as Luke debated whether or not to pull on his wool topcoat. He decided to go out in just his robe and slippers. *It's only to the end of the driveway and back.* Sneakers trotted out ahead of him but almost immediately stopped and hesitated, noticing the wet pavement under his paws. He looked mournfully at Luke.

"I know," Luke said. "But what can we do?"

Starting down the driveway, he realized he should have worn his coat. The robe felt as flimsy as tissue. The wind gusts were like ice on his face. "Careful," he said, steadying himself, walking backward in baby steps, his knee hurting again.

Stooping to pick up the *Tidewater Times*, he heard tires spinning into motion where the road tucked into the tall brown marsh grasses and veered east.

A white Audi skidded to a stop on the pavement beside him.

The tinted passenger window whirred down.

"Luke?" the driver exclaimed, as if startled to find him in front of his own house.

"Jackson?"

So he'd been right.

"How you been, Luke?"

"Good."

"Thinking about you. You doing all right?"

Jackson Pynne set the car in Park and got out, leaving the driver's door wide open, the engine running. Walking vigorously around the front to shake Luke's hand, as if that was the important thing—that they shake immediately. He wore an expensive-looking cashmere overcoat, his scarf tucked inside, resembling an ascot.

Pynne still moved with the swagger of a young man, his arms swinging out to the sides, as if he was used to people giving him a wide berth. His face was striking, as always, hinting of drama as he stretched out his arm. For all that, though, it was a soft hand-shake, which had always struck Luke as peculiar for someone so forceful in other ways.

"So, how you been?" he asked again.

"Still good."

"How's Charlene?"

"Charlotte? She's fine."

"Good. You holding up okay?" he said, patting Luke on the shoulder, his breath turning to vapor.

"In what sense?"

"That business down at the church. Jesus Christ, I just heard about it."

"Yeah," Luke said. He glanced up for a moment at the branches moving in the wind. "What brings *you* here, Jackson?"

"Just driving through. Looking at a piece of property." He nodded vaguely over his right shoulder, as if the property were across the road. "I'm on my way out of town, actually. Working on something down South. Just thought I'd swing by, say hello. Figured you might be walking your dog or something. Dumb luck finding you."

Luke turned so his back was to the wind. He wondered how long Jackson Pynne had been parked around the corner, waiting for him to come out to retrieve the newspaper.

As he turned again, he noticed that Sneakers had jumped into Jackson's car and was now sitting in the passenger seat, watching them.

"So, what's the story down at the church, anyway?"

"The story?"

"Yeah." Pynne pushed his hands into the pockets of his overcoat. His eyes shifted, becoming colder all of a sudden, as if he were about to rob him. "I saw the thing in the paper yesterday. And then today." He nodded at the paper Luke held tightly in his hand. "Neither one really said anything."

"I guess there's not much to say yet."

"But *you* found her?"

Luke nodded, tightening the belt of his robe.

"She was *killed*, right? I mean, it wasn't suicide, an accident? Natural causes? Nothing like that?"

Luke shook his head. His teeth were chattering.

"They find anything? A car, personal belongings, anything like that?"

"I don't think so. But I'm sure the police could tell you more than I can." He tucked the paper under his other arm, shivering. Sneakers's head was sticking out of the open passenger window of Pynne's car. "Can I invite you in for a cup of coffee, Jackson?"

"Nah, I'm in a rush." A note of impatience in his tone.

"Sneakers! Come here," Luke called.

Pynne turned his head partway, uninterested in what was happening with Sneakers. "And she was, what are they saying, early thirties? Asian features?"

"Mm hmm," Luke said, although the original report in the paper had said "Caucasian." A mistake that had struck him as odd, although the local paper was known as much for its mistakes as anything else.

"Asian features?"

Luke nodded. Pynne turned his head and said something, *"Dammit!"* maybe. The wind blew strands of hair onto his forehead.

"You knew her," Luke said.

"What?"

Pynne turned to him, his eyes wet from the cold, or maybe emotion.

"You knew her."

"What?" He feigned a laugh. "Who said anything about knowing her?"

"No, I was just asking."

"Yeah? Well, you're asking the wrong question, then. Okay?"

"Okay." Luke added, "I'd be glad to talk with you about it, if you'd like, Jackson."

"Nothing to talk about, Pastor. And it's really none of your business anyway."

"Okay."

After a moment Jackson Pynne forced a smile, probably realizing that his response was inappropriate. Sneakers had jumped back out of the car and was sniffing tentatively now at Pynne's shoes.

"Look," he said. "Don't get the wrong idea here, Pastor, okay? I'm just making conversation with you. I haven't seen you—what's it been? A couple of years? I'm making conversation. What is this, you're giving me the third degree?"

"Sorry."

Pynne pretended to laugh, but another version of himself had emerged and he couldn't just put him away. Luke had seen this often in the past; anger was Pynne's problem, the thing that got him in trouble and kept him from being where he wanted to be. Years before, he'd been charged with assaulting his ex-wife, a detail Luke had forgotten until now.

"Anyway, good to see you," he said, reaching to shake his hand again.

"If you want to talk, I'm here."

"I heard you the first time, Pastor," he said, smiling stiffly. "Okay?"

"Sure."

"Okay." He walked around the car and got in.

"Oh, and Pastor?" he said through the passenger window, trying out a new demeanor—polite, reasonable. "I'd greatly appreciate it if you didn't tell anyone we had this conversation. Or that you even saw me."

Luke watched him.

"Can we agree on that?"

"I guess we could," Luke said. "Do good things with your life, Jackson."

"We agree, then."

"Where are you headed?"

"South," Pynne said. "Okay? I'll be in touch."

Luke heard him pick up speed as soon as he rounded the corner, the Audi's wheels spinning on the wet pavement, heading inland, it seemed, although with Jackson it was impossible to know.

Chapter 14

HUNTER WOKE IN darkness, disoriented, her alarm rattling insanely on the bed stand. *Was it really morning?* She shut off the alarm and blinked at the clock. Winston, sitting on her desk, meowed his approval that she was up. No doubt he was thinking already of his morning tuna.

By the time Hunter finally stepped outside for her run, a cold light was streaming through the clouds and glinting on the marina waters. She started slow, her legs stiff, her eyelids feeling pasted together. But the chill of the air—wet with a trace of snow—soon got inside of her and began to force her awake. Running north on the marina road, she found a rhythm, Maroon 5 cranked on her iPod as she strode through the long shadows of the shipyard, where crab and oyster boats were mounted on cinder blocks. She stretched out her stride on the long incline to Seven Shoals Road, beginning to sweat finally. Coming to the overlook where the road dead-ended, she slowed to catch her breath and ran in place, looking out at the glittering scales of the Chesapeake, the fringes of foam down along the beaches of the bayfront houses. She turned in circles a couple of times, punching her fists in the air as Radiohead blasted in her ear, shouting twice, "We're going to solve this thing!"

It was Hunter's version of a "Rocky" moment.

As she ran back, morning light gilded the tall grasslands and blushed the narrow creeks and tributaries to the east. She let her stride unwind full-tilt on the downhill, feeling inspired now, really starting to think that this might be the day the case would break open.

"HEY!" SHIPMAN SAID, waving Hunter over. He'd bought her meal and set her place with a couple of napkins and a spoon. Their breakfasts here were always the same: fruit and yogurt parfait with orange juice and a side of hash browns for Hunter; the Big Breakfast with hotcakes and a large Diet Coke for Ship.

"So," he said, "you got my message."

"I did."

Noticing a smear on Shipman's eyebrow, Hunter touched her own brow instructively as she sat.. "You have something."

"Oh. Thanks." Ship swiped quickly, missing it, and picked up his fork again.

"No, other side."

He touched his other eyebrow, showing a little-boy expression of mock annoyance.

"Here." Hunter leaned across the table and wiped what appeared to be a bubble of dried shaving cream away with a napkin. "Okay," she said. "All gone."

"Actually, I was saving that for later," he said, and they both laughed heartily. Somehow, Shipman's jokes always made Hunter laugh, even when they weren't funny.

"So, anyway," he said, his eyes going back to the hotcakes and hash browns. Sometimes, Shipman acted as if he had important news to convey when all he really wanted was to meet. "I wanted to tell you, something changed last night over in the Sheriff's Department."

"Oh?" Hunter felt a quick rush of anger at the mention of the Sheriff's Department.

"Yeah, there's been a shift in the case."

"What kind of shift?"

"Not sure," he said." He lifted his soda and slurped.

Jackson Pynne, Hunter thought. The sheriff must know about him now, too. Pynne would slow down the rush to indict Robby Fallow. So maybe it was a good development.

Shipman took another bite, and made a face indicating he had to finish chewing before he could speak again.

"The other thing I'm hearing?" he said. "They're pretty sure now there were two people involved."

Hunter shook her head. "And I'll bet Robby Fallow's still one of them."

"Fallow's one of them, yeah. From what I hear, the sheriff has something solid on him now."

"Oh? And what might that be?"

"Well." He was sawing a sausage link. "Supposedly, they found a .22 caliber shell in Junior Fallow's cottage. Robby owns a .22 handgun. Which, as we know, was the weapon involved."

"But they haven't shared that with us."

"I know."

"This *is* our investigation, right?"

"Right."

Hunter looked out at the traffic, forcing herself to calm down.

"So what's the theory du jour, then?" she said finally.

"The what?"

"The sheriff's theory."

"Oh. That Junior Fallow got into a fight with this woman. Who was an escort."

"But an escort working where? There are no escorts in Tidewater County. And Fisch hasn't found evidence of any escorts anywhere else."

"I know, I'm just saying—"

Hunter shook her head. "I don't think so," she said. "If the Fallows killed an escort, they would have dumped her somewhere, they wouldn't have broken into a church and posed her. Although I can't imagine them being involved with an escort in the first place."

Shipman cleared his throat, nodding.

"Is it possible the sheriff would do something to, let's say, enhance the case against Fallow?" Hunter asked.

Ship momentarily stopped chewing, his eyes widening as if he were a student who'd been asked a difficult question. "Well," he said. "I mean, do I know that he's ever done anything like that before? No, I don't. But, I mean—is it possible? Sure, I guess it's possible."

"And do they think they have enough to convince a grand jury?"

"Well, I mean, it doesn't *take* a lot, right? Will they have enough to indict? Probably. Convict? I don't know. But you know what?"

Hunter realized that her cell phone was ringing. Luke Bowers.

"Excuse me," she said. "Let me take this."

"Oh, okay. Sure."

She turned away from Shipman: "Hunter."

"Good morning," he said. "In case you're interested, I just spoke with Jackson Pynne. He came by my house. I got the impression he knows the woman we found in the church."

"*Really.*" Hunter stood and walked toward the window. "Please. Tell me more."

He did. Hunter let him talk, glancing several times back at Shipman, who was hunched over, eating the last of his pancakes, straining to listen.

"And what was he doing in Tidewater County?"

"He said he was passing through, looking at a piece of property. I almost got the idea that he came here to talk with me. To ask about the woman in the church. He said he was working on some kind of deal down South. I don't know that it means a lot, but I thought you'd like to know."

"Yes, I do. Thank you for telling me. I'll call you later," Hunter said, watching the sparse morning traffic, figuring out where to go with this.

"Jackson Pynne," she told Shipman, setting her phone down on the table. "That's the new development."

"Really? Are you sure?"

Hunter nodded, and explained. Afterward, Ship got a look in his eyes, one she recognized.

"Tell me what you're thinking."

"Just that Pynne had a connection with Fallow," he said. "Pynne tried to buy his property a few years ago, when he was living here."

"Haven't a lot of people tried to buy it?"

"I guess."

Hunter put the lid on her empty parfait cup.

No, she thought, looking past Shipman to the highway. The case *is* shifting. But not necessarily in the ways the sheriff thinks it's shifting.

"Actually," she said to Ship, "I don't think we're looking at the right things yet. I think maybe we need to go in a completely different direction."

Chapter 15

THE SOUTH COUNTY Sheriff's Substation was an old four-room fisherman's cottage at Linley Point on property owned by the county. During the early summer months, some of the largest blue crabs in the world were pulled from Linley Creek, and the deputies would often hang crab traps from a dock in the morning before they went on patrol and then carry dinner home in their trunks at the end of their shifts.

Sheriff Clay Calvert squinted unpleasantly at Hunter, who was standing now in his doorway, surprised she had finally cornered him. He closed his laptop. There were several magazines on the desk, including *Time, People, Sports Illustrated,* and the *National Enquirer.* He seemed to be the only one working today. If that's what he was doing.

"Sheriff. How are you this morning?"

"Doing fine."

"Pretty quiet out this way."

"Yep. What do you need?"

"Just thought we might talk. Glad I finally caught up with you."

He didn't respond or offer her a seat.

Hunter took in the room. The furnishings were old and utilitarian. Metal office desk, file cabinets, bookshelves. The only personal item a photo of his wife and son. Sheriff Calvert's wife Shana worked for the County Records Department, a pretty, brassy-looking woman with big blond hair, who'd grown heavyset over the past few years. The night before, sitting home, Hunter had told Winston the cat that she might try to flatter the sheriff, as a way of getting him on the team; but seeing the resentment in his face now, it no longer felt like an option.

"I've left several messages for you since Tuesday morning, sir," she said.

"Have you? Been a busy couple of days. Also, my wife's not been well."

"I'm sorry to hear that."

His nose crinkled as if picking up a bad smell. "So, what can I do for you?"

"Just thought we might lay our cards on the table. About Robby Fallow. Before things escalate anymore."

Hunter waited.

"Do what now?"

"I visited Robby Fallow yesterday. He wouldn't talk with me."

"Well, I guess that's his right, isn't it?"

Hunter met his smile. "Yes, except that we're working together here, as a task force, to solve a homicide case." She felt her heart begin to thump. "Or supposed to be. I know you've talked with Mr. Fallow and I'm told you may have found some evidence at his motel. He seems a little rattled by it all."

"Robby?"

"Robby."

"I've talked with Robby about any number of things," he said, still pretending to be confused over what she was saying. "I couldn't comment on whether or not he's rattled."

"Mind if I sit?"

"Help yourself."

She did. "Sheriff, is there anything you'd like to share with me? Anything that might be considered evidence that was found in Junior Fallow's cottage? A .22 caliber shell, for instance?"

"No, ma'am." His eyes went flat. It reminded her of how quickly her cat Winston could look feral when he felt trapped. "These were private conversations," he said. "I've known Robby since we were little boys. I knew his daddy. Went to school with Robby and his wife, rest her soul. Do we talk from time to time? Why, of course we do."

"Sir, you're aware of the agreement with the county regarding homicide investigations. If you're withholding evidence or deliberately not cooperating with this investigation, I can go to the county commission and ask to have you removed from this task force."

He stared at her. Then he pulled out his trash can, leaned forward and spit into it, his saliva making a hard pinging sound on the metal. He slid it back under his desk and nodded, giving her his attention.

Hunter went on, "I'm told you wanted to hold off releasing information about the numbers in the woman's hand to other agencies. Perhaps we should talk about that. Because that would have to be at my direction."

"Do what, now?"

She repeated herself, using slightly different language, her voice nearly cracking at one point. The sheriff sighed as she finished, and Hunter saw something she'd never seen before—a trace of sadness in his eyes. For just a moment she almost felt for him.

"No," he said. "I wouldn't have an opinion on that. I'm sorry if someone gave you the wrong impression."

"Sir, why were you concerned about releasing the numbers carved into her hand to other law enforcement agencies?"

"Well." He softened his voice into a near-whisper, showing the edges of an unpleasant smile. With the scars on his face, it made him a little scary. "Between you and me, Sergeant? Because that may be exactly what Robby wants." Emphasizing the last four words. "All right?"

"Sir?"

"I just don't want us—any of us, and least of all you—to be manipulated by Robby Fallow. You understand? It's possible—and I'm not saying I have any direct evidence of this yet—but it's possible Robby may've carved those numbers hisself to throw us off."

"Where would you have gotten that idea?"

"Didn't get it anywhere. Why don't you ask *him*, if you're going to question everything I say?"

"As I just said, he won't talk to me. But *you* talked with Robby about it," she said.

"That's right. I did. But as I say, you have questions, you need to take them directly to Robby, not to me."

Hunter took a breath, lost somewhere between a Kafkaesque labyrinth and an Abbott and Costello routine. "Evidence to the contrary, Sheriff, we *are* on the same team."

She smiled, to shift the tone. But also to keep her cool.

Sheriff Calvert surprised her by chuckling and shaking his head, gazing off toward the creek, letting his smile fade slowly. "You know something, Sergeant?" He took a long moment to reach for his crotch and elaborately adjust himself, something he did every time she'd met with him one-on-one. "Let me just share something with you. I've been at this a little while, all right? And I can see exactly what you're doing here."

Hunter let him engage her in a brief staring contest. "And what is it that you think I'm doing?"

"I know *exactly* what you're doing, Sergeant. You're acting like you want to solve this case, bring justice to the community. But you know, and I know, that's not what you're doing at all." His eyes hardened. "You know and I know that you're using this job—and this county—as a stepping-stone. You're not invested in Tidewater County. You don't even own property here. Don't even own one square inch of dirt in this county. You don't want to solve this case, you want to make a big splash so *Amy Hunter* comes out a little hero and rides off into the sunset on a white hearse."

She blinked at him several times, wondering if he'd really said *hearse* or if she'd mistaken his pronunciation of *horse*.

"And all the things that you think *we're* doing? Well, *you're* doing the exact same things," he continued. "Don't think we haven't figured that out. You're withholding evidence from *us* because you don't want us figuring anything that might take any of the credit away from *Amy Hunter*. When you get right down to it, it's pretty goddamn obvious what you're doing."

Hunter just looked at him, a little stunned, partly because he had never spoken to her like this and partly because there was a kernel of truth in what he was saying.

But there was something about this last accusation that got to her.

"What do you mean, withholding evidence?"

He smiled, his face becoming handsome, the pockmarks all

disappearing. "Well, you tell me. Sounds like you know exactly what I mean."

Hunter wasn't sure. *Was he referring to the Psalms? Jackson Pynne? Or was this just a bluff?* She hadn't told anyone at the debriefings meetings about the Psalms. Hadn't told anyone, in fact, except for Ben Shipman. But that was her prerogative. It was her case.

"Just for your own edification. Miss Hunter, I was born in this county, as was my daddy. My daddy was an arsterman, was out in that bay every morning at five-thirty. And there's no place me or my family plans to go, or wants to go, 'cept right here. This is my home. It also happens to be, far as I'm concerned, the greatest place on earth."

"Okay, sir, that's all well and good," she interrupted. "I respect that you've been here a long time and I'm sure you know many things I don't know. But none of that changes the simple fact that our unit is in charge of this investigation. And I'm in charge of the unit. I'm sorry, but that's the reality we all have to deal with. You may be upset about what was done to you by the county commissioners. But that's not my doing. I'm just abiding by the way things are. And if you or anyone else isn't able to deal with that, we'll have to make a change."

"Is that a threat, little missy?" he said, giving her his angry squint.

"No," she said. "Just the way it is."

Her body was shaking as she climbed back into her unmarked police car and started the engine.

Chapter 16

"This is Detective Mike Gale returning your call," the voice at the other end said, speaking in a country drawl, using only five or six syllables.

Hunter was back at her desk, still a little shaken from her meeting with the sheriff. She scrambled to find the folder with printouts from the Delaware arson/murder that had been e-mailed to Sonny Fischer. "Thank you, I appreciate you calling back," she said. "I'm, uh, investigating a Jane Doe here in Tidewater County. And looking at other cases in the region for possible similarities. I don't see that there has been an update on the case there in several days."

"Right. Nothing to update," he said. "Insurance investigator has it right now."

She scanned the case summary: a storefront wax museum in a small town about a half hour from Dover. The badly burned body of an unidentified woman found inside, among melted wax figures of presidents and comic book heroes. Dental and DNA tests hadn't drawn an ID so far. Nothing from missing persons reports.

"What similarities do you see, you don't mind my askin'?"

"I didn't say there *were* similarities. I said I was looking for them." Hunter glanced through a news clipping about the case. "This was a wax museum?"

"Little historical museum, uh-huh. It's known as the Haunted History Museum. *Was* known. The owner bought a few cheap wax figures, I don't know, ten, twelve years ago. Abraham Lincoln, George Washington. Then added an Elvis, which wasn't quite life-sized—and wasn't authorized by the Elvis estate, either, I'm told. And then Wonder Woman. Batman."

"And the woman who died?"

He coughed. "No ID yet. No connection to the museum we've been able to determine. Strange case."

Yes, Hunter thought. He gave her more, speaking in a slow cadence with drawn-out vowels: the fire probably started around two or three o'clock in the morning. An accelerant, kerosene, was found among the charred remains. Latex glove prints on a wall near the rear entrance. It had rained that night and all the next morning, so footprint and tire track evidence behind the museum had mostly been washed away.

"Who owns the museum?"

"The owner's name is Mervin Coleman," he said. "He was charged a few years ago in a tax fraud case involving the museum, so—off the record?—yeah, we've treated him as a possible suspect. But so far nothing ties him to the fire. He was on vacation down to Myrtle Beach when it happened."

Hunter wrote the name on her legal pad. Something about this detail bothered her, she wasn't sure why. She looked up, saw a pair of Canada geese flapping in the bright sky above the pine trees beyond the parking lot.

"Could've been anyone, though," the detective continued.

"Might've been a drifter, broke in the back door. Maybe just some-body wanting to keep warm. It's been brutal cold this winter, I don't have to tell you. May have even been an elaborate suicide. Or an elaborate dump job."

"There wasn't any writing left behind, was there?" Hunter asked. "Any numbers, letters, at the scene, anything like that? On the body, on the premises?"

Detective Gale coughed, and then there was a long pause. Hunter could hear him breathing.

"Excuse me?" he said.

"There wasn't any writing left behind, was there? Any numbers or letters, that kind of thing?"

"Why you askin'?"

"Sir?"

"I'm not sure I understand your question. Or that I want to talk about it over the phone. I normally like to see who it is I'm talkin' with. Face-to-face, so to speak. No offense intended."

"None taken. All right," Hunter said. She glanced at her desk clock, figuring how long it would take to get there. "Can I meet with you, then? I can be there in less than an hour and a half."

"UNUSUAL CASE FOR US," Detective Gale said, poking his pencil point on the open case file. "Homicides, we've had, what, three now since I've been here? That's in eleven and a half years. Three including this one, I mean."

"Were the other two solved?"

"Other two was cut and dry. One the husband, the other the boyfriend."

"But this one isn't."

"No, that's right. This one isn't."

They were interrupted by the whoosh of a toilet flushing next door. Gale waited awkwardly for the whining of the filling tank to stop. Although his voice contained the gruff inflections of someone much older, he looked to be in his mid-thirties, a small blotchy-skinned man who wore thick-lensed tortoiseshell glasses. His hair was blond and thin and he sported a slightly lopsided brush mustache. The detectives bureau was a small office at the back of a dingy brick-facade municipal police station downtown.

Detective Gale gave her the basics of the case again, seeming to enjoy having a visitor in his office, all the while opening paper clips and bending them every which way until he finally broke them. It didn't take Hunter long to figure out that Michael Gale was the *entire* detectives bureau for this town.

"But anyway," he said, interrupting himself. "You asked me about some numbers."

"I did."

"I don't see any reference to numbers in the Tidewater County case."

"No," she said. Hunter suspected he'd been studying the church case since they'd spoken on the phone. She said, "I don't see any reference to numbers in the arson case, either."

"Well, that part's under investigation. Insurance investigators have it. And I don't know that it means anything." He cocked his head and opened another file. Pulled out a glossy photo and looked at it. "This is the victim," he said, grimacing as he handed it to Hunter. "Lovely, isn't it?"

The corpse did not look human. Just the blackened shape of a head and a partial skeleton.

"Did she die in the fire?"

"No, ma'am, she didn't." He was holding out his hand, waiting for the photo back. "But we haven't released that yet. According to the medical examiner, there was no monoxide in the tissue that was recovered."

"So she was deceased before the fire started."

"Well, we know that she didn't burn to death, anyway, that's right. May have been a gunshot. Looks that way, in fact."

Hunter handed the photo back. "If it was a gunshot, that would be another similarity with our case."

He pushed up his glasses again, interested.

"What about numbers?" she said. "Were there any numbers left behind?"

Instead of answering, he lifted a third file from a corner of the desk, opened it and passed a photo to Hunter. Then another.

"I can't tell you what this means, but here you go. We thought it might just be something that came on the glass. It's an unusual paint, though. Fire resistant, gold paint. The owner says he knows nothing about it. Never saw it before."

The first photo showed the front of the museum, after the arson, the glass and wood soot-blackened. Arced letters on the glass spelled out *Haunted History Museum*. The second photo was from inside, a close-up of four numbers, maybe an inch and a half tall, painted in gold in the lower right-hand corner of the window: 6823.

Hunter studied it.

"And those numbers weren't there before the fire?"

He shrugged. "The owner, Mr. Coleman, says he has no idea where they come from, as I say. We haven't spoken to anyone who recalls seeing those numbers before Friday morning."

"And the fire was Thursday night."

"Yes, ma'am."

Four days before the Tidewater County Jane Doe was discovered.

Hunter fixed him with a look. "So then what do you think the numbers might be?"

"Well. We checked with the glass companies. Not something they would've done. We looked at a few other things." He smiled. "Our police chief thought for a while it might be something gang-related."

"Gang-related how?"

He made a face and shook his head. "There'd been this thing—this rumor going 'round that gang members were randomly shooting at motorists on the I-68 for a time. Some kind of initiation thing. Turns out it was just a story, what they call an urban legend.

"Then we had a numerologist look at it," he went on. "Gave us a bunch of ideas. The number sixty-eight is supposed to be a symbol of loyalty, she said." He shook his head and one side of his mouth smiled. "Bunch of crap, frankly," he said. "But if you have any other ideas, I'm all ears."

Hunter handed him back the photos. *There's something very creepy about this case; familiar-creepy.*

"Can we go look at the building?" she said.

"Sure."

Chapter 17

UNLIKE TIDEWATER'S MAIN Street, this one had several boarded-up storefronts. Only an attorney's office seemed to be open today in the block where the wax museum had been.

Sheets of plywood covered the front windows of the museum. Gale twisted a key in a padlock and pushed the plywood-covered door. The museum's gift shop in front was mostly intact, though the walls were soot-blackened. The room still reeked of burnt wood and plaster.

Gale clicked on his flashlight, pointing the beam at the entrance arch to the museum, then led her in, swinging the light back and forth over the floor. The museum had been a single large room, he said, showing her with the light beam what was left of it. The flashlight picked out a figure she recognized as Superman, his legs now foreshortened, most of his face and arms gone.

"Started the fire at the back of the museum in here." Gale swished the light beam against another doorway to a small rear office. "Probably using paper and plastic and stuffing from the sofa cushions."

"So he carried her in through the back door?"

"Back door, that's right. Probably parked right behind the door. Broke in. Set up the fire. Then carried the lady in. Set her body on fire. Left the door open when he left."

"Single point of ignition, then?"

"No, ma'am." He pointed the light among the various-sized stubs of the wax figures. "Arson report says that they believe there were four separate points of ignition."

The detective's demeanor had changed, Hunter noticed, as soon as they'd entered the museum. His voice had become more halting; his pauses seemed reflective. Scenes of unexplained killings had always felt a little haunted to her, inhabited still by the mystery of what had happened and by the presence of the victim. Hunter could tell this crime still affected him deeply.

As they stopped again in the center of the museum, she felt a gathering sense of recognition—the way the killer had staged the scene to create a dramatic impression.

Hunter smelled the wet leather of Gale's jacket as he moved closer to her, his sleeve touching hers.

"Were there security cameras?" she asked, stepping away.

"Disabled." He aimed the light toward the storage area. "Motion activated. We figure he came in through the office and deactivated them there."

"So he would have had to know the setup."

"That'd be a reasonable assumption."

"Where was the victim, exactly?"

He pointed the beam at a spot near the center of the room. "Seated about here. One of the points of origin." He moved closer, so he was directly above the spot where the victim had been found. "Accelerants poured on her body, evidently." He drew a dash of light on the floor. "She was between the figures of Wonder Woman." He moved the beam several feet to the left. "And Batman. Both of which burned down to almost nothing, as you can see."

Hunter watched, imagining the man setting her there, pouring the accelerant, then igniting it with a cigarette lighter. She had seen sloppy arsons over the years; this one wasn't sloppy. It was a studied, carefully planned crime. The perpetrator knew how it would burn. He had left the back door open, knowing how the oxygen would impact the fire; that the cold air would fan the flames but then would also help extinguish them, leaving the front of the building intact.

Detective Gale clicked off his light and moved back toward the gift shop. Hunter stood in the darkness for a while, taking it in. *The perpetrator's comfortable working at night. In darkness.*

"There you go," Gale said, shining his light on the lower corner of the front window.

Hunter crouched down to examine the numbers. Deliberately subtle, it seemed. *As if the perpetrator didn't want his puzzle to be figured out too quickly.* Gale moved the light beam slowly over the numbers, back and forth, left to right, right to left.

They seemed almost even, as if the killer had used a stencil. Hunter traced her fingers over the gold paint.

"Strange, huh?"

"Yeah, very."

She stood.

"Why bring her here to a wax museum, do you think?" she asked when they stood on the sidewalk in front.

"That's the question, isn't it?"

Hunter took a deep breath as Gale padlocked the door. The air was wet, and above the brick buildings she saw stray snowflakes.

She zipped her army jacket, and they walked into the wind around the building, Hunter picturing where the killer had parked in the alley before carrying the woman's body inside.

"When will the insurance company sign off on this, then?" she asked when they'd returned to the police station.

The detective pushed his glasses up on his nose. He shrugged. "Next week?"

"And are you still looking at the owner?"

"Not really. Not much to look at."

"Can I call you tomorrow?"

"Don't see why not. Why?" he said. "What are you thinking?"

"I don't know yet," she said. "Hunches."

"Okay."

Detective Gale gave Hunter printouts of the case-file photos and walked her out to the parking lot. As they stood by her car, he pushed his glasses up on his nose and sunk his hands in the pockets of his leather coat. Hunter saw his eyes examining the inside of her car.

"Think it's going to snow?" he said.

"Feels like it."

They both looked up at the sky.

"Too late for it, really. It's been a strange season," he said.

"It has."

"What kind of hunches?" he asked, looking at her directly again through the thick lenses.

Amy Hunter sighed, not wanting to say anything yet. "I just have a funny feeling about this," she said. "I think maybe you and I are dealing with the same killer."

This didn't seem to surprise him. "That's why you came," he said. "Tell me about the numbers."

"I will."

"When?"

"Let me check on something first," she said. "Then I'll call you."

LUKE WAS LOADING suitcases into the back of their car when Charlotte yelled from the front porch that the "inspector" was on the line.

"I'm on the road, in Delaware," Hunter told him. "Heading back to Tidewater. Could you meet me in fifty minutes?" She added, "It's urgent."

"Oh, okay." Luke glanced at his watch. Their plan had been to leave in seven minutes. "Actually, we're just about to get out of town. We're going away for a couple of nights, down into the mountains." He heard Hunter's car engine accelerate. "We'll be back Saturday, early afternoon."

"Can I ask you to delay your departure? I've just found something I need to share with you."

"Well, then, sure. I suppose. Although I'll have a restless mixed Lab to contend with. He's a traveling fool. A true road dog. We should've named him Kerouac."

"I'm sorry, but can I meet you at the church in fifty minutes?"

"I'll be there," he said.

Luke walked back into the house, feeling a charge; it was as if some of Amy Hunter's excess energy had been transferred to him through the phone line. He tripped going up the steps and nearly fell face first onto the porch. "Jeez," he muttered, looking back to see what he'd tripped over.

Charlotte was in the kitchen, filling Sneakers's travel bag with toys and chew treats. Classical piano music was playing on her CD—maybe Liszt, Luke thought, but probably not.

"You're not going to believe this," he said.

Chapter 18

AGGIE CARRIED IN a steaming mug of coffee, set it on the coaster on Luke's desk, straightened his stapler and flipped his desk calendar to the correct day. She was dressed in a lovely black outfit today, her hair styled, frosted, and sprayed enough to withstand a Category 2 hurricane.

"Thank you, Ag."

"My pleasure."

Five minutes later she was back.

"Amy Hunter is here again?" she said, her voice just above a whisper. "I informed her I didn't know if you were available. Would you like me to say you're on a conference call?"

"No, please have her come in."

Hunter walked in, her hair wildly disheveled. Luke stood to greet her.

"Thanks, thanks for seeing me."

"Sure."

She exhaled as if she had run the last half mile. One of her collar points was up, the other flat. Luke gestured for her to have a seat.

"I hit on something today," she said, sitting on just the front edge of the chair, "that's starting to freak me out a little bit. I'd like to share it with you, if I could."

"This is something besides Jackson Pynne?"

"Right, something besides that."

She placed a nine-by-twelve envelope on his desk.

"I have to put this in context first."

Luke nodded. Hunter told him what she'd learned about the Delaware arson case from Detective Michael Gale: The unidentified female victim. The medical examiner's ruling that she hadn't died as a result of the fire. The owner Mervin Coleman and his conviction for insurance fraud.

She showed him the laser printouts Gale had given her of the window glass.

Luke studied the image: 68 23.

"I already looked up Psalm 68, verse 23," Hunter said. "Doesn't fit."

"Okay."

"I just wonder if there's another one. Or something else it could be."

Luke reached for his Bible and opened it. He knew that the only books with sixty-eight chapters were Psalms, Isaiah, and Jeremiah. He went to Isaiah first, then tried Jeremiah. Then he turned to Psalm 68 and checked anyway.

Line 23: *That your foot may crush them in blood.*

No, she was right, it didn't fit.

He felt the texture of the familiar thin paper between his fingers. The attic rafters creaked loudly in several places, as if parts of the building were communicating with one another. Hunter, leaning her elbows forward on his desk, watched intently.

"What theories do they have in Delaware about the numbers?" he asked. "Anything?"

"They don't know. They thought maybe gangs for a while. I think they're probably just going to chalk it up to not meaning anything."

Luke looked at the open Bible and got a different idea.

Change the punctuation.

He went back to Psalm 68 and tried verses 2 and 3.

He looked at Hunter's expectant, light brown eyes, her smooth cheeks still pink from the cold. Then he turned the Bible around, pushed it toward her and let her read.

As smoke is driven away, so drive them away, As wax melts before the fire, So let the wicked perish at the presence of God But let the righteous be glad; Let them rejoice before God; Yes, let them rejoice exceedingly.

Hunter's eyes went back to his. "Holy crap," she said.

Luke half smiled.

"Sorry," she said.

He pulled the Bible back across the desk and read the words again. The idea of getting away into the mountains suddenly wasn't as enticing as it had been an hour ago.

"You want to know something?" she said. She was standing now, her eyes looking out through the window glass like restless thoughts. "The first time you mentioned this?—the Psalms thing?—I didn't really buy it. Not all the way—"

"I know."

"I mean, I thought it *could* be something. But it also might just be coincidence. Like we were reading too much into it."

"I wondered myself."

"I still don't know that I'm a hundred percent." Her right hand was a fist softly pumping the air. "But if it's a coincidence, it's now two coincidences. And that's freaking me out a little bit. You know?"

"I know. Me, too."

He could see that she was anxious to get away, as if there were someplace specific she must go—and maybe there was. "Anyway. I'm sorry to have kept you from your trip. If you think of anything else, please call me, okay?"

"I will. Although we're going to be in the mountains, as I said, and may not have service."

"All right. Well, have a safe trip."

Luke stood to shake her hand. But she surprised him by coming around the desk and giving him a quick hug, her face cool and smooth against his. His eyes reflexively went to the outer office, where Agnes Collins was seated behind her desk.

"THE THING ABOUT Pynne is that he knows how to hide," Gil Rankin was explaining to Kirby Moss. "Okay?"

Moss had arrived at the house on Jimmy Creek just after four-thirty, more than an hour late. Something his client wouldn't have allowed, but what could he do about that? The two of them were seated on leather armchairs in the living room, a room that reminded Rankin of a private club, lots of leather and dark wood, maritime oil paintings on the walls. Blinds and drapes drawn.

Moss held a Diet Coke on his right leg. "Can't hide forever," he said, sounding unconcerned.

"That's not the point," Rankin said. Pynne owned a town house in the county, a summer rental property on the water, southwest of there. If he returned to Tidewater, that's likely where he'd go. So Moss needed to keep surveillance on it.

"Of course." Moss trying a smile.

Rankin didn't tell him that he'd been to the town house himself on Tuesday. That he'd broken into the garage. Only the Client knew that part of it. Such was their agreement, "as it was written." Although, of course, no part of the agreement was in writing.

"At the same time, poke around," he told Moss. "Stay inconspicuous, but keep your eyes open. *Listen.* It might take a couple of days for him to return, I'm told. There's even a chance he'll show up to church on Sunday."

"Scene of the crime."

"Right, so you need to be there. In case it happens."

"If we haven't found him before then."

"Right."

"And if he doesn't show at all?"

Moss drank his soda, keeping his eyes on him. Funny looking man, Rankin thought, round face, crew cut, eyes that darted around a lot. Moss wanting to start a conversation, while he wanted to keep it strictly business, not wanting to hear about Moss's family in Massachusetts because then Moss would want to know about his. Talking about his wife and sons would be the same as getting them involved. And that wasn't going to happen. No, sir. That wasn't any of Moss's business.

"If I need to, I've got a way of getting his attention," Rankin said. "Okay? But that's between me and him. Let it sit a day or two. I don't want him going to the fucking police."

"Gotcha." Moss went to his soda again, although Rankin was sure he didn't know what he was talking about. He even wondered for a moment if he really needed Kirby Moss in order to finish this thing.

Chapter 19

SNEAKERS SAT LOOKOUT in back, panting almost continuously as the slow movement of Saint-Saëns's third violin concerto played and the mountains rose up in the distance. Travels with Charlotte tended to be unpredictable, but in a good way. Being on the road was an evolving adventure, never a means to an end; it wasn't unusual for her to see a sign for an antiques shop or a fruit stand twelve miles off the highway and decide to pay a visit. This time she took what became an eighteen-mile detour to a country store near Fredericksburg that advertised homemade jams. Charlotte and the owner, a petite, animated gray-haired woman, spoke at length about the process of making and canning preserves, while Luke walked Sneakers down an unpaved country lane. They drove away with a case of blueberry jam in the trunk.

Continuing south by southwest, Luke gazed blankly out at the gray-green fields, scenery that rested his eyes and kept his thoughts far away. If the Tidewater County killing was connected to another case, it was likely connected to others as well, which was what he had suspected from the beginning. But if the Psalms were a message, who was the intended recipient? And how might the victims be connected? What did a middle-aged woman in Delaware and a thirtyish-year-old found in his church have in common?

"You're obsessing, still," Charlotte said, turning down the music.

"Am I? I guess I was so obsessed I didn't notice."

"So let's talk about it."

"We don't have to."

"What if I want to?"

"That's different."

But then neither of them could figure out what to say first.

"I think the case has taken a very strange turn," Luke said at last.

"Yes, I know," she said. "So, is it really about the Psalms? Is that what you're thinking?"

"Starting to."

"Is she?"

"Hunter?"

"The sergeant."

"Starting to."

She switched lanes and passed a semi trailer. Then another, more aggressively, the speedometer needle climbing above eighty. For some reason, Charlotte always drove faster when they were talking, her hands steady at two and ten o'clock on the steering wheel. Sneakers lay down across the seat in back now and occasionally whimpered when he felt she was driving too fast. Luke felt the same way at times, but kept quiet.

"It's the sheriff who's been spreading those stories about Robby Fallow."

"I think so," Luke said. "The sheriff and his proxies. Maybe Barry Stilfork."

"I don't get it. Why?"

"Because he senses opportunity, I guess. The sheriff's profoundly resentful about what happened to him last year. That's my theory anyway. He thinks this could change things back."

"Tidewater County is a peculiar place."

"People keep telling me that."

"What sort of opportunity, exactly?"

"A chance to make a case against Robby Fallow and have it stick."

"But if this is about the Psalms, he can't do that."

"That's right."

"It would also mean they're dealing with a serial killer."

"Yes," he said. "That, too."

She switched lanes to pass again. A town appeared ahead with a gas station, traffic signal, white wood-frame houses, an old Baptist church. The case *had* taken a strange turn. If this was a serial killer, there was something wrong with the setup, Luke sensed. An idea kept playing in his thoughts, trying to take a shape.

Charlotte slowed as the road narrowed to two lanes and then became a residential street, snaking past houses and a public green, then an antiques store, hardware, minimart. Sunlight backlit the gray clouds above the mountains ahead.

"Why Psalms?" she said, wanting to draw Luke out. "I mean, is this someone trying to justify what he's doing? Meting out punishment, so to speak?"

"Meting?"

She turned the music off. "Tell me more about Psalms," she said.

Luke glanced at her, seeing that she was fully engaged now. If she can't stop me from obsessing, she'll join me. Okay, he thought.

"What do you want to know?"

"Everything?" He looked at her. "But condensed."

"'Kay." He formulated a topic sentence as she picked up speed again. "The Psalms, in a sense, encapsulate all of the scriptures, old and new. And cover the whole range of the human condition."

"Old and new?"

"They predict what comes in the New Testament—although, of course, they were written hundreds of years earlier. Psalm 22, for example, tells the story of the crucifixion, Psalm 16 the resurrection. Psalm 110 has the savior at the right hand of God. The Psalms were the first prayers used in Christian liturgy. Thomas Aquinas said the Psalms contained the essence of Christian doctrine in poetic form."

"How are they different from the other books in the Old Testament?"

"They're different because they don't tell stories. The Psalms are divinely inspired songs, poems, and prayers written over a period of about a thousand years. Telling us how we should live our lives. Originally, they were meant to be sung."

"And they were written by David."

"Mostly, yeah. Many of them reflect events in David's life. God famously called David 'a man after my own heart.'"

"There's a lot of eye-for-an-eye stuff in the Psalms, though, isn't there?" she said, flooring the accelerator as they returned to divided highway. Sneakers scrambled to a standing position to see what was going on.

"Yes. Lots of 'smiting enemies.'"

"Could this be someone in the clergy, then? Doing the smiting?"

"I wondered that," Luke said. "Possible, but I don't think so. I think an FBI profiler would probably say that this is more likely a lone-wolf sociopath. Someone who doesn't interact well with others. Who has time to create an intricate fantasy world, with twisted interpretations of Bible verse. Maybe transferring his own feelings of persecution. It also sounds like someone who doesn't understand the Psalms."

"How so?"

"The Psalms were beautiful Hebrew poetry. They were a part of ordinary daily life for the Israelites. If this is really about the Psalms, they're being cherry-picked for a very different purpose—to justify violence and anger."

"And how would Jackson Pynne be involved? Is this him?"

"I don't know." An unsettling feeling rippled through him. "All I know," he said, "is that he has some connection with the woman in the church."

"But no idea what."

"Not yet."

She passed a stream of cars and coasted back into the right lane.

"Strange name, Jackson Pynne. Always reminds me of Jackson Pollock."

"Well, actually, his thinking process resembles a Pollock painting."

"Ha ha. Could *he* be the killer?"

"No, I don't think so," Luke said. "But I have a funny feeling he might be able to tell us who is."

"Why hasn't he gone to the police, then?"

"Good question. He's scared of something. Or someone, maybe. I don't know, I don't get it yet."

They drove in silence for a while, pondering that. Woods, clearings, fences, farmland. Luke wondering what Jackson Pynne had done with himself these past few years. What he'd thought about and dreamed about. How he'd strayed from his goal of creating luxury coastal developments. Had he been able to find simple pleasures in the ordinary, as he had often urged Jackson to do?

"You know what I think," Charlotte said after a while. "When we return, they'll have ID'd the woman. Found Jackson Pynne. And solved this whole thing."

Luke nodded.

"Yes, and maybe the Democrats and Republicans will have agreed to put aside their differences and settle on a new budget deal."

CHARLOTTE HAD RENTED a two-bedroom condo with a fireplace and a sweeping back-deck view of the Blue Ridge Mountains. They'd made a pact: no television or Internet during the trip, and once they reached the mountains they would not talk about the church killing anymore. At least not until Saturday. Charlotte brought her cell phone, but it was only for incoming calls.

On Thursday night, walking with Sneakers on a wet, winding mountain road, Luke finally began to disconnect from the case. It felt exhilarating walking through the cold mist in this strange locale, smelling the pine and spruce trees, seeing the moonlit shapes of mountains in the distance. Hearing nothing but their footfalls and the dog panting.

"We did some good male bonding," he reported to Charlotte as Sneakers trotted across the kitchen to his water bowl.

"Did he encourage you to stop obsessing?"

"More than encourage. He pulled me into the woods and refused to walk back unless I gave my word."

"I trained him well."

Luke could see that Charlotte felt at home here, her eyes finding something in the mountain scenery that seemed to satisfy the wilder parts of her soul. He liked that.

In the morning, they all went on a trail hike through the woods, discovering a narrow waterfall cascading down a cliffside. He and Charlotte sat beside it and ate egg sandwiches, feeling the spray in the cool breeze, while Sneakers ran from point to point, sniffing the ground. The mountain air was a tonic, and the peacefulness in this place that Charlotte had found gave Luke a feeling of interior peace as well. Only occasionally did he think about the woman in the church pew or the peculiar way people had looked at him in the days after he discovered her.

Both evenings, he and Charlotte role-played—as they often did while vacationing. On Thursday, Charlotte was a forest ranger, checking the area for a giant brown bear reportedly roaming nearby. On Friday, Don Kendall, the local sheriff, showed up looking for a female prisoner who had escaped that afternoon. Sneakers ignored them through it all, having better things to do, chief among them lying on the throw rug, his face catching the heat from an air vent.

Friday night, sitting wrapped in blankets on the screened deck, they finally talked about the "things" that Charlotte had mentioned. Luke hoped the conversation might somehow excise the private sadness that had seemed to creep into her thoughts—and the vague restless feelings he'd had lately in the middle of the night. "Things" came down to logistics, mostly: Methodist pastors averaged five to seven years in one church, then they were moved, traded to another city like pro athletes to another sports team. Luke didn't want to do that forever, nor did Charlotte. Both of them wanted to purchase a home eventually and to live their life in one place.

"If we feel it's important," he told her, "I could give up the ministry and move on to something else. I don't know what exactly it would be. But, I mean, there are plenty of other things I could enjoy doing."

"Such as?"

"Teaching. Counseling. Writing. Pumping gas."

"Are people still paid to pump gas?"

"In Oregon and New Jersey they are."

Her lips formed a faint smile, as if she didn't believe him. It always surprised Luke when he knew something that Charlotte didn't, particularly when it was about America, her subject as historian.

"I mean, it *would* be sort of nice to live a more certain life," she said. "In one place. Right?"

"Yes," he said. "And we will—whenever we feel it's the right thing."

Luke reached for her hand; after a moment she rested her head in the crook of his shoulder, and he breathed the scent of her shampoo. The only problem with changing their life was the implication that there was anything wrong with it as it was, and neither of them believed that. Charlotte loved the freedom to write each day and to find homes for the animals at the Humane Society; and, as she'd said many times, where they lived didn't matter a lot to her. Luke enjoyed the duties of being pastor, meeting people, helping members of the church, and working to expand the congregation. Still, they were planning to visit Charlotte's parents next week, and it was always a good idea to address this issue beforehand, because it nearly always came up at the Carringtons'. Charlotte felt a gentle—sometimes not so gentle—push from her parents, her father in particular, to produce children. Maybe that was what lay behind her recent moments of sadness. Or maybe it was the ghost of her brother—her "soul mate," she had called him—whose death seemed to still haunt her family.

They sat on the deck long into the evening, sipping wine, watching the clouds drift like cold smoke over the dark mountains, the conversation lapsing to a comfortable silence.

"So, we've had 'the talk,'" she finally said.

"Yes. And we're still married."

"Hallelujah."

CHARLOTTE'S PHONE DID not ring until early Saturday, when Betsy Anders, the church organist, woke them to ask Luke if he was okay with her revised prelude and postlude selections for the Sunday service. It was the first time she'd ever sought his approval; but it was also the first service since the "church killing."

"She just wanted to make sure they were appropriate," he explained to Charlotte, who was lying in the giant bed hugging Sneakers, probably wondering why someone would call at eight o'clock on a Saturday morning. "Considering everything."

"It's good to consider everything."

"Yeah. Although it takes a while."

"True."

Luke got back in bed, tugged the blankets and finally closed his eyes.

"Don't worry about Betsy," Charlotte said. "She's a Methodist."

"Oh." Luke opened his eyes. "What's that supposed to mean?"

He turned in time to see her shoulders shrug as she pulled the covers back toward the side she occupied with her canine partner. Luke looked out: gray clouds hanging in the distance, rain or snow nesting above the mountains. "You know," she said. "Just that Methodists tend to not like the minor keys—as much as, say, Presbyterians or Catholics."

"Really?" Luke said, wide-awake now. "I love the minor keys."

"I know—and I'm glad your Catholicism stops there." She added, "Flagellation, as you know, is frowned upon in the Methodist church."

He saw her shoulders shaking under the covers and realized that she was laughing.

HEARING BETSY'S VOICE made Luke think of Tidewater again, as he lay there: Jane Doe's beautiful, vacant face as he walked across the empty sanctuary toward her. Jackson Pynne's whiskey-colored eyes darkening as he stood at the base of his driveway with no place to go. The Jane Doe in his dream, trying to dance, her damp flesh sticking to his fingers. And the scenario he could only imagine: Someone swinging a bat several times, splitting the bones of the dead woman's legs and ribs. And, later, carrying her damaged but well-dressed corpse into his church, setting her up in a rear pew and posing her so she faced the altar.

When they returned home that afternoon, and Luke read the news that they'd missed, he learned that the woman had not been identified and that there was still no arrest in the case, although Sheriff Calvert had told a reporter that investigators were "pursuing several strong leads."

Chapter 20

"SERGEANT HUNTER?"

"Yes." She recognized immediately the flat, direct intonation of the sheriff's voice.

"It's Clay Calvert. I know you're very concerned about this being a 'team effort' and all. So I just wanted to make sure you heard about this right away."

Hunter waited. *What was he up to now?*

"We're at the murder scene."

"The murder scene."

"That's right."

"The murder scene has been discovered?"

"That's correct. I'm at the location right now, along with a couple of my deputies. CSI just arrived. We've secured the scene."

"Where?"

"We're at the old Jenkins cottages down to Oyster Creek. Deputies responded to a call from the owner some forty minutes ago. We're just starting to process evidence."

So why wasn't I called immediately? Hunter almost asked, but she knew the answer, of course. As soon as she hung up, she called for Ship, who came half running into the hallway.

A maintenance man had entered the cottages that morning to check the window air-conditioning units. The mattress on the bed in Cabin 6 seemed to be stained with blood, and there was a stench in the room. Evidence techs had also found what appeared to be blood on the floor, the shower tiles and grout.

"There's something else, too," the sheriff said over the phone. "Which I'll tell you when you get here."

Hunter let Shipman drive. Oyster Creek was in the southeastern part of the county, a low-lying maze of creeks, streams, tributaries, and tall marsh grasses that formed the labyrinthine boundary with Chesapeake Bay. Yellow crime tape blew among the scraggly pine trees by the road, where a gaggle of onlookers and two reporters had gathered.

The killing had occurred in the last of a dozen cottages on a mud beach beside the creek. The Jenkins cottages were built in the late 1940s, originally for fishermen and families interested in an outdoors vacation; now, like Robby Fallow's Ebb Tide Inn, they were often vacant, rented out by crabbers in June and July and hunters in the fall. The road to the cottages was one lane and gravel. Small driveways were slotted beside each of the cabins. Two sheriff patrol cars and a state police evidence collection van were parked near the end of the cabin drive. Hunter studied the scene, quickly noting the various footprint and tire-track patterns that hadn't yet been marked as evidence, including a series of footprints extending from behind Cabin 10 to the rear of Cabin 11.

The footprints had been tramped over by fresh prints, she could see, probably from the sheriff's deputies.

Hunter looked back up the drive, figuring what might have happened. A four-wheel-drive vehicle had been parked beside Cabin 12. Two men walked from the drive to the cabin and then walked back out.

"The locks aren't real secure on some of them doors," the sheriff said, startling her from her thoughts. "If they were locked at all. I'm told they get transients in there occasionally."

"Kind of like at the church."

Calvert squinted at her. Wind gusted up the shallow creek, carrying the smells of muck and dead fish. Shipman was at the top of the gravel drive now, talking with Barry Stilfork.

"What's the something else?" Hunter asked.

"Do what?"

"You said there was something else you'd tell me, when I got here."

He nodded, but took a moment to survey the creek first, his eyes narrowing in the dull light. "State police recovered a Chesterfield cigarette butt up in the woods. At the top of the drive. Barry'll show you when he gets back. As you know, we also found a Chesterfield cigarette outside the church.

"I'm also looking at some of them shoe-print patterns," he added, "and thinking they look mighty familiar."

"But with a difference," Hunter said.

"Oh? And what difference would that be?"

"There are two distinct footprint patterns this time," Hunter said. "There was only one at the church."

The sheriff looked her up and down, and then turned to see what Stilfork was doing.

Hunter walked up the steps to Cabin 12. A rusty spring creaked as she pulled the screen door. It was a single-room cabin, with an old musty smell. The bed was at an odd angle and an armchair overturned, as if there'd been a fight. Two evidence techs were dusting surfaces—a small wooden chest of drawers and a nightstand. She stood just inside the door, looking at the massive bloodstain on the bed, which seemed to have spread from a single point.

"Tell me about the shoe prints you found," Hunter said to one of the techs, a tiny woman with dark hair and nervous eyes.

"Several well-defined prints so far," she answered

"Different prints?"

"No. One."

"Matching the prints outside?"

"Haven't checked those yet."

"Please do," she said. "Before the sheriff's deputies tramp over them."

Surprisingly, the woman turned her head and gave Hunter a knowing smile.

Hunter studied the room for several minutes, and eventually noticed something else. She walked to the wall on the other side of the bed, traced her fingers around the edge of a small hole in the wood panel.

"You see this?"

The woman looked up and froze. The other tech, a short heavyset man with hair like steel wool, walked over.

"Bullet hole," Hunter said. "No shell casings here, were there?"

"Nope."

Hunter nodded. She walked back outside, calculating the trajectory of the gunshot. It took about seven minutes for her to find it, embedded in dried mud beneath a sprinkling of pine needles. A .22 caliber bullet. The probable cause of Jane Doe's death.

Two cabins away the sheriff was standing with evidence techs who were taking tire track impressions. It wouldn't have surprised Hunter if they were taking impressions of their own vehicles.

"WHAT DO YOU think?" she asked Ship as they drove back, threading the maze of creeks and coves and back bays.

"Too many people involved. Evidence contamination."

"What did Deputy Stilfork tell you?"

"He thinks the case is looking pretty solid. They're banking on the Chesterfield cigarette now and the shoe prints. In both cases the same as at the church."

Jackson Pynne, in other words. The shift in the investigation was palpable, yes. Just as Shipman had mentioned at breakfast the day before: The sheriff's primary suspect appeared to be Pynne now, not Robby Fallow. And Calvert seemed to be embracing this new scenario just as avidly as he had pushed the one about Fallow—as if it was something *he'd* discovered. Maybe he believed he had.

Was this another version of "necessary outcome"? Sheriff Calvert liked to reach conclusions quickly, Hunter knew. Mistakenly, he considered it a sign of competence.

"Why, though?" she said. "Why would he have taken her to the church? Why would he have carved those numbers in her hand?"

"You know what Beak thinks?"

"Fortunately, no."

"He thinks that Robby Fallow and Jackson Pynne were in on this together."

Hunter gave him a look: *come on.* Shipman's smile vanished.

"I'm just saying."

"How imminent are charges now?"

"Couple of days? Maybe middle of the week. What about this Psalms thing, though?" he asked. He looked at her. "Is there anything to that?"

"I don't know." Hunter recalled the sheriff's accusation that she'd been "withholding" evidence, and decided not to tell Ship any more about Psalms right now. The only people who knew about Psalm 51:8 were the pastor and Ben Shipman. As much as she loved him, and thought of him as a brother, she sometimes worried about Ship's divided allegiances.

They fell into silence for a while, as the road wound north toward farmland. Then Ship put on his Beatles CD, nodding his head to the music. "Lady Madonna, baby at your breast, wonder how you manage to feed the rest . . ."

Hunter imagined the advice her father might have given her. *Go with your instincts. Don't let anyone throw you off your game.* Pep talks. Her dad seeming to have all the answers, wanting her to play sports, become an athlete. He'd never have imagined she'd be investigating homicides now, playing poor man's chess with the local sheriff. The world her father had tried to prep her for was out there somewhere, it just wasn't the one she lived in. She thought again of the filmy eyes of Jane Doe, above clasped hands in a church pew. The faces never went away; Hunter knew she would still be seeing those eyes years from now.

"What are you thinking about?" Shipman asked, turning down the music.

Hunter glanced at his steady freckled face and her suspicions about him evaporated. There was something irresistibly companionable about Shipman. He became uncomfortable when people were upset or quiet for too long. "Sorry," she said. "I guess I was thinking about my dad. Thinking what he might've said about all this."

"What would he have said?"

"Stick with it. Go with your instincts, stuff like that."

Ship was silent for a few beats. "He died suddenly, didn't he."

"Heart attack. Forty-three. Yeah, no one saw it coming."

"Sorry."

"Weird, the impressions our parents leave on us, isn't it? Even all these years later."

Then, after a pause, Shipman said, "Mine died young, too."

Hunter glanced at him, and felt bad that she had never asked about his father. She knew he'd been a waterman and that he was no longer alive, but little else; the narrative about Ship's dad always seemed to begin and end there. It was something he seemed uncomfortable talking about.

"Yeah, he was a deep sea crabber," Ship said. "His boat started taking on water forty miles offshore. Off the coast of North Carolina. I was thirteen."

"I didn't know. I'm sorry."

"Nah, it's okay, I never talk about it."

Hunter watched the road unfolding in front of them, the cloud-tinted light in the fields. When Shipman spoke again, his words were a complete surprise: "Tribulation leads to perseverance, perseverance to character, character to hope. And that's how it goes."

"What's that?"

"Thing my daddy used to say a lot," he said, keeping his eyes on the road. "It's from the Bible."

Hunter made a mental note to look it up. "Your dad grew up in Tidewater."

"Yep, born and raised. Tried to leave a couple times. Like me. Something about the air here, I guess, the water. Draws you back. Some people, they think they can leave their worries behind if they go somewhere else. Doesn't work that way. My ex- thought that. She moved to North Carolina, thought she'd start over, her problems would disappear. My daughter Becca, she tells me Donna's just the same as always, though only worse. She's bipolar, we think. Everything's fine for a while then it's like, whoa, look out."

"Well, I'm glad you came back," Hunter said.

"Yeah. Me, too."

It felt comfortable going into silence after that. Faintly, Hunter heard the Beatles, the chorus on "I Am the Walrus." She began to think about the case again, about what she'd seen in the woods at Oyster Creek, the game the sheriff was playing.

Finally she said, "Jackson Pynne's company owns a town house here in Tidewater County, you know."

"Does it?"

"A rental. I think it might be a good idea if you went over and had a look at it.""

"Okay. Sure." He turned the music off. "Why? Do you think he's been staying there?"

"No," Hunter said. "But I think we might find something."

"Okay." After a pause, he said, "What do you think we might find?"

"I don't know," Hunter said. "For starters, maybe a pair of shoes."

Chapter 21

JACKSON PYNNE HAD taken the narrow back roads out of Tide-water, south through the corn and bean fields to Virginia, determined again to disappear. He'd thought a few times about going to police, telling them what he knew. But it was too risky. Tidewater County was poison now and would be for a while. If he stayed, he might not get out. Better to put some distance between himself and what had happened. Try to figure things out on his own.

He kept imagining her face—the way she had looked at him that last time, with her dark, complicated eyes, portals to a world full of secrets, most of which he'd never learn now. He kept thinking there must be some way of changing it, reversing what had happened. Of bringing her back.

Pynne made it as far as Selma, North Carolina. Exit 97 on the interstate. He stopped in a parking lot on the commercial strip, for a hamburger and a smoke, to think about what he was doing, where he was going.

He lowered the windows and lit a Chesterfield. Watching the thick cumulous clouds over the chain motel roofs and the giant green interstate signs. Breathing the Carolina air. The slight irritation was there in his throat again as he smoked, and he wondered, as he often did, if he had throat cancer. Then he closed his eyes and tried to just savor that breeze. It made him feel good—the fast food smells, the asphalt and diesel, the pinewoods, the rushing sound of traffic, the taste of the cigarette.

His cell rang as he was driving back toward the entrance ramp. And when he answered, he heard her voice again. Just as if she were still alive. Just like that.

But not talking to him.

"No, please," she said. "You're not going to do this. Please don't."

Jackson pulled to the shoulder and jammed the car into Park.

"No, no no!" he heard her say, followed by a loud, percussive sound.

Jackson Pynne came out of the car and vomited his lunch in the gully beside the road. Knowing now. Knowing that this plan to disappear would never work. They would find him. Wherever he went, they would be following. *Until they find me.* He was never going to get away from what had happened.

Chapter 22

ALAN BARKER WAS the chief of detectives in Bridge County, West Virginia, a rural mountain community near the borders of Maryland and Pennsylvania. A Jane Doe had been found there at the bottom of a wastewater containment pit, wrapped in a bedsheet, her hands, ankles, and neck bound with duct tape. Dead from a single .45 caliber gunshot wound just below her right ear. The woman was white, appeared to be in her late thirties, five feet seven, 160 pounds. Wearing jeans and a black T-shirt. A small amount of marijuana in a Baggie was found in her front pocket.

Sonny Fischer had left four messages with Barker, Hunter saw from the Tidewater case log, going back to Wednesday. Barker had called once, after the second try, leaving a message, but there was nothing after the third or fourth calls.

Hunter brewed a pot of coffee and settled at her desk, the door closed, looking out at the parking lot, the trees shaking in the wind near the halogen lights. The offices were mostly empty tonight, just a couple of dispatchers, a desk sergeant, emergency call handlers in another wing of the building, someone moving around in the detective division. She liked the quiet, the lack of interruption. She was going to work on this as long as it took. *Not stopping until I find something.*

First up, West Virginia. There was no home number listed for Alan Barker, but she found listings for several other county officials. It took her four tries to reach one. The assistant county attorney was a Patricia Pembrook, whose voice was so deep that Hunter thought at first she was talking with a man.

"All I can tell you," she said, "is if it's Saturday night, there's a good likelihood Barky's having dinner over at the Red Lobster."

"Excuse me—Barky?"

"Al Barker. Isn't that who you're asking about?"

"Right."

Hunter found the number for Red Lobster. The girl who answered sounded like she was ten years old.

"I'm trying to reach a Mr. Alan Barker," she said. "I believe he's having dinner there right now." She listened to the confused utterances on the other end, then added, "This is urgent. It's actually an emergency."

Hunter looked at her watch. Six minutes passed before a man's voice came on the line.

"Hello?"

"Mr. Barker."

"Who's calling?"

Hunter explained.

"Well, geez Louise," he said. "I'm having dinner with my family right now. Could you call my office on Monday? I don't even know who this is I'm talking to."

"I just told you, sir," she said. "And we did call your office. We left multiple messages. Four messages, according to my log.

This is an urgent, high-priority case." She tried softening her tone slightly. "I just need a minute or so of your time, sir."

Barker sighed dramatically, twice. Then his voice became more measured. "What is it you need to know?"

"I'm looking at the file from the Jane Doe case there. I'm looking at a possible connection with a Jane Doe here in our jurisdiction. I need to know something, sir. Were there any numbers left behind at the scene where the body was found—or on the body?"

"Numbers."

"Yes. On or near the body? Anything like that?"

"Who told you that there were?"

Hunter felt a surge of energy. "No one," she said. "It's speculation, sir. As I say, it's possible it might tie our case with yours."

"Do you have a phone number where I can reach you?"

"Yes, sir," she said, and she gave him both of her numbers.

"And your name again?" Hunter told him. "All right. I'm having dinner right now. I'll have someone call you if we find anything. Thank you," he said, and hung up.

Then Hunter opened the case file from the Central Virginia John Doe murder and read through it, front to back. The victim was a white male, found beside a rural stretch of State Road 736. Shot in the chest at close range with a .22 caliber handgun. Fisch had talked with two detectives in the case, but they provided no useful information beyond what was in the files, except that they considered the killing drug-related, most likely a "retribution killing," the missing tongue meaning he'd been a snitch.

Hunter heard something and looked up. A door closing. Out the window, stray flakes of snow glittered up above the halogen lights. She heard the beep of a car door lock. Listened to the mechanical sounds around her——clock, coffeemaker, the heating. Then she got an idea.

SHE FLIPPED BACK to the case file for Jane Doe in West Virginia. The medical examiner was named Carroll Sternwilder, and a *C. Sternwilder* was listed in the white pages on Slope Lane. A male voice answered when Hunter called.

"Mr. Sternwilder."

"Yes?"

"This is Amy Hunter, I'm calling from the homicide unit in the Tidewater County Special Investigations Office in Maryland. I'm looking at a homicide case here and referencing your open Jane Doe investigation. I'm interested in the numbers that may have been left behind with the victim."

"Hello?"

Hunter heard a television in the background—a buzzing sound that she finally began to recognize as engines in a Nascar race. She repeated most of what she'd just said.

"I'm not authorized to make any statements to the media," he said in an even-sounding, high-toned voice.

"Sir? I'm not the media. I'm the chief investigator for the state police homicide unit."

"I'm not authorized to talk about it."

Talk about *it*. Hunter took a breath.

"But there were numbers."

"Nothing that's relevant to the investigation."

"But there *were* numbers."

"Could you give me your name and phone number, please."

She did, and Carroll Sternwilder hung up.

Several minutes before nine her cell rang. A West Virginia number came up on the screen.

"Hunter."

"My, you're a busy little beaver," the voice said.

"Excuse me?"

"I understand you just called our chief medical examiner at home?"

It was "Barky," back from Saturday night at the Red Lobster. "Sir, I think there may be a connection between our Jane Doe case and the Jane Doe case there. I think you'll want to hear what I have to say."

"And what do you think that connection might be?"

"I won't know until you tell me if there were any numbers left behind," she said.

Hunter heard a rattle of papers.

"*Were* there numbers, sir?"

"Well, I've just pulled those files, and the only thing I see is that there were some numbers tattooed onto the small of the woman's back. If that means anything."

"Was this sent out to other law enforcement agencies?"

"Statewide, yes."

Statewide. Meaning they assumed the woman was from West Virginia and that the crime had a local solution. Same as in the Delaware arson case: thinking, for obvious reasons, that the wax museum owner may have been the perpetrator. Local assumptions, local solutions.

"Could you describe it, please? The numbers."

Hunter felt adrenaline pumping into her blood as she waited.

"Well. It was sort of funny." He drew a long breath. "The numbers on her back? It was sort of crudely done. We thought at first it might've been 666. You know, the mark of the beast, from the Bible? We thought maybe they'd tried 666 and just done a bad job. But we eventually decided—it's pretty clear, in fact, they're eights. Two of 'em."

"Eights."

"That's right. Eight. Eight. And a six," he said, drawing out the sound of each number. "That mean anything?"

"I'm not sure."

"If this is somehow connected to another homicide case, why, naturally that would be of interest to us."

"Of course," Hunter said. "One of your investigators told us that you already had a theory about this case?"

"Well, no," he said. "We have *ideas*. We have a person of interest. But, frankly, we don't have the evidence at this time to make a case against him."

"Could you elaborate on that, sir?"

"Well, we have reason to think that this is a drug-related crime. Not far from where this woman was found, there's a drug house, place that's been raided a few times over the last—I don't know, six, seven years. Man's been charged with possession of cocaine and paraphernalia, on three separate occasions."

At the far end of the parking spaces, parallel to the building, a Tidewater County sheriff's patrol car whipped into a space. Its lights went out.

"How might this other case be connected?" Barker asked.

But Hunter's thoughts were racing. "Listen," she said. "I need to check on something. Can I call you back?"

"Well. I suppose."

"Thank you, sir."

Drug-related. She paged back through the Virginia file. The mutilation. Detectives there believed that the killing was drug-related, too, although the circumstances were very different: in West Virginia, marijuana had been found in one of the woman's pockets, but there were no drugs in her system. Could the drugs have been planted to make it *seem* drug-related? To divert attention from what might've really happened?

Hunter considered this new evidence: a three-digit number, crudely tattooed on the woman's back. Not a number left behind like a calling card, though. A number tattooed there: 886.

This time, Hunter didn't need to call the pastor.

She opened her Bible. A Bible from Hunter's childhood, her signature on the title page. Amy L. Hunter.

88:6.

This time she got it on the first try.

886 was Psalm 88, verse 6.

A simple message. Succinct description of the fate of this woman, who'd been discovered at the bottom on a waste pit on a hillside in West Virginia.

Hunter read it, several times.

You have put me in the lowest pit, in the darkest depths.

Chapter 23

THE COLD AIR and silence felt insulating as Hunter walked across the parking lot. But as she reached her car, she heard an engine starting behind her. At the other end of the asphalt strip, a patrol car's headlights lit the trees as it reversed from the space and accelerated toward her.

The car stopped behind Hunter's, blocking her way. The driver's window was lowered. It was Barry Stilfork.

"Sergeant."

"Evening."

"Working late?"

"Just tying up some loose ends."

His eyes loitered on the folders she was carrying. Technically, she wasn't supposed to take files from the building without logging them out. Was he going to make an issue about that? Stilfork's heavy-handed attitude seemed to her a distorted reflection of where he'd come from. Ship had described him as something of an outcast in school, a tall kid who never laughed, whom people made paths around if they noticed him at all. Hunter had heard Stilfork say that his parents, now deceased, had worked in the "food service industry." But Ship told her they'd never worked anywhere but at McDonald's up on the highway, which was where they'd met; his mother a food fryer, his father working his way to manager.

"You live down by the marina, don't you?" he said.

"Pardon?"

"You live by the marina?"

"Why?"

"There was a report of vandalism there earlier tonight. Just thought you ought to know."

"What sort of vandalism?"

"Broken window. Someone driving around with their lights off. Just wanted to give you a heads-up."

His eyes stayed with her. There had been several late night vandalism reports over the past few days—rocks through a window, four or five cars broken into, tombstones overturned at the cemetery. No clear suspects yet. It was as if the church killing had spread a dark fever of mischief through the county. Hunter wondered if Stilfork himself, the only officer on patrol through the night, had any role in it.

"Thanks," she said. "I'll be fine, Lieutenant."

"Well, I'll probably be patrolling the area some later. I'll check on your building."

"No, there's no need for that."

"Just be careful," he said, his tone a threat as much as an expression of concern.

It was nine-seventeen as she started her car. Pastor Bowers

would be home by now. Had been home, probably, for hours. Hunter sat in her car and called him. Stilfork's patrol car idled at the entrance of the parking lot, as if he was waiting for her.

Bowers's wife answered. Hunter waited as she called him; it almost sounded as if she said, *It's Nancy Drew!* Probably just, *It's for you!* "Hello?"

"You were right, god damn it," she said.

"Pardon?"

Hunter inhaled deeply. "Sorry. Let me start again. It's Amy Hunter. You were right. There *is* a third case. Psalm 88, verse 6. I just found it. I'm going back further now."

"Okay."

"Can you meet me first thing in the morning?"

"Uh, sure I could." Hunter wanted his opinion on the Virginia case now, too. "Of course, I do have a prior commitment tomorrow morning," he added.

"Oh."

"Could it be after the service?"

"Yes. Sorry. I wasn't even thinking."

AT FBI HEADQUARTERS in Washington, D.C., Supervising Special Agent Dave Crowe skimmed through the details of the peculiar John Doe case from Central Virginia: well-dressed middle-aged man, lips sliced off, tongue cut out.

It wasn't his case. Probably had nothing to do with what he was working on, except that he was checking all missing person cases in the region, on the off chance he'd find a piece that fit the jigsawed image in his head. This one didn't. But the description was unsettling. It would stick with him; he would come back to it later—after he'd learned that the pieces he was collecting belonged to a different puzzle than the one in his head.

For now, though, Dave Crowe closed the file and moved on. He had something much more immediate to deal with.

PART 2

Praying Woman

"Behold, I tell you a mystery: We shall not all sleep, but we shall all be changed—in a moment, in the twinkling of an eye, at the last trumpet."

—1 Corinthians 15:51

"Sometimes the question is complicated and the answers simple."

—Dr. Seuss

Chapter 24

OVERNIGHT, A LIGHT snow dusted the roads, lawns, and fields of Tidewater County. As the sun rose over the farmland, fog hung like Spanish moss in the loblolly pines by the coast. A low thunder rumbled at intervals, making odd sonic reverberations through the bayside cliffs and coves.

Luke Bowers had asked Aggie to call in two extra ushers and to print fifty additional church bulletins, anticipating a larger than normal crowd. But no one expected the attendance to more than double. By the time Betsy Anders began her organ prelude, the pews were filled end-to-end, with more than thirty people standing in the back of the church and in the doorways. Only the pew where the dead woman had been found, set off by tape marks on the floor, was empty.

"I must say," Luke began, "I have never seen so many people here on the third Sunday in March." A nervous titter rippled through the room; the sanctuary air was scented with damp hair and clothing. "I suspect that a few of you may have come here this morning more out of curiosity than a desire to worship. And that's fine. I'm happy we're all here, together. Which is a roundabout way of bringing me to today's message.

"This week," he said, glancing at his notes, "our church, and our community, was visited by tragedy. It came to us under cover of darkness early Tuesday and slipped away unseen, and without explanation. In the hours and days since then, many of you have asked the same questions—of yourselves, of one another, and of me. Who was the young woman found here in our sanctuary Tuesday morning? What path brought her to us under such unfortunate circumstances? Why did this evil visit our gentle little community of Tidewater?

"We ask these questions because it is our nature as human beings to want to explain the events in our lives, in particular the tragedies. And it is our nature to expect that such events always *have* explanations.

"But what happens when there are no simple answers to our questions? Or when the explanations don't appear as quickly or as clearly as we would like? That's what I'd like to talk about this morning. Because, sometimes, what is human nature and what is God's nature are two very different things.

"We meet here this morning on the shores of hope—not in despair or confusion, but through the grace of God. Often, we talk here in this room on Sunday mornings about faith. And living with questions is a necessary part of our faith. Did you know that Jesus was questioned more than eighty times in the Gospels? Our questions remind us that a questioning faith is a living faith. When our faith has run out of questions, it becomes not faith but dogma.

"The scriptures implore us to seek, but they also invite us to ask questions. In the famous passage in Matthew, the apostle says, 'Ask and it will be given to you; seek and you will find; knock and it will be opened to you.' But Scripture also tells us that we must learn to be discerning in *what* we ask—and to be patient as we wait for answers. Faith is full of trials and tribulations, in other words, and it is often through these trials and tribulations that we grow in the spirit."

Several times during his sermon Luke noticed a round-faced man with smoky blue eyes and a dark buzz-cut sitting on the aisle end of a side pew, wearing a dark raincoat. The man appeared to be staring, opening his eyes wider, into small saucers, whenever Luke looked at him. There were no rules on eye contact during sermons, and Luke had drawn a few "starers" over the years—nearly always women, including those Charlotte called his "groupies." This one was beginning to make him uncomfortable, so he finally stopped looking that way.

"Our questions sometimes become the central mystery of our faith," he continued. "And the way those questions are answered—or not answered—sometimes shapes our beliefs. But we must remember that what we receive, when we embrace faith and patience, is often the gift of wisdom. So let us ask our questions. But let us be patient and listen—and really listen—as we wait for answers."

Luke paused for effect; in the silence, a long rumble of thunder shook the floorboards of the church building. He looked out across the congregation.

"I think even those *not* wishing to listen heard that," he said.

As if in reply, the thunder rumbled again, louder and longer. A wave of laughter rippled through the sanctuary.

"So. We continue to ask questions," Luke said, in summary. "But as we wait for answers, let's use this uncertain time as an opportunity to grow—to deepen our capacity for patience, faith, and understanding. And to deepen our commitment to this community, to our families, and to one another. Let's remember that evil can reach us anywhere, as it did this week. But when it does, we must meet evil with grace.

"Now, please join me as we pray for the woman who was killed and left here in our sanctuary on Tuesday." Looking quickly out at the congregation, he again noticed the intense-looking man with the crew cut. The man's eyes met his—pale blue, unrelenting.

Luke bowed his head in prayer.

FILING FROM THE church, congregants and visitors waited in line to greet Pastor Luke. Charlotte stood by the adjacent doors, meeting guests with her easy cheer. There were many here Luke had never seen in church before: the impeccably dressed Congressman Morton Sand and his heavily made-up wife Carlotta; Donald McFarland, the tall, cherubic-faced mayor of Tidewater, and his tiny wife Petra, who reminded Luke of an elf; Buddy Read, the leathery skinned charter boat captain who always referred to him as "Pastor Bers"; State's Attorney Wendell Stamps, his lovely wife Janine, and their two tall blond daughters; Anna Havram, seller of computer cartridges, whose small eyes seemed to light up with amusement whenever anyone spoke to her; the philanthropists Harold and Blanche Ganders, a charming British couple who owned the county's largest home and whose hobby was drinking; the snowy-haired painter Wendy Singh, whose portrait of Eleanor Mondale was owned by the National Portrait Gallery; several jean-clad Buntings, from the newspaper, one of whom tried persistently, but unsuccessfully, to interview Luke; the pouty-lipped Debbie Cosgrove, who managed the movie theater, and her current fiancé Bobby Bell, who uncharacteristically wore a suit jacket, but also sported a black eye this morning; and the severe-looking service station owner John Patterson, who, as always, seemed to be waiting for things to end.

Also present, but uninterested in chatting today, were former Secretary of Defense Donald Rumsfeld and his wife Joyce, who lived the next county over, and who came here occasionally because they liked the old church building and its perch above the bay.

But the peculiar, crew-cut man in the black raincoat was nowhere to be seen; Luke wondered how he'd managed to do that—to vanish.

Bringing up the rear of the line was Amy Hunter, her army jacket collar turned up unevenly, her hair sticking out on one side.

"Pastor," she said. "When you have a second, could I talk with you?"

"Of course. Oh, Charlotte, have you met Amy Hunter?" he said, introducing them. "State police homicide investigator?"

Charlotte offered a limp handshake. "Enchanted," she said.

Luke gave her a frown. Charlotte mouthed the word *What?*

"Good sermon," Hunter said, looking out at the parking lot with restless eyes.

"Thanks."

"I imagine people *do* ask you a lot of questions," she said, assessing Charlotte for a second. "And expect you to know the answers."

"Well, as long as they don't ask me about probability and statistics, I do all right."

He saw that she kept glancing at the sheriff's deputies, standing out in the entrance drive.

"Could we meet somewhere away from the church?"

"Sure, I don't see why not."

"How about the Blue Crab Diner, in thirty minutes?" she said.

"Okay."

When he looked back at Charlotte, she was glaring at him.

GIL RANKIN WAITED in his car in a far corner of the parking lot under a sycamore tree, as Kirby Moss emerged from the side door of the church and needled his way through the vehicles, looking conspicuous in his dark raincoat and 1950s haircut. The man wasn't as subtle as he thought.

Rankin watched the people streaming into the parking lot. Young families, old couples. *Clueless souls.* Everywhere he went, he saw people like this, it seemed, wearing nearly the same clothes, the same expressions. *Not paying attention. Corrupted and afraid. None of them has an inkling what's going to happen. Thinking they're so civilized when they treat their poorest citizens so shamefully.*

Shame has a smell, too.

Rankin suddenly realized that these were not even his own thoughts he was thinking, they were the Client's thoughts.

Jesus Christ! What the hell was happening? Would he eventually not be able to tell the difference?

He looked up again at Moss. He could read the expression on his face well before he reached the car. No need to ask what had happened. Moss opening the passenger door, sliding in next to him. "Not there," Moss said, as if he was telling him something.

"Didn't think so."

Moss reached for his seat belt but had trouble getting it to reach all the way across. He tried twice and then a third time before he got it.

So we'll wait, Gil Rankin thought. Okay. We'll just wait a little while longer. And he drove away as if he were in the car alone.

Ship called as Hunter was headed for the diner on Main Street. "You were right," he said. "Jackpot."

For a moment she didn't know what he was talking about. Then she got it.

"You visited the town house?"

"Yep. Nothing inside. But I found muddy boots in the garage. The sole patterns seem to be a match, or close to it," he said. "How'd you know?"

"A hunch. What'd you do with them?"

"Nothing. I'm standing outside right now. Do you want me to bag them and bring them in?"

"No. Summon the evidence techs, if you would."

"Sure."

Hunter went silent for several seconds, figuring what had happened. Then she said, "Okay, yes, call the techs. Have them go over the garage and the town house thoroughly, inch by inch. Take their time. I'm more concerned about what else might've been left there than the boots."

"Ten-four," he said. Sounding uncertain.

"And don't broadcast it. If possible, don't let the sheriff know."

Chapter 25

LUKE PARKED TWO spaces from Hunter's white Camry in front of the Blue Crab Diner. His eyes found her in a booth, facing away from the door, two file folders on the table. The smell of hamburgers and fried potatoes made him realize he was hungry.

"Hello again." She half rose to shake. "How was your trip?"

"In a word: relaxing."

"Excuse my enthusiasm last night," Hunter said as Luke sat across from her. "I guess I was freaking out a little."

"No harm in a little freaking out," he said. "Jesus had a freaking out with some money changers, as you might recall. Whipped them right out of the temple."

"Good. Makes me feel better."

Luke smiled.

"Anyway, you were right," she said. "There are three cases now. Three that we know about."

Luke waited. Hunter's seemingly unquenchable intensity was, again, a little contagious.

They ordered coffee and bagels. After the waitress left, Hunter began telling him about the Jane Doe case in West Virginia, then opened one of the file folders and slid him photos. They showed a bullet wound on the left side of the woman's head, just below the ear, and the exit wound through the top of her right ear. Then the numbers on her lower back.

"Guess this scuttles the grand jury plans," Luke said.

"It's probably a few hours from becoming a federal case," Hunter said. "I'm just being careful how I proceed. I'm a little concerned about sheriff and the deputy."

"What could they do now?"

"I don't know, but I don't trust Calvert. I know he wants to come out of this benefiting somehow. In a big way, if possible. And he's been talking with the state's attorney." Luke turned the photos face down as the coffee and bagels arrived.

"Of course, we're still missing a few of the essentials," Hunter said, reaching for her bagel.

"You don't know who the woman I came upon is, in other words. Or why she was left in the church."

"Yes, those essentials." She spread cream cheese on half a toasted bagel. So, tell me more about Jackson Pynne," she said. "Is he a violent man?"

"Violent? Not really." Luke thought about it as he tipped sugar into his coffee. "He has a temper. But it tends to percolate awhile before boiling over—although then it can be pretty scary." He sipped his coffee. "Which isn't to say that I think he did this."

"Because you don't think he did."

"No."

"Why?"

"Because of who he is. And because of how he acted when we talked."

"But what if he was pushed—if his temper boiled over."

Luke tilted his head, as if to say, *It's possible, but not likely.*

Hunter told him about the new evidence found at the cottage on Oyster Creek—the cigarette butt and the shoe prints, both seeming to link Jackson Pynne to the killing.

Luke listened, surprised but unconvinced. Too obvious, he thought.

Why would someone want to frame Jackson, though?

He was trying to find a less obvious thread linking the different cases, some kind of unifying motive that would reveal not only what the perpetrator wanted them to find but also what he *didn't* want found.

He wondered, too, if Hunter was weighing the question of disclosure. If they released information about the Psalms now, could it prevent another murder? Or would it just prompt the killer to become smarter and change his M.O.? Or spook him into disappearing, spoiling whatever chance they had of catching him?

"It's odd, though, isn't it?" he said.

"What is?"

"The dissimilarities. I mean, if the numbers were calling cards, why were they left in such inconsistent ways?"

Hunter hunched forward, elbows on the table. "Okay, what are you thinking, then? That it's not the same person?"

"Or maybe this is just the way that he's decided to reveal what he's doing."

She nodded for him to go on.

"I mean, look at the three calling cards we know about. The second one we found—paint on a corner of the glass—was more subtle than the numbers carved into her hand."

"Okay."

"And the third even more so than the second."

"So maybe that's a deliberate pattern, you're saying?"

"It could be. I mean, if these are calling cards, it's highly unlikely that detectives in Delaware would have looked at those numbers on the glass and thought anything about the Book of Psalms. It's just not something that would have ever entered their minds."

"Okay, agreed."

"And probably less likely in West Virginia. You said the local officials there didn't think the numbers meant anything. They thought they were a tattoo. It sounds like they never would have said, 'Gee, I wonder if that could be a reference to the book of Psalms.'"

Hunter nodded. "Okay, so, in other words, without first knowing what happened here, there's no way of figuring out the other two."

"That's right."

"And you're saying it was done that way intentionally—progressively apparent, so to speak. So that they would only become calling cards after the fact?"

"It's an idea."

"Why, though?"

Luke shrugged, handing back the photos. *That was the question.* "I guess because he doesn't want the pattern to be discovered until later."

"Maybe not until after he's stopped."

"Maybe."

Neither of them spoke for a while. A gregarious couple from church came over to say hello, and Hunter closed the file folder. She opened the other folder as soon as they walked away.

"This is Virginia," she said. "John Doe. I wanted you to see it. One of our investigators talked with the lead detective there. There was no number left behind in this case. But, I don't know—I have a funny feeling about it. There's one very odd detail, which seems to be a different sort of calling card. Have a look."

Luke skimmed through the printouts in the case file.

John Doe. White male. Age 45-55, 5' 10", 193 pounds. Spotted by a motorist in the woods beside a rural highway in north-central Virginia. Wearing dark suit pants, a white dress shirt and a print tie.

On the surface, he saw little linking this to the Tidewater case, except that the victim had been mutilated and his identity was unknown. The nature of the mutilation seemed meant as a message: the man's upper and lower lips had been sliced off with a sharp blade, maybe an X-Acto knife, according to the medical examiner, and his tongue had been cut out. The state police investigator told Fischer the killing was probably drug-related.

"Detectives in West Virginia think their Jane Doe was drug-related, too," Hunter said. "An assumption that probably kept them from casting a wider net."

"So maybe the perpetrator wants it to *seem* like a drug case?"

"Possibly. Which would mean less chance of connecting it with the other murders. At least for a while."

Luke nodded, figuring if the Tidewater Jane Doe came from somewhere else, the others might have, too. Maybe the dump sites were selected randomly. Another way of obscuring what the perpetrator was actually doing. Whatever that was.

He glanced out at the parking lot and noticed that an unmarked Crown Vic was now parked in the space between Hunter's car and his. The driver, sitting behind the wheel, seemed to be watching them.

"Don't look now," he said, closing the file, "but I think your friend the deputy is outside."

Hunter waited before glancing, discreetly.

Beak Stilfork elaborately got out of his patrol car and looked carefully at the other cars in the lot, as if counting them. He came into the restaurant with his peculiar, stiff-legged gait. Taking a quick inventory of the patrons, half nodding as his eyes moved past Luke.

He talked to the waitress behind the register without smiling—ordering coffee to go, most likely—showing his long-nosed profile. Finally, he walked over.

"Sergeant," he said. "Pastor."

Luke stood and shook his hand, then sat down again..

"Good crowd this morning."

"Yes, it was," Luke said, good-naturedly. "Much larger than I'd have expected."

Stilfork's eyes went to the folder on the seat bench beside Hunter. Then to the other file on the table.

"Here for lunch?"

Luke smiled. "Just coffee and bagels."

Hunter raised her eyes. "How'd you make out with the vandals last night?"

"Say what?"

"I saw you parked outside my apartment building at about two-forty in the morning. I assume you were staking out vandals?"

Stilfork's eyes turned to Bowers's. Then he nodded goodbye and left without saying another word . He paid for his coffee and returned to the patrol car.

Luke waited until he finally drove off before opening the case file.

Images of the crime scene and victim were in a separate envelope inside. Eight were crime scene photos, six from the medical examiner's office. Hunter was right. There were no numbers, or any other sort of calling card, besides the mutilation itself. But he recognized two similarities between this case and the others. There was only a small amount of blood at the scene, and the wounds had been postmortem, according to the medical examiner. "So he was killed and mutilated somewhere else and dumped here."

"Yeah. That's the odd detail," she said. "That's why it feels connected."

Hunter sipped her coffee. She set the cup back in the saucer.

The front-on photos were gruesome—the man's mouth open grotesquely, an oval of coagulated blood where his lips had been. Dried trails of blood down his neck and shoulder. Eyes closed.. The victim didn't look like a drug dealer, let alone an addict. His appearance suggested an attorney or an accountant.

Luke imagined what the killer had done: parking somewhere off the highway, carrying the man's body into the woods, propping him against a tree. But the Virginia victim was a big man; it would have required two people, probably, to carry him. Surprisingly, he saw nothing in the report about shoe-print evidence.

"Wait," Hunter said, touching his wrist. She flipped back through the photos and pulled one out: the man's clothing and watch, laid out on a stainless steel table at the medical examiner's office.

"My God," she said. "I completely missed that."

"What."

"Look at these two pictures. This one was probably taken several hours after the first."

Luke studied the images she'd set side by side in front of them.

"Do you see what's wrong with them?"

At first he didn't. Then it became obvious.

"The wristwatch."

"Yeah. The wristwatch. The watch shows the exact same time in both pictures."

Meaning it had stopped. Or been stopped. Luke drew a breath.

"Let me see what this says about the watch." Luke waited as Hunter paged through the CSI case report, her eyes intently scanning lines of text; he felt her energy like heat off a summer pavement.

"'Wristwatch, stopped, twelve twenty-three. Watch intact,'" she read.

That was all. None of the local detectives had attached any significance to it. Just a stray oddity. But Luke already had his phone out and was Googling Psalm 12.

Chapter 26

TWELVE TWENTY-THREE.

Luke scrolled through the verses of the Twelfth Psalm.

But there was no verse 23.

Psalm 12 consisted of only eight verses.

He scrolled to the top and read the summary: "Man's Treachery and God's Constancy." The author, once again, was David.

He read from the beginning, stopping after the third verse. Feeling a chill race through him. He looked at Amy Hunter, her light brown eyes fastened on his, rotated the phone and handed it to her.

"Psalm 12," he said. "Verses two and three."

He watched as she read.

They speak idly everyone with his neighbor; with flattering lips and a double heart they speak.
May the Lord cut off all the flattering lips And the tongue that speaks proud things.

Luke glanced out at the gray, scudding sky above the 1960s movie marquee and the slanted awnings and brick facades of Main Street. Hunter pulled the photo of John Doe's arm from the folder and looked at it again.

"Shit," she said finally. "And it fits your theory, too."

Yes. It traced the pattern back one more notch: the earliest, and subtlest, of the four John/Jane Doe messages. *Progressively apparent*, as she had called it. Any lingering sense that this might be some bizarre coincidence had just evaporated, Luke realized. Clearly, they were dealing with a serial killer, someone who had carried out his crimes in a brilliantly methodical fashion.

"Shit!" she said again. "This is what he wants, isn't it? This is exactly how he wants us to discover this."

"He?"

"The Psalmist. That's who this is. That's how he wants us to perceive him. He's playing us. This is really twisted." Her eyes were wild with energy now. "And it's big, much bigger than Tidewater County."

"What are you going to do?" Luke asked.

"I'm going to end the grand jury talk, first," Hunter said. She pushed the photos back into the envelope and closed the folder. "Then call the FBI. Have a profiler come out. They'll bring in a team from Behavioral. It's a new game now. It'll be a federal case probably by tomorrow morning."

"Okay."

She stood. Revved up. Already off to somewhere else in her thoughts.

"Let me call you later, okay?" she said.

"Sure. All right."

They shook hands, Hunter's grip firmer than before, as if she were more directly engaged with life now. Luke sat back down. He touched the stem of his coffee cup and thought about another bagel as he watched Hunter drive off, wheels spinning through the gravel.

Closing his eyes, he considered the four cases again. The same person had committed four murders. Leaving behind clues so subtle, clever, and interconnected that they would never have been identified individually. Why? Who was intended to see them, and for what purpose?

Chapter 27

HUNTER STRODE DOWN the long corridor to the state's attorney's office, her thoughts narrowed to this: four sets of numbers, four Psalms verses. It was the only evidence that seemed to matter anymore; they were like a blinking buoy light just before dusk, the thing you couldn't take your eyes away from.

Wendell Stamps's administrative assistant, Connie Elgar, with her jowly bulldog's face, looked up as she came in.

"Is Mr. Stamps in?" she asked.

"No, honey, I'm sorry. He's not. Do you have an appointment?"

"Could you ask him to please call me as soon as he gets in?"

Connie Elgar smiled, amused by Hunter's urgency, and lowered her eyes instead of answering. Hunter walked back to her office. She closed the door, hung her jacket on the coat stand and called the FBI field office in Washington. She left a message for John Marcino, saying she needed his help on a serial killer case. Marcino was a criminal profiler she'd worked with on two prior homicide investigations. She trusted him and wanted him to be her first point of contact with the federal government. Marcino was good about calling back; Hunter figured she'd hear from him within an hour.

He told her he would bring out a team and the Bureau would take the lead. She knew she'd have to accept that, though she felt deeply invested now and wanted to stay with the case. She wanted to see the investigation unwind; to learn what might have motivated someone to kill four human beings so elaborately and cruelly. Marcino would probably allow that. For now, though, she felt restless, involved finally in a complicated multistate case but at the mercy of other people's schedules, strategies, and whims. It was the part of her job she didn't like.

Waiting, unable to connect with anyone, Hunter reviewed all four of the killings. She studied the photos of the crime scene at Oyster Creek. Then those from the Methodist church—wondering again what might have led this victim, and killer, to Tidewater County. She imagined, as she had many times before, how Luke had felt walking into the sanctuary early Tuesday and discovering the dead woman in a pew, thinking at first that she might be praying.

Then she saw the blur of the state's attorney, his navy three-piece suit whooshing past.

Hunter put away the photos and walked back to Stamps's office. Before she had a chance to speak, Connie Elgar said, "I'm sorry, sweetie, he's on a call. I can have him phone you."

"I'll wait."

Lowering her eyes, Elgar pursed her lips disapprovingly. Hunter stood by the door of the state's attorney's plush office. "No, no, I understand," she heard Stamps saying. "That's good work, Clay. Right. Let me go now. All right. Good job. Right-o. Thanks, Clay."

When he hung up, Hunter was inside his doorway. Stamps's impassive eyes widened, as if he were mildly amused by the intrusion.

"Hunter."

"Talk?"

He nodded once and she sat.

"I just want you to know what's happening, sir. That our Jane Doe case is about to become a federal investigation."

"Oh?"

"Yes. So whatever information the sheriff may have, or thinks he has, this is no longer a local crime. We've found connections now to three other homicide cases, in three other states. We're evidently dealing with a sophisticated serial killer."

What might have been a smile flitted across his face.

"The numbers in the victim's hand were a calling card, not a red herring," she went on. "We've found similar calling cards in those three other cases. We're just beginning to understand what it means."

"Who's we?"

"The task force."

"You and the pastor?"

"Sir?"

"No, I'm sorry." He shook his head and lowered his eyes in a gesture of contrition. Very occasionally, Stamps did this—breaking his neutrality to toss a barb, but then quickly backing off and apologizing, as if it had just slipped out involuntarily, like a stomach growl. It was rare enough to always throw her off.

"Hold on," he said, swiveling his executive chair away from her. "Let me check something here first. Just a second."

Hunter waited, glancing at the computer screen on the cabinet behind his desk. He seemed to be scrolling through his e-mails. "Are you hearing me, sir?" she said. "We're dealing with a serial killer."

"Here we go." He hit several keys in quick succession. "Hold your calling cards for a second, Hunter, okay? We just got an ID a few minutes ago."

"Sir?"

"On Jane Doe. We've just ID'd her."

Chapter 28

WEARING HIS FIXED, unfathomable expression, State's Attorney Wendell Stamps slowly retrieved a sheet of paper from his printer and seemed to be studying it.

"Here we go," he said at last. "Came in as a tip to the sheriff's office less than an hour ago. He just called as I was driving over here. You should be receiving a photo by e-mail momentarily."

He handed the paper to her and Hunter looked: it was the image of a woman's face. Clearly the woman from the church, although she appeared younger. Smiling slightly. Steady eyes. Still alive. A pleasant face.

"That's her, isn't it?" Stamps said, seated again.

Hunter read the identifying information below the picture.

The woman's name was Kwan Park.

Age thirty-two. Almost exactly one year older than Hunter.

Resident of Sharonville, Ohio.

"Yes?"

Hunter took a breath and sighed, reminding herself that this was still her investigation. "Yes," she said. "Okay. We'll need a briefing with the task force, then. Have local officials contacted her next of kin?"

"You'll have to follow up with Clay on that. Apparently, there's some problem there that's delaying the release of information."

"What problem?"

"I don't know. You'll have to follow up with Clay on that," he said again.

Hunter rose to leave, so enraged she felt the blood rush to her face. Stamps stood, too, and his frown seemed to become a smile. As if he could see that the game was changing in his favor.

OVER THE NEXT fifty minutes Hunter, Shipman, and Fischer assembled a rudimentary profile of Jane Doe, now identified as Kwan Park. They spoke with police detectives in Ohio, the manager of the convenience store where Park worked, three coworkers, and two neighbors. No one, it seemed, really knew Kwan Park. She was described by acquaintances as polite but aloof, almost a phantom presence in her neighborhood and at the store, a woman with no real friends, who'd left her family in Korea seven or eight years earlier.

Stamps forwarded a copy of the voice-mail tip that had been recorded on the sheriff's nonemergency line. Male voice, with a slightly Southern accent: "I wonder if the woman found in the church is the same woman who worked at a convenience store in Sharonville, Ohio. If so, her name would be Kwan Park.'"

He spelled it.

"Trace?"

"Phone company's on it. Clint Fogg's following up," the state's attorney said.

It was, at first, difficult for Hunter to stay focused on Kwan

Park, knowing about the muddy boots and the .22 caliber handgun found in Jackson Pynne's apartment and what she'd just learned about the Virginia and Delaware Psalm verses—information that appeared to be of little interest to the state's attorney. For now, they seemed separate narratives; although, of course, they had to be connected.

But all the same, Hunter didn't want the details of the serial murders to be shared yet with everyone on the task force. It was all right to compartmentalize, she decided. To stay focused on the Tidewater case until after the victim's name was released to the public.

There was one detail in particular, though, that surprised her about Kwan Park. It surely would change the case in a way the state's attorney didn't see yet. Several minutes before the task force was scheduled to meet, she closed her door and called Pastor Luke Bowers.

It was something he needed to know.

SUNDAY WAS CHARLOTTE'S day off from writing, although she liked to work for an hour or two in the evening after they'd shared an early dinner, reviewing and editing what she had written the previous week.

After church, she dressed casually—in her old Georgetown sweats, usually—and often went on a long, early afternoon walk with Sneakers—sometimes all the way down the beach to Conners Point, where in summer the three-hundred-year-old Admiral's Inn served giant lump-fin crab cakes and fried oyster fritters that were so delicious people would wait more than an hour to be seated.

Sneakers's tongue always wagged from the side of his mouth

after these walks and he trotted across the kitchen to his water bowl as if he had just crossed a desert.

Afterward, Luke and Charlotte shared the *New York Times*, spreading it over the living room floor, swapping sections and discussing articles. Then Charlotte went to the kitchen and into her nearly impenetrable "cooking zone," as Luke thought of it, listening to classical music as she prepared dinner. Tonight they'd have baked tilapia filets crusted with almonds, cooked with Dijon mustard. Sneakers, whom she'd appointed her "food taster," parked himself contentedly at Charlotte's feet.

Luke was camped in the living room reading an article about Noam Chomsky when Charlotte came in with her laptop and plunked it in front of him; Sneakers trailed behind her with his head lowered.

"Did you see this?" she said. "They're applauding you."

"Who is?"

The *Tidewater Times* website had posted a story: PASTOR BINDS COMMUNITY. There was a blurry photo of Luke at the top—arms raised like a fundamentalist preacher, not really himself. Strange: he hadn't seen a photographer in the church.

He read:

> Pastor Luke Bowers gave reassurance this morning to a community still in shock over the unexplained murder of the "mystery woman" discovered Tuesday morning at Tidewater Methodist Church.
>
> Bowers, who discovered the woman in a pew, urged the overflow crowd Sunday morning to use this tragic event to draw closer together as a community.
>
> Citing the many unanswered questions surrounding the

killing, Pastor Bowers said, "As we wait for answers, let's take this opportunity to deepen our capacity for patience, faith, and understanding. And to deepen our commitment to this community, to our families, and to one another."

Police, meanwhile, continue to pursue leads but are still unable to identify the woman or determine why she was at the church.

He stopped reading as the phone rang. Charlotte picked up in the kitchen. Sneakers languidly followed her back in, in case it was for him.

"You," she said, handing over the phone. She didn't have to say who it was. Luke could see by her pinched expression.

"We have an ID!" Amy Hunter said.

"On?"

"Jane Doe. Name, background, the whole nine yards. It's all going to be released to the media in about an hour."

"Okay," Luke said. He was surprised that she'd be calling *him*, but listened with interest as she breathlessly relayed the known details about Kwan Park.

"And here's the thing," she said. "You were right about Jackson Pynne. He did know her."

"He did."

"Yes, he was a co-owner of the convenience store where Kwan Park worked. In Ohio. He sold his interest last year. Right about the time she started there, apparently. It's possible Jackson Pynne may have even been the one who hired her."

"Really."

"Yeah, I just wanted you to know. That part's not for public consumption yet."

Luke blinked at the darkening afternoon sky. He couldn't picture Jackson owning a convenience store.

"We're having a press briefing on the woman's identity at five," Hunter said. "I'll have more later."

Both Charlotte and Sneakers were staring as Luke walked back into the kitchen, the phone in one hand, Charlotte's laptop computer in the other. He placed the phone in the cradle, feeling stunned. Wondering again if he'd been wrong about Jackson Pynne.

"I think they're going to need to update this story," he said, handing the lap back to Charlotte.

Chapter 29

BY THE TIME the Homicide Task Force gathered around the conference room table at four-fifteen, the skies were swollen with snow clouds. The forecast now was four to six inches, beginning early in the evening as flurries and continuing through the night, with much of it expected to melt away the next afternoon.

There were eight people in the conference room this time, besides Hunter. State's Attorney Wendell Stamps sat at the head of the table. Also present were state police homicide detectives Ben Shipman and Sonny Fischer; Sheriff's Deputy Barry Stilfork; the sheriff's public information officer, Kirsten Sparks; Tidewater Police Chief Arthur Law, an honorary member of the task force; and state's attorney investigator Clinton Fogg. Hunter's boss, Henry Moore, was also in the room—still solidly but quietly supportive.

"Okay," Hunter said. "We have an ID now on Jane Doe. Her name is Kwan Park. K-W-A-N. P-A-R-K. She lived in Sharonville, Ohio, a suburb of Cincinnati, for the past five months."

Hunter went on, careful about what she said and how she answered questions. She wanted this to be about the victim, she'd decided, not a serial killer. Not yet. Not in this company. Saying anything in front of Barry Stilfork was the same as saying it in front of the sheriff. That information wasn't for this group, it was for the FBI. But in her own thoughts, Hunter was working through puzzles. Over the past several hours she'd begun looking at the case differently. *Who were these four people who'd been killed, and what, if anything, connected them? Would knowing the identity of one now cast light on the identities of the others?*

"Ms. Park worked as night manager at the Sharonville Quik Gas store since early October," she said. "We're still gathering information on her background prior to that.

"She was not reported as a missing person, evidently, because no one considered her missing. She had told a coworker, a neighbor, and her supervisor a week before she was found that she was going to visit family in Korea for two months. She was supposedly driving to Cincinnati, with plans to fly to JFK. And from there, to Seoul, South Korea. Her coworkers assumed she had already left the country. So far we have no record of airline reservations in that name.

"Kwan Park was evidently a very private individual. She rented a three-bedroom house in a nice part of town. Drove a leased Mercedes C350. At this point the car's unaccounted for. Her house, we're told, was immaculate. Designer-furnished. Almost like she didn't live there.

"We haven't yet been able to locate family or any contacts in Korea. But we will," Hunter said. "The contact names she gave her employer—so far, at least—do not check out. Again, there aren't a lot of known details at this point about the woman's personal life.

"And, we don't know what she was doing in Maryland, either at Oyster Creek or at the church."

Except, perhaps, for Jackson Pynne. Hunter wasn't going to stress that, but she'd decided she would mention it. Otherwise it might look—later—like she was concealing something. She glanced at State's Attorney Wendell Stamps before going on.

"There is one connection we know of with this county," she said. "One of the former co-owners of the Quik Gas corporation has a summer rental property here. His name is Jackson Pynne. Some of you know the name, I'm sure."

Several of those in the room exchanged looks.

"Is he a suspect?" asked Kirsten Sparks. Momentarily, she stopped chewing gum.

"No. Not at this time," Hunter said. "We're attempting to reach him. That is on the QT at this point, okay? His name should not be mentioned to the media or to anyone else until after we've located him."

"So, is he considered a suspect?" Sparks asked again.

"It's too early to label anyone a suspect," Hunter said. "It's really not a relevant question at this time. We're still gathering information."

She began to chew again. "What's the nature of his involvement, then? Do we know?"

"Just as I said. He was a partner in the corporation, but sold out his interest last year. And, again, that's *not* to be released." She looked at Fisch and Ship. "He's someone we need to find and talk with."

"And she was manager of this store?" Sparks said.

"Night manager."

Sparks kept watching Hunter as if they were the only two in the room. "How was she able to live so well if she was working in a convenience store? I don't get that."

"Or why was she working in a convenience store if she was able to live so well?" Hunter said. "We don't know yet. It's one of the things we'll be looking at."

"How much of this *are* we going to release, then?" Sparks asked. She was looking at the state's attorney now, not Amy Hunter.

"We announce that she's been identified," Hunter said. "Name, age, address. Place of employment. Make and license tag of the car. That's all. Nothing else at this point."

"Okay, but why *was* she in Tidewater?" Sparks said, again eyeing Hunter. "I mean, *that's* what the media's going to ask."

"Yes. And as I just mentioned, we don't have the answer yet. We have no comment on that." Hunter was reminded then of the pastor's sermon about questions and answers. *What we want we often don't get: simple answers to complicated questions.*

"Except we believe she was probably en route to somewhere else. Right?" Sparks said.

"No," Hunter said. "There's nothing to indicate that. The car is missing. We issue the make and license tag of the car but that's all. And that's all we have for the media at this point."

AFTER THE PRESS conference, Hunter retrieved the voice-mail messages from her office. She'd missed a call from the FBI in Washington just minutes earlier. But it wasn't John Marcino, the profiler she had called. It was Special Investigator Dave Crowe, a man she'd worked with, and known, years earlier. Hunter felt a strange mix of apprehension and excitement as she prepared to call him back.

Chapter 30

SHE WAS WALKING through the late afternoon shadows, her collar up against the wind, when Agent Crowe came on the line.

He greeted her familiarly—"Hi, Hunter"—although it'd been probably seven years since they had spoken. "We just got the news," he said, "on your Jane Doe ID. We'll have a team coming out."

"Really? Why?" He couldn't know about the numbers, could he? The release had said nothing about Kwan Park being connected to other homicides. Did the FBI already know this? No, it was more likely that John Marcino had passed her message on to him. Although it was odd that Marcino hadn't called first.

"I'll fill you in when we get there," Crowe said.

Hunter started her car, shifting to reverse. She'd known Dave Crowe during training at the FBI Academy in Quantico. Four years her senior, Crowe had been something of a mentor to her. They'd gone out a few times, to dinner and twice to the movies, although it was over a long period of time and she'd never considered it dating. They'd both been seeing other people at the time, which Crowe didn't consider a problem. Hunter did. Ironically, it was *her* relationship that had broken off, not his. He'd gotten married to the woman he was dating then; as far as she knew, they were still together.

"You're coming *here* with a team?"

"Right, I will be. I'll call you once I get on the road."

THE SNOW BEGAN just before dusk, flurries mixed with light rain at first, quickly becoming a veil of thick wet flakes. Hunter had printed out the four Psalms verses in fourteen-point type and tacked them to the corkboard above the desk in her study. Beside them was a map of the mid-Atlantic states, with notes pinned to the four locations where the killer had left calling cards.

> *Saturday, March 2, Central Virginia, John Doe*
> *Tuesday, March 6, Bridge County, West Virginia, Jane Doe*
> *Friday, March 10, Delaware, Jane Doe*
> *Tuesday, March 14, Tidewater County, Jane Doe, now ID'd as*
> *Kwan Park*

Would there be more? The pattern revealed an interval of four days between killings, although there hadn't been one on March 18, at least not that they were aware of. It also told her that the killer appeared to be nocturnal. All of the killings had occurred in the middle of the night. Two or three o'clock in the morning, probably.

Hunter didn't recognize the caller ID number when her phone rang shortly after seven, so she let the voice mail pick up. It was

Crowe: "I'm on my way out now, Hunter. I thought maybe we should meet."

"Hey," she said, picking up.

"Hi, Hunter."

She wasn't sure how to address him: *Dave*? *Agent Crowe*? Or just *Crowe*? She'd never really gotten the knack of using last names.

"Look," he said, "I don't know if you're in for the evening or what. But it might not be a bad idea if we met and talked about it tonight. This is all moving very quickly."

"What's moving quickly?"

"As I said earlier, I can't get into it over the phone. Tomorrow's probably going to be a zoo, though."

This felt familiar—and familiarly disorienting: Crowe alluding to some pressing offstage drama, probably exaggerating its importance. Hunter tried to decide if she could trust him—and also wondered a little if she could trust herself.

He'd be staying at the Old Shore Inn, about twenty miles from her place at the marina. If she wanted to stop by, they could discuss it tonight.

"Why a zoo in the morning?"

"The press, for one thing. They're probably a day behind us, two days at the most. And that gap will certainly tighten by the a.m. There are a lot of moving parts to this thing and I'm afraid it may blow up quickly."

"Why are you interested in what happened here?"

"We're interested in Kwan Park. But I'm not going to get into it now," he said. "I spoke with your sheriff briefly, by the way. Earlier. Sounds like quite an interesting place there." She could hear the wink in his voice. "We meet for a drink, I can lay the groundwork for you. Otherwise, we do it tomorrow morning with everyone else present. Your call."

Hunter turned to the window, surprised to see the snow coming so thick, slanting against the marina lights. No, she thought, it wouldn't be particularly smart to get on the road now, at the start of what was predicted to be a substantial overnight snowfall.

"I THINK I'LL go check the doors at the church," Luke Bowers said.

"And windows."

"Those, too." He looked out at the snow, moonlit through the birch and pine woods. "I just need to go over the books for a few minutes. Fix all the things that Aggie straightened out for me."

Charlotte gave him a faux scold. "Be nice. We need to invite her over sometime."

"You're right. Let's do that soon."

Luke looked at his wife and felt a ripple of affection as he turned to go. She was one of the most naturally kind people he'd ever known, despite her inherent inwardness; it was never something she had to work at the way he did. Once, Charlotte had told him, *If you can't be happy, be kind. Happy will follow.* He had slipped those words into a sermon a few days later, even though he worried some in the congregation would find them corny. But the church members seemed to unanimously love it; some still repeated it as if it were a famous biblical passage.

The drive along the bay road was lovely, the snow dense to his left, already sticking in the farm fields and sparse woods, swirling to his right out over the Chesapeake.

He parked in the gravel lot under the overhang and ran into the offices, entering through Aggie's work space. He flicked the lights on and walked down the long corridor linking the offices and sanctuary, breathing the warmer, musty air. Entering the church through the choir door, he left the lights off, then sat in the front row and watched the stream of snow patterns on the walls and across the floor and the rows of pews. He loved the effects of snow through the rear windows and stained glass of this old building. It always stirred dormant feelings, reminded him of how it felt to walk into falling snow as a child, to soak in the quiet dignity of all that nature. In a sense, that was what his work was all about, he'd told Charlotte—trying to recapture the sense of joy and wonder that we surrender to adulthood.

Luke was aware of another presence in the sanctuary this evening, though. The thing that had invaded Tidewater County almost a week ago was still here. A certain kind of evil. He turned his head toward the place where he had discovered Kwan Park's body, hunched over the pew back, facing the altar. He watched the cascade of snow through the second-story rear windows as the old building moaned and its shutters thunked faintly. And he saw a long arc of light flash across the south wall like a shooting star.

What was *that*?

Luke stood up and listened, hearing the rafters strain in the wind.

A minute later he heard something else, louder and more deliberate.

Knocking.

Someone was banging on the front doors of the church building.

He stepped back through the choir entrance in the dark, and

the knocking came again, harder. An insistent, muffled *bap-bap-bap*.

Luke stopped several feet from the doors, wondering if he'd remembered to lock them. He saw the handle jiggle back and forth.

The knocks came again. A question being asked. He reached toward the door and opened it.

Chapter 31

Jackson Pynne stood in the doorway, his long cashmere overcoat flecked with snow.

Luke let him in and closed the door. Pynne brushed his shoulders and sleeves. He stomped his right shoe, then his left.

"Fucking snow," he said.

"I thought you were leaving town, Jackson."

"I came back."

"I can see. Let's go to my office. It's warmer there."

Pynne's rubber soles squished on the wooden floor as he followed Luke down the dark corridor to the church offices, walking in that slightly cocky way he had. Luke clicked on the desk lamp in his office.

"Have a seat, Jackson."

He didn't. He stood in the center of the room, taking in everything, the snow melting from his coat. "I understand the police've been looking for me," he said. "Bothering my sister."

"Have they?"

"Our little conversation the other day was supposed to've been in confidence. Right?"

Luke clasped his hands on the desk.

"I trusted you on that, Pastor," Pynne said, pointing an index finger at him. "I like to think I can take a person at his word."

Luke sighed. "Please. Have a seat, Jackson."

This time he did, reluctantly, his long legs jutting up from the card-table chair in front of the desk.

"So, it turns out you *do* have a connection with this woman who was found in the church, after all," Luke said.

Pynne's expression didn't change. Luke watched the shadows of falling snow on his face.

"She worked for a Quik Gas franchise in Ohio. Which, it turns out, you used to co-own. That's what I was just told this afternoon. I didn't know you were a franchise owner of Quik Gas."

Jackson Pynne watched him. He said nothing.

"The police figured that out by themselves, I assure you. From what I understand, they're looking for you."

"Yeah?"

"That's what I understand."

"Jesus Christ," he said, turning his eyes to the window.

"They want you to tell them what she was doing here in Tidewater. What might've happened to her."

Jackson sighed dramatically, fiddling with the buttons on his coat. The tension had shifted; his concern now was defending himself rather than accusing Luke.

"Well, I can't. And I'm not going to," Pynne said, anger rising in his voice.

"Which one is it?"

"What?"

Jackson sat up straighter again. He crossed his legs at the knee and jiggled his foot. Then uncrossed them.

"What happened?" Luke said. "Who was she?"

"Kwan Park."

"Yes."

He turned away, as if he didn't know where to look or what to do. "I was helping her," he said, his voice sounding humbled all of a sudden. "Okay? What do they *think* happened?"

"I don't know."

He kept glancing out the window, at the place he used to inhabit; like a man in prison, Luke thought.

"If you want to talk about it, please feel free," Luke said, summoning the most reasonable tone he could.

"I'd rather you do the talking here, Father."

"I'm not a father."

"Pastor."

Luke shrugged. "Okay, what should I talk about?"

"Tell me what you know." He reached for something inside his coat. Then tried the other pocket. Luke wondered for a second if he might be carrying a handgun. "What the police think *my* connection to this is?"

"Police think this woman Kwan Park worked for you."

"Okay." Pynne finally found what he was after: a pack of Chesterfields.

"They think maybe you were having a relationship with her."

"Yeah?" He tamped out a cigarette. Felt for matches or a lighter, nodding for him to go on.

"They also think her murder might be connected to several other homicides."

The cigarette was halfway to Jackson Pynne's mouth when his hand froze.

"Several other *homicides*?"

"Yes." They stared at one another across the desk for a while, the snow shadows creating an illusion of distance. He's come here for a reason, Luke thought. Information, yeah, but something else, too.

"What happened to Kwan Park, Jackson?"

Pynne shook his head, but his eyes, uncharacteristically, seemed to glisten. Luke noticed the front of the matchbook as he finally pulled the match between the striking surface and the cover. Gonter's Crabhouse. The end of his cigarette flared red. He slipped the matches back into his pocket. His fingers unsteady.

"I had nothing to do with what happened," he said. "You understand that, right? I was trying to help the woman. I loved that woman."

"Okay." Pynne's eyes were on the end of his cigarette as he inhaled. "You can understand why police would want to find you, though, right? The fact that she worked for you—they're going to want to ask you questions. I think you ought to be prepared for that, Jackson. I mean, if you didn't have anything to do with it, you still have—"

" 'If' I didn't have anything to do with it?" he said, bolting forward in the chair.

"I'm sorry."

"I just *told* you I didn't have anything to do with it."

"Yes, you did. I'm sorry."

Luke let him cool off. Smoke hung in the office now, the smell reminding him of other paths his life might've taken.

"Who's after you, Jackson?" Luke finally said.

He shook away the question.

"Do you know?"

"Yeah, I know." He looked out the window. Luke waited, understanding they were in delicate terrain now.

"What's this about, Jackson? What do you think happened?"

Pynne took his time, seeming to work through a problem. Finally, his eyes slid back to Luke's and held steady. "I got into something, okay?" he said. "A little mess. But I didn't kill anyone."

"What kind of a mess?"

"Just—a business deal that went wrong." He hunched forward, placing his elbows on his knees, holding out the cigarette in his right hand. "But it's not what I did so much as what I know. What I figured out. Or what they think I figured out."

"Okay." Pynne inhaled on the cigarette, letting smoke flow slowly from his nostrils this time. "And you don't want to go to the police with what you know. Not even anonymously?"

"Right."

"Why?"

"Why?" His mouth flexed unfamiliarly. "Because I say anything, it'd be the same thing as shoveling my own grave. You understand?"

"Not entirely," Luke said. "But, as I say, I'm sure the police are looking for you right now, Jackson."

"*Are* you?" He feigned a laugh and shook his head. Looked out the window. "Fucking snow," he said, lifting the cigarette slowly to his mouth.

"I know," Luke said. "Just understand that if you want to talk, I'm here."

"I heard you the first time, Father."

"I'm not your father."

"Pastor." He pointed his cigarette at Luke again and held it; snow shadows twisted patterns through the smoke. "Tell me about those other homicides."

Luke drew a deliberate breath; he probably shouldn't have mentioned that.

"Go ahead, goddamn it," Pynne said, lurching forward again. "Tell me about that. Who they were. Describe them."

Luke thought of the computer printouts, the death scenes, the victims, the man whose lips and tongue had been removed. "As I understand it, there are three other cases, Jackson," he said. "Which police think might be related. I don't know a lot of details."

"Tell me what you know. Describe them."

"Two women and a man."

"Describe them."

"Okay. A woman in Delaware. Maybe forty-five years old. Her body found burned beyond recognition in a wax museum fire. Then a woman in West Virginia, late thirties. Shot in the head, left in a waste pit, wrapped in a bedsheet and bound in duct tape. And a man in Virginia, around fifty, wearing a business suit. Shot in the chest. Left in the woods beside a rural highway."

A shadow of recognition swept his face, Luke thought.

"Go on."

"That's all."

He slowly rose from the chair. Walked through Aggie's office to the front door. He took a long final drag on his cigarette and flicked it outside, the wind blowing the red sparks into the office. He walked back through Aggie's space, his eyes wandering, both hands shoved in his coat pockets, bringing a breath of cold air back with him.

"Let me tell you something, then, Pastor," he said, still standing. "All right?"

"Yes, please."

"I'm going to give you three names, okay? If you want to tell the police about them—anonymously—go ahead, see if they mean anything. Just don't call anybody right away, you follow me? Give me a couple of hours."

"Why?"

"Why. You don't listen, do you?"

"Not always."

"Not often."

"Okay."

"At this point, my name doesn't enter into it. Not in any way, shape, or form."

"If that's how you want it."

"It is." Luke waited. "Okay. You got a pen?"

Luke reached for the church ballpoint pen on his desk and held it up.

Jackson Pynne gave him three names then, spelling each. Luke wrote them in his spiral sermon book: Mark Chandler, Sheila Patterson, Katrina Menken.

"Look into their backgrounds if you want. Where they worked."

"Why? Who are they?"

Pynne stared back at him. Luke thought he was about to become angry again. Instead, he flashed a smile. "You mean, who they are right now?"

"Okay."

"Right now they're nothing. Lighter than vapor."

He stepped toward the window. Peered out, ducking his head slightly to see better, the set of his face somber again.

"The thing is," he said, "I was trying to do something honorable. You know?" He turned, hands in his pockets. "You ever read 'The Killers'?"

"You mean the Hemingway story?"

"Yeah." He smiled quickly, surprised that Luke knew this. "Well, that's who I am. Old Ole. They're coming to collect now. Trumble's people are coming to collect."

"Collect from you?"

"Yeah, right." Luke saw an ambiguous half smile in his reflection on the glass. "Remember how we used to talk, Pastor?"

"Of course I remember."

"And how I always told you I was looking for something? Something I could do that would make a difference. Help other people. Maybe give me redemption, in a way. Remember that?"

"I think so,"

"Well, you know what? I finally found a deal like that. And it had to do with Kwan. It was about us. We were going to do some good and then maybe have a life for ourselves. Somewhere down South."

Luke felt an enormous sadness for Jackson Pynne all of a sudden, Pynne looking up at the snow.

"What I recommend, Jackson, is that you talk with the authorities," he said. "They're going to find you eventually, you know."

"Yeah, I do. I do know that, Pastor. And you know what: they can *fuck off*, okay?" He gave Luke an unfriendly smile. "But I want to tell you this. I actually prayed for this goddamned thing to work. With me and Kwan. And you know what? Despite all that, the whole fucking thing blew apart, you follow me? The whole fucking thing!"

Luke waited a moment, looking at his desk.

"Would you like to tell me about it?"

"No. I wouldn't."

"Why not? You were just saying how we used to talk."

"Why *not*? Because I said so, okay? I can't. Not until I'm sure about a couple of things."

"Okay."

A few minutes later Luke watched Jackson Pynne striding through the snow to his Audi, scanning the grounds of the church. Taillights brightened as he braked around a bend of trees. Luke tracked his direction, waiting for the taillights to disappear in the snow. But before they did, he saw from the north a pair of headlights, slicing a path that came into line behind Jackson's car. And for a few seconds there were two sets of taillights, moving in tandem, south and east, before both vehicles seemed to become engulfed, swallowed up by all that snow.

KIRBY MOSS FOLLOWED Pynne's Audi as it pulled out from the church lot. *Finally*, he'd found him. Mostly by dumb luck and happenstance. He'd been staking out the town house from a distance and Pynne had eventually shown up, parked for less than a minute, and then driven on. Police evidence techs were inside by then, processing the unit. No way was he going in.

Moss had followed. He'd tailed Jackson Pynne driving north, back toward the church. Back to the scene of the crime, just as Rankin's client had predicted.

The fact that Pynne had spent this time in the church might become a problem now, Moss figured. But it wasn't *his* problem. His problem was to keep Pynne in sight, to find where he was going to stay tonight. Then Rankin would make sure they ended this thing in whatever way he saw fit, so they could all go home. It was even possible they could finish it before morning. Moss felt a warm current of satisfaction course through him, thinking about it.

Then Rankin would have to make a decision about the man at the church. The pastor. It was too bad Pynne had decided he was going to involve a pastor in this deal.

Chapter 32

"It becomes easier, then, doesn't it?" Charlotte watched Luke across the sofa, as snow continued to settle on the lawn and trees around their cottage. "I mean, there's a pretty clear line beyond which you can't protect him. Right?"

Luke nodded, although it didn't seem quite so simple to him. Coming up the drive, his tires losing traction on the snow, he'd seen the pastel-orange glows of lampshades inside and felt a deep sorrow for Jackson Pynne again, who had no such rooms or people—or even pets, as far as he knew—to return to. *Did Jackson commit this crime?* He didn't think so. But he seemed guilty of something, something that was persecuting him.

"It's just that he asked me not to mention him. In any way, shape, or form."

"Which is asking a lot."

"Yes."

"If he had insisted you not identify him in any way or shape that would've been bad enough," Charlotte said.

"I know."

"But adding form in there."

"Pretty cruel."

They shared a smile, Charlotte trying to draw him out, a skill she'd honed pretty well over the years.

"On the other hand, he told you those names for a reason," she said.

"He wants them known."

"Yes."

"So. Maybe I'll send them to her anonymously, by e-mail." He had tried calling Amy Hunter as soon as Jackson left, but only got her voice mail. Which struck him as odd.

"'Her' being the sergeant? Nancy Drew?"

"Yes." Luke turned to his wife. "You're quite the comedian, have I ever told you that?"

"Sorry, I misspoke. I meant Amy Hunter. She likes you, you know," she added, batting her lashes provocatively. "You do know that, don't you?"

Luke laughed incredulously.

"I just hope you don't think of her the same way," she said.

"She doesn't 'like' me. And I'm interested in no one but you. I'd be the world's biggest fool if I was."

"Good. Because you know I'll scratch her eyes out if she tries anything."

"A very Christian sentiment."

"Well, no, more Old Testament." Charlotte smiled, irresistibly. Normally self-assured, she was capable of surprising insecurities. "She does have chutzpah, I give her that," she said. "Going up against the sheriff and the state's attorney the way she has."

"She has moxie, too," Luke said.

"Yes, that, too. Not to mention pluck."

He set up an e-mail account in several minutes using the name Anonymous777. Charlotte looked on while he typed in a message. *These three people are somehow involved in the killings you are investigating,* he wrote, followed by the names that Jackson had given him: *Mark Chandler, Sheila Patterson, Katrina Menken.*

"Think they might be the three victims?" she asked after he'd sent it.

"Could be."

"But Jackson Pynne isn't responsible. Is he?"

"I don't think so. He's involved in some way, because of Kwan Park. I think he loved her very much. But for whatever reason, he isn't ready to talk about it. I don't understand that yet."

Luke was flashing again through the images Hunter had shown him of the victims. "It's peculiar, though," he added. "Something about these crimes seems wrong to me."

Charlotte filled their wineglasses and returned to the sofa. The wind gusted against the cottage, rattling shutters and the side door latch. Sneakers, lying on his rug by the heat vent, his favorite toy—a tiny, slobber-stained reindeer—beside his nose, growled as he slept, but didn't raise his head. He was still in postsupper siesta mode.

"Okay," she said, "so what is it that seems wrong?"

"This isn't how serial killers operate."

"There's a rulebook?" Charlotte sipped, sliding her eyes to the snow for a moment. "You're talking about the victims."

"Uh-huh. Serial killers usually target a certain type of victim, don't they? To take some of the better-known ones: the Atlanta killer went after little boys, the Hillside Strangler guy killed prostitutes, Ted Bundy young women and college girls, Jeffrey Dahmer gay men."

"The Hillside Strangler guy was actually two guys."

"Okay. You're right."

"But anyway, so there's no pattern like that here, you're saying."

"There doesn't seem to be. One's a well-dressed Asian woman, early thirties, who worked in a convenience store. Another is a woman in her late thirties, wearing jeans and a T-shirt, with drugs in her pocket. One's a man in a business suit, about fifty. And the other is a woman, mid-forties. The methods and locations are all different, too."

"Okay, professor," she said. "So are you saying he's *created* a pattern to make them *appear* to be serial killings? That's what the Psalms verses are?"

"Maybe," Luke said. "Or maybe the Psalms obscure a different pattern that's not as obvious."

Charlotte held his gaze, tracking with him. "Like maybe the killer knew these four people."

"Mmm hmm." Charlotte nodded with just her eyes. "That's what I'm wondering. It's an idea, anyway. Jackson said police might look into where they worked. So, what if they worked for the same person, or the same organization?"

Luke stood, setting his wine on the side table.

"Where are you going?"

"I just thought of something else. I'll be right back."

Charlotte tilted her head expectantly when he returned. Sneakers continued to snore, the vent air ruffling the fur around his neck.

"Yes?" she said.

"Right before he left, I asked Jackson who those three people were. He said something like, 'Now? Now, they're nothing. Lighter than vapor.'"

"Okay. And?"

"It's from the Book of Psalms." Charlotte's eyes deepened with interest. "'Lighter than vapor' is Psalm 62:9. Well-known Psalm." He read aloud:

> "Surely men of low degree are a vapor,
> Men of high degree are a lie,
> If they are weighed on the scales,
> They are altogether lighter than vapor."

She held her wineglass thoughtfully. "Okay, and high degree means something like highborn? Rich?"

"Yes."

"But why would Jackson Pynne be quoting from the Book of Psalms? He never struck me as someone interested in the Bible."

"I don't know that he was consciously quoting from Psalms. I had the feeling it was a phrase he'd heard someone else use and maybe liked the sound of it."

"Huh." Just then a loud thumping sound startled them—twice, then three times, against the front of the cottage.

Sneakers lifted his head and went into his slow, sinister growl—a sound known at times to intimidate the wind. All three of them waited and it came again, the sound resembling Jackson Pynne's urgent knocking on the church door. Luke felt his heart racing. Then he recognized it: the shutter had come loose again at the front of the cottage. "I'll go fix that," he said.

Chapter 33

AMY HUNTER WAS at that moment sitting across a small white-clothed table from FBI special agent Dave Crowe at the Old Shore Inn, an elegant hotel/restaurant on a tongue of land jutting into the Chesapeake. The room was lit only by candles and a fire in the fireplace across from the dining area. They were the only people in the restaurant. Having ordered drinks and dinners, Hunter still waiting for Crowe to "lay the groundwork," as he'd promised. But she could tell he wanted the food to arrive before he got down to business. He drank a seven and seven, she a pinot grigio.

Dave Crowe reminded Hunter of her past. Of a version of herself she'd long since grown out of. It wasn't an entirely pleasant reminder, although some of it was. Crowe was still a persuasive and attractive man, but he seemed a little too sure of himself around her.

"So you're liking Tidewater County?" he asked again, his dark eyes dancing in the dim light.. Crowe had always reminded her a little of early Tom Selleck—a smaller, less charismatic version.

She cupped her glass, nursing the wine. "As I say, it's a great place in the fall and spring. Particularly if you like sailing and crabs. Busy in summer. Politically, there's something a little disturbing about it. Something that feels kind of upside down. From another time. And maybe a little corrupt."

"For example?"

"This case," she said. "Kwan Park."

"How so?"

Hunter looked out, marveling at how heavy the snow was coming down, and that it seemed to have turned a shade of blue. She wondered if the roads were still drivable. "The sheriff and the state's attorney have been pushing for a local solution from the moment the body was found," she said. "Half of the county seemed ready to buy into it. A 'necessary outcome,' the sheriff called it."

Crowe nodded slightly—the psychology of small-town justice still interested him , Amy sensed, the quiet conspiracies and intrigues that seemed to go on everywhere.

The food arrived before she had a chance to explain—grilled steak for Crowe, salmon salad for Hunter, and then a second basket of hot rolls.

"So, how were they going to do that?" he asked.

Hunter followed his eyes, saw that he was studying the waitress's derriere as she walked away.

"They had some evidence. Alleged evidence. A .22 caliber shell, supposedly. A strange local man named Robby Fallow and his son were the prime suspects. They were trying to hurry it along to the grand jury, even though it was a weak case."

Crowe cut a piece of steak, his eyes on hers. "And what changed their minds?"

"We did."

"How so?"

Hunter broke apart the salmon filet on top of the greens. "We found evidence that poked a hole in their theories," she said. "Although I'm not sure I should be talking about that. You were going to tell me about your case first."

Crowe laughed robustly.

"What, is this going to be a bartering session? I show you mine?"

"Could be."

He laughed through his nose, then concentrated for a while on eating, chewing with what seemed like exaggerated bites. Hunter reached for a roll and tore it in half.

"It's okay by me if it is," he said. "I mean, I'm sure we can help each other." He looked up just long enough to seem suggestive.

"How's married life treating you, by the way?"

"Not so great, actually." Before Hunter could come up with a suitable reply, he added, "I've got a little girl now."

"Oh, I didn't know. Congratulations."

"Yeah, she's my pride and joy. Makes everything worthwhile."

Hunter went back to her salad, deciding it wasn't such a good idea to have broached this subject. The topic of marriage made her feel funny. Her own love life had been disastrous at times and she was fine not worrying about it.

Something about Dave Crowe made her feel vulnerable, though, even all these years later.

"What kind of evidence did you find?" he asked.

"Oh. Evidence linking this case to three others."

Now he looked up in earnest, holding his fork above his food. "*Three others?* What are you talking about? Murder cases?"

"Homicides, uh-huh." The appearance of crinkles around his eyes surprised her. "You don't know that?"

He had stopped chewing, the corners of his mouth drawn down. "No," he said.

Hunter didn't get it. "What's going on?" she said. "Isn't that why you came out here?"

But he was just looking at her, his face blank.

"Then what the hell are you investigating?"

DAVE CROWE ORGANIZED the food on his plate with his fork, as if reconvening his thoughts, wanting to put things into some kind of proper order and context. Charm time was over.

"We're here because of a convergence," he said.

"Okay, I don't know what that means. What convergence?"

"Kwan Park. Her body showing up in your church here. Which, unfortunately, we didn't know about until the ID went public this afternoon."

"Why would it interest you?"

He patted his mouth with the napkin. "Because." He glanced out at the empty dining room as if to make sure no one was in listening range. "We've been looking at Kwan Park for the past several weeks. We thought she had left the country."

" 'Looking at her.' Meaning what?"

She waited, as he moved his tongue against his back teeth. "Look, here's the deal," he said. "I'm in the middle of a major fraud and racketeering case right now. I can't go into a lot of details. But it's a big case, involving several agencies."

"Okay." Hunter had stopped eating now, too.

"But, just in very general terms: We've identified a criminal enterprise, which, for a long time looked like a number of iso-lated, independent entities. We now know they aren't. It's all con-nected in a convoluted way, through untraceable shell companies and banking havens. We're in the process of piecing it all into a whole."

"Okay." She took a minisip of her wine. "And where does Kwan Park come in?"

"Kwan Park worked for this organization. For the man running it."

"Huh," Hunter said, waiting for more. He enjoyed these circumlocutions, she knew, and dangling morsels of information while withholding the bigger pieces. Sometimes, when he'd had a few drinks, he used to say more than he should. "This is in Ohio?"

"In Ohio, Maryland, Delaware, New Jersey. In Texas. Maybe elsewhere. It's a small organization with a wide reach."

"But the fact that she turned up here, dead, was a surprise."

"Total. Not on any script we'd imagined. As I say, we thought she'd left the country."

"Your case doesn't involve Tidewater County, then."

"It *didn't*, no," he said. "Now it does, sure."

His eyes went to hers and stayed. Hunter wondered how much she should tell him.

"So *this* is what the media's been following?" she asked. "The story about this organization."

"Right."

"And you can't tell me how it involves Kwan Park?"

"Mm mmm." He went back to eating, cutting his steak into small pieces, chewing them longer than seemed necessary. She continued eating too, but only picked at her salmon salad. When Crowe finished, he set down his knife and fork, one over the other, and surveyed the room again. They were still alone.

"I *can* tell you this, because it's public record, anyway: do you know where Kwan Park worked?"

"Of course," she said. "Quik Gas, in Sharonville, Ohio."

"Yes. Wonder why the lady worked in a convenience store?"

"A little."

"Dig deeper, you might find that her store was in the news a couple of times in recent months."

Hunter nodded. "You mean, for selling two multi-million-dollar lottery tickets?"

He blinked at her, and looked back at his plate. "It wasn't just the store, though. It was her. In January she sold a lottery ticket worth fourteen point four mil. Last month, same store, she sold a ticket worth eighteen point two. There were a few others, for smaller but still substantial, amounts. Last week she quit and—we thought—left the country."

"Okay."

"Last year," he said, "a store in Texas sold three multi-million-dollar tickets. One for twenty-one million. Same setup. Also a Quik Gas. Might've even been the same woman working there, using a different name, we don't know."

"What kind of setup? And who's this man you're looking at?"

He smiled, reaching for his drink.

"You've heard the standard arguments about the government getting involved in the lottery business, I assume."

"Sure," Hunter said. "The lotteries are a regressive tax on the poor. They peddle false hopes. Etcetera, etcetera."

"Right. You don't hear those arguments quite as much these days as you used to, of course, because gambling is more or less entrenched now across the country. The opposition softened in most places years ago. Funneling lottery revenues into education programs was pure PR genius. It's made government-sanctioned gambling palatable just about everywhere in the country."

"It *is* a regressive tax in a way, though, isn't it?"

He shrugged. "In the sense that the poor spend a larger proportion of their incomes on the lottery than anyone else, sure. I mean, there are some who say that gambling has corrupted the idea of the America Dream—the old American Dream was about hard work; the new American Dream is about picking the right numbers or buying the right scratch-off."

"So are you saying this enterprise involves a conspiracy to steal from state lotteries? I didn't know that was possible."

"I didn't say that." He caught the waitress's eye and pointed a forefinger at his drink and then hers. "But, yeah, it's possible. It's been done. Of course, it's possible. Without giving away any trade secrets: Most scratch-off lottery tickets are manufactured by a handful of companies. They create algorithms that determine the winning tickets. It's not random, it couldn't be. It has to be systematic, so at the end of the day the governments come out with a predetermined amount of payout and profits.

"Over the years, we've investigated several cases where individuals cracked the algorithms and funneled away hundreds of thousands of dollars. It's happened. Then things always tightened up. This one's a little different. This is the first organized deal we know about where the same group's been working it in five or six states, maybe more."

"Presumably, they'd need someone inside the lottery commissions, then, to make it work?"

He nodded, finishing his drink. "Minimum of three people in each state. Someone who buys the tickets, someone who sells them, and, yeah, most importantly, someone on the inside, selling information."

The new drinks arrived. Hunter poked at the remainder of her salad.

"So that's what you're working on," she said. "That's what this organization is doing."

"No," he said. "That's a part of it. Half of it. The smaller half."

"What's the larger half?"

He took a long sip of his new seven and seven. "Between us?" Hunter nodded. "What's the federal government's biggest vulnerability to theft right now? Have any idea?"

Hunter frowned and pretended to be thinking hard.

"Don't know?"

"Not sure."

"Income tax," he said. "Fortunately, not a lot of people know that. But enough do. This one's a little more embarrassing, of course. Each year, the government sends out billions of dollars—on the order of three to four billion—in fraudulent tax returns."

"I didn't know that."

"They don't advertise it." His almond-colored eyes seemed to harden. "But, just to give you an idea. The Inspector General's Office last year identified one and a half million tax cases where the government issued refunds on fraudulently filed returns. And, of course, once the checks have been issued they can't get them back. We're always looking at it, putting in more safeguards. But for years it was open season."

"How do they do it?"

"Lots of ways. They steal identities, generate phony W-2 forms. There are actually tens of thousands of individuals trying this kind of scam each year. Still."

"But this group is doing it in an organized way, you're saying."

"Right. And on a large scale."

"So this organization is stealing millions of dollars from the government, you're saying. Through lotteries and through income tax fraud."

"Right. And the thing about it is—in their minds, what they're doing isn't really a crime. Because there's also an ideology behind it. They consider what they're doing a kind of payback. Retribution for what the government, state and federal, does to its poorest citizens."

"Wow," she said. "And so who's benefiting from all this stolen money?"

He smiled and straightened his knife and fork several times.

"I can't go into it. But I'll just say this: Six days after the winning lottery ticket was cashed in Delaware? Anonymous donations totaling three million dollars were received by a dozen homeless charities in a seven-state region, okay?"

"Not a coincidence."

"No. Two of the checks came from an organization called the Sherwood Forest Foundation, which was also the name of the company that purchased the winning ticket."

Hunter nodded, getting it. "So instead of stealing from the rich and giving to the poor, they steal from the government and give to the poor."

"Something like that." He reached for the roll basket. "Do you want this last roll or can I?"

"Please, take it."

He seemed to focus all of his concentration on buttering it.

"And so what's the name of the man running this organization?" she asked. "The man you said Kwan Park worked for."

His smile appeared very slowly, but his eyes stayed with the roll in his hand; she guessed he was starting to realize he might have told her too much.

"Can you share that?"

"Not really."

"But the newspaper knows."

"The newspaper knows. It'll most likely be out in a few weeks." He watched her carefully, then, while chewing, said, "Very brilliant character, this guy. He's set up half a dozen or so charitable foundations that are really just fronts for this organization. Has even more corporate entities and holding companies. But he's clever; it isn't easy tying anything back to him, or even finding him. The man's more elusive than Howard Hughes."

"And Kwan worked for him, you say."

"Mm hmm."

The waitress returned and took their plates. Hunter looked out at the snow. I'm going to have to spend the night here, she thought.

"The thing is, we think he knows that we're on to him now," Crowe continued. "We think he's probably in the process of disbanding most of the organization. Shutting things down. We think that's why Kwan Park was leaving the country. And we think part of his end game may involve telling his story. On his own terms. Making himself come off like some kind of hero—an outlaw hero anyway." He allowed a quick smile. "And we want to make sure we stop him from doing that." He winked.

"So why was Kwan Park going to Korea?"

"We think he paid her. To go away, be quiet. A severance, if you will. More than enough, probably, to live comfortably for the rest of her life."

Hunter sipped her wine, considering this new scenario. *But*

where would Jackson Pynne figure in it? And who would have
brought Kwan Park to Tidewater County, Maryland, of all places?
It made less sense to her now than it had before Crowe started
talking.

"Anyway," he said. "It's your turn."

Chapter 34

THE YELLOW LIGHTS of a snow plow spun through the thick-falling snow along the entry road to the Old Shore Inn. Hunter sipped from her third glass of wine, feeling the currency of information now connecting the two of them—or maybe it was just the drink. Crowe liked this, of course—saying a little more than he should, using the drip of information as a form of control. She felt the same danger being with him now that she had felt years earlier, never knowing exactly how things would turn out.

"Okay, so let me ask you a hypothetical," she began. "What if the end game isn't what you've just suggested. What if it was actually something very different?"

"'Kay."

He stirred his new drink with the swizzle stick, avoiding any noticeable reaction.

"What if this person is closing it down, but *not* paying them a severance. Not even letting them get away," Hunter said, sharing a hunch that had just come to her.

Crowe continued to stir. "What do you mean, like a leave-no-witnesses deal?"

"Yeah."

"Not his M.O. This fellow harbors a vendetta against the government. Federal and state. Big-time. But he's not a killer."

"Okay." Hunter waited a beat. "You've seen the M.E. report on Kwan Park, right? You requested a copy this afternoon."

"I've seen it."

"You saw the numbers that were carved into Kwan Park's right hand?"

"I did. Weird. What's that about?"

Hunter drew a deep breath. *He doesn't know.*

"The pastor who found her actually figured this one out, not me. The numbers reference a line from the Book of Psalms."

Crowe pulled his head back, giving her a *come off it* look.

"That's the evidence I mentioned earlier."

"What are you talking about?"

"That's the evidence."

He grinned quickly, as if he didn't believe her. "What, linking this to three other homicides?"

"Yes, three other homicides where numbers were left behind. They all refer to the Book of Psalms." Crowe's face squinched; he looked like a boy whose toys had been snatched. "And that's just between us, too, of course," she added.

"Show me."

"What?"

He dropped his napkin onto the table. "Hold on, I'll be right back."

Hunter took another small sip of wine, wondering for a crazy instant if she would end up sleeping with Dave Crowe tonight. No, huge mistake, she thought—although she could see how comfortable Crowe was; he hadn't said a word about her driving back twenty miles in the snow, as if it wasn't going to be an issue. The fire popped, startling her out of her thoughts. Then Crowe was back, walking with his efficient, clipped stride across the dining room, carrying a Bible.

Hunter showed him the four references.

The Tidewater case, Psalm 51:8. *Make me hear joy and gladness, That the bones you have broken may rejoice.*

The Delaware arson/murder, Psalms 68:2 and 68:3:

As smoke is driven away, do drive them away,
As wax melts before the fire,
So let the wicked perish at the presence of God
But let the righteous be glad;
Let them rejoice before God;
Yes, let them rejoice exceedingly.

The woman at the bottom of a West Virginia waste pit, Psalm 88:6: *You have put me in the lowest pit, in the darkest depths.*

And the stopped watch on the Virginia John Doe, Psalms 12: 2 and 12:3:

They speak idly everyone with his neighbor; with flattering
lips and a double heart they speak
May the Lord cut off all the flattering lips,
And the tongue that speaks proud things.

Four murders, four calling cards. Progressively apparent. Crowe looked at her for a long time, but didn't say anything. Hunter liked him this way.

"So?" she finally said. "What do you think?"

"Frankly?"

He looked at the Bible, then at her.

"Frankly."

"This guy," he began. "I've spent some time studying his background—"

"The guy running this organization, you mean."

"Yeah, right. I've spent a lot of time trying to know him, figure him out. Trying to get inside his head. To understand his obsessions, what drives him."

Hunter nodded. "And?"

"And, it so happens—that's one of his obsessions."

"What is?"

"*That.*" He raised his hand and pointed his index finger at the Bible as if it were a dead rat. "The Psalms. In a way, Trumble—this fellow—seems to fancy himself as some kind of modern-day David. He used to talk about the David and Goliath story. How David slew Goliath because he found a chink in Goliath's armor. Goliath's forehead was unprotected and David went for it. That's kind of how he saw himself."

"Goliath being the U.S. government?"

He cocked his head affirmatively. "Right. This fellow—he was prosecuted for tax fraud thirteen years ago. Went to prison for eight months. Getting back at the government has been a vendetta ever since."

"Wow." Crowe nodded, watching her, his eyes dancing. "But you just said he's not a violent man. That's not his M.O."

"No. Not historically anyway. But he has a security team that can play rough." He sighed, tilting his glass. "Or so we think."

"It sounded like you just said Trumble," Hunter said. "Is that his name?"

Crowe looked at her blankly. Clearly, he hadn't meant to say it. He shrugged quickly, like it didn't matter.

"It sounds familiar," she said. "Wasn't there a story about Trumble once—on *60 Minutes*?" The rest of his name suddenly came to her. "August Trumble."

"Yeah, right," he said, his eyes surprised again. "Why, what do you know about him?"

"Nothing. Just that he was a very brilliant and clever man, as you said. Wasn't he the guy who developed a system to beat the casinos?"

"Yeah, right." He took a long sip, looking off. "Once upon a time, the man was a statistics professor, at Princeton. In the early 1990s he figured ways to fish millions out of the casinos in Atlantic City and Vegas. When the casinos banned him, he trained other people to go in, do it for him."

"Was this card counting?"

"Card counting, that was part of it. He worked other games, too. But it was more than just casinos. He also became a high-stakes confidence man. He began to set up deals, working cons against the government, looking for weak spots. He had sort of a cult following after the *60 Minutes* thing. Which was done without his permission. And which we wish had never happened. I've talked to a few people who saw him before the tax fraud thing and after. When he got out, he was a very different man. The whole idea of government-controlled gambling became a kind of an obsession for him."

"Where is he now?"

"No one knows. For a brief time we had a source—two sources—inside his organization. But even when they were giving us information, they couldn't tell us where he was."

"What happened to the sources?"

He shook his head tightly, indicating the subject was off limits. "He's a very elusive character, as I say. His organization is small, but loyal. He seems to have a certain power over the people who work for him. You know the saying 'Everyone has a price'?'

Hunter nodded.

"We think that's what he does. He finds what a person's price is, and he pays it." He pushed open the napkin on the bread basket, as if there might be another roll. "He's a master manipulator, in other words. Has an eye for people's vulnerabilities. But we don't know much about him that's of value anymore. He's pretty good at altering his appearance, from everything we've heard. So we don't even really know, for sure, what he looks like these days. There isn't a known photo that's less than ten years old.

"Anyway," he said, folding the napkin back into the bread basket. "You're looking good." He kept his eyes on her, showing a hint of smile; a strange smile. "You've grown. You've gotten bigger."

"Not really."

Her terse reply amused him. "No, no," he said. "I don't mean physically. I mean—you've grown in your work. You take up more space now than you used to. I'm impressed."

"Oh, I see. Well. Thanks, I guess." She liked what he was trying to say, even if she didn't particularly care for how he was saying it. She showed him a quick, exaggerated smile.

JACKSON PYNNE PULLED his Audi into the garage of the condo on Tompkin's Neck. He was a half mile over the county line, certain that he had eluded his tail—for now, anyway. Pynne had purchased this unit five years ago under a fictitious corporate name for occasions like this, when he didn't want to be found— although tonight was the first time he'd ever actually had to use it that way. His other property here—a town house owned by his development company—was off-limits now, maybe forever. He'd gone there for the last time late Wednesday, to retrieve the Audi.

Jackson had noticed he was being followed as soon as he'd pulled from the church lot, but he should have noticed much earlier. His advantage was that he knew these old county roads and the strange turns of the creeks and tributaries and back bays. He'd put on his signal at Bayfront and Route 21 as if he were going to join the highway, then cut his lights and went the other way— down an unpaved access road, to what had once been a private boat ramp. It was a sheltered space where he used to go to think. Where he'd taken his wife many years ago to look at the lights of the harbor across the water and talk about his plans, the projects he was going to build here one day. And where he had expected to take Kwan Park.

Tonight he'd waited there watching the snow slant above the waves. He'd lowered the window a couple of inches, breathing the ice-cold air, thinking about Kwan, recalling the pleasure and purpose she had given him. He'd watched the lights of a freighter way out on the bay, and the chimney smoke rising from the houses down the coast. Knowing in a few weeks, it would be warm again, it would all be starting over, and he wouldn't be there.

HE SAT NOW in the darkness of his condo on Tompkin's Neck with a glass of bourbon and ice, looking out at the light of the high round moon across the marshlands. He felt nostalgic for this place, for the simple life he thought he'd find here again. *Chesapeake Nights.* If he were a songwriter, he'd've written a song called that. He thought about August, the ripest month, how when things got real quiet at night, you could hear the voices of everyone in the county, it seemed, the families eating suppers in their kitchens, the couples laughing by the water, the kids running barefoot on the streets; all the windows open to breezes and cross drafts.

But that was summer. Jackson figured if he stayed inside, he might get by for another day or two, not much more. He felt something dissolving in his thoughts, his certainty maybe. Someday he'd find what he was meant to find, but it wouldn't be here. Tidewater wasn't a place he could live anymore. He was beyond that now, beyond everything he used to think and expect. Beyond the law. Everything felt sad tonight, and very temporary.

Chapter 35

Amy Hunter ran hard down the center of the marina road, where the plows had cleared a single lane, the snow banked on either side, Radiohead blasting in her ear buds, the wind burning her face. The fields, bright already with melting snow, hurt her eyes; the sky was a rich, nearly cloudless blue. As she warmed to the morning, the air became a fuel, lifting her spirits, her life seeming to slide into sync with the natural world again. She felt guilty that she'd almost stayed with Crowe last night, but pleased with herself that she hadn't—although driving twenty miles in the snow after three glasses of wine wasn't smart. Nor was accidentally turning off her cell phone and missing a call from Pastor Luke.

She sprinted the last straightaway, past the boatyards and the commercial harbor, returning to her apartment damp and invigorated, tethered again by work. She was excited about all she'd learned the night before and the new paths this case would take.

"We're going to solve this," she said to Winston, who sat on her desk awaiting his morning tuna as she peeled off her sweats. "Do you hear me? We're going to solve it."

Elllll!, he rumbled, jumped down and trotted, tail up, to the kitchen.

Hunter did her morning chores, feeding Winston and changing his litter, emptying the trash and the dishwasher. Then she took a long hot shower and drove to work. There, she checked *The Post* website first. Nothing. Then she went to the *Tidewater Times.*

Associate Editor Karen Bunting had written an update.

CHURCH HOMICIDE VICTIM IDENTIFIED

> *Police yesterday identified the so-called "mystery woman" found in Tidewater Methodist Church last Tuesday morning.*
> *The Sheriff's Department identified the woman as 32-year-old Kwan Park, of Sharonville, Ohio.*
> *Federal investigators have now reportedly joined the search for the woman's killer. Sources say the woman may have worked for a Baltimore-area escort service, although police and sheriff's spokespeople refused to comment.*

What? Hunter thought.

That had to have come from the sheriff's people. Still pushing their escort theory. And still thinking they could somehow tie Robby Fallow to this crime.

She scrolled through her e-mails hastily, going back to one from Anonymous777. The subject line grabbed her attention: *Information re. Kwan Park.*

Her heart quickened as she read the message, feeling a cocktail of adrenaline and caffeine.

These three people are somehow involved in the killings you are investigating: Mark Chandler, Sheila Patterson, Katrina Menken.

Nothing else. The e-mail had been sent to her anonymously. Hunter called an IT tech in to try to trace it. Then she began running data searches on the three names. Two possible connections turned up quickly: there was a Katrina Menken who worked for the Ohio Lottery Commission. And Mark Chandler was a Washington-area-based attorney representing several accounting firms in Virginia and Maryland.

"'Morning, interrupt for a second?"

Hunter nearly jumped.

Dave Crowe was standing behind her.

"Oh," she said. "Good morning."

"'Morning." There were dark crescent moons under his eyes. "Interesting talk last night. Glad you made it back okay. Meeting's canceled, by the way."

"Why?"

"I'm going back to Washington. Changing tactics," he said. "I'll try to return this afternoon. Please say nothing to the media. I don't want us being tied to this in any way at this point."

"Kind of late for that."

"Yes, I'm sorry about that sentence in the newspaper. I've called them and asked for a correction." He added, "There are two other agents who will be here for the briefing this morning at eleven. In the meantime, please keep the Psalms thing under your hat."

Hunter nodded. "So I'm part of this investigation."

"Right. You are. We'll talk about that later."

Great, she thought. There was an edgy undertone in his voice, though, something he wasn't telling her.

"Wait," she said. "I thought you might want to look at this."

Hunter scooted away to give him room and watched as Crowe read the message on her screen. She smelled his aftershave as he leaned down in front of her, his hand on the back of her chair. After a long moment his head jerked back as if he'd just read that China had invaded the U.S.

"Where in hell did this come from?"

She shrugged, mimicking his normally cool demeanor. "Anonymous e-mail," she said. "Why? Another convergence?"

"Yeah," he said. "Big-time."

"You know who they are?"

He looked at her as if he hadn't heard the question. Then he said, "I know who they are. Two of them. Where did this come from?"

"Don't know. Which two?"

"Chandler and Patterson." Then, lowering his voice, he said, "Both of them worked for August Trumble's organization, okay? Why the hell didn't you tell me about this last night?"

"I just got it."

"When?"

"Just now. Five minutes ago."

He closed the door to her office and sat in the chair beside her desk.

"Look," he said. "Here's the deal. There are a few things I didn't tell you last night."

"What a surprise."

He shot her a look, and then sighed deeply, as if to make it clear that he really didn't want to tell her what he was about to say. "You know how I mentioned that he's made himself impossible to find? How he's like a Howard Hughes figure?"

"Trumble."

"Yeah. Well, for whatever reason, it was a characteristic of some of the people who worked for him, too. Or part of the requirement to work for him. Kwan Park, for instance, almost certainly isn't the woman's real name. Her fingerprints turn up nothing. There's no family that anyone can trace. We think Trumble's organization *became* her family, in a sense."

"Sort of like a cult."

He shook his head. "In a way, although we don't use that word anymore."

"Okay. Let me ask you something, then," Hunter said. "Do you think Jackson Pynne, the developer, could be involved in this organization in any way?"

His eyes began their dance. "Jackson Pynne."

"Yeah."

"Why would you ask that?"

"He's been seen in the county over the past week. I'm just curious."

"Really." Crowe gave her a hard, less-than-friendly look. "Anything else you're not telling me?"

"No. That's all I can think of."

Hunter waited, but that was evidently all he had to say.

Moments after Crowe left, she called Pastor Bowers at the church. Aggie Collins put her on hold for more than three minutes before she heard his voice.

"It's Amy Hunter," she said. "Can I talk with you?"

"Of course. But check your messages," he said. "I've been trying to reach you since last night."

"I'm sorry, nothing yet," Kirby Moss said again. He was parked in the snow beside the road by Pynne's town house, a plastic twenty-ounce bottle of Diet Coke between his legs. "I have a feeling he's not coming back here. Not after the police went in."

"So where is he?"

"I'll find him."

"I know you will, but where is he?"

"I'll find him," Moss said. "Just give me a little time."

Okay, Gil Rankin thought, trying to hold his anger in check. Moss had found him last night and then lost him. Lost him in the snow, he'd said. *Jesus Christ.*

"Don't worry about it. I'll find him." Good-natured, ignoring the possibility that he might be upset.

"Right," Rankin said. "Don't call me again unless you have."

"*Until.*"

Yeah, yeah. Rankin snorted. The morning light was making him irritable.

"What about the pastor?" Moss asked. "Do you want me to do anything there? See if he can tell me anything?"

Rankin didn't even feel like answering. "Worry about Pynne. I'll worry about the preacher."

"Okay."

Rankin hung up. He blew a long stream of air from his mouth, thinking about the preacher. There were several ways of dealing with him, if it came to that. He could scare hell out of him if he needed to, keep him so off balance he couldn't walk a straight line. And he could have some fun doing it. But he had to be careful.

Sometimes, he got sidetracked, going after the wrong people. Easy targets. Just because he *could*. It was one of his weaknesses. He knew that.

This wasn't about the preacher, it was about Jackson Pynne. Rankin knew Pynne was a snake, that he was difficult to trap. The man had a knack for disappearing, then slithering back when you didn't expect him. Pynne's life, in a way, was a fucking perpetual comeback story.

This time there wasn't going to be any comeback. That was the one thing Gil Rankin knew for certain. Because it was time now for him to go home. He wanted his family back. That was all that mattered. To satisfy the Client and go home. Reclaim his life.

Chapter 36

LUKE WATCHED HUNTER'S Camry pulling in the drive to the church, tires crunching in the snow. She took the shortest route to his office, walking with her purposeful stride through the snow, wearing the oversized army jacket, jeans, and work boots that had become her uniform. Luke went out into Aggie's office to meet her and usher her in.

Hunter took a seat, pulled a folded piece of paper from her jacket and opened it on his desk. "I received this overnight," she said.

"Okay." Luke looked at a printout of the e-mail he had sent her. Hunter was breathing heavily, her face pink from the cold.

"I've got techs working a trace. Looks like we might have an angel here trying to help us."

"Hmm," Luke said. He nodded and handed it back. "Pretty concise."

"Yeah, it is."

Luke could feel her watching him.

"And do you know who they are?"

"Two of them." she said. "Two of them may be victims of our serial killer. We're trying to verify that now."

"Huh." Luke nodded again. "I wouldn't spend too much time trying to find out where the e-mail came from, by the way."

"Oh?"

His eyes finally drifted back to hers.

"What are you talking about?" she said. "*You* sent it?"

"It was supposed to be anonymous. I tried to reach you first. A couple of times."

Her face reddened. "I know, my cell was off. I apologize. I screwed up."

"That's okay."

"Why?" she said. "What's going on?"

"Jackson Pynne came to see me here last night," he said. "He gave me those names. That's why I was trying to reach you. I didn't really want to give that information to anyone else."

"I appreciate it. I'm sorry," she said. "What else did he tell you?"

"He told me that he knew Kwan Park. He said he was trying to help her get away from the organization she worked for. He mentioned a name. Trumble, I think it was."

"Yeah," she said. "August Trumble."

"You know who that is?"

"Now I do."

"That's who Kwan Park worked for."

"Yes." Her eyes seemed to brighten. "He's the common denominator in all these killings. It's about to become a federal case. I expect Dave Crowe of the FBI will be out to talk with you later. I wanted to give you a heads-up."

"How later?" Luke said.

"I'm not sure, why?"

"Because—actually, I'm going out of town this afternoon. *We* are. Just over to Charlotte's parents' in D.C."

"Charlotte?"

"My wife."

"Right."

AS PREDICTED, BY high noon much of the snow was melting across Tidewater County, running down the curbs and blacktops, dripping from drainpipes. An afternoon rain shower was expected to wash away the rest of it.

Luke turned off his laptop and packed his sermon notebook into a knapsack, where he also had a change of clothes and toiletries.

He clicked off his desk lamp, surprised to see Aggie standing in the doorway, wearing her stylish new two-button pinstripe pants suit.

"There's a call from a Mr. Jackson Pynne?" she said. "Should I tell him you're gone for the day?"

"Oh. No," he said. "Thanks, Aggie. I'll take it."

He sat back at his desk, genuinely pleased to hear from Pynne. "Hello," he said. "Jackson?"

But the voice on the other end wasn't Jackson Pynne's. It was a heavy, deeper voice, with what sounded like a mid-Atlantic accent. "Sorry to disappoint you there, Preacher. This is not Jackson Pynne. Although I'm hoping you might help me find him."

"Who's calling?"

"This is a friend of Jackson Pynne. Like I say, I'm trying to reach him."

Luke listened to the man breathe, a raspy sound. "Well," he said, trying to remain good-natured, "I'm afraid I can't help you there."

"Actually, I think you can." An edge now in his voice. "Because I know that Jackson visited you last night. There at the church. And I'm sure, if you give it some thought, you could probably give me an approximation of where he might be."

"Who is this?" Luke said.

"This is not a business you want to get involved in, Preacher, you understand me? And you also don't want to go to the police. You understand? It's important that we keep this communication just between the two of us for now. You hear me? Because I know where you live. And where your wife lives."

Luke was silent.

"You just think about that and I'll call you back, on your cell next time."

"How do you know my cell number?"

"I don't. But you're going to tell me."

"I don't think so."

Luke listened to his breathing again. "That's your choice. But I'm sure you don't want to cause anyone to get hurt, do you? Now, go ahead and tell me your cell phone number and we'll end this on a civil note."

He did, and the line went dead.

Luke sat in his unlit office afterward, squinting at the bright sunlight out the window, the snow melting in the woods, wondering if this might just be a prank. Was the sheriff trying to warn him away from Jackson Pynne? Or were his and Charlotte's lives really in danger? There was something darkly credible in the caller's voice.

Luke closed the door all the way. He sat at his desk, lowered his head and prayed, at length, for guidance and for protection. As he was finishing, he realized that Aggie was tapping on the door. "Are you all right, Pastor?"

Chapter 37

As Charlotte drove them to Washington, Luke told her all he had learned from his Google searches about August Trumble. He didn't mention the telephone call, but carried his cell phone in his right front pants pocket, ready for the promised follow-up, feeling a rush of emotion each time he thought about it.

Sneakers spent most of the drive sitting in back, panting steadily. Luke envied him a little.

"You know what—I think my father might've *known* August Trumble," Charlotte said at one point.

"Oh," Luke said. Charlotte did this sometimes—she came up with some astonishing tidbit of information that couldn't be true—but in fact often was. "No," he said, "I don't think so."

"Or met him."

"I guess it's possible. Unless you're thinking of someone else."

Charlotte went quiet, passing a fast-moving semi. "Didn't August Trumble go to Yale?"

"Well, yes. He did, as a matter of fact."

"Yeah, I think my father knew him," she said. "You could ask."

She turned, offering up a nice, hopeful look. "That would give you fellas something to talk about, wouldn't it?"

"Besides our future," he said. "Yours and mine, that is."

"Yes," she said. "Besides that."

THE CARRINGTONS LIVED in a rambling, 1906 Tudor-style home in the suburb of Chevy Chase, Maryland, less than a mile from the D.C. line. It was an old-moneyed neighborhood of oaks and elm trees and narrow winding streets, with lots of Lexuses and Mercedes parked by the curbs.

Both Judy and Lowell Carrington were retired, although Charlotte's father "dabbled" in real estate, as he put it, which in fact had become a thriving second career. In his first career he had been an economics professor at Georgetown, and served as a White House adviser during the Reagan and Bush 41 administrations. He was a tall, genteel man who seemed in no hurry to cede any ground to the new generations; his untamed white hair suggested the stereotype of a mad scientist or eccentric filmmaker, although he was in fact very grounded and very conservative.

As they arrived in her old neighborhood, Charlotte became perkier—and then a little giddy—as if the narrow, tree-crowded streets were the secret path back to her childhood, not just to her parents' house.

There was a pattern to these get-togethers—beginning with cocktail hour in the ornate living room, during which Charlotte would become loose and animated in ways he never saw at home. Eventually she would volunteer to help her mother with something in the kitchen or else go off to look at her mother's latest art purchases, strategically separating the sexes.

Sneakers, meanwhile, was exiled to the basement, because of

Judy Carrington's various allergies, where the dog slept, watched television, and occasionally made vocal pleas for attention.

Lowell Carrington was a man who could talk with ease about nearly anything, from golf to health care to French restaurants to the latest conflicts in the Middle East—although, inevitably, it seemed, conversation eventually swung to Luke and Charlotte's "plans" for the future. Charlotte and her father seldom if ever had substantive talks anymore, their opinions too often at odds for civilized discourse. But with Luke, her father was less cautious, considering him a conduit to the rooms of his daughter's inner world where he couldn't go by himself.

This time it took only a few minutes before he asked, "So, have you and Sharley given any more thought to buying a place?" Her father was the only one who called Charlotte "Sharley."

"A little," Luke said.

"I know Sharley's mentioned it a few times recently."

"Hmm." Luke was all but certain that Charlotte had not said anything to her father recently about buying a place. "We just don't know that this is the right time for it," he said, offering a variation of his standard answer.

Charlotte's father got to his feet, his long body unfolding. "Of course, people say that their whole lives, don't they?" He smiled deferentially. "And before long they find they're stuck. Another glass of wine?"

"I'm fine."

He walked to the wall cabinet that functioned as a bar and slowly fixed himself a scotch and ice. Their living room resembled an offbeat museum—antique French chairs roped off along one wall, classical busts on the glass-fronted bookshelf and pedestal table, original paintings by Robert Rauschenberg, Frank Stella, and Damien Hirst. Charlotte's mother was the art collector. Lowell Carrington had once conspiratorially confessed to Luke that he considered her collection "high-priced yard-sale-quality art," adding that he nevertheless "respected its value" as an investment.

"You know, we have a rental place down in Turks and Caicos," he said, his tone faux casual. "It's going to come available in late April for a couple of weeks. South Caicos, directly on the water. Lovely place, really. I haven't said anything yet to Sharley, but, I mean, it'll just be sitting there. Jude and I aren't able to go this year. She has museum business and I'm in the middle of this tax deal."

"Ah," Luke said.

"So, I mean, it'd be a good opportunity, just the two of you, to get away."

"Well, that's very generous," Luke said. He pulled out his cell phone and checked, just to make sure he hadn't missed a call. "Of course, April tends to be a very busy time at the church. Lent, Easter."

Lowell's expression hardened. He seemed to have the idea that Luke and Charlotte just needed a little time alone to discuss their future, and then they'd be able to make the necessary decisions and changes. He was well aware of a pastor's salary and had offered more than once to help Luke switch his calling to real estate.

"Well, we'll certainly consider it," he said cheerily.

"You have an assistant pastor, I imagine, who can take care of the service and things like that?"

"Yes, although I already had her take over for me for a couple of weeks in the fall. When we went on the missionary trip."

"A *woman*?"

"Yes, the assistant pastor is a woman. Melissa Walker."

He smiled privately. "I didn't know that."

"Yes, in fact she took over when I took the trip to Kenya last fall."

"Oh, yes." He grimaced slightly, as if the taste of his drink wasn't quite right. Luke suspected it was his mention of "missionary" work in Africa. The Carringtons' idea of charity was tithing. Going into the streets and helping people in a troubled nation seemed show-offy.

"So what in God's name happened out there at your church, anyway?" he asked, lowering his voice as if broaching a forbidden subject. "Was it homicide?"

"It's under investigation. I can't really say much about it."

A peculiar sound came from his throat. "We're family here, Luke."

"No, what I mean is, I can't tell you much because I don't *know* much."

"Oh, I see." Lowell sipped his drink. "Sharley tells me they've got some young kid running the investigation."

"No." Luke smiled, at Charlotte's mischief. "She's in her thirties, I think. Trained with the FBI. Head of the state police homicide unit for the region. Has two master's degrees."

"Well. You and I both know what that and sixty-five cents'll buy you nowadays."

He winked and went into his laugh, an out-of-character, bawdy nasal guffaw.

The women came in with their drinks then.

"What's so funny?" Judy Carrington showed her crooked, surprised smile. She often seemed self-consciously on the other side of things.

"We were just having a debate over the future of the Tea Party," Luke explained.

Judy stared at him for a moment before breaking into a smile. "You were *not*."

Luke smiled. She didn't get him, but at least she recognized when he was kidding.

"Did you tell him about our place down in Caicos, dear?"

"I just did."

Charlotte looked at Luke and rolled her eyes.

THE DINNER PHASE began with a prayer. Luke asked for blessings for the food and their family and offered thanks for their health and good fortune. The Carringtons bowed their heads, both with uneasy looks on their faces, and half whispered "Amen" before reaching for their forks and knives.

Dinner conversation centered on the Carringtons' travels and on Judy's growing art acquisitions. For a time Lowell tried to talk about his investment properties, but no one carried the other side of the conversation except Luke. Judy smiled strangely as Luke complimented her on the meal. She was a sweet woman but difficult to talk with, particularly after she'd had several drinks.

During dessert a loud, guttural sound startled everyone. Charlotte's mother looked at Luke as if he had slapped her. The sound resembled the bark of a sea lion at first, Luke thought; then it morphed into what seemed to be random notes on a French horn, then it sounded as if the sea lion and the horn were mating.

"What on earth?" Judy Carrington said.

"Oh," Charlotte said.

"Our son," said Luke, pushing back his chair.

The cries came again, louder and even more bizarre.

"Jesus," said Lowell Carrington.

"He just wants to join the fun," Luke said. "Nothing another chewy won't fix. Excuse me. Thank you, Judy, for a wonderful meal."

Luke took Sneakers for a short walk in the small yard behind the Carringtons' house, which was wet with melted snow. Then he sat with him on the basement floor for several minutes, rubbing his belly with a towel as they watched the old Mary Tyler Moore show on MeTV.

"I know," Luke said. "I don't always like it here, either. Sometimes in life, though, we have to put up with what we don't enjoy. It builds patience and character and keeps our wives happy. Anyway, we'll be finished in a little while and then we'll go for another walk, okay? All three of us this time."

Another brief segregation followed dinner, as Charlotte helped her mother clean up and load dishes. Charlotte was comfortable around her mother, able to laugh and talk easily about personal things. With her father she summoned a sociable, daughterly demeanor but was more guarded. They were still fighting old wars.

Sitting with him in the living room, Luke saw his chance to raise the subject of August Trumble.

"You know," he said, "Sharley—Charlotte—mentioned earlier that she thought you may have known August Trumble at one time."

"August Trumble. August *Trumble*," Carrington said, sounding out the words as he got more comfortable in his chair. "Now there's a name I haven't heard in a while. Quite the troubled genius, wasn't he?"

"But you knew him?"

"No."

"Oh. I thought Charlotte said you knew him."

"Nope." He sipped his scotch, as if no further explanation were necessary. Then he said, "Oh, we both went to Yale. But at different times. I believe I was an undergraduate while he was in graduate school. Don't think I ever saw him. Tom Griffin knew him."

"Tom . . . ?"

"Griffin. One of our neighbors."

"I don't think I know him."

"You don't. He lives right up the street." Luke made a note to pass this name along to Amy Hunter. "Of course, Trumble kind of went off the rails some years ago, didn't he?"

"That's what they say."

Lowell raised his glass in a toastlike gesture. Luke was surprised he hadn't asked why he was interested. "Anyway, I think it's time Sharley became a little more settled," Carrington said, "now that she has some momentum with her writing. And you know what?" He twirled his drink. "On this one, I think she actually agrees with her old man."

"On which one is that?"

"Settling down. Buying a place."

He gave Luke a pointed look.

"Actually, moving about has its merits, too," Luke said, just for the sake of argument. "I mean, when we moved to the shore five years ago, she became interested in its history, in particular in Frederick Douglass, who was one of the Eastern Shore's great residents." Lowell Carrington squinted disagreeably, as if waiting for heartburn to pass. "That's how she got started on her current book. Quite a project. Jefferson and Douglass."

"Well," Lowell said, with a sinking note of skepticism. "So if your next church assignment takes you out to Kansas, she writes the history of winter wheat in America?"

"Or, perhaps a biography of Fatty Arbuckle," Luke said cheerfully. "He was a Kansan."

Charlotte's father looked down and wiggled his glass. "No," he said. "No. I see her work as more important than that. A little more important than whichever way the *wind* blows."

"I do, too," Luke said. Unable to resist, he added, "Although, of course, the wind can takes us to some interesting places. As I sometimes tell people in the congregation, we shouldn't try to control too much in our lives."

"We should try to control whatever we *can* in our lives," Lowell said, as if speaking to a student. "What we *can* control we *should* control."

"Ah."

"You don't, life passes you by. And then what do you have?"

"I don't know. Existential angst?"

Lowell Carrington surprised Luke by smiling broadly. "You're a good man, Lucas. And you're smart enough not to take me too seriously." He leaned over and gave him a playful jab in the shoulder. Luke looked up and saw Mrs. Carrington, standing in the doorway, holding her drink, a crooked smile on her face.

DURING THE TEN o'clock news Charlotte drank herbal tea while Luke and the Carringtons refreshed their drinks. Luke checked his cell phone during a stop in the restroom. Still nothing.

Midway through the news, Judy Carrington went into a series of sneezes, an event that occurred nearly every visit, usually at about the same time.

"My, I must be allergic to something," she said.

By the end of the newscast, Luke noticed, she was asleep, her vodka and tonic still in her right hand.

Lowell leaned over and plucked it from her. "Well," he said, "I guess we'll be calling it a night. Looks like Jude's gotten a little head start on me."

He kissed the side of his wife's face and she snapped awake. "Oh my goodness," she said, her eyes turning to Luke and then to her husband. "I must have dozed off for a second."

Luke smiled politely and she smiled back.

"Thanks again, Judy," he said. "The salmon and the peach cobbler were wickedly good."

Once her parents were safely upstairs, Charlotte said, "Go for a walk?"

"Shall we bring the opera singer with us?"

"Please."

It was a lovely evening, clear and not nearly as cold as it had been the night before. They walked hand in hand through the night shadows down the hill toward the creek, letting Sneakers trot ahead, sniffing at the bushes and lawns but not finding anything worth stopping for.

"I love this old neighborhood," Charlotte said.

"I can tell. I like it, too."

They stopped at the bottom of the street and listened to the creek in the woods. He watched Charlotte's breath rise, misting in the streetlight. As they kissed gently, he felt something buzzing in his pants.

Charlotte's face became a frown. "You brought your cell phone? Why?"

"Oh," Luke said.

He pulled it out, his heart racing, ready now to tell Charlotte what had happened.

Except he saw that this wasn't the threatening caller from earlier, as he'd expected.

It was Amy Hunter, of all people. By the time Luke got the phone open, he'd missed her call. "Hunter," he said. "That's odd."

"Go ahead. Call her back." Charlotte was standing on a rock now by the creek. Sneakers lowered his head and tentatively licked at the water. "I'll just hover about and pretend I'm not eavesdropping."

Luke smiled.

"I mean, unless there are some personal issues the two of you need to iron out. Maybe you had a tiff before you left?"

"Funny."

She walked alongside the creek, giving him a little space. Sneakers was beside her. Hunter answered right away.

"Hi, it's Luke Bowers."

"Yes, thanks for calling back. I just left you a message."

"Oh, okay." It grew quiet. Luke looked back up the hill, saw the lights upstairs in the Carringtons' house, someone moving behind a curtain. A dog barked twice. Sneakers's head rose and tilted alertly; he was considering whether to go into his growl.

"I wanted to tell you: They're bringing charges in the Kwan Park case. Probably tomorrow."

"Really," he said. "Federal?"

"No. Local."

"Not against Robby Fallow?"

"No," she said. "Not Fallow. Against your friend, Jackson Pynne."

"Oh." Luke suddenly felt ill. The silence seemed to thicken. "Well," he said, "they may have a difficult time finding him."

"No, they won't," she said. "He just turned himself in."

"What?"

"Yes. And he's asking for you."

"Me."

"Yes. He says you're the only one he'll talk to."

Chapter 38

TUESDAY, MARCH 21

THE VISITING ROOM at the Tidewater Correctional Facility was stark white, newly painted, with metal tables and benches bolted to the floor, fluorescent lighting overhead. Luke Bowers had done prison ministries here for several years, and as he walked through the series of doors from the processing center to the visiting area, he was struck, as usual, by the contrast between the bright surfaces and the hardened, diminished demeanors of so many of the inmates.

Jackson walked in wearing an orange jumpsuit. They sat across from each other at a small square table, maybe two feet by two feet. Pynne had refused so far to talk with the state police and the sheriff's office and insisted that his meeting with Luke could not be recorded. So it wasn't an interview, just a conversation. Although, of course, Luke could ask whatever he wanted.

"Hello, Jackson."

He nodded hello, his face expressionless.

"You look good," Luke said. An inane remark, although he wanted to start with something positive. In fact, Jackson didn't look so good. He needed sleep and a shave.

Jackson shifted his feet, then folded his hands together. His eyes took in the room, the other two inmates who were meeting with family members, the two guards.

"Would you like to pray first?" Luke asked.

He shrugged and leaned forward, arms on his knees, looking up from under arched eyebrows. Luke lowered his head and prayed for him.

Jackson seemed to be staring at him when Luke opened his eyes again. "Tell me what they have," he said in a small voice. "Evidence, I mean. What's the case?"

"Well, they're charging you with speeding, I'm told, and interference in official acts. Resisting arrest. And they may be adding a weapons violation. You were carrying an unregistered handgun?"

"Kwan's murder," he said brusquely. "What evidence do they have?"

"Oh." Luke cleared his throat. "From what I'm told, your DNA and shoe prints were found at the church and also at what they're calling the murder scene—a cottage at Oyster Creek—"

"What's the DNA?"

"Cigarette butts. Chesterfields."

He nodded slightly, keeping his head down, like a boxer absorbing punches.

"Jackson, you told me you didn't do this, right?"

"Right."

"So do you want to tell me what happened, and what's going on?"

His eyes lifted, but he avoided looking at Luke. There was

something slightly off about him, Luke thought; Jackson wasn't quite as upset as he should be.

"Abridged version?"

"Okay."

"All right, abridged version." He took a deep breath and began. "It goes back three years—or, let's say, more like two and a half, okay? I started a company with two partners. They came to *me*, actually, I'd worked with them before. We took over the operation of four Quik Gas stores, two in Ohio, one in Delaware, one in Maryland. It was basically hands off for me. Just a place to park some cash. The stores did all right—gave us a steady income for most of that time. I was planning to start a new development company in north Florida at the time, eventually sell my interest in the stores. But before that happened, this attorney contacts us, last summer, says he's representing an investor. Offers to buy the stores. His offer was good, too good to turn down." Jackson coughed, a smoker's hack.

"I met Kwan at our Sharonville store," he went on. "She started there, like, within a week of when we sold it. I stopped in a couple of times, just to pick up some cigarettes, lottery tickets. Shoot the crap, just friendly back and forth. I admit, I took a liking to her right away. There was something about the lady that was very intelligent, very classy. But at the same time, kind of aloof, if you know what I mean. Private, in some ways, and I guess that sort of interested me. Anyway, it didn't take long for me to figure out that something wasn't right about the setup."

"What do you mean, wasn't right?"

"Just something about the business, something that was bothering her." He shuffled his feet. "And so, anyway, before long we sort of became kindred spirits. I mean, I'm fifty-six years old, right? She's what, thirty-two?" His eyes misted with emotion as he looked off. "But it was one of those things, had nothing to do with age, really."

"What was bothering her about the business?"

"What was bothering her? Well, I don't know—I mean, why did they want those stores so badly in the first place?"

"Tell me."

He shrugged, and shook his head, meaning he wasn't going to say. An inmate three tables over stood and walked toward the vending machines with his two visitors; mother and sister, Luke guessed. Jackson exhaled dramatically, his eyes glazing over. He waited until they passed. "But so, anyway, one night we meet outside of work, okay? Meet for a drink. And that's when I really began to see how scared she was. A very lovely lady, although she made herself hard to see sometimes, if you know what I mean. But a very lovely lady."

"What'd you *think* was going on?"

"With the store? Or with her?"

"Either one."

He shrugged a shoulder and made a face, pushing out his lower lip. "No idea. Drugs? Money laundering?" His eyes did a quick inventory again of the visitors' room. "I mean, I've been around that kind of thing before. It could've been anything. But I guess what really made me take notice was the lottery thing. She got very nervous about that."

"About selling the winning lottery tickets. With multi-million-dollar payouts."

"Yeah, right. Absolutely didn't want to talk about it."

"And did you have any idea what was behind this organization that bought the stores?"

"Later, I did."

"When, later?" Luke said.

"Months later. I mean, gradually she began to reveal little things here and there to me about the setup. And about the man running the thing. And I began to understand why she was frightened."

"The man running it was August Trumble."

"Yeah, right." He showed a tiny smile, looking at Luke. "Trumble."

"Why was she telling you this, Jackson? What did she want you to do?"

"*Why* was she telling me? To get it off her chest. Because she wanted out. It was like, the walls were starting to close in. That's how she described it."

"Explain. Why were the walls closing in?"

"*Why?* I don't know, maybe she'd outlived her usefulness or something. She was scared of this guy, everyone was, but she also depended on him. I mean, he paid her six figures, right? Took care of her health care. Paid her rent, leased her car. But then they also expected her to behave a certain way. It was like the old song—you sell your soul to the company. But then Kwan decided she wanted it back again. And he didn't want to give it to her. Thought it was his."

"Seems odd for a company that owns convenience stores to operate that way."

"Well, yeah. Exactly."

"So what happened?"

"Long story short: I offered to help her. As I got to know her, I found out there were a few other people who were just as scared as she was. They'd become this sort of secret alliance, I guess you might say. And so I helped Kwan and the others come up with a plan to get away."

"Were those the three names you gave me at the church the other night?"

He turned his eyes to Luke and nodded.

"So you made a plan for her to quit and get away, you're saying."

"Right."

"And what about the others?"

"They were on their own. My concern was Kwan."

"Okay. But something went wrong."

"Well, yeah, obviously."

"How was it supposed to work?"

"How was it supposed to work?" He waited for the other inmate and his guests to pass again. "Kwan was supposed to drive to the airport in Cincy, fly to Reagan Monday morning, get on the Metro. I was going to meet her in Virginia. Pick her up, we'd go from there, catch 95 south, I'd arranged a place for her to stay." He looked at the floor between his knees, his eyes glistening. "Then I get an e-mail Monday evening says, 'Let's meet tomorrow morning in Tidewater instead. In front of the Methodist church.'"

"And so what'd you do?"

"What did I do?" He gave Luke a sharp look. "I tried to reach her, obviously. I couldn't. And so finally I came out. Drove through, just in case. Then the next day, Wednesday, I read the thing about the woman in the church. In the newspaper."

"You didn't do this, Jackson. Right?"

"I told you, Pastor."

"Okay." Luke watched him, trying to understand his expression, and what he wasn't saying. Jackson Pynne could be something of an omission artist, Luke knew, and this didn't seem to be the whole story. "How do you think your DNA ended up at the two crime scenes?"

"Couldn't tell you."

"Take a guess."

"Anyone could have followed me and saved my cigarette butts. I have no idea."

"Could Kwan Park have saved your cigarette butts?"

He shook his head and turned toward the wall, his eyes shining vulnerably again.

"How about the shoe prints? The shoes that made them were found in the garage at your town house here in Tidewater County."

He blinked rapidly. "I don't use that town house. It's a summer rental, the real estate agency handles it. The shoes? No idea. Maybe they were planted there."

"By whom? Who would have planted them?"

"No idea." Jackson lowered his head again. "Look," he said. "The thing is, this wasn't really about us, okay? Just to be clear. What Kwan really wanted was to blow the whistle. I was going to help her—"

"Blow the whistle on?"

"On what this organization was doing. Not just about stealing money from the government. I don't think any of us gave a shit about that. But what they were doing to their own people."

"Their own employees?"

"Yeah." His face took on a faraway look. "And I guess they must've found out what we were doing, and considered it disloyalty or something. Which, to them, is kind of like a capital offense."

"They who?" Luke said.

"Trumble. Trumble's security people."

"Is that who's after you?" Pynne shrug-nodded. "Why *you*, Jackson? You weren't part of this organization, were you?"

"Never. It's because of what I know—or what they think I know. And because I helped plan this thing. I was part of the betrayal."

"You need to tell this to the police, Jackson. They need to know what you just told me. Okay? You need to talk to Amy Hunter, the lead investigator. Will you do that?"

He shook his head.

"Why not?"

"Don't want to."

"Why?"

"Because I don't need to. Because I feel safe here, okay? I walk out of here, I wouldn't make it to the county line. Guarantee you. That's why I turned myself in."

"Then stay here. But you still need to tell your story. So they can find who actually did this."

Jackson said nothing. He looked back at the floor. He seemed to be waiting for Luke to disappear now. Luke finally signaled the guard across the room.

"Anything else, Jackson?"

"Yeah, one thing," he said. He sat up straighter. "What did she look like? When you found her?"

"She looked beautiful." Jackson was watching him attentively. "Until I got up close."

"Then what?"

"She still looked beautiful. But then I could tell that she'd been hurt."

He nodded, as if this was what he'd wanted to hear. Both men stood, Luke first. Then Jackson reached to shake his hand.

"She *was* beautiful," he said, holding on weakly. "I can't believe anyone would think I could've hurt her. I mean, I'd be the last one. The *last* one."

Chapter 39

THAT SOMEONE HAD been detained overnight for the church killing hadn't made the newspaper or television news, but it was all over the streets of Tidewater County that morning. At the wooden booths and Formica-topped breakfast tables on Main Street, patrons kept their papers folded, sharing the real news over coffee, bacon-egg specials, and crab omelets.

Luke picked up a carry-out coffee at the Blue Crab Diner and fended questions from several of the regulars, surprised that no one seemed to know, yet, that he had just talked with Jackson Pynne.

Driving in to the church, he called Amy Hunter. The late morning sun was bright, melting the patchy remnants of Sunday's snow.

"How was he?" she said.

"He was pretty open. About Kwan Park, anyway. Not about everything else."

"Where are you?"

"Headed to the church."

"I'll be right over."

AGGIE COLLINS, DRESSED in a brand-new navy pinstripe suit with a purple print scarf, went through the usual formalities before allowing Hunter to enter Luke's office, to be seated in front of his desk.

"Could I get either of you anything to drink?" she asked. "Coffee? Water?"

"No thanks," Amy said.

"I'm fine," Luke said.

"You sure?" Her eyes went back to Hunter. "Tea?"

"We're fine," Luke said.

When the door finally closed, they shared a smile. Then Luke began to tell Hunter all that Jackson Pynne had told him at the jail that morning. Hunter looked on without reaction, her eyes alert.

When he finished, she looked out the window and grimaced.

"So?" Luke said. "Will they have enough to bring a case against him?"

Her eyes were back with his "*They* think so. It's a tricky case. The evidence is all circumstantial, of course, but there's a lot of it. We're dealing with a serial killer and we need to connect the four crimes in order to show what really happened. But the state's attorney is resisting that. He has what he considers a strong case against Jackson Pynne now and he wants to proceed, get it over and out of Tidewater County."

"Without involving the other three murders, you mean?"

"Yeah. And what you just told me, about them being lovers, only makes it stronger." Hunter sighed. "The wild card in all this is what the FBI is going to do. And for some reason, I don't have a very good feeling about that, either."

Hunter looked away out at the marshlands, thinking private thoughts. Moments later she stood and moved toward the door.

Luke could see she had something else to say to him, although he couldn't imagine what it might be. She stopped by the door, her hand on the knob, her eyes roaming his office.

"You know what," she said at last. "There's something I said to you the first time we talked here that I've regretted a little ever since."

"Oh?"

"Yeah."

Somehow, Luke knew what she was going to say next. "You don't mean about being a devout secularist?"

"That's right." She showed a rare smile. "How'd you know?"

He shrugged.

"It just seemed a little flip," she said, "and also not entirely true. I guess I'm not really sure what I believe."

"Nothing wrong with that. I'm not a proponent of absolute certainties," he said. "Or of anyone following a religion that doesn't have some deep-rooted meaning for them. The nice thing is, we can come to faith from many directions."

"Yeah." Hunter smiled again, her hand still on the doorknob. "Good," she said.

Luke thought of several things he might've said then, questions he wanted to ask about her life. But this didn't seem like the time for it.

"Anyhow," she said. "Talk with you later."

LUKE HAD PROMISED himself that he would address the short stack of congregants' comments before lunch. Many were cheery observations about the church staff, his sermon, or the music selection, although there were always one or two challenges in the deck. Germaine Holland, for instance, requested that the church ask the Mickelson family—although she didn't refer to them by name, only as "the newcomers"—to "refrain" from sitting in the second-row pew, which had been Germaine and Bob Holland's "regular" seat for close to ten years. Luke moved her note to the bottom of the stack.

Easier to handle was this anonymous comment: *For two weeks, the same dead cockroach has had been lying in a corner at the very back of the church. Please REMOVE before Sunday!!*

Luke decided he'd handle this one himself, before taking on Germaine Holland.

He pulled a tissue from the box on Aggie's desk. "I'm going off on a mission," he told her mysteriously, and then he walked off into the church. He spent several minutes trying to locate the offending bug, but without success. Maybe Martha Cummings, the church custodian, had beat him to it.

As he headed back to the offices, Luke felt his cell phone vibrating. The ID read: UNKNOWN CALLER.

He stopped in the darkened corridor between the sanctuary and the offices, his heart thumping.

"Hello?"

"Hello, Preacher." It was the thick voice from the day before. "Did you visit our friend Jackson Pynne this morning?"

Luke said nothing.

"It's funny, because I thought you told me you didn't know where he was"

"I didn't. Police called me last night and said he wanted to talk with me."

"And what did Mr. Pynne tell you?"

"Not a lot."

"What did he say happened to the woman? Kwan Park."

"He doesn't know."

"You're not leveling with me now, are you, Preacher? What did he say happened to Kwan Park?"

Luke remained silent.

"You don't think someone other than Jackson Pynne killed this woman, now do you, Preacher?"

"I wouldn't know."

"I sure hope you don't think that." Luke could hear him breathing. "Because that would be a big mistake. If you did. Big mistake."

Luke thought of Charlotte. "That's really not my business," he said. "That's police business."

"Yes, exactly right. That isn't your business. So don't try to play hero now and become involved any more than you already have. Because if you do, you might discover some carvings on your wife's body."

"What?"

"I think you understand what I'm saying, Preacher. She's a very pretty lady," he added, a chuckle in his voice. Then the line went dead.

Luke stood there staring down the dusty wooden corridor. Then he called Amy Hunter.

"Hi," he said. "You probably didn't expect to hear from me again so soon."

SEATED IN HUNTER'S small office at the Public Safety Complex, Luke reconstructed his two conversations with the anonymous caller. The threat against Charlotte had immediately changed the equation for him. After the first call, he'd prayed and wrestled with what to do. But not after the second. Even if this was someone associated with the sheriff trying to scare him away from

Jackson Pynne, the caller had crossed a line by threatening Charlotte.

Hunter watched him with the quiet empathy of an experienced listener. It was almost as if their roles had become reversed, Luke's intensity absorbed by Hunter's calm. She'd been around, he could see. She'd been through things she didn't talk about.

"I guess I should have told you right away," he said when he finished.

"It's tough to know what to do sometimes. Just don't let this get to you," she said. "Go about your normal day-to-day activities. We'd like to send regular patrols by your house, if you don't mind. And I'd also like to put a trace on your phones."

"Sure," he said. "Thanks."

"It's probably best that you don't involve yourself in the case anymore, in any way, from here on out. Don't talk with Jackson Pynne again. If he calls, refer him to us."

"Okay."

Luke watched her, feeling humbled. ."Who do you think this is?"

"I don't know," she said. "It could be someone connected with the sheriff, as you say. Or it might be someone involved with this organization that Kwan Park worked for. Either way, the motive's the same."

"They want to make sure Jackson is prosecuted for the murder."

"Right, that's what it seems like. Which is sort of interesting in itself."

"It is,"

Hunter showed a cautious smile. Luke could see from her eyes that she was way ahead of him, already playing out the chess moves in her head. He felt a little sad that he wasn't going to be involved anymore; but he also knew that's how this had to go. His only role now would be to pray. And to wait.

GIL RANKIN WATCHED the pastor's wife from a distance as she walked from her BMW to the front door of the cottage, carrying a small bag of groceries. She's a stylish woman, he thought, pretty and slender. Nice hair. Comports herself nicely. If he'd had to rough her up, he would've enjoyed doing it.

But it was too chancy to start on anything like that at this stage. Until they knew for sure what was happening with Jackson Pynne, he needed to be more careful. He'd shaken up the preacher now, that was good enough.

Rankin knew that his problem was too much empty time again. He needed to work out, to get his mind on something else.

You do as you see fit, that's not my business, his client had said. *I just need to ascertain the end results.*

I wish we didn't have to do it this way, Gilbert. These people, they were like children to me, you know that. But they have that stench now. Betrayal has a smell. So, we have no choice anymore.

Rankin started the engine of his Jeep. It wouldn't be long before police began to monitor the pastor's house. He couldn't come near here again.

Driving back toward Jimmy Creek, he turned up the radio to drown out the Client's voice playing in his head

But it was still there, as tangible as the road and the fields: *You do as you see fit, that's not my business. I just need to ascertain the end results.*

I wish we didn't have to do it this way, Gilbert. You know that.

Chapter 40

STATE'S ATTORNEY WENDELL Stamps agreed to delay filing murder charges against Jackson Pynne until Amy Hunter met with him at three-thirty the next afternoon. This was good and bad news for Hunter. Good because it gave her a twenty-four-hour window to make a case that might change his mind; bad because twenty-four hours wasn't enough time to do that. It would have helped, of course, if Jackson Pynne had agreed to talk with her. But Pynne was still refusing her requests for an interview. Ben Shipman had, uncharacteristically, called in sick that morning, making their work even more difficult.

Hunter enlisted Sonny Fischer's help to track down Pynne's movements on Monday and early Tuesday. She wanted to create a timeline, proving that he couldn't have killed Kwan Park or left her body at the church. But the surveillance video told a different story: Pynne's pickup truck had crossed through the Bay Bridge toll plaza at 6:07 on Tuesday morning en route to the Eastern Shore. Meaning he could have been in Tidewater County at the time Kwan Park's body had been placed in the church. State troopers had found his truck two days ago, in a shopping center parking lot, but no sign of his computer or any other personal items.

Several times, Hunter tried to reach Dave Crowe, who was apparently still in Washington. She eventually left him a message saying she had important information to share about Jackson Pynne.

It was a few minutes past five when he finally called back.

"Just a heads-up," he said, by way of greeting. "Between us? We found something this morning on Mark Chandler. We think he may be the John Doe from Virginia. The mutilation, with the lips and tongue missing?"

"Yes."

"He was an attorney. Represented several accounting firms, including the one that did the books for the Quik Gas franchise. He was one of the three names you gave me."

"Right, I know all that."

"Okay, but you don't know this. We've searched the hard drive on one of his home computers. Over the past few weeks, he'd been diverting funds from a Delaware firm that has a pipeline to August Trumble's charities."

"Really."

"Mmm mm. We're talking several million dollars, all told, funneled from illegal tax returns through shell companies." He paused. "Electronically transferred, then redistributed to four separate accounts. One of the accounts was absorbing the bulk of it."

Hunter turned away from her desk, letting that sink in. Funny that Crowe was talking so openly over the phone all of a sudden. "So, what are you saying—you think Chandler was embezzling from Trumble's corporation?"

"I didn't say that. This is still preliminary, Hunter. You can draw whatever conclusions you want. I'm just giving you a heads-up."

Hunter had a sinking feeling. "So you're thinking Kwan Park was one of the four accounts? That maybe she and Jackson Pynne were together embezzling from Trumble's organization? And that's why she was killed?"

"We don't know that. We don't know who was accessing the fourth account. We know it existed, that's all." Crowe took a deep breath. "It's early yet, but I think you can see where it's heading." After a moment he added, "I understand Jackson Pynne's been arrested but isn't talking?"

"That's right. I've been trying to reach you."

"Sounds like they might have the right man this time," he said.

"Oh? Why would you say that?"

"We'll get into it later."

"When?"

"The morning."

Hunter sighed. "So what's happening with the investigation?" she asked. "Is this federal yet?"

"The murder of Kwan Park? No. But we can talk about that in the morning. Sit on this for now."

"On what?"

"On everything I've told you. From when we first spoke the other night."

"Why?"

"We'll talk in the morning. The case is taking a turn. That's all I can say. I'll be back out there in the morning and we'll discuss it."

"Why can't we—"

But he'd hung up. Hunter sat there, holding the phone. After a while she realized she was studying her own reflection in the window and not liking what she saw. She imagined what she'd look like in twenty-five years, where she'd be. They were not thoughts she needed to be having right now.

"You DID THE right thing, telling her," Charlotte said. "It's in their hands and you don't need to worry about it."

"I know." They were all in bed together, under the covers—Charlotte, Luke, Sneakers—the three amigos, the room lit only by a night-light. A state cruiser was parked up the road, police keeping the cottage under surveillance. First thing in the morning they'd have alarms installed on all the doors and windows.

"But promise me you won't be involved anymore," she said. "Let's not even talk about it."

"Okay."

"Promise."

"Promise."

She leaned on her elbow. He could sense her eyes watching in the darkness.

"What."

"Say it again," she said. "This time with feeling."

"*Prom-miss,*" Luke said. She kissed him and then snuggled closer, getting comfortable. Moments later, Sneakers, sensing three was a crowd, burrowed out from the covers and settled in his own bed for the night.

Charlotte had a way of making bad things disappear. It was one of her talents. As he lay in bed listening to the wind, Luke thought about the first time they'd met. She had come alone to a Methodist service in the D.C. suburbs and chatted him up in the parking lot afterward—talking about Joseph Campbell, Madeleine Albright, Plato's *Republic,* and rapper Coolio, all of which he'd somehow managed to include in his sermon. They laughed easily together in a way that—he now knew—wasn't quite natural for either of them. Several weeks later they went out for dinner, and began dating. It was a respectful, lively, and platonic relationship. Then, several months in, after a dinner of yellowtail snapper at Charlotte's house, she asked, "You didn't bring your pj's, by any chance?"

"Should I have?"

Charlotte shrugged and for the first time gave him the mischievous look that he'd come to love.

Tonight, they fell asleep holding each other. But Luke woke several times and turned over, recalling the menacing intonations of the caller's voice. He listened to Charlotte and Sneakers breathing in rhythm like secret jazz musicians. He lay with his hands behind his head for a long time, watching the moon through the curtain as it hung high above the marsh grasses, wishing he could just close his eyes and join them.

Chapter 41

RETRIEVING THE MORNING paper, Luke waved to the state police trooper parked up the road. The trooper—a large, pleasant woman he recognized but couldn't name—nodded but didn't wave back. The morning sky was bright and cloudless, the temperature probably pushing fifty degrees, the snow long gone. He heard echoes of people who were already at work—hammering nails, scraping barnacles from boat-bottoms. The world felt delicate and kind of precious this morning.

He unfolded the paper on the kitchen table. Jackson Pynne was there on the top left-hand side of the first page: DEVELOPER HELD ON CHARGES.

Charlotte stood at the stove in her moose pajamas, making cheese and mushroom omelets, Sneakers at her feet, sleeping soundly. A sweeping symphonic music played from her CD box.

On the top of the right-hand side, Luke saw: PRAYING WOMAN CASE STILL A MYSTERY. The subhead read: *FBI to Take Over Investigation.*

"The AP picked up on the story, evidently," he said. "They're calling her 'Praying Woman' now."

"More interesting than mystery woman," she said, turning down her music.

"I guess."

"Next stop, the tabloids."

"Might be good for tourism," Luke said.

"Maybe."

She dished the omelets from the skillet onto plates, then set their breakfasts on the table, along with glasses of orange juice and a plate of wheat toast.

"So," Charlotte said, when she had his attention, "feeling any better?"

"Some. I finally got back to sleep around three-thirty, I think."

"Good," she said. "We'll be fine."

They ate for a while in silence. It felt funny not being able to talk about the case anymore.

"I feel better with the trooper out there," Luke finally said.

"Deanna."

"Must get a little boring for *her*, though."

"I was going to see if she wanted some breakfast or a cup of coffee."

"Good idea," Luke said. "Maybe we could send the opera singer out to entertain her."

"Too bad he only performs in my parents' basement."

"Yes. A shame."

Charlotte looked at Sneakers, lying beneath her, who was snoring faintly. They finished in silence.

HUNTER DROVE TO work thinking about the phone call and

wondered what the caller's next move might be. It was an added wrinkle: for whatever reason, someone was worried about what Jackson Pynne might say to police if he decided to talk.

At her office she found another voice message from Theresa Kincaid, the AP reporter who'd come up with the "Praying Woman" tag for Kwan Park. Hunter ignored it and went back to the case files. Her phone rang shortly after nine-thirty. Dave Crowe.

"Think you could you come up to the conference room at ten-ten?"

"I suppose. Are you here?"

"I'm in the building. This has to go a certain way, Hunter," he said, his voice sounding comically officious. "'Kay? Just trust me on it, I'll fill you in later. But I need you to be with me on this."

Hunter felt her defenses flare up, and fought the urge to challenge him. At five past ten she dutifully walked down the hallway and up the steps to the small conference room on the second floor. Wendell Stamps was already there, along with Deputy Stilfork, state's attorney investigator Clinton Fogg, and public information officer Kirsten Sparks. Seconds after Crowe closed the door, Sheriff Clay Calvert slipped in and sat at the other end of the table. Hunter felt her neck bristle as he sat down.

"Good morning. Thanks for coming on short notice." Crowe gave everyone the same quick, all-business look. "I just want to provide a brief update. As you know, the local paper is reporting that the federal government is taking over the Kwan Park investigation." He waved a copy of the *Tidewater Times* and dropped it on the table. "Not true," he said, glancing at Sheriff Calvert and then at Kirsten Sparks. Sparks seemed to be mimicking his facial expressions as he talked. "Just to bring everyone up to speed: the

FBI is *not* taking over the Kwan Park investigation. We are offering assistance if and when it's requested. But this is *not* a federal investigation. I've spoken with the local media and we'll be issuing a general press advisory to that effect later today."

Hunter felt a flash of anger. *Why didn't you just tell me?*

"To further elaborate—and, please, this isn't for the media." He winked at Sparks, who lowered her eyes and, for some reason, fought back a smile. How long has this been going on? Hunter wondered. "Two things: First, I'm satisfied this is a local crime and that the prosecutor and the local and state investigators"—here he nodded at Sheriff Calvert, and then at Hunter—"have that under control. Second, we are currently involved in a separate, ongoing federal case. Completely unrelated to this murder. Kwan Park, the victim here, is—was—also a tangential figure in the federal investigation."

"What sort of federal investigation?" Sheriff Calvert said gruffly, as if perceiving this as some sort of personal affront.

"An ongoing federal fraud and racketeering investigation. I'm not at liberty to go into details."

"Is it related to this county in any way?" the sheriff asked.

"No, it is not."

This seemed to appease Sheriff Calvert. Moments later he cleared his throat and then slipped from the room.

"So the numbers found carved into Kwan Park's hand are not part of any larger case, you're saying?" Hunter asked, surprised by the attitude in her own voice.

Crowe's face seemed to tighten. "I don't think they are, no."

Hunter's heart was racing now.

"Okay?" Crowe looked at each of those in the room, one at a time, his eyes sliding quickly past Hunter. "That's all, then."

Stamps nodded, Hunter noticed, but in his usual understated manner. Kirsten Sparks seemed to blush as Crowe's eyes stayed with her a little too long.

CROWE WALKED DOWN the hall with his clipped stride, deliberately keeping a step or two ahead of Hunter.

She followed him into her own office and closed the door, angry energies roiling inside of her. Crowe feigned a smile. He settled into her guest chair, folded his hands behind his head.

"Why didn't you just tell me this?" she said. "You know this is my investigation."

"I asked you to bear with me, Hunter. I told you I'd explain later."

Hunter remained standing.

"Why is the Bureau trying to shut down the larger case? I don't understand that."

"We're not."

"Sure you are."

"We've got to protect *our* case, Amy. Nothing more than that. I'm trying to keep this going a certain way."

"I can see that."

Hunter finally sat. But she didn't cool down.

"Let me take a wild guess here," she said. "The Bureau doesn't want the embezzlement story out there because it might make Trumble seem like the victim?"

"Something like that."

"And you think maybe that's how Trumble *wants* this to play? That's how he wants his story told? He wants to come off looking like a victim? Victim of Jackson Pynne and Kwan Park? And you think that story is a form of misdirection."

Crowe shrugged. "You're good," he said.

Hunter looked out at the pine trees. "So *was* Kwan Park embezzling money from Trumble's organization?" she asked. "And was Jackson Pynne part of the deal? And did they then have some sort of fight over it? Is that what you're thinking now?"

"It's the $64,000 question, isn't it? I can't answer it yet. I'd like to ask Pynne about it. But, as you know, he won't talk with me, or the sheriff. Or the state police. He won't talk with anyone."

"Except the pastor."

"Right, so I hear."

"But, just to be clear," Hunter said. "We *do* have four murders that are clearly related. Right? As we discussed the other night."

"I *don't* know that," he said.

Hunter took a deep breath, wondering what else he wasn't saying. Crowe was like two people—one a player, the other a suit of armor. The difference, usually, was a couple of drinks.

"Look," he said, "you're smarter than these people, Hunter. We both know that. I've gone into lots of little jurisdictions like this over the years where someone's in a power play and doesn't want to let go. The Bureau's not getting into the middle of that here. We can't. Let it play itself out. Just let the case go forward. If there are others, we'll take them one at a time. That's the way this needs to go down. There are a lot of moving parts to this thing."

Hunter felt a fresh surge of anger. He was getting pressure from Washington to pursue the Trumble case a certain way, she suspected. *That's* what this was really about.

"Tell me the rest, then," she said. "Does this have something to do with your informants? Tell me what's really going on."

"I will," he said. "In time." He sat up straighter and gave her a flinty look. "Okay?"

Then he slapped his hands on his thighs simultaneously to punctuate the conversation, stood and walked away.

Motherfucker, Hunter thought, watching him go.

But she said nothing. And afterward she was glad she hadn't. Although it had been mighty tempting.

Chapter 42

Hunter sat in Wendell Stamps's waiting room while he finished a phone call. Hearing him say, several times, "I want to do everything I can to help you, Everett, you know that."

"The Wait" was part of the state's attorney's style. Hunter, like everyone else, was used to it.

She'd studied the case files that afternoon as if cramming for a final exam, but something about this still felt unwinnable. Being right wasn't enough; she had to prove it in a convincing way, which seemed all but impossible as long as the state's attorney wouldn't consider linking this case to the other three.

Finally, at 3:41, Wendell Stamps called her in. His large glass-topped desk was polished and immaculate, as usual. He stood and nodded as she sat, but in a detached way, as if his thoughts were still with the phone call. Or maybe with his next order of business.

"Let me just say at the outset, Amy," he began, "that I don't want any bad blood between us. I just think we need to move forward in the most efficient and effective manner possible. I want us all to be on the same team here."

Hunter nodded. He'd taken her line about being on the same team, one of Stamps's favorite techniques. Calling her "Amy" was a calculated touch, too; it was as if they were not only teammates now, but also friends. Stamps was a shrewd prosecutor and a good judge of character. Unlike the sheriff, there was no question Stamps would be reelected in November. Sheriff Calvert was a maverick, who rubbed some people the wrong way and drew oddball challengers every election. The state's attorney was even-tempered and diplomatic, cordial with everyone. No one had bothered to run against him for his past three elections.

He presented the case much as Hunter expected, beginning with the morning of the crime: Jackson Pynne's truck was seen parked by the church about an hour before Kwan Park's body was discovered. His shoe prints and DNA were later found at both the church and at the alleged murder scene on Oyster Creek. The truck was recovered from a parking lot up on the highway. Boots matching the shoe prints were discovered in the garage at Jackson Pynne's town house.

The state's attorney spoke clearly and convincingly, as if rehearsing his opening argument to a jury, which Hunter supposed he was. After presenting the evidence, he explained Jackson Pynne's motive: Pynne and Kwan Park had been lovers, but their relationship was troubled. The prosecution would produce a co-worker from the convenience store in Ohio who had witnessed them arguing in front of the store days before she disappeared. On Monday they met at a parking lot near the Cincinnati/Northern Kentucky International Airport, where Kwan Park left her car, and then drove together to the Eastern Shore of Maryland. Five hundred twenty-six miles, a ten-hour drive. They arrived at the cottages on Oyster Creek late Monday afternoon or early evening.

They got into a fight that evening over their plans for the future. It escalated, became violent; he shot her and beat her. Pynne then loaded her into his pickup truck and drove back to the Western Shore. But feeling remorse, he returned early Tuesday morning, taking her to the Methodist church, which Pynne had once attended, where he left her body.

"That's where we are," he said, folding his hands.

Hunter nodded.

"The problem is, it's too perfect," she said. "And there are too many details you're leaving out."

Wendell Stamps lifted one eyebrow slightly, meaning, *Go ahead, tell me what you've got.* He leaned forward, elbows on the desk, his fingers tented.

Good, Hunter thought. He's open.

"There's no evidence, for instance, that her body was ever in his pickup truck."

"That's right," Stamps said. "But we *are* able to place the truck in front of the church Tuesday morning, as you know. And we've got the shoe prints and cigarette butts at both scenes. And the boots in his town house."

"The boots weren't his," Hunter said. "Both the boots and the cigarette butts were planted. And with a little more time to process evidence we'll be able to show that conclusively."

Stamps nodded, seeming unconcerned. "But is that just him talking, or can any of that be proved?"

"We will be able to prove it, sir. We just need a little more time.

Stamps watched her, but said nothing.

"You're also leaving out the fact that she was beaten postmortem," she continued. "That wouldn't follow from a fight that 'escalated.' Nor does it indicate there was any remorse afterward."

The state's attorney tilted his head as if these were unimportant distinctions. "Remorse following passion," he said. "He's a volatile character. We both know that." Hunter saw his eyes studying her, showing nothing. "Go on," he said.

"And the idea that he left cigarette butts behind? If he was otherwise so careful not to leave fingerprints or DNA, would he really leave cigarette butts at both locations?"

"Why would someone want to frame him, though?" Stamps asked.

"That's the larger story, sir. I believe this killing is connected to a dispute over a complicated embezzling operation, and that Pynne was the man chosen to take the fall. We need a little more time to pursue that angle."

Stamps sighed, a long drawn-out sound. "Again," he said, "if we had any evidence to indicate that might be true, I'd be only too happy to consider it. You know that."

"You have no evidence showing he was in Cincinnati Monday, either," she said. This, she thought, was among the most speculative parts of his case. "No surveillance video, no witnesses."

"And there's no video showing he was in Washington on Monday."

"But there will be," Hunter said, her eyes going anxiously to the clock. "We're working on that. There are still hours of tape to go through."

"Either way, we know he was *here* early Tuesday morning. And that he left evidence at both crime scenes."

"No, sir, we don't." Hunter took a breath. "My concern is that we're rushing into this before we've had time to process all of the potential evidence."

He breathed elaborately.

"And what if the defense brings up those numbers carved into her hand?" Hunter continued. "How do you respond? What do the numbers mean?"

"Who knows?" He was growing impatient, Hunter could see. "You know, a character study of Jackson Pynne bears out the fact that he's a rather unusual fellow. Generous one minute, angry and delusional the next. And, of course, logic and order don't always explain motives in murder cases. I don't have to tell you that. "

Hunter nodded, seeing that he was giving her a peek at the rest of his prosecution: they were going to put Jackson Pynne's odd personality on trial—his anger problem, his obsessive-compulsiveness, the occasional delusions of grandeur.

"And the other three cases?"

"Not germane," Stamps said. "We just don't have strong enough evidence tying any of them together." He opened his hands for a moment. "Although in the case of the wax museum, it turns out Pynne does have a connection to that part of Delaware, doesn't he? He used to live one town over." Hunter nodded; she didn't realize he knew this. "But those other cases, that's something of a Pandora's box, Amy—which we don't need to open right now."

"But when the defense brings up the numbers in her hand, what do you say? What if they're able to tie them to these other cases?"

Stamps said nothing at first. This, she had thought, was probably her best argument. The state's attorney's reaction wasn't what she'd expected, though; instead of engaging with her, his eyes glazed over and he leaned back.

"I don't know, a red herring? Like we thought from the beginning."

"Why, though?" He lifted a corner of his mouth, as if it didn't matter. "What if they go there? Five-one-eight. What does that mean? What do the numbers mean?"

"A date? May eighteenth, maybe?" It surprised Hunter how quickly he said this. "I'm going to speculate that five/eighteen is a date that means something to the two of them. Maybe it was a date they were planning to go off together. Maybe they planned to get married. Who knows? But, frankly, I don't anticipate a case being made about the numbers. If they even were numbers."

"*If* they were?"

"*If* they were."

"All right." Hunter took a breath. She leaned toward the desk. "Then here's why I think you'd be making a mistake going forward, sir. This case has the potential to draw national attention. If you prosecute it this way, you're ignoring additional evidence from three other murder cases that, I believe, will take the Kwan Park case in a different direction—and only end up embarrassing this office. I think we'll find evidence to prove that the four crimes are related and that Jackson Pynne couldn't have committed any of them. We haven't yet exhausted those avenues of investigation, sir. And, with all due respect, I think it's reckless going forward until we do."

Hunter was wired now. But she could tell that Stamps was fighting a yawn. She understood what he was doing. He wanted to prosecute this thing and put it behind him. Have it over by the time the weather turned, before the gates opened to the summer tourist season. And he knew he probably had the evidence to do that.

"And you're basing this on?" When she didn't reply right away, he held up his right hand. "You don't have to answer. I know what you're basing it on. The Psalms. You think this is about the Psalms." Watching her without blinking. "Correct?"

Hunter tipped her head to the side, acknowledging it. "Yes," she said. But who told him? Crowe? Shipman? Or had the detectives in the other jurisdictions begun to put it together and talked to him or to Clinton Fogg, Stamps's investigator?

"That's not my case, though," he went on, showing a practiced smile. "That's not for me to prove. I'm looking to prove a particular crime that occurred within the borders of Tidewater County, based on available evidence. Period.

"Candidly?" he added. "I don't buy the Psalms theory. I've looked at all four cases very closely, and I don't, frankly, think it holds water. The one with the watch and the one with the tattoo? I'm not convinced those mean *any*thing. The numbers on the glass? Who knows? To me, it's like playing a Beatles record backward and finding a clue that Paul is dead."

Hunter was silent. How did he know those details? That was the case *she* was going to make to him. The case he didn't want to hear.

"But regardless," he went on, "they're separate crimes. It's not uncommon, as you know only too well, for someone to be prosecuted for murder in one jurisdiction and later be found guilty of a separate killing in another jurisdiction.

"No case is perfect, Sergeant. Would I prefer to have video footage, DNA in the pickup, eyewitnesses? Why, of course. But I think we have more than enough here to meet the burden of proof, and that's what matters." He let her look at his reasonable face for a moment. "But if you can give me a good, specific reason not to go forward, other than this somewhat convoluted conspiracy theory. Some piece of evidence I haven't considered. Then, of course, I'll listen."

Hunter's eyes misted with frustration. But she also began to sense that he had something else—some sort of ace in the hole that he wasn't telling her. Something about his demeanor seemed too unconcerned.

"Could you give me twenty-four hours?"

Stamps didn't react at first. But his silence told her he'd go along with it. Hunter had walked in thinking she would ask for forty-eight, but knew now that would be pushing it. "End of day tomorrow?"

He puckered his mouth slightly and looked at the clock. He was an effective conciliator who wanted everyone to be happy, when possible. Hunter respected that. Despite what the sheriff had said, she wasn't looking for personal glory; and unlike what Calvert had implied, she wasn't trying to overthrow the old guard. She was just interested in justice, in finding out what had happened. Who had killed Kwan Park.

"Okay," he said. "Fair enough. Five P.M. tomorrow, then."

SEVEN MILES AWAY, in the house on Jimmy Creek, Gil Rankin sat in afternoon darkness, waiting for news from Kirby Moss. Pynne was in custody now. Not an outcome Rankin would have chosen. But at least it would create an opportunity. If Pynne was charged, there'd be an arraignment at the courthouse; if not, they'd let him go. Either way, they'd at last be able to get to him.

This needs to happen as soon as possible, the Client had told him. *Otherwise, Pynne endangers the whole enterprise. Take care of Pynne, it closes the door, and we all move on.*

I'm very saddened by what has occurred, Gilbert.. You know that. But this is as it's written. We had no choice. They received the just fruits of their disloyalties. You understand that.

Rankin did not know the "whole enterprise," but he knew

enough. He'd heard the stories about enormous "tax returns" benefiting various East Coast charities. He'd read about multi-million-dollar lottery payouts and knew that the Client was behind some of those as well. Rankin was part of a larger story, but a small, kept-in-the-dark part. That was the nature of the bargain they'd struck.

Certain things were beginning to bother him, though. The killings were fine. A job was a job. But the mutilations—lips removed, bones broken—and the numbers left behind, none of that made any sense. Either the Client was testing him or else he was coming unglued, as some of his employees had been saying. But either way, he knew there was nothing he himself could do about it. Nothing at all. So he needed to think about other things.

He took the photograph of his wife and sons from his wallet and set it on the table in front of him. *Think about the good things, Gil. The things that are coming.*

Chapter 43

A DELICIOUS AROMA of sherry-cooked oyster chowder permeated Chez Bowers as Luke came through the front door, following his afternoon visits to Memorial Hospital and Tidewater Hospice. Classical music played very softly from the kitchen, something he recognized as baroque. Bach, maybe, or perhaps Handel.

Charlotte and Sneakers were nowhere to be seen, though. Luke knew that meant one of three things: she was having a great workday, she was having a bad workday, or else she was going to seduce him.

He could tell as soon as she spoke that it wasn't option three. Not today.

"I'm in here," she called from her study. "I'll be out in a minute."

"Take your time," he said.

Luke got a local-brewed Chesapeake beer from the refrigerator and walked into the living room. He looked through the window at the bay, which was yellow and orange with the sun. Sneakers finally came out to greet him and to collect his neck, head, and belly rub.

"Damn!" Charlotte said, twice.

"Everything okay?" Luke called.

"Oh, crap, I just lost part of a file. *Damn* it!"

"Anything I can do?"

Luke and Sneakers hovered for a moment in the doorway to Charlotte's office. But he knew better than to try to help. Normally, she had the most wonderful temperament. But occasionally she became wildly flustered over some minor problem. The best response, Luke had learned, was to give her space to work through it.

He walked out onto the deck, thinking about his day, feeling grateful for having Charlotte and Sneakers and for the gift of this life he'd been given. Sunset blushed the wetlands, the light sharpening, the air cooling. He kept thinking about Jackson Pynne, wondering what was going through his mind right now.

Charlotte finally joined him, with a glass of wine. The air was breezing up and there were still five or six minutes before sunset.

"Sorry," she said, giving him a kiss. "I found it."

"Good," Luke said. "So everything's hunky-dory again?"

"Everything hunky-dory," she said, leaning against him. "Except we haven't eaten yet."

"I know. But we can't waste the sunset."

"No."

Several minutes later they went in, Sneakers following, and settled for dinner.

Luke told her about his visit that afternoon with Millie Blanchard at the hospice, as they ate oyster chowder and corn bread. And then, to his surprise, Charlotte asked him about Jackson Pynne, even though she'd made him promise not to talk about the case anymore.

"What I heard," she said, "is that Jackson is going to be charged with the murder in another day or two. And it seems that people know about the numbers in Kwan Park's hand all of a sudden now, too."

"Well, how about that," Luke said. "Although, of course, we're not supposed to be talking about the case, right?"

"No, that's right."

"But what else did you hear?"

A sly smile animated Charlotte's face. "My friend Claire, at the Humane Society, told me this. 'He's capable of it,' she said. But isn't everyone?"

"Capable of it? Some more than others, I'd say."

"They're saying he might be responsible for these other murders, too," Charlotte said.

"They may be saying it," Luke said, "but it's not true." He wondered if Amy Hunter knew how these new rumors were flying.

The sun was gone now, and he could see lights along the docks at the harbor and the crab houses brightening across the cove.

When they finished, Luke cleared the table. Then he scooped out cups of chocolate chip ice cream for dessert.

"How are they keeping him in jail, anyway?" Charlotte asked. "Don't they say on TV crime shows that you can't hold someone beyond twenty-four hours? Or is it forty-eight?"

"He doesn't want to leave," Luke said. "And no one's in a rush to throw him out. He says that if he leaves, he won't make it to the county line."

"Very dramatic."

"Yes. I know. He doesn't want out. He wants police to solve the case while he waits."

"You want to help him, don't you?" Charlotte said, her pale blue eyes softening as she watched him.

"I wish I could," Luke said. "I feel bad for him. I think he really loved this woman."

"Kwan Park."

"Yeah. I think for him this was a real love story. He wanted to have a life with her. He expected to."

"Despite the age difference."

"Despite everything," Luke said. "Part of it was the impossibility of it. I think that's what appealed to Jackson. That's how he is. He saw it as something real, a real love story. And then it was all pulled away from him. And now, on top of that, he's being accused of killing her. I feel bad for him."

Sneakers's head suddenly shot up, for no apparent reason. He produced a very subdued growl before he let his face ease back to the floor.

Luke realized after a moment what he must've heard: his cell phone was vibrating in the living room.

"Wonder who that is."

He didn't get there in time, but saw that the call had come from the Tidewater Correctional Facility. Which could only mean one thing: Jackson Pynne wanted to talk.

PART 3

Violent Man

"See, I have set before you an open door, and none of you can shut it."

—Revelation 3:5

"The hunter is taken in his own snare, as the great Psalmist says."

—Bram Stoker, *Dracula*

Chapter 44

"AMY HUNTER."

It was Crowe, calling from Washington. "Have you seen the latest? The AP's saying there may be a connection between Tidewater and West Virginia."

"I just saw it, yeah."

"Where do you think that come from?"

"No idea."

He went silent for several seconds. "If it keeps spinning out like this, they'll have the Psalms thing in another day or two."

"Why do you think that?"

"Because. More than one reporter knows about the numbers now, from what I'm hearing. *You're* not talking to the media, are you?"

Hunter said nothing.

"I mean, not even off the record?"

Hunter didn't respond. She suspected Dave Crowe was into his cups early today and had gotten a wild hair about her deliberately leaking information—a way of tripping up the local investigation, maybe. She had actually thought about it, but not very seriously.

She considered hanging up on him as she pulled into the marina apartments and parked in her space. She saw the curved outline of Winston in the living room window, waiting for his Fancy Feast tuna dinner. She felt a warm glow of affection for him.

"Regardless," Crowe was saying, "the detectives you've talked with in the other jurisdictions are letting it out in dribs and drabs. No one's muzzling them, and the press is starting to put it together. How much have you said to them?"

"I haven't told anyone about the Psalms," she said.

Hunter cut the engine. She watched the boat masts tipping in the early evening mist.

Crowe snorted. "We didn't want this story out there, Hunter. You know that. *That's* why I've been trying to keep it at the local level."

"Yes, I figured that out." But it was obvious to her what was happening. Crowe was getting heat from his higher-ups to contain this story, and he was taking it out on her. "Look," she said, exaggerating her anger. "I don't appreciate this. I haven't and wouldn't talk to the media. End of discussion. All *right*?"

"All right," Crowe said quietly.

"Is that all you're calling to tell me?"

"No. In fact, I was calling because I'm told that Stamps's investigator—Clint Fogg—went down to Virginia and found a couple of things that the state police there apparently missed. Did you hear about it?"

Hunter took out her keys. "No, what do you mean?"

"You didn't know? I thought you would have heard."

"What did they find?"

"DNA, apparently, and shoe prints again. Tying it back to Jackson Pynne."

So *that* was why the state's attorney wasn't worried about finding a different result in the other cases? If so, he hadn't even bothered to tell her. *A lie by omission is still a lie.* She felt her heart
racing as she walked into the apartment. Winston looked up and
ran away, pretending he hadn't been waiting for her.

"What kind of DNA? What are you talking about?"

"A drink container in the woods, apparently."

Hunter made a scoffing sound. "I've got to go," she said. "We'll
talk later."

She dumped her files on the kitchen table, poured herself a tall
glass of red wine and took a drink. She spooned out half a can
of tuna dinner for Winston. Then, as he devoured it, she settled
in the living room and began to sift again through the case files.
There were enough ingredients there to cook it into something
that might satisfy a local jury. Hunter knew that. The argument
that this had been a lovers' quarrel almost made sense, except
for the bizarre postmortem beating. A jury—and the Tidewater community—would probably accept the idea that Jackson
Pynne was the killer. But not the idea that he was a serial killer,
who'd left behind calling cards. So she needed to show conclusively that this *was* a serial killer. It seemed a simple enough
resolution; but simple and easy were two different things. Would
the news story implying a connection between Tidewater and
West Virginia make any difference? Would it have any impact
on Stamps's resolve to move forward? Probably not. She knew
that, too.

Hunter wondered who *had* told the reporter about the connection, and decided it had to be Alan Barker. "Barky." The West
Virginia homicide detective whose Red Lobster dinner she had
interrupted. Maybe he got off on the idea of being involved in a

serial murder case—particularly one with the potential of going national. She had known police detectives like that.

"Any ideas?" she asked Winston, who had curled up against her on the sofa. She patted the top of his head and Winston made a loud but indecipherable reply.

When the phone rang that evening, Hunter was on her third glass of red wine and staring out the window. Winston snored softly in one of his wicker sleeping boxes. She picked up when she heard Pastor Luke's voice on her answering machine.

"Hi," he said. Still uncomfortable calling her Amy. "I'm sorry to bother you."

"Hey, no, I'm working," Hunter said. The sound of his voice was a pleasant contrast to Crowe's earlier. "I need to keep on this."

"Maybe I can help. I received a message from Jackson Pynne," he said. "He's agreed to talk with you. He *wants* to talk with you. I'm no longer involved, of course. But I said I'd pass it along."

"Great," she said. "When can we talk?"

"Can you meet him tomorrow morning? Nine-thirty?"

JACKSON PYNNE'S WORLD had shrunk to nine feet by nine feet. Just a bed, toilet, and attached sink. Stale air, the sounds of human bodies. There was nowhere he could take his anger anymore, nothing he could do with it. At first it had consumed him, being stuck with it in this box, knowing he'd been outmaneuvered by something he didn't understand. That they had taken everything from him again, and in a way he'd never seen coming. First Kwan, now his freedom. Not even knowing who *they* were, exactly. But then, gradually, he began to see his circumstances as a different kind of freedom; freedom in reverse.

Jackson believed that he could turn this thing around, and trap the men who had killed Kwan Park. That he might even be able to come out of it as a good guy in some way. Maybe even a kind of hero.

And during that long night, as he tossed on his metal bed, listening to the sounds of other men sleeping, he began to nurture a new idea. A redeeming one. The idea began to play itself out in a seemingly endless series of variations, giving him surges of hope. And finally, a couple of hours before dawn, it even allowed him to sleep.

Chapter 45

HUNTER DROVE PAST the courthouse, the grocery, the 1960s movie palace, the Blue Crab Diner and Holland's Family Restaurant, the antiques shops and the Baptist church, then into the corn and bean fields of farm country. She was thinking of the questions she needed to ask Jackson Pynne.

There were only two, really.

The pastor's call the night before had felt like a gift, her chance to finally learn what Jackson Pynne knew about Kwan Park's death. And, probably more significantly, to learn exactly where he'd been on Monday and early Tuesday.

She waited for him in the small concrete-block interview room, reading through the list of questions she'd stayed up past midnight writing out—more than she'd have a chance to ask. Luke Bowers had warned her not to push Jackson Pynne. "He has to tell you things on his own terms or he shuts down." This time the conversation would be digitally recorded. Whatever Pynne said would become part of the case against him. Or, she hoped, it would form the basis for a different case.

He came in accompanied by an armed guard, wearing an orange jumpsuit, walking with a slight bounce, as if happy about something. The guard stood across the room by the door. Around the metal desk were four stacking chairs.

"Good morning, Mr. Pynne," Hunter said.

Jackson seemed surprised from the moment he saw her. Shaking her hand, he held on longer than expected, although his grip was surprisingly weak. A roguish smile etched his mouth as she laid out the ground rules, his eyes roaming her face.

Hunter was used to all that. He was reacting to her physical appearance and to her age. She wondered what he'd expected.

"Okay?" she said. "So we're on tape here."

Jackson Pynne nodded. And then he began to tell his story, keeping his eyes on her the whole time. Pausing occasionally to give her what he must have imagined were meaningful looks. Hunter nodded at intervals. She could feel him performing a little as he spoke, overgesturing at times. Punctuating his narrative with "as you know" and "as I already told the pastor." Often the sly smile appeared just as his eyes turned to hers, and she would nod instead of smiling back.

The story ended with his return to Tidewater County last week, and his talk with Luke Bowers, "the only person here I trust anymore."

Once he finished, Hunter said, "The state's attorney is planning to charge you tomorrow morning with the murder of Kwan Park. First-degree murder. How do you feel about that?"

Pynne watched her. Still smiling slightly.

"Sir?"

"I don't feel anything about it."

"But you didn't kill her."

"No, that's right, I didn't."

His eyebrows arched as if he were going to say something else.

"Here's their case," Hunter said. "This is the prosecution's theory: You met Kwan Park in Cincinnati on Sunday night or Monday morning. You drove together to Tidewater County, on your way to somewhere else, probably somewhere down South. You planned to stay in a cottage at Oyster Creek. Laying low. You argued. It escalated. You killed her. You beat her. You took her to the church."

"No."

"None of that's true?"

"None of it. I was never in Cincinnati. Or Oyster Creek. I was in D.C. all day Monday, as I already told the pastor."

"Okay. And they have nothing to prove you weren't. But can you prove you *were*? Where specifically were you Monday? Think about every street you drove down, every store you entered, every phone call you made, every conversation you had. Let's start first thing in the morning when you woke up and go through the day. We need to check out the whole day, for witnesses, surveillance video, traffic cams. That's how we win a delay, and that's how we get you off. Okay?"

The pastor had told her that Pynne's attention span was limited, so she wanted to get this on the record right away. Jackson took his time, enjoying talking to her. He gave a detailed account of what he'd done on Monday: all morning he'd been at his apartment in the Maryland suburbs, watching television and reading. Kwan was supposed to fly into Reagan National just before noon, he said. He drove to a Virginia Metro stop to meet her.

But Kwan never showed up. She didn't answer her phone, didn't e-mail. He waited more than an hour and returned home. He repeatedly tried to reach her, without success; then, at about eight-thirty, he received the e-mail, asking him to meet her in front of the Methodist church in Tidewater County the next morning at seven.

Hunter knew that cell phone and e-mail records would be able to prove or disprove much of this, although she'd need stronger evidence to clear him.

Jackson told her he rose before sunrise on Tuesday and drove across the Chesapeake Bay to Tidewater County. He idled in front of the Methodist church but never went in. He was sure something was wrong. The e-mail didn't sound like Kwan, and he knew she would've called if she'd been delayed.. But he didn't begin to understand what had really happened until later—when he read the news Wednesday that a woman had been found dead inside the church.

Hunter felt satisfied with the details of his timeline. It gave them a number of specific times and locations to check and to run through computer forensics. But behaviorally it didn't quite add up.

"Why didn't you go to the police?" Hunter said.

He shook his head.

"Mr. Pynne?"

"Jackson," he said. "A lot of reasons."

"Okay." She nodded for him to go on.

But Jackson again shook his head and said nothing. Hunter looked at her questions. "A couple of weeks ago," she said, "Mark Chandler transferred funds from a corporate account to a private bank account, then distributed it into four separate individual accounts. More than six million dollars in all. Three of those accounts have been frozen. The fourth was emptied on Monday, the day before Kwan Park died. Did you and Kwan Park have access to that account?"

He was looking at the backs of his hands, giving no indication he'd heard her.

"Sir? Did you have access to that account?"

"Jackson," he said.

"Jackson."

"No."

"Did you know about it?"

"I had nothing to do with that."

"But did you *know* about it?"

Only his eyes moved as he looked up at her, slowly. "Kwan told me, yeah," he said. "The day before she disappeared."

"Okay, what did she tell you?"

"Just what you described."

"About the embezzling?"

"Yeah."

"And what did you think about that?"

"What'd I think? It's like—if someone finds a briefcase full of money on the street. Do you turn it in or do you keep it? It was a test of loyalty, that's what I thought. That's what *she* thought. They were leaving a briefcase of money for us, just to see what we'd do. But I didn't take it.."

"What do you mean? Who was it that left the briefcase of money?"

He shrugged.

"Could that be the real reason she wanted you to help her disappear?" Hunter asked. "Was this about stolen money?"

"No." He added, "Not to my knowledge."

"So you're not sure."

His eyes seemed to fill with anger for a moment, and Hunter could see she'd maybe pushed too hard. There was a contained quality to Jackson Pynne that she was afraid could blow up any moment.

"Did you *know* Chandler?" she said. "Had you agreed to help the others, too?"

"I didn't know the others, but I met Chandler once. He was the attorney who came in the office to buy the stores. We met with him and he negotiated the deal. The others? Never. Was Chandler the John Doe in Virginia?"

"Yes."

He nodded.

Hunter said, "Why would someone want to kill Kwan Park and why would they want to frame you for it? I don't understand that."

He hunched forward slightly, his elbows on his knees, fingers clasped, looking intently at the floor. He said nothing.

"You told Pastor Bowers yesterday that if you got out, you didn't expect you'd make it to the county line. Why would you have said that? Who is after you?"

Jackson opened his mouth in a strange fishlike motion. His eyes seemed busy now finding patterns on the concrete. He'd forgotten about flirting with her.

"You also told Pastor Bowers that this person or these persons are after you because of what you know. Not what you did, but what you know."

"That's right."

"So you know something about this organization that they're afraid you're going to talk about."

He shook his head almost imperceptibly.

"This was something Kwan Park told you?"

He shrugged, meaning, *Could be.*

"Tell me about it. What did Kwan Park say to you about the setup?" Jackson cleared his throat and coughed. He said nothing. "And why didn't she go to the police or the FBI with this?"

"She wanted to get out first, okay?" he said. "We had a feeling that someone had already gone to the FBI, told them some things. She thought it was Patterson."

"Sheila Patterson."

"Yeah. And we know how that ended."

Hunter suddenly realized something. "How did it end?"

"You know how it ended. She wasn't supposed to talk. None of them were. That may have been what ruined it."

"How do you mean?"

Jackson exhaled dramatically. "Just because—he finds out about things. I don't know how, but he does. And he thought one of them was betraying him, one of the four. He may not have known which one, but he knew it was one of them. And he probably thought they were talking to each other. So he had all four of them taken out. He considered them all betrayers."

"Trumble, you mean."

"Trumble, yeah."

Hunter decided to try something else. "You didn't do the Psalms to make it look like Trumble?" she said.

Jackson's face went blank.

"You knew that Trumble had an obsession with the Book of Psalms, right?"

He looked at her a long time before answering. "What?"

No. He doesn't know about the Psalms. She could tell. *He doesn't have a clue.*

"You said 'like vapor' to Pastor Bowers the other day," she said. "Where did that come from?"

Jackson blinked several times in rapid succession, as if they were now speaking different languages. "What?"

"You said, 'Right now they're like vapor.' Where did that come from?"

"Oh." A faraway smile rose to his face and vanished. "That was something Kwan said. She was quoting the security guy. The big guy who used to come around, those last couple of weeks."

"What big guy? Who was the 'security guy'?"

"Guy that did security for the organization. There were two of them. There was a guy named Kirby, a funny looking guy, and a guy named Gilly, who was his boss."

"Was Gilly the big guy?"

"Yeah." He began to pick at one of his nails and made the strange motions with his mouth again. "Not a friendly guy. The Violent Man. That's what Kwan called him. I only saw him once."

"What was Gilly's full name?"

"Don't know."

"Kirby's?"

He shook his head. "Never came up. They just started coming around the last few weeks. Two or three times, maybe."

"Together?"

"Together, separate. Whatever they wanted."

"To do what?"

"Nothing. Check up on her. Scare her."

Hunter waited. She could see something else was going on.

Finally Jackson said, "He has a connection here, you know."

"Who does?"

"Trumble."

Hunter waited. She wondered if this was just a way of changing the subject. "What do you mean—in Tidewater County?"

He nodded. "Take a close look at property records, you might find something. His company, anyway, had some property here. Probably still does."

"You're saying Trumble's a player here in Tidewater County?"

"No, I'm saying he has a connection here."

"Okay." She could see he wasn't going to elaborate.

"Who did this murder, Mr. Pynne?" she said. "What are your instincts telling you?"

After a long time he said, "Between us?" Hunter nodded. "The security man."

"Gilly."

"Yeah." His eyes looking up at her slowly. Hunter tried to remember who he reminded her of. Someone well known. An actor, maybe.

"Why?"

"Because he was Trumble's enforcer. Trumble wasn't violent, but he needed someone who could enforce the law. Trumble's law. He obeys something he calls the 'higher law.' People who work for him, he tells them they have immunity from the laws of society— but not the higher law. And part of his job, at the end, was to keep an eye on Kwan. Because he thought she was breaking some of that." His eyes seemed to lose focus. "Sometimes, this security guy took things too far, roughed people up, raped a couple of the women. That's what Kwan said."

"Did he rape *her*?"

Jackson looked down, tilting his head at a funny angle. Answering by not answering.

"When did he rape her?" Hunter said, feeling a charge of adrenaline. "When and where did it happen?"

"He went to her home." His eyes suddenly glistening. "Three or four days before she disappeared. Just showed up in the middle of the night."

"And what happened?"

"It was a night she wasn't working. She went to bed at two or three. Hadn't been asleep more than an hour, I think, and he showed up, banging on the back door, trying to get in. Woke her. Told her that something had come due. That there was no way she was going to be able to prevent it from happening. She'd been talking too much, not being careful."

"Was that the real reason she wanted out?"

"Mmm mmm." He nodded, briefly closed his eyes.

"Talking too much to who—you?"

"Maybe."

"Was this done on Trumble's orders?"

"The rape? No. The rest of it, probably. I'm sure the rape was his own idea. But it was within the parameters of what was allowed."

"Allowed."

"In the organization, yeah."

Hunter felt a surge of anger—but also a new sense of purpose. "What's this man Trumble like?" she said. "What did Kwan say about him?"

"Not much. Subject she didn't want to talk about. Just—that he's invisible, basically."

"Invincible?"

"Invisible." He smiled at the misunderstanding. "He lives his life among ordinary people. That's what she said. He's the man who checks our groceries at the supermarket, who sells us tickets at the movie theater, who makes our lunch at the sandwich shop. He's just there, *invisible*, watching everything." He lifted his eyes to hers again. "But Gilly, he wasn't like that. He took care of business. Worked after dark always, she said. Big guy. Ice in his eyes."

"Why was your DNA found outside the cabin in Oyster Creek, do you think?"

He blinked and looked off, caught by surprise. "No idea. I wasn't there. I loved Kwan," he added. "She was a kind and classy person."

Hunter nodded, believing him. He was becoming restless, she could see, probably about to cut her off. "What else? Is there anything else you need to tell me? Anything we should know?"

"Yeah." He rubbed his hands together. Seemed to smile at something. "One thing."

"All right."

"If they let me out, I'm willing to work with you."

"I thought you didn't want out."

"If they *want* me out. If *you* want me out, I'll work with you."

"Okay. How so?"

"As bait. I'll stay in the county, as long as you want. Just set me up in a house somewhere, keep me under surveillance, twenty-four/seven. I guarantee, they'll come for me. Sooner rather than later."

"Why are you so certain?"

"Because." He looked off again, at stuff she couldn't see. "That's how it works, okay? Like I say, they think I know things. And in their world, too much knowledge is considered a capital offense."

"Okay." They exchanged a long look. "We'll consider that, sir," she said, standing.

"Jackson."

"Jackson. Thank you for talking with me."

As SHE DROVE back into the open farm country, Hunter felt lit up. The most important details were on tape now—where he'd been Monday and who he thought committed the murders. She had arranged with the state police to produce an electronic transcript of the interview from the digital recording and have copies available to her and Fischer by the time she returned to the Public Safety Complex. She called Fisch on the way, telling him how it had gone, asking him to begin checking the surveillance tapes.

They had six and a half hours now to derail the state's attorney's case.

Chapter 46

WALKING TO HER office, lost in thought, Hunter nearly collided with Wendell Stamps, who came barreling out of the men's room.

"Oh, excuse me. Good morning, Hunter," he said, sidestepping her. It was rare that he used the public restrooms; the state's attorney had the largest and nicest office in the building, complete with a private toilet.

"Good morning, sir." He exaggerated a nod and tried to keep going. She said, "Oh, sir. I understand you found some additional DNA evidence? In Virginia? Tying the case to Jackson Pynne? Were you going to share that with me?"

He frowned as if he didn't know what she was talking about. "Oh," he said, "didn't Clint Fogg tell you?"

"No."

"My gosh, I wonder why not? *I'm* sorry." His face was, as usual, largely impenetrable, although his eyes seemed amused, as if saying, *Your move.*

"That only makes me wonder again why you would want to

prosecute this locally without looking more closely at the other three cases."

"Didn't we have this conversation yesterday?"

"A version of it."

"Look, what you're talking about, Hunter, is very complicated," he said. "A jury, frankly—this isn't their natural way of processing information. I know this county, Hunter. I know the circuit judges. Believe me, I'm looking at what will work."

"I see," she said. "So, do it in a way that is fast and simple and will get it out of our backyard?"

He smiled quickly. Rather than engage with her again, though, he looked at his watch. Making his point: she had six hours and twelve minutes.

HUNTER PICKED UP her copy of the interview transcript from a desk sergeant in Records and read through it in her office as she ate the Swiss cheese sandwich she'd packed for lunch. Looking up several times to study the mug shot of August Trumble tacked to her corkboard beside the driver's license photo of Kwan Park. Wondering what he looked like now, today.

Crowe finally called, just as she got to a particularly interesting part.

"So," he said, "what did he give you?"

"Who?"

"Stamps."

"Oh. Twenty-four hours." She glanced at the clock. "Now down to less than five and a half. I talked with Jackson Pynne this morning," she added. "In jail. Found out a few things you probably ought to know. But you need to bring me in all the way."

"Ours is a separate case, Hunter. I told you that."

"I know. But why don't we drop that now? I need to know the rest of what you're not telling me. And we need to work together to solve this thing. Jackson talked on the record, by the way," she added. "You're welcome to look at the transcript, of course."

"Can you e-mail me a copy?"

"Sure."

She waited twenty-five minutes after e-mailing the transcript to Crowe and called him back. She was surprised when he answered.

"What do you think?"

"Interesting," he said.

Hunter waited. "As you probably noticed," she said, "Jackson thinks Sheila Patterson talked to the FBI before she was murdered. She was the woman who was found in the wax museum, right?" Crowe said nothing. "So was *she* your source on Trumble? One of the two people you told me was on the 'inside'? Is that what's behind this?"

Crowe was silent. Then he sighed. Not once, but twice.

"Look," he said, "I can't talk about Sheila Patterson, okay?"

"Why?"

"I can't get into it."

"But she *was* your source."

After an awkward silence Crowe said, "Let me tell you why this is sensitive."

"Please."

"We think Trumble's finally starting to understand what's going down here, okay? What he's up against. He's finally beginning to hear the footsteps, in other words. And he probably knows that if we do prosecute a racketeering case against him—which we will—it's going to put him away for a long time. The rest of his life, probably. It won't be eight months this time."

"So?"

"So the theory is that he's jettisoning his organization and maybe he wants to take a few people down in the process. People he doesn't trust." *Exactly the theory she had suggested to him the other night and he'd rejected.* "Okay? Inside people he thinks might be enticed to talk to us in exchange for immunity."

"Like Sheila Patterson."

Crowe ignored her. "But frankly I don't think this is him doing these killings, okay? I think it's someone else, trying to make it look like him."

"Who?"

"We're not sure."

"Why, though? Explain why someone else would be doing this."

"I will. But I want to give you a document first, okay? This is just between us, but it'll provide you a little background. And then you can draw your own conclusions."

"All right," Hunter said.

"How about I drop by your office in an hour? I'll be out that way anyway. To see the state's attorney," he said. "One hour?"

"Okay." Hunter had no idea he was back from Washington. "One hour," she said.

HUNTER WALKED NEXT door to check in with Sonny Fischer, who was seated, as usual, ramrod straight in front of his monitors. He'd already contacted the relevant agencies in Virginia and Maryland to obtain electronic security tapes that, with some good fortune, would soon prove that Pynne had been in D.C. alone on Monday, not with Kwan Park.

"Nothing yet, I guess?"

"Working on it"

"Okay, good."

FISCHER'S LOOK SEEMED to linger, as if he were pleased to see her. Which was strange, because Fischer seldom seemed pleased to see anyone. He not only wasn't a diplomat, as Ben Shipman could be, but he seemed unaware that diplomacy mattered. To him it didn't.

"Got something else, though," he said as she was turning to leave.

"Oh?"

"Ship will tell you."

"How *is* Ship?" she said. "He called in sick yesterday and I got a message that he'd be in late today, but I haven't seen him."

"He's fine. He'll be in in a few minutes. He's been working on something."

He turned back to his monitors, closing down the conversation. Hunter understood. That was Sonny Fischer: cool, the coolest man she knew, although, of course, she *didn't* know him. But she could see that in his own way he was excited about something.

Back in her office, Hunter discovered that Theresa Kincaid, the AP reporter, had left three more messages. The first were like the earlier ones, which she'd ignored. The third sounded more urgent: *I'm on deadline right now and need to run something by you. Could you please call before three.*

Wondering how much she knew, and where she might have heard it, Hunter decided to call as she waited for Crowe and Shipman.

Kincaid came on the line sounding out of breath but happy to hear from her. Hunter heard her flipping pages in a notebook.

"Okay, first off, the Praying Woman thing. Did the victim in the church killing actually appear to you to be praying? Would that be an accurate description?"

"But you've already reported that in your earlier stories," Hunter said. "*You* called her the Praying Woman."

"Right, and I'm just triple-checking now. For verification. Would that be an accurate description?"

"I suppose." Hunter heard the clicks of computer keys. "Who told you that?"

"A source."

"Law enforcement source?"

Theresa Kincaid made a clucking sound with her tongue.

"Information comes easier when it flows both ways," Hunter said. "This is someone here in Tidewater County?"

"Mmm."

"And what else did the sheriff tell you?"

She could hear Kincaid covering the phone and saying something to herself, or maybe someone else. When she spoke again, her voice sounded deeper and more officious. "Can you verify that the Tidewater County case is being investigated in connection with three other homicides?"

"Off the record?"

"Okay."

"Yes."

Keyboard sounds. Good that she knows this, Hunter thought. But where had she heard it?

"All right. And is it true that there were numbers left behind at the scene?"

This, too, surprised—and pleased—Hunter. But where was it coming from? The sheriff certainly wouldn't have told her *that*.

"Can you say anything about what the numbers might mean?" the reporter asked. "And is the church killing being investigated as a serial murder?"

Dave Crowe strolled into her office then, stopping when he saw her on the phone. But not leaving. She smiled at him and turned her back. He'd brought in a smell of bathroom hand soap.

"No," she said, lowering her voice, "I can't comment."

"On which question?"

"Can we continue this later?" Hunter said.

"Okay. One last thing: is Jackson Pynne going to be charged with the Tidewater County murder? That's what one of my sources is telling me."

The sheriff. Hunter looked at her clock. "Off the record?" she said, lowering her voice. "I would hope not."

"You would hope not. Meaning?"

"That I would hope not. Okay? Maybe we'll talk later."

Crowe was looking sideways at the phone as Hunter set it down. "Anyone I know?"

"Probably."

Crowe grinned. He took the seat beside her desk and stretched out his legs, crossing them one way at the ankle then the other. He was holding a white nine-by-twelve envelope.

"'Kay," he said. He tilted his head in a conciliatory manner as he handed it to her. "Partners, then? Here it is. This is what one of our sources on the Trumble operation gave us."

"Sheila Patterson," she said.

Crowe shook his head. "I'm not going there, Hunter, I told you, so don't ask me again who it is. 'Kay? Just have a look." Before she could open the envelope, he added, "There's one other part of this equation that you don't know about. But you'll see it when you read the transcript. Trumble, over the last year or so, has supposedly been unraveling. Paranoia, erratic behavior, memory problems. Serious mental decline, from several reports. Or at least that's the impression he's giving. It's possible it may be a performance, we don't know. But we think someone may have seen that as an opportunity." He stood and turned to leave. "Someone like Jackson Pynne and Kwan Park. 'Kay? Anyway, have a look. Tell me what you think."

HUNTER OPENED THE envelope as Dave Crowe walked away. Inside, she saw a twenty-three-page document, a partial transcript of three interviews with a source identified only as "Subject A." Subject A had been August Trumble's former "business manager," she read. She, or he, had met with an FBI agent in a Northern Virginia hotel room on three separate occasions to talk about Trumble's organization. Hunter skimmed through the transcript, then returned to the first page and read it carefully.

The transcript painted the picture of a person who had been drawn into the belly of Trumble's organization and then didn't know how to get out. Who lived in a "multi-million-dollar home" but whose life had become "miserable." Several passages particularly interested her, and she went back and reread them.

It really just happened gradually, I guess . . . I had a little accounting business, in Pennsylvania. We'd been audited the year before, so I had some issues with the IRS . . . I was contacted by someone claiming to be an IRS investigator, but he wasn't. He was someone from this group . . . I know now that's how they recruit. They look for a certain kind of person, who I guess has a certain vulnerability, or whatever. Has issues with the government. . .

He began to give me things, and I got to feel comfortable with it. That's how it works. By the time I began to understand what was really going on, I was in too far. . . .

I worked for him directly at first. Then not so much. For the past year and a half, I worked for this other man . . . Mark Chandler, who basically took over what I'd been doing . . . I got the impression he was kind of like the no. 2 man in the organization. . . .

What was Trumble like? Smart, but manipulative. Kind of a genius, that's what I thought at first. Everyone did. There was something about him, his eyes, the way he looked at you, that stays with you. And some of the things he told you got inside your head and you couldn't get them out. Made you look at the world differently. Made you look at authority differently. It was weird. Scary weird. . . .

I just got to feel very uncomfortable about the whole thing . . . because once you're in at a certain level, it's like you can't just walk away from him. That's the thing. Like, you had to act a certain way, sign nondisclosure agreements, not contact family members . . . And, of course, the majority of the people who worked for him were women. I think he enjoyed having that power over women. Half of them looked like Playboy bunnies from the 1960s to me . . . But they were smart. He was able to pick women who had a good work ethic . . . But the other thing was, I felt that deep down he really just wanted to be normal. . . .

The elephant in the room, as far as I was concerned, was that you couldn't ever just walk away. Sometimes people disappeared, and you weren't supposed to ask about them or mention their names ever again or whatever . . . But I did once. There was this woman Beth-Anne Childester. I had worked with her, we'd sort of gotten to be friends. I still don't know what really happened . . . But I know he has these security people. And some of them are, like, pretty scary . . . I always kind of felt they represented the other side of him in a way. Like an alter ego or something?

They've begun to shut down some of the offices, yeah. And there've been stories going around that he's out of it half the time, paranoid, blaming people for shit they never did . . . There are a lot of stories. I never saw him, though, the last year. But you hear things. . .

Noticing a shadow, Hunter looked up and saw Ben Shipman. He was standing inside her doorway holding a file folder.

Chapter 47

"HEY. HAVE A few minutes?"

"Sure." She slipped the transcript back into the envelope. "How you feeling?"

"Feeling," he repeated, as if he didn't know what she was talking about.

"Come on in. Please."

Ship crossed the room with his endearing, somewhat clunky walk. He stood by her desk, feet spaced evenly, like a pupil about to recite a speech.

"I know you've been sort of avoiding me," he began, watching her wide-eyed. "And I can't really say as I blame you."

Hunter frowned, not getting it. For the past two days Ship had been missing in action, out sick one day, working from home today. "No," she said. "It's just been busy."

"And I know what you're probably thinking." His eyelids fluttered. "So I just wanted to say I'm sorry."

"Sorry for what?" She glanced at the clock.

"*I* told the sheriff and state's attorney about the Psalms." Shipman's face reddened, accentuating his freckles. "I'm sorry. I gave them background information about our investigation. And showed them the interview logs."

Hunter was deeply surprised. "Why?"

"They asked me," he said, bowing his head. "I should've told you about it, but I didn't. The sheriff sort of wanted me not to say anything. I kept wanting to, but it just never felt like the right time."

She nodded. *Still loyal to the old guard.* It was okay. In fact, it was a little touching that it mattered so much to him. "Why are you telling me this now?"

"I guess because I feel bad."

"Okay. Thanks," she said.

His face seemed to recalibrate. "But there's something else, too," he said, and Hunter could see that what he had come here to tell her was in the file folder. "I went back through the evidence these past couple of days. From the very beginning of the case? And I found a couple of things—some pretty significant things, actually—that we missed. Which makes me think the sheriff—or someone—may have messed with evidence."

She nodded to the chair. Shipman remained standing.

"Remember how we talked before about planting evidence?" he said. "Whether the sheriff would do something like that?" Hunter nodded. She saw the hard resolve in his eyes. "I don't think it's about what they planted. I think it's about what they left out. Here . . ." He opened the folder and pulled out unevenly stapled sheaves of paper. He laid them side by side in front of her like solitaire piles, showing a sense of order that didn't come natural to Ben Shipman. "This is the trace, fiber, and biological report that you were given last Tuesday, okay? And these are the preliminary evidence logs from the police techs at the church. They're not quite a match."

Hunter looked, wondering what he was getting at. It was true she hadn't seen the preliminary documents, only what had been processed into an evidence report. That was the procedure the state police and sheriff's office followed for county crime scene investigations, despite the change of law for homicide cases. "Three discrepancies," Ship said. "There was a small amount of DNA on Kwan Park's body and a couple strands of hair on her clothing that didn't make it into the evidence report. And also, a fingerprint out at the Oyster Creek cabin."

"Why was that evidence left out?" she asked.

Shipman shrugged. "Procedure. State CSI has always worked with the sheriff to prepare the evidence report. That's how they process it. In this case, it looks like they just neglected to log in certain pieces of evidence. When we submitted the first round of evidence for our meeting on Penn Street," he said, meaning the medical examiner's office in Baltimore, "for whatever reason the DNA and hair strands were left out. The fingerprint wasn't logged in anywhere. I found out about it through one of the techs who was on the scene."

"Why?" Hunter asked.

"What they'll say with the fingerprint is it's not relevant to the investigation. Hundreds of people had been in that cottage, right? Who aren't relevant to this crime."

"Which is probably true."

"Yeah. Except in this case, it *is* relevant," Ship said. "We've run the prints and come back with a hit for one on the national databases. Still waiting on the DNA and hair."

"Really."

"Yes. The fingerprint at Oyster Creek belongs to a man named Kirby Moss."

He began to pull loose papers from his file folder, placing them on top of one another before Hunter had a chance to see what they were. "Kirby Moss was arrested thirteen years ago in Connecticut for assault with a deadly weapon and attempted second-degree murder. Both charges dropped for lack of evidence.

"Here's why it's interesting: They also found a fingerprint at Jackson Pynne's town house on Sunday, inside the boots, that appear to be a match."

"With Kirby Moss?"

"That's right."

"Holy crap," Hunter said. "*That's* interesting."

Kirby. Kirby was one of the names Jackson Pynne had mentioned. One of the "security guys."

Shipman's freckled face watched her expectantly.

"And the hairs and DNA were left out of the evidence log that was forwarded to the task force, you're saying?" Hunter asked.

"Yep."

She played it forward in her thoughts, wondering if this could lead to obstruction charges against the sheriff, or if it would just be seen as incompetence.

"Here's more of what I found on Kirby Moss," Ship added, handing her the last, stapled report.

Hunter motioned again for Ship to sit. This time he did. She leaned back and paged through the document for several minutes, realizing that Fischer must've had a hand in this, too, maybe more than a hand.

Kirby Moss had served in the U.S. Army in the mid-1990s. For the past eleven years he'd worked as a private security consultant.

In his mug shot, he wore a crew cut, had startled, saucerlike eyes. What caught Hunter's attention was something several pages in— something that may have seemed incidental to Fischer and Shipman. Moss had been employed for about two years by a Florida firm called Private Excelsior Security Consultants. A corporate statement from nine years earlier showed that the company's CEO was an R. Gilbert Rankin.

Did that complete the circle? Could Gilbert Rankin be Gilly? Trumble's "enforcer"?

The Violent Man. Big guy. Icy eyes.

Possible.

"Does Stamps know anything about this yet?"

Shipman shook his head. "Uh-uh. No one knows."

Hunter felt the adrenaline pouring into her blood, knowing that this missed evidence could change the case. If Rankin was the head of security for Trumble, then they might be able to establish a link now between Trumble and the killings. And, in the process, exonerate Jackson Pynne.

Why would the sheriff have suppressed this evidence, though? She paged back through the report. *Would he really have been so reckless?* It seemed unlikely. Except—if he'd always gotten away with controlling the evidence-processing, he may have become conditioned to believe he could do whatever he wanted; it was a common enough human failing. And at the time, he'd already decided that Robby Fallow was the perpetrator.

"Great," Hunter said, closing the report. "But we need to shift gears now. I'd like you and Fisch to drop everything else. I'm less interested in Kirby Moss than I am in Gilbert Rankin. I think that's Moss's employer. I think that's where we need to focus next." She glanced at the clock. "We've got four hours."

"Oh," he said, still staring at her. "Really?"

"Yes. I'm not sure yet, but I have a feeling the DNA's going to come back as a match with his. I think Gil Rankin might be our man."

Shipman blinked at her several times. "Which man?"

Hunter just looked at him.

"Oh," he said. "Ten-four."

Chapter 48

WENDELL STAMPS'S BROAD, pale face held its sober neutrality as Hunter walked into his carpeted office. This time the Wait had been eleven minutes.

"Have you got something?" he said, unruffled as always.

"I think I do." Hunter sat, and opened her folder on his immaculate desk. Data reports, bios, information the three of them had put together over the past four hours. "New evidence," she said. "Evidence missed earlier."

"Oh?"

"Yes. I don't fault anyone but myself for this," she said. "When several agencies are involved in collecting and logging evidence, sometimes there's confusion and mistakes are made. It shouldn't happen, but occasionally it does. I'd like to think that we'll learn from this and in the future streamline the evidence-collection process to avoid this sort of thing. But I take full responsibility for it."

"Is it relevant?"

"Relevant? Yes."

"Okay." He leaned forward, a way of indicating interest. Hunter showed him the report on the fingerprints at the murder scene and at Jackson Pynne's garage, identified now as belonging to Kirby Moss, and the still unidentified DNA found on Kwan Park's body and the hairs on her clothing. And then she told him about the connection between Moss and Gilbert Rankin.

When she finished, Stamps leaned back in his executive chair, still expressionless. "And you're saying a procedural mistake is going to jeopardize the outcome of this case?"

"No, sir, I'm not. I'm saying evidence was suppressed. Evidence that, in my opinion, points to a different perpetrator."

"Suppressed how?"

"I don't know. It was apparently removed or left out of the evidence log on Tuesday before the reports were submitted to the task force. The fingerprint belongs to Kirby Moss. We know that. And we believe Moss worked for a security consultant named Gil Rankin.

"The reason that's significant," she went on, "is because Kwan Park worked for the same organization that Gil Rankin worked for. So, they're all connected."

His eyes narrowed and he glanced for several minutes through the reports that Fischer and Shipman had prepared. Finally, he looked up.

"And you have evidence that this Gil Rankin was involved? Because I don't see anything here."

"Not yet, but we will," Hunter said. "I suspect the DNA on Kwan Park will come back as his. But it's also significant, you understand, because the other three victims—I know you don't want to make them part of your case, but I think you're going to have to now—also worked for the same organization. August Trumble's organization. That's what ties these killings together. So I don't see how we *can't* make them part of the case."

"But I don't see that here."

"No. But you will," Hunter said. "We're working on it."

Stamps frowned. "But Jackson Pynne's DNA was at the crime scenes here and in Virginia. And possibly in West Virginia," he said. "And this man's fingerprint was in *his* town house. So you're saying Pynne did this in collaboration with these other two men?"

"No, the opposite," Hunter said. "His DNA was planted, as I said earlier, by these men. The boots, two cigarette butts, a plastic soda cup. That's what we have on Jackson Pynne. That's what you're basing your case on. Sir, we can't go forward with charges against Mr. Pynne."

Stamps's face remained stoically blank, as if he were thinking about something else, even though Hunter suspected he was beginning to sense the case was crumbling.

His eyes went to the clock on the wall. Hunter looked, too.

"Is the FBI aware of this?"

"Not yet."

He nodded, as if that meant something. "Who is this man, Ralph Gilbert Rankin?"

"Gil Rankin." She handed him a two-page fact sheet that Fischer had prepared, the last document in her folder. "He's a former police detective from New Jersey. He retired after allegations that he had planted evidence in a drug case and roughed up a potential witness in another case. No charges were filed in either incident, although there were internal investigations. He later worked security for Exxon for two years. He runs a very high-end security consulting firm now, called Private Excelsior Security Consultants, based in South Florida. From what we're told, his main client—probably now his only client—is August Trumble's organization."

"But you don't have any evidence confirming that?"

"No, sir. Not yet."

"Huh." The state's attorney nodded. He closed his eyes for a moment and rubbed his temples. "But so—what are you thinking? I mean, motivewise. Can you tell me that again?"

"Jackson Pynne didn't do this, sir. I believe Gil Rankin did, on orders from August Trumble. And I think they've come here now to silence Pynne, thinking he knows more than he does. And then tie this up in a bow and go home. Except things haven't worked out quite the way they expected."

As Stamps continued watching her with his impassive expression, Hunter began to entertain a wild idea: what if the state's attorney was in on this, too, in some way? Stamps was evasive by nature, far cleverer and more deceptive than the sheriff, but every bit as much a protector of the old order. And he'd had issues with Jackson Pynne years earlier, too. What if Trumble's organization was paying him to see that things went a certain way?

"Go on," he said.

"There's no more, sir."

"Okay." He glanced at the reports on his desk. "Then let me review these and give it some thought. Can I hold onto these?"

"Yes. Those are your copies."

"Thank you, Hunter. I appreciate your efforts."

She felt a charge as she walked out past Connie Elgar and back down the long corridor to her office at the other end of the building. The play of sunlight in the glass arcs of the hallway, the luminance of the clouds, took on a sudden magnificence. The details of the investigation had just rearranged themselves into something that resembled a final form. This was the championship now, and nothing else mattered to Hunter—not next season, not the rest of her life. She had a real opponent at last, a single target—and a clear sense of what had happened. It was one of the best feelings she knew.

She whipped out of the parking lot that afternoon onto empty blacktop and drove west, speeding toward the Methodist church. But then she remembered the threats against Luke and his wife and slowed down, deciding it was best not to go there.

HUNTER WORKED INTO the night, determined to learn all that she could about Gil Rankin. She'd brought two cans of Red Bull and her iPod to the office so she could blast Maroon 5 and Ani DeFranco to periodically recharge her energies.

Pulling together a profile of Rankin wasn't easy, though. There was almost no information about him for the past ten years, other than an address in Miami, Florida, and his listing with Private Excelsior Security Consultants. The only photo was twelve years old. She sensed he'd been deliberately sheltered working for Trumble. According to Pynne, Rankin had hurt people and raped women. But he had no criminal record. Hunter also wondered if maybe *he* wanted out of Trumble's organization now. Maybe that's what this was—an elaborate breakout on Rankin's part?

Fischer and Shipman stayed late in their respective offices, like separate tenants, still combing through surveillance tapes and running data searches. Three other state homicide investigators from out of the region were pitching in as well, reviewing tapes. It was busywork again, but it wasn't strictly a Tidewater County case anymore, despite what the sheriff and prosecutor thought.

At 9:20 P.M., Ship came in and plunked himself in her guest

chair, hooking his right leg over the arm. He did this occasionally, often under the pretense of needing to borrow a pen or an Altoid, but really to compare what he was thinking with what she was thinking. Fischer never did; she couldn't recall the last time he had entered her office.

"So, we having fun yet?" he said. His usual opener.

"Not yet."

"Figured everything out?"

"Some, not everything."

"Good." Shipman exhaled as if he were exhausted. Finally, he asked his question. "You don't think Pynne was involved, do you?"

"No, I don't. As I said earlier. I think Gil Rankin did this."

He nodded. "Why, though? I don't get it," he said. Then he asked a better question: "Why this way, I mean?"

"Well." Hunter glanced at Trumble's old mug shot again on her corkboard, next to Kwan Park's picture. "I don't have it all figured out yet. Except I think they were creating a specific narrative that Jackson Pynne had helped set up an embezzling scheme involving these four people. Which is why there were four accounts. And then, for some reason, a conflict arose among the partners. He got greedy or paranoid and ended it. The narrative also involved a fight between Pynne and Kwan Park."

Ship was nodding ever so slightly, meaning he was with her. "But that's not the real narrative."

"No. I think it's designed to conceal the real narrative."

"Which is?"

Hunter realized that he was waiting for her to explain what he'd probably been sitting in his office trying to figure out for the past hour or so. "Well," she said, "that Trumble felt his organization was threatened by these disloyal people, that they were planning to betray him and maybe ruin him. And so he decided he needed to have them eliminated."

"But so—why leave behind the series of calling cards?"

She smiled. "We're still working on that, aren't we?"

"Right." Ship absently swung his leg up and down. "You don't really think the sheriff or the state's attorney might be involved?"

"Well, I don't know. Anything's possible."

Shipman continued to watch her, his eyes hungry for more.

"Anyway," she said, "we should get back to work so we don't have to speculate like this anymore."

"Right. Okay. Ten-four," Ship said, rising from the chair.

It was at about a quarter past eleven, after Shipman had gone home, that Dave Crowe called. He'd again waited hours before getting back to her.

"Where've you been?" she said.

"Sorry," he said. "My girl at the *Post* just called. She asked me what I could tell her about Ralph Rankin. What am I missing here?"

Hunter said nothing at first. Serves you right, she thought.

But then she summoned a reasonable tone and said, "I'm not sure what you mean." She needed Crowe on the team, after all. Also, she was curious why the *Post* reporter would have asked about Rankin. Was the timing just coincidence?

"I read the interviews with your source," she said.

"And?"

"At one point, she—or he . . ." Hunter cleared her throat and waited for Crowe to clarify, but he didn't so she continued. " . . . talked about being afraid of Trumble's security guys. Pynne mentioned them, too. And Jackson gave me two specific names—a man named Kirby, and another named Gilly."

"Okay, I read that."

"I think Gilly is Ralph Gilbert Rankin. He goes by Gil. Gil Rankin." When Crowe didn't respond, Hunter said, "You knew that, right?"

"I mean, sure, we know about a man named Ralph Rankin. Security man employed by Trumble. One of about eight or nine we've identified over the years. We don't frankly see him as being a big player in this case."

"I think he is."

"Why?"

"As I just said, I think Rankin is Gilly. The big guy. And I think he did this."

"Did what?"

"The murders."

Crowe laughed, a nasally high-pitched sound that didn't seem like it could have come from him. "Why?" he asked. "Because Jackson Pynne said so? Of course he'd say that. Look at what he's facing."

"No," she said. "Because of new evidence. And because it makes sense. It ties everything together."

"The evidence is against Pynne, though."

"Not any more."

Crowe went silent. Were his sources that bad? Hunter wondered. Or was he deliberately being steered away from Rankin by his bosses at the FBI?

Then she flashed on something else: If Sheila Patterson was the FBI's informant and she'd been murdered, was the Bureau now trying to cover its ass in some way? Is that what this was all about? Was that the real reason the case had to go "a certain way"?

"What's the new evidence?" Crowe said.

Hunter glanced up at the trees bending in the night winds, debating whether to tell him anything. Remembering how reluctant he'd been to share information the first night he phoned. But not telling him now would be counterproductive. She needed them to work together.

Crowe listened as she explained—completely silent, diminished, it seemed, by these new details, recognizing not only that this evidence was going to change the case, but also that the story he had been pursuing—about August Trumble—might in fact be the wrong story.

JACKSON PYNNE WAS tired but unable to sleep, tossing for hours on his tiny bed. He'd said what he needed to say to the homicide detective, but he didn't feel good about it for some reason. Something about her had thrown him off.

For the first couple of days, Pynne had felt protected here. Now, the idea of spending months, or years, in a cell with these human sounds and odors felt deeply disturbing. He wanted to be out again, speeding down the highway with the windows open, a Chesterfield between his fingers. *We'll be known by the fruit of our actions,* Pastor Luke used to tell him. *So our lives should be about producing good fruit.* Amen, that was what it all came down to. He understood that now.

Jackson stared at the ceiling and thought about the detective some more. *Amy Hunter.* He actually sort of liked her. He liked her determined eyes and her hand gestures, the set of her mouth— the way she didn't seem to miss anything. The way she came at you head-on. It reminded him a little of Kwan. He liked what he couldn't quite see, her spirit, which felt kind of brave. She'd done something to him—*infected* him a little, it seemed, with a feeling that was intoxicating and maybe sort of dangerous, like the lost energies of his own youth.

For some reason, everytime he got to thinking about his future—or about anything serious—his thoughts turned to the homicide detective. *Amy Hunter.* It was as if she knew the secret that could get his life back onto the right path. And he wouldn't know what it was until he saw her again.

Chapter 49

THE CLIENT WATCHED Rankin, moving through the night shadows on the lawn of the house across the lane, and he considered what he must be thinking. What was churning inside of him.

A whiff of doubt. Disloyalty, perhaps. Is that what I am picking up? Will you eventually join the others, Gilbert?

He turned away and studied his own naked image in the full-length bathroom mirror—an image he much preferred to that of Gil Rankin. And he thought of the "others." The tragedies their lives had become.

Mark, you were a decent man when you came to me. But, of course, you were asleep. I woke you, didn't I? I taught you. You learned how to think, and you became a good soldier. And a very wealthy man. For a while you believed in what we were doing; for a while you had everything you wanted, didn't you? Everything. You told me that. But such a busy little mouth, saying all those things about me, talking with the others. We finally had to remove the lips and the tongue, didn't we? You can see now that we had no choice.

Sheila, you had a "burning" devotion to us at one time. To me.

Your words, not mine. But you were the worst traitor of all, weren't you, dear Sheila? You wanted to hurt us, to destroy us, and God knows you tried, talking with the "authorities." You thought it was all happening out of sight and you would never be discovered. It was quite fitting that we arranged a wienie roast for you in that wax museum, don't you think? Yes, I know you do. Although your real fire will be an eternal one.

And poor Katrina. Lost sheep Katrina, off on the crooked path when you came to us. I gave you a chance to find your way, and for a while you did, and you helped us, didn't you? You found riches, you said. But your greed, Katrina, your betrayals, they earned you the chance to dig for more treasures in that pit, didn't they?

And Kwan. Sweet Kwan. You were so happy for a while. You, too, had all you ever wanted, you told me. Working for such a worthwhile cause, helping poor souls. But then you broke your promise and tried to run away with the corrupt Mr. Pynne. Such a bad mistake. We had to break your legs. You understand that, don't you? Broken promises, broken legs. A fair exchange, wouldn't you say, Kwan?

And now your broken bones rejoice, just as the others rejoice. Because you are finally free, aren't you? This is all as it was written. None of it is my choice. I am the Lord's Psalmist and I have been called to fulfill the law. These are the verses that I have been asked to share—that each of you may now consider for your eternities. Oh, it is a humbling task. I am saddened by it, but much more so by what you became.

You understand me, don't you, Gilbert? Or will you join the others?

Chapter 50

HUNTER WOKE BEFORE dawn and immediately began to pull on her running gear. She needed to get her blood pumping, her thoughts alert and focused. It was suddenly cold again in Tidewater County. Bay winds gusted along the coast, spitting an icy rain, as the new sunlight spread shimmers of color through the creeks and wetlands. It was a magnificent blue morning, and she ran hard against the wind coming back.

She fixed a protein shake and checked the news online while Winston sashayed back and forth, wanting her to gently grab his tail—although he acted mortally offended every time she did. Theresa Kincaid's story had been posted an hour earlier. Already a dozen news sites had picked it up.

NEW CLUES IN 'PRAYING WOMAN' MYSTERY

A series of numbers carved into the hand of murder

victim Kwan Park, the so-called Praying Woman, may hold the key to identifying her killer, police sources say. Investigators in this idyllic bayside community would not comment on the record, but sources who spoke on condition of anonymity confirmed that the numbers carved in Park's right hand appear to be a "calling card" left behind by the person who killed her and may be connected with at least three other murders in a tristate area.

A homicide detective investigating one of those murders said he has been in contact with Tidewater County detectives and is considering the possibility that the same killer may be responsible. He would not elaborate on the investigation, however, or on details about the so-called "calling cards."

Former Tidewater County developer Jackson Pynne, meanwhile, has been held in Tidewater Correctional Facility since Thursday evening on unrelated charges, and police sources have told the Associated Press that Pynne is considered a "person of interest" in the murder of Kwan Park. However, when asked yesterday if Pynne would be charged with Park's murder, an investigator familiar with the case said, "I hope not."

Ugh, Hunter thought. Well, she probably deserved that.

But she also knew that this story would change the game. It would alter the public's perception about what happened and probably spoil the sheriff's and state's attorney's plans for a quick local resolution.

Feeling a surge of satisfaction, she drank down the last of her shake, as Winston stared intently up at her.

Afterward she clicked into her e-mail account and saw that

Shipman had left her an e-mail with only a subject line: *Breakfast 8:15?*

Okay, she thought. Game on.

"Hey." Ship held open the door to McDonald's, his mouth full of breakfast, a napkin stuck to the left elbow of his lumberjack coat. He was wearing a tie this morning with his wrinkled dress shirt and jeans. Ship was hustling now, part of the team again; she could feel how wired he was, even though his eyes were bloodshot from lack of sleep. Hunter liked nothing as much as working in top gear like this.

He'd taken the liberty of ordering her a yogurt parfait and orange juice and setting her place with a spoon and two napkins.

"Optimistic that I'd show," she said.

"Yeah, well, I had to be."

"Why? What's up?"

"Two things."

"Okay." Ship let her settle before explaining. He watched as she took the lid off the parfait and mixed the yogurt. A file folder was on the table beside his breakfast.

"Go ahead," she said.

"Two big developments."

"Tell me."

He was waiting for her eyes to turn back to his. "Gil Rankin and Kirby Moss were in central Virginia the day Mark Chandler was killed. The lips and tongue case? We've got verification now."

"How?"

"Security tape in a convenience store. The tape was pulled by Virginia State Homicide."

"Okay, great."

"The second development's even more interesting," he said. He wiped his hands again, pulled photos from the folder and pushed them to Hunter. One of his collar buttons, she noticed, was undone. "This was taken last night, right here, at the South Bay Market. The man in the passenger seat—there's a better view of him here." He showed her, pointing. White Jeep parked outside a convenience store, the passenger door open. A big man sitting in the passenger seat. A smaller man, with a round head and close-cropped hair, opening the driver's door. "We think that may be Rankin on the passenger side. The car is registered to PSL Associates in Baltimore."

Hunter nodded. "That would be Private Excelsior Security Consultants, headquartered in Miami, Florida."

"Okay . . ."

"And is the other man Moss?"

"That's what we're thinking, uh-huh."

"So, presumably," she said, "unless they left overnight, they're probably here in Tidewater County right now."

"Yep." He handed her a printout, a computer-generated map that Fischer had probably produced. "These are all of the entry points to the county," he said. Hunter studied it, going back to her parfait as Ship went back to his pancakes.

So, do we try to close off the county? Set up roadblocks at all the exit points? Or try to track him down surreptitiously? They were in tricky territory. She didn't want to alert the sheriff right away—or to alert Rankin to how much they knew. But she didn't want him to slip away, either.

"Tell me more about this," she said, tapping the map printout.

"Mmmmmm." Ship took a moment to finish chewing. "Okay. According to the register log? They purchased beer, deli sandwiches, orange juice, sodas, and microwave popcorn. Security camera shows they then drove off to the south.

"There's a flashing light intersection two and a half miles down the road, at Whistling Swan Drive," he continued. "They could have gone north from there, but it's a long ways to anywhere. So most likely they kept going straight or, probably, took the road south."

"To?"

"South is Jimmy Creek. There are about a dozen homes and two condo buildings that way. Close to eighty units, probably, although at least three-fourths of them are empty."

Unless it's a deliberate diversion, Hunter thought.

"Were you up all night on this?"

He shrugged.

"You haven't talked to the AP reporter by any chance, have you?"

His eyes fluttered, just before he shoveled a last forkful of food into his mouth. Hunter raised a hand to change the subject. "Doesn't matter," she said. "Good work."

"Oh, and one other thing." Shipman accelerated his chewing again so he could talk intelligibly. "You saw what the AP story said? Word's getting out that the case against Pynne maybe isn't going to stick."

"Wonder where they got that."

"Well, the sheriff's people are conveniently blaming the task force now. For having picked up the wrong guy again. That's the word down at the Blue Crab. It's all over Main Street by now, I expect."

"But of course we *didn't* pick him up."

"I know. I'm just saying."

"Okay. Doesn't matter," Hunter said, pretending it didn't sting a little that the sheriff was still playing the rumors against her. He'd probably do it again when "Gilly's" name got out to the media: Keystone Cops task force now on its third suspect. Payback for the cold case she had solved over the winter.

"I mean," she said, feeling a crazy rush of anger, "are we more interested in solving this crime and bringing the perpetrator to justice? Or in controlling how the *media* spins it?"

Shipman stopped chewing for a moment and his eyes widened. Looking like a student called upon in class, he answered, "Solving it."

LUKE BOWERS WAS driving away from the coast into a clear, cold morning, Amy Hunter beside him, her leg pressed against his, her hand tightening on his thigh each time they hit a bump. Emo rock rattled the dashboard, Hunter nodding to the beat, the music so loud there was no point in trying to talk. Ahead, nothing but miles of blacktop and blue sky. But then, wham, a huge pothole; Luke's eyes jolted open.

He blinked at the rosy morning light through the curtains. Then lifted his head, remembering where he was. He leaned on his elbow, admiring the elegant curves of Charlotte's mouth and chin as she slept. He suddenly felt very guilty.

Sneakers, he noticed, was sitting, not lying, at the foot of the bed, looking directly at him, as if he knew.

Maybe he does.

"Come on," Luke whispered, allowing a moment for the hard edges of the dream to soften. "Go out for a walk?"

Luke let Sneakers romp through the moist morning shadows beside the marshlands. They followed the trail along Harmon's

Creek, which in summer was sometimes teeming with turtles, walking all the way up to the bluff, where they stood together and admired the bay, the water glittering with thousands of sun sequins.

Why had he dreamt that, anyhow? What was it Charlotte had said the other day? *She likes you, you know that, don't you?*

It wasn't true. He didn't believe it at all. Not in that way. During the long walk back, Luke decided that he'd offer to prepare dinner for them that evening. One of his three dishes: seafood tacos, crab chili, or the old faithful, spaghetti.

Classical music thundered dramatically from the kitchen as they entered the house. Charlotte stood at the stove, stirring egg batter, preparing French toast. Sneakers hurried past her to his water bowl and lapped furiously.

"Good news," Luke said. "Guess who's making dinner tonight?"

"My two men?"

Chapter 51

When Amy Hunter arrived at the Public Safety Complex, she saw Crowe's car with his Virginia government tag in visitor parking. He was waiting for her in the first floor conference room. He wasn't alone. Another agent, a woman, was with him. They'd taken over the room, clearly intending to be there awhile, the table covered with laptop computers, printouts, file folders, phones, coffee and pastries from Holland's Family Restaurant.

"Hunter, have a few minutes?"

"Sure."

He introduced the female agent curtly. Her name was Wendy Jennings. She looked a few years older than Hunter, big-boned, with probing eyes, thick dark hair, and a distant smile. Hunter could tell right away that she tolerated Crowe but wouldn't abide by any of his nonsense.

"Go to your office?" Crowe said, clearly meaning the two of them, not Wendy Jennings.

"Okay, sure." Walking a half step behind him, Hunter said, "I think I know what you're going to say."

"Yeah? What am I going to say?"

"That this is federal now."

Crowe grunted.

"I'm just surprised it took this long," Hunter said. "So the local solution is off the table? Just like that? Jackson Pynne is off the table?"

"I didn't say that," he said. "Pynne is involved. We just don't know how, exactly."

"But he isn't the killer."

Crowe said nothing. Clearly, though, there had been a reassessment overnight. The Bureau now realized that Gil Rankin *was* in fact a major player in the Trumble organization. And locating him was suddenly high priority. Hunter could almost feel the twin pressures working on Dave Crowe: from Washington and from the media, which was on the verge of turning this case into a national story.

In her office, Crowe took a seat and stretched out his legs, as he always did, placing one ankle over the other, then switching. Hunter passed along what Shipman had just told her over breakfast. She showed him the surveillance photos of Rankin and Moss in Tidewater County the night before.

Crowe said nothing at first. He handed back the photos.

"Nice job," he said.

"It wasn't me. It was Ben Shipman and Sonny Fischer who figured this out. The homicide division."

"Fisch and Ship."

"Right."

"Okay. So let's make some assumptions," Crowe said. He sat up, crossed his legs at the knee and jiggled his left foot. "If we were to seal off Tidewater County. Surveillancewise—"

"We've already mapped it," Hunter said. She gave him the map Fischer had prepared. "There are eight points of entry and exit. Two monitored by cameras. We can work with state police, post someone at the other six points."

"Roadblocks, you mean?"

"No." Hunter had been thinking about it on the way in. "How about as a surveillance operation first? And we don't release his name or image to the public right away."

Crowe's brow creased.

"I mean, for a few hours, anyway," she said, softening her tone.

"Why? What are you thinking?"

"That if we put his name out there, we may lose him."

"And if we don't, we might unnecessarily endanger the people living here."

"Yes, I know."

When Hunter said nothing else, he asked, "Why wait a few hours?"

"Strategy. A different way of doing things. Not instead of, but in addition to."

Crowe's eyes crinkled. "Okay, I don't know what that means," he said.

"Meaning: nothing's happening with Jackson Pynne, right?"

"Correct. He's free to go. So?"

"So, Jackson Pynne made an interesting offer yesterday," Hunter said. "I've been thinking about taking him up on it."

"What offer?"

"He offered himself," she said. "As bait."

Crowe held his frown. "What are you talking about?"

"We set him up in a house in the county. Someplace secluded, where he'd seemingly be vulnerable. Only we make sure he isn't.

Provide round-the-clock surveillance and security. Monitor the surrounding roads and properties."

A trace of dimples appeared on his cheeks. "And you think your friend Gil Rankin would just walk into a trap like that? I doubt it."

"Jackson thinks so. He seems convinced that Rankin will come after him right away if he's let out. Maybe overnight."

"Why?"

"Because that's what he's been told he has to do. They're afraid Pynne knows too much and is going to talk. I don't fully understand it. Except this organization operates under its own peculiar set of laws. Which maybe don't always make sense to people like you and me." Crowe's forehead remained wrinkled. "But Pynne seems to understand them. Better than I do. Pynne's involved in this in some way, as you said, right? I think his instincts are at least worth paying attention to."

"Sounds pretty unorthodox."

"I know," Hunter said. "That's kind of what I like about it."

Crowe let out a long sigh. He was probably with her, Hunter figured, just didn't want to give in too easily. Plus, he'd need to run her idea by Washington before he agreed to anything. "I think I'd want to talk to Jackson Pynne first."

"Me too," she said. "Why don't we go see him."

HUNTER WAS SURPRISED by how agreeable Jackson Pynne sounded when she called him about a follow-up interview. His voice on the phone seemed nearly giddy at first, as if he'd been waiting on pins and needles to speak with her. Yet, when he came walking into the interrogation room at ten minutes past two, he looked almost like another person. His face was pale, his hair disheveled. But his eyes brightened as soon as he spotted her.

"How are you, sir?" Hunter said, reaching to grasp his extended hand.

He again held her hand longer than he should have. But his face dropped when he saw Dave Crowe standing behind her.

Hunter introduced him as "the FBI agent now heading this investigation." Crowe, dressed in a dark blue suit, no tie, reached out to shake.

Pynne nodded a terse hello and sat. For some reason, he wouldn't shake Crowe's hand.

"Sir, you understand that no charges are going to be filed against you," Hunter said once they were all seated. "They're dropping the interference charge. So you're free to go."

Pynne scooted back his chair, trying to get comfortable.

"If I may," Crowe said. "I've read the transcript of your conversation from yesterday, Mr. Pynne. We're trying to get a better fix on the people who are after you. Gilbert Rankin: is he the man you said is pursuing you? Is he Gilly?"

Pynne looked steadily at Hunter as Crowe spoke, giving no indication that he heard anything Crowe was saying. Then the corners of his mouth turned up slightly. She could see that he wasn't going to answer.

"Can you tell us a little more about Gilly Rankin," she said. "Why do you think he's going to come after you?"

"Why?"

"Why."

"Because that's his job. The man's got an assignment, he does it, no questions asked. That's the way this organization works," he said. "His assignment is to take me out."

"Do you know that for certain?" Hunter asked.

"Do I know it for certain? No, not for certain. But that's the only thing that makes sense. I can see now how this thing was set up."

"Okay, how was it set up?"

Pynne shrugged. "It's obvious. They planted evidence. Tried to frame me for these murders. That was the setup, right? They thought I was going to run, do something stupid, maybe self-destruct. But I didn't, and so now they think maybe I know too much. Maybe I'm going to tell you what I know. So they decide they need me out of the picture, sooner rather than later. I'll cause them more trouble if I'm prosecuted."

"How would you cause them trouble?" Crowe asked.

Pynne, continuing to look at Hunter, said nothing. Clearly, something about Dave Crowe rubbed him the wrong way. It was like a dog picking up vibes.

"How would you cause them trouble?" Hunter asked.

"By talking," he said. "Because they think I know things." A faint smile animated his face. "I *don't*. But that's what they think. Because of Kwan."

"And so the assignment is coming from August Trumble, you're saying?" she asked.

Jackson shrugged: *Who knows?* Hunter sensed that, for whatever reason, he wasn't going to open up as long as Crowe was in the room. There was something about Jackson Pynne that she liked, she realized, a mysterious integrity about him.

"Are you still on board with the idea of helping us out?" she asked. "Being bait?"

"Sure," he said. Pynne smiled as if she had just asked him to the prom. "What've you got in mind?"

Hunter told him the plan she'd worked out with Dave Crowe and the state police commander. Pynne would be released from jail that evening and transported to a residence on Sherman Creek. Police would provide round-the-clock protection, monitoring the house and grounds and all points of entry with visual and digital surveillance. "You won't have to leave the house. Just stay inside, watch television, read. Tell us whatever you need. Give us a list of groceries."

He seemed to like that. "All right," he said, chuckling at something.

"And you believe he'll come for you," Hunter said.

"Do I believe he'll come for me? No," he said, "I *know* he will."

"Okay."

"So what time would the release be?" Crowe asked.

Hunter looked at Jackson. "Eight o'clock?"

"Okay," he said. "Eight o'clock. Only thing I ask is that the pastor be there when I'm released."

"Oh." Hunter looked at Crowe, who was shaking his head. "All right," she said.

She knew that Gil Rankin operated at night. All of the Psalmist killings had taken place under cover of darkness. Chances were good that he'd come for Jackson Pynne overnight, which was what Jackson believed, too. By then they'd have night-vision surveillance in place on the property, and patrol cars, officers, and agents staking out the surrounding roads, ready to take him.

"We'll put it out on the five and six o'clock news, then, that you're being released. And see what happens," she said. "Everyone okay with that?"

Pynne nodded.

"Good," Hunter said.

GIL RANKIN AND Kirby Moss went over the details of their plan at the house on Jimmy Creek late Friday afternoon. It didn't take long. When they finished, Rankin told Moss to go to his room and watch television. Moss was making him nervous.

"Think I'll take a nap," Moss said.

"Okay."

"Is that all right?"

"As long as you don't sleep through this thing."

Moss gave him a look, hoping Rankin would smile.

Rankin lifted the blinds as soon as Moss left the room. He moved his armchair to the window and gazed out at Jimmy Creek for a while, the sunlight rippling bright silver slivers on the water. Scenery to rest his eyes. It was a nice place, this Tidewater County, but Gil Rankin didn't expect he'd ever come back again. Kirby Moss never would, either. He was pretty sure of that.

He sat alone with his thoughts, and pretty soon they began to gnaw at him again. The way this assignment didn't feel clean anymore, didn't feel like any of the others. Rankin knew he wasn't supposed to think about it. The motives behind the assignment weren't his business. Those were the terms of the deal. *But how could he not think about it?* This one had seemed simple enough at first—take out four disloyal employees; make Pynne the fall guy. *Disloyalty*, the Client had said, *is one of the greatest earthly evils.*

But taking out Pynne now also meant taking out the fall guy.

That was the part that didn't make sense. That was the thing that was gnawing at him.

You're the only one I can really count on to complete this, Gilbert. You understand that.

But Gil Rankin, left with too much time to think, wasn't sure if he *did* understand it.

CROWE AND HUNTER established a command post for the operation in the makeshift FBI office at the Public Safety Complex. The house they'd chosen at Sherman Creek was surrounded by wide-open lawns on three sides, wetlands on the other. It would be impossible for anyone to get close without being seen. The house was a summer rental property, a faux Victorian, owned by a cousin of the county clerk. Four state police officers would be on the grounds, monitoring the drive in from the highway and along the creek. Four officers would be inside the house. Cameras covered all points of the lawn. There should be no blind spots.

It was Hunter's idea that Louis Gunther, a local DWI attorney known for his tacky TV commercials, would drive Pynne to the house. Gunther's involvement would add to the sense of Pynne's vulnerability.

Hunter, Fischer, and Shipman were in the six o'clock operational meeting along with six state troopers and five Bureau agents. The room smelled of coffee and perspiration. By design, sheriff's deputies weren't invited. Crowe wanted the operation to be as streamlined as possible, and he'd learned enough by now about the workings of the Sheriff's Department to keep them out of the loop.

"Pynne will be released from the county jail at eight P.M.," Crowe said. "He'll be met by his attorney, Louis Gunther, and driven to the Sherman Creek property. We believe that our suspect, Gilbert Rankin, will come after him there overnight. Probably sometime after midnight."

"Wonder what Gunther's being paid for this," one of the troopers said quietly, trying to make a joke.

"Don't worry about it," Crowe said tersely.

The image of Rankin on his laptop was grainy and not very

useful, but it was all they had—a nondescript man with a wide face and receding hairline. The only other available image was a twelve-year-old Florida driver's license photo that looked like a different person.

"We believe he has another man, Kirby Moss, working with him. We are not releasing either name to the public until the morning at the earliest. We don't want Mr. Rankin to know what we know. 'Kay?

"We believe they're driving a white Jeep Cherokee." The surveillance video from the convenience store came on the screen. "But it's possible they will be using another vehicle before they approach the house. It's possible they could use tear gas or explosives to force him out, but that doesn't appear to be their M.O. We'll be ready for whatever they try, though."

He paused for effect before going on. "Obviously, there are a few ways this can go. If they get wind of what we're doing, or see the patrol cars parked near the borders of the county, they may change plans. They might abort. Either way, it's likely they will switch vehicles at some point. It's possible that, if they feel pushed, they may carjack a vehicle, maybe attempt to kidnap somebody. So we have to be prepared for all eventualities and remain diligent.

"Now, these are the positions we have staked out," he said, calling up a surveillance diagram.

It was funny that Crowe was talking with such authority, Hunter thought, when twenty-four hours ago he'd known almost nothing about Gil Rankin.

"We think Rankin may be based in the southern portion of the county at this moment. We have several locations under surveillance, but haven't found anything yet. That's ongoing as we speak.

Needless to say, if we find him before Pynne is released, that saves us all a lot of trouble. Questions?"

HUNTER WALKED OUT of the meeting with Ben Shipman, who seemed unusually subdued. She wondered if he still felt bad about giving information about the Psalmist to the sheriff. When he got quiet, Shipman was hard to read.

"This is all happening because of you," she said, clapping him on the back as they stood beside his car. "You know you've done a great job."

"We all have."

"We all have, right."

Shipman zipped up his jacket, giving her a cordial look. "But it's not over."

"No, it's not," she agreed.

He glanced off at the scenery, his freckles prominent in the late afternoon light. It was possible that he felt left out now, after providing the crucial information on Rankin and Moss. Hunter wasn't sure.

"Anyway," Shipman said, forcing a level of enthusiasm. "I'll see you at the jail at seven-thirty. I'm going to look at a few places before then, grab an early dinner."

"All right," she said. "See you later."

"Ten-four," he said.

Chapter 52

GIL RANKIN SAW it on the six o'clock local news: they were going to release Pynne at eight o'clock that night. His attorney, Louis Gunther, saying his client was "absolutely innocent and anxious to get on with his life." The attorney some weasely little character wearing a peach-colored jacket and a crooked bow tie.

Moss had just returned from scoping out the countryside and brought Rankin a different sort of news. Not the kind of news he wanted to hear. It only confirmed what he'd been thinking earlier.

"A bunch of federal agents seem to be gathered over at the county safety complex," he said, staring at Rankin with his wide eyes. "State police have set up surveillance at exit points out of the county."

"Fuck it," Rankin said.

Moss looked at him, unsure what he meant.

"Do we need to rethink this?"

"'Course not. Don't worry about it."

"Okay." Moss knew better than to say anything else.

But Rankin was worried. *What* did *this mean? That they knew who he was?*

Or were they setting a trap for someone without knowing what they'd get? Was this all based on something the snake, Jackson Pynne, had said?

There was little doubt anymore about one thing: For the first time since his client had hired him, Rankin was working an operation that had big problems. Worse, he was involved in something that could adversely impact his family. It could jeopardize the life he'd built for himself over the past ten years, and for them.

Yet he couldn't walk away. He had to finish it. He had no choice. That was the nature of the deal. Those were the terms. If he walked away, the Client would come after him.

"What are you thinking?" Moss asked, hovering across the room.

Rankin ignored the question. "You gonna be ready?"

"Of course."

"Okay. Make sure you're ready. Don't ask me what I'm thinking."

"All right."

"Jesus."

Moss walked back into his room. Everything about Moss made Rankin's skin crawl now; everything except his special skill, which was the reason Rankin had hired him again. Moss was a nervous man who asked asinine questions. But he was good at one thing, and that was what mattered.

Out the window, a reflection of something in the late sunlight caught Rankin's attention.

A car.

Jesus! A car was crunching slowly down the drive toward the house. *What the fuck?* Stopping halfway. Parking. The door opening. Rankin sat forward, his attention fully engaged.

"Hey!" He called for Kirby Moss. "Get up," he said. "Something's happening. Come in here. Quick!"

LUKE SERVED UP generous portions of what he called his "original recipe" veggie and crabmeat chili, his secret penance for the morning dream. Sneakers, having already dined on a beef and chicken combo served over dried Purina, lay beside Charlotte snoring contently.

"So," she said as they dug in, "when exactly were you planning to tell me what the big secret is."

"The—hmm?" It was difficult to fool Charlotte, about anything, always had been. "What big secret?"

"The one you're not telling me?"

"Oh. That one," Luke said. "What makes you think it's big?"

"Detective work." She looked at him with her knowing blue eyes. "That's where the clues are all pointing."

"Which clues are these, now?"

"For starters, you're not drinking beer or wine tonight."

He looked sheepishly at his glass of water.

"Secondly, there's this dinner."

"Yes, but it's unrelated," Luke said. "Just a way of showing my appreciation."

"And, third: I can't think of any reason why you'd want to go back to work on a Friday night. Unless . . ." She batted her eyes theatrically.

"Unless?"

"Unless you're planning a tryst with Nancy Drew."

"Oh. Funny."

"Thank you," she said. "And so? That leaves just one question."

"Okay."

"What's really going on?"

There was no smile in her inflection this time. Luke scooted his chair slightly, realizing he shouldn't have tried to keep anything from Charlotte. Sneakers briefly lifted his head and looked up, as if he, too, wanted to see what Luke would say. "Sorry," he said. "Well, yes, of course you're right."

She nodded.

"The killer's here in Tidewater County right now, it turns out."

"The Psalmist."

"Yes."

"My gosh."

"Yes. Apparently, they're setting a trap for him this evening. Jackson has offered to be the bait. They're letting him out at eight o'clock and they're going to set him up at a house in the county and keep it under surveillance."

"And here I thought you were no longer involved," she said. "Silly me."

"I'm not. But he says he wants me to be there when he gets out."

"Okay," she said, with a note of disapproval.

"I'm not *going* to be involved, I'm just going to be there."

Ignoring that, Charlotte said, "And the killer's just going to walk into this trap, and not be suspicious?"

"Well, Jackson thinks so. Someone's been assigned to kill him, he believes. And it needs to happen quickly. That's what this is all about."

"According to Jackson."

"Yes."

Charlotte frowned at her wine. "Why didn't you tell me earlier?"

"I guess I didn't want you to worry. After what happened before. I'm sorry."

She drank the last of her wine, looking away. "And whose idea is this?"

"Jackson's."

Her forehead squinched.

"I know," he said.

"Well, then, I have just one request," Charlotte said.

"Anything."

"I'd like to go with you."

Chapter 53

THE ANTENNAS OF three television news trucks poked above the razor-wire spirals outside the entrance to the Tidewater Correctional Center. Hunter drove Crowe through the gates, past a small gathering of print, radio, and TV reporters. The entire Bunting clan seemed to be there, she saw, as well as television and print reporters she recognized from Annapolis and Baltimore.

"You didn't do this, did you, Hunter?"

"Didn't do what?"

"Get all these media people here."

She rolled her eyes. Crowe was joking, but only sort of. She could read him well enough to know that he was apprehensive about the whole arrangement—in part because they were going into unfamiliar territory, and in part because it hadn't been his idea. By morning, if nothing had happened and they hadn't found Rankin, they'd release his and Kirby Moss's names to the media. And do it Crowe's way.

"Just kidding," he said. "Although I still don't know how my girl at the *Post* got Rankin's name."

"She must've had better sources than you did."

Crowe harrumphed.

"Just kidding," Hunter said.

"No, it's probably true. You were right about Rankin. There's more to it than we were looking at." *Right about Rankin.* She decided to let that one go. She parked and they walked to the visitors' entrance.

They were escorted to a gravel yard inside the gates but outside the rear port of the jail. Jackson Pynne would come out there once he was released. Two vehicles were waiting, engines idling: Louis Gunther's Town Car and a Bureau Explorer. A Bureau agent would accompany Pynne and the attorney to the house on Sherman Creek. Hunter and Crowe would follow in the Explorer.

Television and print reporters were mingling in the dusk on the other side of the prison fence when the doors opened at two minutes past eight. Actually, she *hadn't* wanted all this media here. Not at all. This kind of attention felt wrong; it might just scare Rankin off.

A guard poked his head out, surveying the crowd, like security after a rock concert or political rally. The television lights immediately went on.

Jackson Pynne came out moments later, with Louis Gunther, behind two state troopers. He wore a long overcoat and walked with his natural swagger, head raised, enjoying the attention. Gunther, a small man wearing a wrinkled blazer and a crooked bow tie, beamed inappropriately.

Pastor Bowers and his wife Charlotte were standing to the side behind the reporters, Hunter noticed. She tried to catch his eye at one point but couldn't. Luke was watching Jackson; everyone was, as if he were a celebrity.

The reporters shouted questions, most of them variations of the same one:

"Mr. Pynne, are you a suspect in the murder of Kwan Park?"

"Mr. Pynne, do you have a comment?"

"Jackson, what happened to Kwan Park?"

Not acknowledging their questions, Jackson scanned the crowd and his eyes finally found Pastor Luke. He strode across the yard, his hand outstretched. For a moment it looked as if he would try to shake hands through the chain-link fence.

But he stopped and waved instead, and then bowed slightly.

Crowe touched Pynne on the elbow and tried to steer him toward the Town Car. Louis Gunther stood by the open driver's door, waiting. Pynne walked several steps and stopped again to wave at the TV cameras.

Hunter joined Crowe at the SUV, just before the prison gates swung open. What they had planned could take hours or it could take longer. She was counting on Pynne's intuition that these were unusual circumstances and that there was an urgency to this deal. And also on the fact that Gil Rankin worked at night, in darkness. She was counting on it happening in the darkest part of the night, tonight. Two or three o'clock. That was when Gil Rankin liked to work. And when he did—whatever he did—they would be there.

EXCEPT NONE OF it happened that way. Jackson Pynne was almost to the open back door of the Town Car when Hunter, standing six or seven feet away, saw his head snap forward and something fly off into the air. Then she heard the gunshot. In that order.

For a moment there was complete silence. Then two more gunshots, in quick succession. *Crack, crack.* People went down, hit or ducking for cover. Screams and panic broke out on both sides of the fence. Crouching beside the SUV, Hunter noticed Pastor Bowers, covering his wife, who'd dropped to the pavement.

She pulled her Beretta 4X and looked out into the dark fields where the shots had been fired—she'd seen exactly where the second and third had originated, not the first. Then she thought she'd heard a fourth one, from a different weapon, a round that hadn't reached the jail lot.

Already a state police car was speeding away on Route 11 into the farmland. Then another.

"Shit! Let's go!" Hunter yelled when she was satisfied the gunfire had stopped. She ran to the driver's side of the Explorer and climbed in.

Crowe finally pulled open the passenger door. She hit the gas as soon as he was in, skidding out through the open prison gates.

"What are we doing?" Crowe said.

Hunter didn't reply. She got on the radio. "Second and third shots came from the McIntyres' farm, just south of the house. Possibly from inside."

By the time Hunter reached the farmhouse property, state police were already in the early stages of establishing a perimeter. "It's going to be difficult for Rankin to escape this," Crowe said. But Hunter wasn't so sure.

She saw nothing moving, in any direction, that wasn't law enforcement.

Both FBI and state police were bringing night-vision equipment to the scene, but they had to shift their attention about ten miles, from the house under surveillance on Sherman Creek to this farm property just south of the jail. *Rankin had planned it that way.*

A sheriff's deputy was responding now from the South County

substation, Hunter could see, even though they weren't part of the operation. Much of the farmland here had been recently plowed. There weren't a lot of places to hide.

Within minutes a state police chopper would be overheard, scanning the fields with spotlights and thermal detectors. But it could take them several minutes to get here. Hunter had a bad feeling about that.

"Shit!" she said. "They caught us off guard. We fucked it up."

She got out and stood beside the SUV, scanning the dark fields to the east and north for signs of a vehicle or figures moving through the darkness.. On the scanner, a state police trooper was reporting something to the south—a car parked on Whistling Swan Road, its lights out, a door open. Then nothing more.

There were two roads down that way, Hunter knew, and a rural route east, out of the county. A state police car was parked on the border at each of the exits, though, waiting. It wasn't going to be easy for them to get out that way. But it was dark across the fields to the east.

Hunter traded notes with the state police commander Gary Martin, trying to pinpoint the location where she'd seen the gunfire.

There was one house on the property and one barn. No lights burning in either one. It was a small farm; the McIntyres grew corn and raised horses. This time of year they were still out of town at their beach property in South Carolina.

Within minutes a SWAT team began assembling to go to the house. Hunter felt something prickle at her conscience as she watched them—the image of Jackson Pynne taking the shot, lurching forward, bouncing against the side-rear door of the Town Car and falling to the pavement.

It was my idea to go forward with this. This is all my responsibility now.

Crowe was silent, surveying everything, hands on his hips—still a little shell-shocked—then walking out to stand beside Captain Martin, the state police commander, whose car had pulled up nearby. The state chopper was lifting, moving toward the McIntyre property now, its lights sweeping the fields.

Hunter was surprised to see the sheriff standing with members of the SWAT team. She turned away. The sniper had been maybe forty yards southeast of where she was now standing. He might've broken into the farmhouse and found his targets through a rifle scope from a second-story window. Or he might've been in the field, maybe on the roof of his vehicle.

She began to walk in the other direction—north, away from the road and into the farm field. The ground, recently turned, was still moist and sticky from Sunday's snow.

"Where are you going?" Crowe called.

"Nowhere," Hunter said, maybe not loud enough for him to hear.

She stopped about twenty yards in and looked east, seeing an occasional shine of moisture in the fields, nothing else.

Hunter listened to the quiet, feeling an icy wetness in the wind. Then resumed walking, deeper into darkness. The sky, to the north, was clear, the moon high, close to full. The air grew chillier as she got farther from the road, breathing the damp-earth smell of the night.

What would Gil Rankin do to get out of here? What route would he take that the police wouldn't notice?

She stopped and listened again, letting her eyes and ears acclimate to the darkness some more. Looking east, south, north.

Lights clustered in the distance, up on the highway. He's out there, she thought. As sirens sounded in the distance, she felt something drawing her deeper into that darkness, away from the investigation. *Gil Rankin is still out here somewhere.* She felt it, like a slow shiver through her soul. She glanced to the south and saw the police lights at the front of the farmhouse.

Hunter zipped her coat and continued walking, her feet occasionally sticking in mud, her breath a vapor. Rankin would have anticipated the perimeter around the farmhouse grounds. That would've been part of his strategy. He must've also known there'd be surveillance video from the convenience store the night before and that police would assume he'd try to get away traveling east and south.

She kept walking, well north of where the shots had been fired, growing more attuned to the night's rhythms. Hunter had long ago trained herself for this—to find glints of light in dark places. On her handheld radio she heard: "White Jeep parked on Highway 16. Subject beside it on the pavement. Approaching." *Crackle, crackle.* Then, "Subject not responding."

One down, Hunter thought. That would be Kirby Moss, she sensed. *The fourth shot, which hadn't reached the jail.* Hunter turned into the faint breeze, looking where she imagined the Jeep had been found—well to the south—but she was too far away to see anything now, like a ship unmoored out at sea.

Moss was the sniper. His usefulness had expired as soon as he shot Jackson Pynne. There must've been two cars. Moss drove south and stopped to meet Rankin, to switch vehicles. Rankin shot him and drove away in the second vehicle. But not in a direction anyone would expect him to drive. Not in a *way* they would expect.

She felt her heart thumping as she walked on toward the dark line in the field that she knew was a road, Highway 7. Taking longer strides as the field briefly grew muddier. Knowing how the roads out here connected. East, and then north. *But what if you invented other routes, diagonal trajectories through the fields that forged new connections. One road linking with another.* In a sense, Rankin probably lived his life that way.

Hunter stopped again, thinking she had heard something. She let her eyes slowly sweep across the fields to the east, looking for an anomaly in the layers of night shadows. Rankin was a creature of darkness. He moved through it easily, taking routes others didn't take, going places they wouldn't look. *He's out there. He'd probably been outside the perimeter before they even began to set it up.*

She stood stock-still in the field and heard it again: a pitched sound that might have been a goose or a swan. But she knew it wasn't.

And then, turning very slightly, she saw it: a faint glimmer of moonlight several feet above the earth, catching something that was moving through the fields; a windshield, maybe.

Hunter waited, not breathing. And heard the sound again. This time she recognized it: a car engine, accelerating in the distance, followed by another sound, what seemed to be tires spinning in the mud. Her eyes inched through the darkness and found it again: two glints, front and back—the shape of a small car, moving in slow motion over the field. *He's driving toward the highway, his lights out, plowing through all this darkness.* She followed his trajectory—at this angle, he would reach the highway east of the police surveillance checkpoint, emerging just past Gracie's Crab House. He'd be in the next county by then, where he could slip into traffic and disappear.

Hunter glanced back at the distance she'd covered—at the lit-up farmhouse and the police activity to the south of it, where they'd found the Jeep. She called Crowe on the radio.

"He's moving outside the perimeter, northeast, less than a mile from the county border, headed right for the highway," she said. "I just saw him. He may be having some trouble with the muddy fields."

"Repeat please."

But Hunter was already running, back to the SUV.

Chapter 54

"How DOES HE get out, though?" Dave Crowe said as Hunter raced the Ford Explorer north through the darkness along Route 11, lights out, windows down. "All of the roads in and out are covered."

"So he crosses where there isn't a road," she said.

"Where?"

Hunter said nothing. She was tracking Rankin's route again through the darkness, but seeing nothing out there anymore: no glints of glass or metal where she expected he should be. Had she lost him? *Maybe he's changed course. Or maybe he's already reached the highway, maybe he's gone.*

She took her foot off the accelerator, letting the SUV coast. Until it finally stopped on its own.

"What are you doing?" Crowe said.

"Just getting my bearings for a second."

"Why?"

"Shhh." She listened, straining to hear anything. She studied the terrain to the north and to the east—the direction he'd been driving. About a quarter mile past the county line on Capsize Creek was Gracie's Crab House. A band was playing tonight at Gracie's Back Room, the club behind the restaurant, the parking lot was packed. Route 11 would've taken him west of the crab house lot, still inside the county boundary. *But what if he'd driven east across the soybean field?* From Route 11 it was a straight shot to the crab house parking lot; and from there he could enter the highway, circumventing the police surveillance checkpoints.

Then she heard it again: the now-familiar whirring sound. Wheels in mud. "Shit!" She held up a hand to silence Crowe, who was beginning to speak. And again—car tires struggling for traction. Hunter turned her eyes farther east.

The muddy fields on the edge of Tidewater County are holding him back. They're trying to stop Gil Rankin from leaving. They're trying to keep him here.

She clicked on the police radio. "Suspect may be en route to Gracie's Crab House from the southwest," she said. "Block entrances and exits. Code one," she added. "No lights or sirens."

"Where? I don't see anything," Crowe said.

Hunter pointed through the windshield, her eyes scanning the plowed bean fields. Wishing she were out here alone.

It was only a minute before she saw it: just west of the creek, a glint of glass and a low dark shadow, the boxy shape of a small car moving north across the moonlit field toward the restaurant parking lot. But having trouble: she heard the whirring again, the high-pitched accelerations of the engine, the whining of tires spinning through the mud. *Tidewater County is trying to keep him,* she thought again, warmed with a sudden pleasure.

"Hold on," she said. Pressing the accelerator, she drove full tilt toward the highway, letting her foot up just for a moment as the car slammed into the recently plowed farmland. Then flooring it again, the SUV bucking and sliding across a soybean field toward the crab house, Crowe protesting. "Jesus Christ!" and "What the—"

Several times they lost traction, too, and the tires spun, but this was a four-wheel drive, better suited for the terrain than the front-wheel-drive car Rankin was in.

Should have taken the Jeep, Rankin, she thought.

She crossed a private drive into the last plot of farmland before the highway and saw his car again on the other side—rising onto the berm before the parking lot. Then disappearing into a jumble of cars and lights. The state police chopper roared behind them and swung low, lighting up the fields, briefly blinding Hunter. She wondered if they'd lost him.

Up on the highway, police and sheriff's cars were sealing the entrances, their patrol lights all spinning. "No! No lights!" Hunter said as she slammed over the berm, stopping just inside the parking lot.

"Jesus H. Christmas!" Crowe said.

Hunter climbed out, pumped up. She surveyed the lot. Dozens of cars, parked every which way. She glanced at the restaurant and then back at the fields.

"I'll see if they have anything," Crowe said.

"All right."

He walked quickly toward the entrance drive, as if wanting to escape from her. Good, she thought. Her body was still pulsing from the motion of racing through open country. It was warmer here, out of the wind, the air scented with steamed seafood. The Explorer was covered with mud, as were her boots; Rankin's vehicle must be, too. She walked along the edge of the lot, her eyes tracing the route he must've taken out of the darkness, finding the spot where his tire tracks had cut into the berm and spun down into the gravel; fifteen yards, maybe, from where she'd entered.

So where was he? She tried to follow the path his car had taken, but saw that it was pointless: the car tracks disappeared quickly into gravel.

There were too many vehicles out here. He could have parked anywhere.

He might be sitting in his car now, or he might be out in the marshland, walking. Or maybe he'd already found a way to cross the highway.

But she didn't think so. There were too many eyes out here now. The Bureau agents and troopers were beginning to fan out through the parking lot. He's here, she thought. He had to be here, hiding in plain view. Amid the chaos.

Hunter walked toward the front deck of the restaurant, taking the safety off her Beretta. She stopped to look back at the dark country they'd just driven through, seeing what the moonlight revealed—plowed soil, marsh creeks, an occasional metal road sign. Nothing else; nothing moving.

She walked the steps to the restaurant, circulating among the people who'd come out onto the deck, curious about what was happening. Shrugging when someone locked eyes with her, as if to say, *I don't know, either*. But feeling a charge again—the nervous excitement of closing in.

Dressed in jeans, work boots, and her army jacket, Hunter could pass as a customer. It gave her a passport to go inside and quickly mingle. But first she leaned on the railing and scanned the lot once again. Saw Crowe near the highway entrance, hands on his hips, talking with a couple of other agents.

She turned then and went inside. Took the steps down to the lobby bar, which was dimly lit and crowded. There were fish nets and captain's wheels on the walls. People were eating dinner at the bar, some waiting for a table. The air was thick with the smells of steamed crabs and boiled shrimp.

She ordered a beer. There was an animated, lubricated mood here, a din of voices. Hunter watched the dining area: people cracking crabs with wooden mallets on paper tablecloths, waiters carrying seafood platters, taking away plates of shells.

She carried her beer to Gracie's Back Room. A band was on stage, a local group she'd seen a couple times, once with Ship; men and women playing music as a sideline to their day jobs as watermen, an auto parts clerk, a hairdresser. A cover band, performing country and classic rock crowd-pleasers. Hunter leaned against the wall and pretended to drink her beer.

The band launched into a song by J. Geils, a favorite here that always drew whoops and cheers after its opening line: "We met in a bar, out on Chesapeake Bay . . ."

But Hunter was surreptitiously surveying the edges of the room—for people in dark places or in crowds. Several of them caused her to look twice. One, a third time.

At a table near the back of the room, a large, wide-faced man wearing a dark jacket and a Baltimore Orioles cap. His chair jutted out at an odd angle, as if he wasn't quite with the others at the table but trying to be.

Or maybe she was just imagining it.

Something else struck her about him: instead of focusing on the band, he kept turning to the entrance, watching people as they came in.

Maybe just waiting for someone.

Then, as she was watching, the man surprised her by looking directly at her. Hunter turned her eyes to the band.

She sipped her beer, waiting. Watched the band.

When she finally looked back, he was gone.

GIL RANKIN FELT momentarily safe, hidden in a sea of unfamiliar faces. *Hide and seek.* He was good at that. But he still had to find a way out; he couldn't go home the way everyone else would tonight. *Those fucking fields, waterlogged from the snow-melt. Mother-fucking fields, had been like quicksand.*

Rankin stepped onto the deck, taking a deep breath of the cold air. Darting glances at the curious eyes, people trying to make sense of what all the police lights were about. No one giving him a second look.

The irony of his predicament wasn't lost on him. This was supposed to be his last job, ten years after he'd first been hired to set up surveillance on the Client's property. And every operation until this one had gone smoothly. All of the others had come off clean.

He leaned on the railing, took a deep breath, the air energizing him a little. He let his eyes drift over the parking lot. Yes, it'd be a challenge for him to slip out of here. But he would. That's what he did. He was a man who didn't get caught. Always had been. He prided himself on that.

He scanned the people again, figuring options. Briefly his eyes connected with those of a man across the deck. A man wearing a knit cap, looking right at him, it seemed. For a disoriented moment he thought it was his client, with those dark, penetrating eyes he had. *Jesus Christ!*

He turned away. *Of course not, it can't be.*

What was the matter with him? He pushed back into the restaurant. In the lobby, he saw the woman in the oversized army jacket again, striding across the room. Looking at him. *What the fuck's her problem?* Rankin changed direction, steering his own ship. He walked toward the signs for the restrooms. There'd be a back exit that way. He'd take it and just walk out of this shitty place. Back to Florida.

And if I don't make it, he thought, for the first time, I don't make it. *It won't be something I'll ever have to worry about again.*

FOUR UNIFORMED STATE troopers made circuitous paths toward the back of the restaurant, their eyes scanning the dinner tables. What are they looking for, exactly? Hunter wondered. Do they even have a good description of Gil Rankin? Just two photographs that probably look nothing like him.

Hunter walked the other way, through the restaurant toward the front deck, where maybe two dozen people were gathered, watching the police activity. Or lack of it. But as she came through the lobby, she saw him again—the big guy in the Orioles cap.

His eyes briefly met hers but he kept moving. Crossing in front of the lobby bar, under an arrow pointing to REST ROOMS.

Hunter couldn't get a fix on him: Was he trying to hide, or was he just looking for someone? Or did he need to use the bathroom?

She continued to follow, at a distance. Stepping into the corridor to the restrooms. Twenty yards separating them now. Hunter felt her heart shift into overdrive. Still not sure.

At the end of the corridor were two doors. Signs reading SOOKS and JIMMIES.

But he wasn't going there.

Just before the restrooms was a door to the outside—a rear exit to the parking lot. The man slowed at the door and leaned into it. *He's leaving.*

But that still didn't mean anything.

Hunter reached for her gun as the door began to open.

"Gil Rankin!" she shouted.

Something, a slight hesitation. Then he turned to look at her.

"Police!" she said. "Raise your hands!"

The man turned slowly toward her, his back to the door, as if he couldn't understand what she was saying. Then he twisted back to the door and his right hand went inside his coat. It came out, gripping a .45 caliber handgun.

Hunter shot first, catching him in the chest. Rankin fired back, off-balance, the bullet just missing her left arm. She crouched and shot again, shattering the window as he pushed out, stumbling several steps into the parking lot, staggering forward and falling onto his right side. Hunter followed him out, her Beretta aimed double-handed.

She stood several feet away, gun pointed. Rankin lifted his head. He seemed to be looking past her now. And then—what had to've been suicide-by-cop—he slowly aimed his gun at her but didn't fire. Hunter shot him once more in the chest, killing him.

There was an eerie silence then—something that would always stay with her: just her and the dead man, together behind the restaurant, the echo of four gunshots pounding in her head, her heart pumping.

And then the world closed in.

Someone was rushing toward her, pointing a gun. A female agent shouting: "Drop the weapon! Down on the ground. On the ground!"

Hunter dropped her gun and went to her knees. The agent took her down, shoving Hunter forward into the gravel. She broke her fall with the palms of her hands. The agent's knee pressing into her back. She heard more running footsteps, cops' voices shouting.

"Get off me," she managed to say. "State police homicide."

In the confusion that followed, Hunter heard the gruff, steady voice of her boss, Henry Moore. And several onlookers trying to explain what had happened—in that nervous, self-conscious and self-important tone that eyewitnesses often adopted. Finally, the agent let her up.

Hunter stood. Her palms were pocked and bleeding slightly from slamming into the gravel. "Sorry," the female agent said, and tried to give her a soulful look. Hunter turned away. Gil Rankin lay crumpled behind her in a graceless pose, his legs twisted, his torso and head facing the fields. What might have been his escape. There was a cliché about shootouts seeming to happen in slow motion; but it hadn't been like that at all. It had all happened very quickly, too quickly to think or feel anything. It was the first time she had killed someone.

"Stand back! Everybody clear out!" a state trooper was shouting. Police were beginning to manage the scene, stretching crime tape to block the back of the restaurant.

Hunter heard a man say, "I was standing right there when it happened! Right behind her!" His voice nearly hysterical.

Diners looked out, their faces pressed to the glass. The band had stopped, the sound of human celebration stilled. The air smelling of steamed seafood mixed now with gunpowder.

Hunter walked with Crowe and Moore to the edge of the lot. She couldn't stop thinking about the agent getting on top of her and putting the gun to her head. It brought back everything that had happened fifteen years ago, when she was a junior in high school, out on a cool spring night in Pennsylvania, a lot like this one. A crime that had shaken her life, the reason that she'd gone into law enforcement, thinking maybe she could prevent that kind of thing from happening to anyone else. Now, she could maneuver in dark places; then, she couldn't; now, she could make an intelligent decision on her own; then, it had been difficult.

She carried the image of Gil Rankin's twisted legs in her head as they walked back, and she felt a strange, fleeting satisfaction, as if she'd finally gotten even for the event that had altered her life, even though this had nothing to do with it.

Ten minutes later she was inside the restaurant, giving a statement to Crowe. This was an FBI case now. Crowe's case.

"Funny how things change so quickly," she said.

"Yes. It is."

An hour earlier the table had been covered with steamed crabs and pitchers of Chesapeake beer.

Hunter was surprised to look up when they were finished and see how the crowd in the lot had thinned to almost nothing. The last of the cars lining up now to go through the police checkpoint. To go home. Police lights still spinning blue and red. She wondered whether Rankin might've slipped away if she hadn't spotted him. Instead, evidence techs were photographing his body behind the restaurant.

"You all right?" Crowe said. The two of them walking through the cool air across the gravel, unnoticed again in the darkness. His hand splayed across her upper back.

"I guess."

"You did good. You did the right thing."

"I did what he wanted me to do," Hunter said.

Her eyes were on the farmland. That's exactly what it felt like. *She'd done what he wanted her to do.* She'd given him an out. Maybe not the one he ultimately wanted, but for him it was better than being caught. Somehow, that made her feel taken advantage of, complicit in his escape.

As they drove back, she imagined what would follow: She'd be placed on administrative leave while a largely meaningless, bureaucratic "internal investigation" was conducted. She'd be assigned a counselor and maybe given some kind of interim desk job. Hunter knew the drill, and it pissed her off. It was exactly what she didn't want. Now more than anything, she wanted to keep working. She wanted to finish this case.

"Did Jackson Pynne die?" she asked as Crowe sped through the dark farmland.

"Critical. They're operating on him."

"Anyone else?"

"One of the guards was hit. In the arm. He'll survive."

"Will Jackson?"

"They don't know yet."

Hunter leaned back and watched the clear sky, the round bright moon, comfortable not speaking, following the turns in the road as if they were leading them toward some great truth at the heart of a larger mystery. She thought about Jackson Pynne, basking in the attention of the journalists moments before he was shot, and the look of sweetness on the pastor's face as he watched. *How innocent that all seems now.*

At her apartment, Hunter ate a Swiss cheese sandwich and drank a glass of red wine. Afterward, she held Winston tightly to her chest. His protests were minimal tonight, as if he knew that she needed a good hug, even if it wasn't reciprocal. Finally, she changed to pajamas, brushed her teeth, and got into bed. She fell asleep quickly, and slept straight through until morning.

When the sunlight woke her, she was surprised to see that it was past eight o'clock.

She lay in bed for several minutes, blinking at the light through the blinds, remembering all of the details from the night before. Winston was sitting on her desk, his normal morning spot, staring at her sternly, anticipating his tuna snack, as if it were any other day.

Even then, though, Hunter knew.

The car that Rankin had been driving was a dark-colored Mazda. She knew that car. She'd recognized the winglike logo design on the back as he rose over the berm into the parking lot at Gracie's Crab House.

That's why'd he'd gotten stuck in the mud.

She rose from bed at last and fixed coffee and toast. After a while her phone rang.

"How are you feeling?" Crowe asked.

"All right, I guess. You?"

"Good. You sleep at all?"

"I slept well. I guess everything caught up with me. Where are you?"

"Down the road. Coming to get you."

"Okay. How's Jackson Pynne this morning?"

"Still in the hospital. We don't know yet."

She could hear it in his voice, too. In the way he paused after saying that. People saying more in their silences than with their words.

"They just now found something out at the house," Crowe said.

"The house."

"Yeah, out at Jimmy Creek. Where Rankin was staying. State police CSI is out there."

Hunter didn't say anything else. She showered quickly, feeling a terrible dread, hoping she was wrong. Then she dressed and went online, just to see the AP's headline: PRAYING WOMAN SUSPECT GUNNED DOWN. About what she'd expected. She signed off and hugged Winston again. "'Bye, sweet Winnie," she said.

The sky was perfect that morning, a luminous blue that reminded her of precious china. A cool breeze pulled through the shadows, but with currents of the warmer air that was coming, that would transform Tidewater County, as it did every summer.

Crowe's car rounded a corner of the marina and pulled beside her. Hunter got in.

They traveled in silence, southeast, into the low-lying maze of creeks and tributaries. Finally, she said, "Go ahead and tell me about it."

Crowe sighed. Hunter watched the fields and the creek paths.

"It's Ship," she said, making it easier. "Right?"

"I'm sorry . . ." he began.

Hunter watched the scenery as he explained, too angry to respond. A chevron of geese flapped lazily overhead, above the breezy tide flats and creeks and narrows, out over a blue bay inlet where the troughs of the waves looked like broken glass reflecting the sky. Her eyes smarted with tears, one of which spilled over and ran down her cheek.

Crowe parked on the gravel drive that ran along the side of the house. A soft wind blew over the sunlit lawn. For a few moments it seemed as if each blade was glowing.

She felt herself tearing up again as she rounded the side of the house, seeing the evidence markers on the ground. State police commander Gary Martin turned to greet her, keeping his head down as he made his way up the lawn with his lumbering walk.

"Hunter."

"'Morning."

"I'm sorry," he said. "They found your partner."

"I know."

"Ship."

"Yeah, I know," she said, an edge in her voice; for some reason, she hadn't wanted him to say his name out loud. Crime scene techs were down by the marsh, combing the grass for evidence. "I'd like to see."

They walked side by side, silently, down to the marsh, and then he led her into the waist-tall grasses at the edge of the narrow creek.

Ben Shipman lay facedown in the shallow water, wearing his lumberjack coat, curls of red hair floating on the surface. He must've found Rankin's hideout shortly before Jackson Pynne was released, she thought. He might've stopped him. He was that close. But Kirby Moss must've cut him down from a distance with his sniper's rifle—the way he'd cut down Jackson Pynne.

"What's he doing *there*?"

"There're two sets of shoe prints. He must've been carried. Looks like there's some blood at the end of the drive. He was probably shot as soon as he stepped out of his car."

Why hadn't he called in to the command post? Hunter wondered. A question with no answer. Who knows? Sometimes people go on strange private pursuits, their own hero's quests, and don't come back. Gil Rankin had taken Shipman's Mazda last night and driven it across the soybean and cornfields after killing Kirby Moss, and it was Shipman's car and the waterlogged soil of

Tidewater County that had prevented his escape. There was some small satisfaction in knowing that. For just a moment it caused her to smile. *Poetic justice.*

She thanked the police commander and walked by herself toward the house, her eyes tearing up again. Everything felt different, a way it had never felt before—the sunlight on the grass, the weight of the air, the rhythms of the wind and the motion of the water. None of it quite real. Or maybe the opposite. Maybe she was really paying attention at last—seeing and hearing clearly. Hunter stopped. That's when she realized that she needed to talk with the pastor.

Chapter 55

LUKE BOWERS SAT in the ICU waiting room at Tidewater Memorial Hospital paging absently through a well-thumbed copy of *Esquire* magazine. He was still hoping to hear from Jackson Pynne's sister and daughter. State police investigators had found a phone number for the daughter and he'd left messages, but so far she hadn't returned his calls. He was the only one in the waiting room now. Earlier, he'd consoled a woman in her forties whose husband's appendix had ruptured early that morning.

Remarkably, Jackson Pynne was going to live, the surgeon had told him. The bullet had cut a path through the side of Jackson's head, just grazing his brain. He was on a ventilator. Doctors had removed part of his skull to allow room for the swelling in his brain. He was unable to speak, but was responding to doctors by squeezing with his hand and holding up his pinkie finger. The nature of his permanent injuries—if there were any—wasn't yet known. The fact that he was going to survive seemed to Luke somehow in keeping with Jackson's peculiar luck, and his uncanny resilience. If his head had been tilted an inch in any other direction, he'd be dead, the doctor told him.

Charlotte had sat with Luke for much of the night. She'd gone out to buy them egg sandwiches and sat with him a while longer, before leaving to take care of Sneakers. Several of the Buntings had found him here and pressed him for an on-the-record statement. Luke had politely declined.

As he got up now to stretch his legs, his cell phone rang: Amy Hunter. Luke hadn't spoken to her since before the shooting. He wondered if she was all right.

"Ben Shipman was killed last night," Hunter told him. "They discovered him this morning. He's just lying in the marsh creek. We're waiting for EMS. No one's said a prayer for him. No one's done anything—"

"Tell me where you are," Luke said. "I'll come right over."

HUNTER WATCHED THE moist shadows along the empty two-lane road at the top of the drive. She couldn't stop thinking about the final moments of Ben Shipman's life—or the last, seemingly inconsequential time she had spoken to him. *See you later,* she'd said. His last words to her were *Ten-four.* He'd walked away from her with his distinctive Ben Shipman walk and hadn't looked back. Why should he have? Something was bothering him, but of course she had no way of knowing that would be the last time they'd ever see each other alive. He must've died instantly, at least, unable to process what had happened.

She waved as Luke arrived. He slid the driver's window down and looked at her with his steady blue eyes.

"You okay?"

"I guess, thanks for coming."

"I'm sorry," he said.

The car slow-rocked down the gravel road to the house. Luke parked and they walked across the lawn to the marshlands.

"I won't ask you why this happened," she said after they stopped by the water. "Because I know you'd say that's the kind of question you can't answer. Or you'd say that there's no place that evil can't find us."

"It's true, unfortunately."

"But when it does, we have to meet evil with grace."

"Yes."

They lowered their heads and Luke prayed for Ben Shipman, for his family, for his soul, for his deliverance. He quoted the verse on tribulation from Romans that she'd told him Shipman's father used to recite—how "tribulation produces perseverance; and perseverance, character; and character, hope."

"In this dark time," Luke said, "we embrace hope not as wishful thinking, but as evidence of our faith in God's plan."

Afterward, Hunter clenched her eyes, feeling empty as she listened to the ephemeral play of the grasses in the breeze, recalling what Luke had said in a sermon about the soul's evolution in silence. *Have faith in silence. Let us empty our souls of distraction and really listen to what God has to tell us.*

She opened her eyes and was startled by how bright everything seemed. She looked at Luke and managed a smile.

"Thank you," she said. "Thank you for coming here."

Luke reached to take her hand. But Hunter opened her arms and pulled him against her, and she felt him hugging her back; holding tight, to something not there. She was pleased to see, after they stepped apart, that his eyes, too, had moistened.

"Thank you," she said again.

DAVE CROWE WAS watching from the porch as Luke crossed the lawn to his car. He stepped out, signaling Hunter.

"Come on inside," he said. "I want to show you something."

FBI techs had gone into Rankin's computer overnight and also pulled evidence from suitcases, briefcases and the Jeep parked by Whistling Swan Drive. They'd already found several electronic records, he said, of elaborate wire transfers from Trumble's charities and businesses into private accounts.

"It's a spiderweb," Crowe said, in officious mode again for the first time since the shooting. They were standing in the living room, furnished expensively with dark wood and leather. "Some of the numbers are lining up with what we found earlier."

"How do you mean?"

"It's starting to look like Gil Rankin may've set up this whole thing," he went on. "Chandler transferred the money, but Rankin was drawing it from the fourth account, the primary account. It'll take a while to sort it all out, of course."

"Wait—you're saying Rankin was the ringleader of the embezzlement operation?"

He tilted his head and raised his eyebrows affirmatively.

"No," she said. "I don't believe that."

"Okay. I'm just telling you what we've found. Between us. Don't pass final judgment until you've seen all the evidence."

Hunter turned away. She didn't believe it. Not for a minute. She believed her instincts. Gil Rankin may have been at all of the murder scenes; he'd probably been responsible for leaving behind the calling cards. But he wasn't the Psalmist. He hadn't ordered the killings. And he hadn't embezzled the money.

She felt angry that she might not be able to prove that. Angrier still at the possibility that the real crimes might become unprovable. And that Trumble might have even planned it that way.

"Have a look at this," Crowe said.

In a drawer of the nightstand by the bed where Rankin had slept was an open Bible.

Hunter leaned closer and saw that it was opened to the Book of Psalms.

"It was there when we entered overnight. We've pulled finger-prints from the cover."

How convenient, Hunter thought.

"August Trumble did this," she said. "Right?"

"I don't know." Hunter could see that, for whatever reason, Crowe wasn't with her anymore. "It's starting to look like maybe Gil Rankin did this. On his own."

No. Hunter walked back up the drive to wait for EMS, her thoughts with Ship again. It still didn't seem real. Not at all. It seemed there must be some way of pulling him back, of rewinding events. She wanted more than anything to call him now, meet him at McDonald's and tell him what Crowe had just said to her. Couldn't she have said something that would have stopped him from coming here? She felt herself beginning to cry. That's our life, she thought; it unwinds and there's no more. At the top of the drive, she turned into the breeze and closed her eyes, losing herself for a few moments in the sweet silence.

As she wiped the tears away, she noticed something weird—the number on the side of the mail box: 1848. Written across the rusty metal with black marker. A very strange detail, particularly since the mailbox right next to it was numbered 134.

Chapter 56

LUKE DROVE TOWARD the bay, feeling sickened by the image of Ben Shipman's half-submerged body untended in the creek. And by Amy Hunter's raw hurt. It was his job to help people through difficult crossings, when faith and grace seemed to abandon them, to walk with his congregants from shattering events that appeared to defy all they'd learned from Scripture. Tomorrow, Sunday, the good people of Tidewater County would again gather in his sanctuary, expecting him to make some sense of a senseless tragedy and to answer questions that he, too, was asking this morning. What could he tell them that would explain it? How could he conjure light from such dark passages? He didn't know, he didn't have a clue. He only knew that somehow, by faith and prayer and divine inspiration, he would do it, that was his job. Somehow, he would tell them about faith and trust, good and evil; together they would pray, and in doing so, would prevent evil from claiming a victory.

On Main Street he stopped at Palmer's Florist to buy a rose for Charlotte.

He smiled at the pretty young woman behind the counter, whose hair was bundled up in a bouffant. She seemed like someone from an earlier time, long before tragedy had come to Tidewater County.

To make conversation, he asked if the owner was around.

"You mean Mr. Palmer?"

"Yes, George."

"No, he's not. He doesn't live here. We never see Mr. Palmer."

"Oh," Luke said. He peered through the plate glass at the street, struck by the absence of traffic or pedestrians. "But he was here last week, right? Last Wednesday?"

"Mr. Palmer? No, I don't believe so. We never see him."

"Oh." Luke had a funny feeling then. A strange intuition. He smiled a goodbye, took the rose and walked to his car, struck once more by the emptiness. Even at the Blue Crab Diner, where there were only two cars out front.

Driving to the bluff above the Chesapeake, he thought, as he often did, about his blessings—Charlotte, Sneakers, his ministry, his friends, his health, his life in Tidewater County.

The sun was higher now, glittering out across the bay. He sat in his car and thought a little more about tomorrow's sermon. *Tribulation. Good and evil.* People had their ideas about that. Gil Rankin would be portrayed as "pure" evil by some, Luke supposed; but evil was usually more complicated than that. It wasn't pure, that was the problem. Thinking of a verse from Romans—about striving to walk in wisdom—he opened his Bible. But instead he turned to the Book of Psalms. Recalling the marker-scrawled number he'd seen on the mailbox as he'd left Hunter and the property on Jimmy Creek, where Gil Rankin had stayed; the number on the box at the top of the gravel lane: 1848.

He flipped pages to Psalm 18, scanned down to verse 48, and read:

He delivers me from my enemies. You also lift me up above those who rise against me; You have delivered me from the violent man.

After a moment, Luke got out. He stood on the edge of the bluff, taking the breeze, looking up the coastline at the docks and marinas and jetties and expensive homes, the restless ebb and flow of the waves, imagining the dark thoughts Hunter was dealing with right now.

He's a violent man. That's what Kwan Park called Gil Rankin, according to Jackson.

So was this Trumble's last message? If so, where was August Trumble now?

SNEAKERS'S PAWS SCRAMBLED on the hardwood floor as Luke came in the house. "How's my boy," he said. The dog galloped clumsily, nudging frantically against him. Luke took him into the sitting room and indulged Sneakers's desire for a vigorous neck and chin rub.

"Where's your mom?" he said after a few minutes of it. "Let's go find your mom."

There was a strange quiet in the house, which seemed to match the quiet outside. Sneakers led him down the wooden hallway into the kitchen, where a seafood stew was cooking. Charlotte was in her study, working, her music playing loudly.

"I'm sorry," she said, looking up. "I didn't hear you."

"No, keep working." She turned down the music. "Anything new?"

"Not really."

But she could see that there was, so she got up and walked to him and they embraced. Even in the saddest times, Charlotte was able to summon the good things. They held each other for a long time, as Sneakers settled by their feet. There was really nothing to say.

Chapter 57

After lunching alone on oysters Rockefeller and a glass of Riesling in the dining room at the Harbor View restaurant, August Trumble stepped out into the crisp Maine afternoon. He was a thin, medium-sized man in his early sixties with silver hair, dark, piercing eyes, and otherwise unremarkable features.

The sun caught him full on the face as he stood in the doorway zipping his jacket, looking at the sky as anyone would coming outside from inside. But what he did next surprised Amy Hunter. His eyes seemed to pick her out and stay with her. Then he twisted his lips into a thin smile, as if he knew exactly why she was there and what was about to happen.

Six FBI agents surrounded August Trumble, guns drawn. The show of force, for such an unassuming-looking man, would have seemed incongruous to anyone who didn't know Trumble's story, a tale that had played out away from public view. But for more than a decade Trumble had been a maddeningly elusive target, according to Crowe. A man with insidiously powerful control over other people, particularly those who worked for him.

Trumble hid in the lives of "ordinary" people. It was Luke Bowers who figured out that one of those identities—which Trumble had invented, and inhabited—was George Palmer, proprietor of a modest florist shop in Tidewater County, Maryland. From that speculation the FBI had managed to follow Trumble here to this tiny island off the coast of Maine, and to one of his other identities. He lived in coastal Maine as Roy Hinders, a likable but very private man who owned only a bicycle for transportation, enjoyed good wines, and ran a very small, part-time tax preparation business out of his home.

As agents cuffed his hands behind his back, Trumble struck Hunter as preternaturally calm and courteous, even while informing them that they had the wrong man.

He was smiling faintly as troopers pushed him into the back of a patrol car. But there was an unsettling afterimage that he left with her. *His eyes.* Dark, probing, as if they could see her fears and motivations.

Hunter rode in the front seat of the car transporting Trumble to a helicopter that would take him to the mainland. Crowe had made a point of making this happen, Hunter riding with him as if it were some sort of prize for her role in the apprehension. Crowe and the Bureau agents followed in three police cars, a state trooper on motorcycle leading the procession. The FBI would place Trumble on a plane to Baltimore, where he would be interrogated and charged. There was enough certainty now and enough people involved that Hunter wasn't worried about him slipping away.

She thought of Ben Shipman again as they rode down the winding two-lane through the Maine pinewoods. Several times a day she still felt the itch to press Ship's number on her cell phone, to ask his opinion on something, knowing it would please him to hear from her. Two days ago dozens of uniformed law enforcement officers from throughout the mid-Atlantic region had turned out for Shipman's funeral, forming a mile-long procession of official vehicles to Ship's final resting spot at the tiny Tidewater cemetery. The moving tributes to Ben Shipman that day, and the military band playing "Going Home" by Dvorak, had reduced many in attendance to tears and raw emotion, including Hunter.

After the funeral ceremony she had spent time with Ship's ex-wife Donna and sixteen-year-old daughter Rebecca, who'd driven up from North Carolina for the service. She'd bonded with Becca in particular, who had Ship's earnest blue eyes, auburn hair, and stocky build. In their car, Hunter noticed the *Beatles 1967-70* CD, which Becca said her father had given her for her fourteenth birthday. Then she and Becca had gone through Ship's apartment together and cleared out his office, filling the trunk and back seat of the car with boxes of his stuff. Before leaving, Donna, who was far less outgoing than Becca, had invited Hunter to visit them in North Carolina. "Any time," she'd said. It saddened Hunter to think about that now. It was the sort of invitation people extended and then forgot about. Visiting would be too sad, she imagined, for all of them.

In Maine, the cars came to a stop in a grass field by the harbor. The driver, a Bureau agent with close-cropped hair and small, hard eyes, stepped out. Hunter opened her door and looked at the dull light over the harbor. There was something about the breeze here, the raw wet smell, that made her feel hopeful. I know the story now, she thought. I just have to make sure that it gets told properly.

Then she realized that Trumble, his hands manacled behind him in the backseat, was saying something to her. They were momentarily alone in the car together and he was asking her a question. "Do you have the time?"

He asked again, leaning forward.

Hunter glanced back. His eyes trying to lock onto hers.

"Time? Twelve forty-seven."

Trumble kept staring at her as he tried to engage her in conversation. Hunter didn't respond, got out of the car and stood beside it. There was something off about the man, something too vibrant and too strange. The smile and the eyes . . . he didn't seem quite human. You could get sucked into those eyes, she thought.

She took a deep breath of the briny air, waiting for Crowe, her primal instincts telling her to keep away from August Trumble. To never even look at him again if she didn't have to.

Chapter 58

UNSEASONABLY WARM WEATHER came to Tidewater County the second week of April, leading many locals to believe—prematurely—that the long cold winter had finally lifted. The weekend streets and seafood eateries were busy again with tourists. Sounds of motorboats, morning lawn mowers, and afternoon baseball carried through the county air. The drugstore aisles smelled pleasantly of garden hoses, rubber rafts, and flip-flops. Everything felt new again.

The shift in mood was a source of apprehension, though, for Amy Hunter—a feeling that the season was passing and the people of Tidewater would soon be occupied with the business of summer, with new, more pressing concerns. Her boss, Henry Moore, had allowed the Kwan Park case to remain open, but local officials were pressuring the state police to close it. Sheriff Calvert, citing the fact that both murderers—Gil Rankin and Kirby Moss—"are as dead as they're ever going to be," told the *Tidewater Times* that it was "a rookie mistake" not to close the case. "I don't know what the girl's thinking," he said in a front-page story.

Dave Crowe, who had become worse about returning calls, seemed uninterested in bringing charges against Trumble for the "Psalmist" killings. And Hunter was beginning to think there might be problems with the federal fraud and racketeering case against Trumble as well. The search of the "Roy Hinders" house in Maine had turned up virtually nothing, other than his fingerprints. And one of the key witnesses against Trumble was wavering about whether she would testify.

Ownership of the house at Jimmy Creek was traced through property records to George Palmer. On the adjacent land, across a gravel drive, was the house where Palmer himself had resided. It had been strange going in, finding the place filled with flowers—plastic and cloth flowers crowding every room, roses, tulips, orchids, hydrangeas, sunflowers, lilacs—along with paintings and photographs of flowers on every wall. A House of Flowers. But nothing to incriminate August Trumble for murder.

To Hunter, the worst part of the case was what the media had made of it—referring now to Gil Rankin as the "Psalmist," portraying him as a conscienceless monster who had betrayed his boss, the reclusive philanthropist August Trumble, then brutally murdered four coworkers who he thought were double-crossing him.

Weighed down by all of these developments, she decided to turn in at the church to see what Pastor Luke had to say. It'd been more than a week since they talked.

THIS WAS TUESDAY, a metallic blue afternoon, the dockside restaurants and oyster bars all doing brisk business, the bay dotted with sailboats. But at the Methodist church there were only two cars—Luke's Ford Fusion and, beside it, Aggie Collins's Lexus.

Hunter was surprised when Luke's dog came bounding through Aggie's office, barking at her as soon as she opened the door.

Aggie immediately stood up behind her desk, as if an alarm had sounded.

"Come here, Sneakers!" Luke called, clapping his hands. "Sneakers! Down. Please!"

Sneakers lowered his head and began to sniff eagerly at Hunter's shoes and jeans, his tail clipping like a metronome. She reached down to rub his neck.

"Sorry, I think he was just startled for a moment," Luke said. "My wife's out of town today, doing some research in Washington. She left me with babysitting chores. I thought it'd do him some good to spend a little time at the church. Come on back."

Luke closed the door to his office behind them, and Hunter took a seat in front of his desk. Sneakers, already tired of her, trotted to the oval throw rug in a corner and settled on his side.

"Hope you don't mind me coming in unannounced," she said. "I just wanted to get your feedback on a couple of things."

"Sure. Which things?" Luke asked.

"The Kwan Park case."

"Oh," he said, "those things."

"Yeah." Hunter sighed. She was reminded of the first time she had talked with Luke, sitting in this same chair, on a cold, windy morning the day after he'd discovered Kwan Park's body in the sanctuary. "Unfortunately, the case has kind of reached a dead end. I have to admit, it's a little disconcerting the way the media's been covering it."

"They've started calling Gil Rankin the 'Psalmist,' I noticed." Luke folded his hands on his desk.

"Yeah, which is just what August Trumble wants, I would imagine," Hunter said. "We're getting a little pressure to close the case. Fortunately, I have a boss who has faith in me. But I sense it has a shelf life. The problem is, there are these two stories out there."

"The one that's being told in the papers and the real one?"

"Yeah, exactly." She liked the knowing look in his eyes; he was right with her, same as before, making this easy. "Unfortunately," she said, "the one that's being told in the papers is stealing all the oxygen from the real story."

"The one that's being told in the papers makes August Trumble seem like the victim."

"Right," Hunter said, "and Rankin the bad guy. Rankin took advantage of Trumble, that's the story. He embezzled millions of dollars from the companies he was supposed to be protecting. He enlisted these four people to help him. Then he became greedy, or mistrustful, or paranoid, and killed them."

"But of course that's not the real story."

"No. Although all of those people are dead now, so none of them can refute it." Hunter's eyes misted for a moment. "The real story starts with what Crowe told me several weeks ago—how August Trumble operates a large, sophisticated criminal organization with a number of untraceable shell companies and banking havens, which has been stealing money from state and federal governments for years, through lotteries and income tax fraud, then pumping some of it into charities."

"Helping the poor and downtrodden, supposedly."

"Supposedly," Hunter said. "Then, at some point, Trumble found out that the FBI had inside information about these operations and was beginning to close in on him. Trumble's plan was to disband the organization before that happened. And to disappear into one of these four or five—or who knows how many—identities he created for himself. Hiding in the lives of ordinary people. In small towns around the country."

"Like George Palmer."

"Or Roy Hinders, yes. And there he could quietly write his story, telling the world who he really is and what his organization has done."

"And in the process, become an outlaw hero of sorts," Luke said.

"Or a modern-day David, as Detective Crowe said. But Trumble must have figured that his only chance to get away safely was to eliminate the handful of people in the organization who knew what he was really doing—who knew his secrets and could hurt him. Maybe he was being paranoid, but it was all very calculated.

"Trumble offered Rankin millions of dollars, presumably, to carry out that operation. Trumble's only stipulation being that Rankin must leave a calling card from the Book of Psalms with each victim. The Psalmist killings were punishments, in Trumble's mind, for what he perceived as acts of betrayal—acts that he saw as sabotaging his worthy enterprise. To cover himself, they then needed to frame someone else."

"Jackson Pynne."

"Yes—who had been Kwan Park's lover and an accomplice to her betrayal. So a very appropriate fall guy, in Trumble's mind. Rankin framed him with the cigarette butts and the shoe prints. He probably collected the butts before Jackson came back to Tidewater. The boots, he or Kirby Moss wore and then placed in Jackson's garage on Monday or early Tuesday.

"That was the plan as presented to Rankin: eliminate four disloyal employees and set up the killings so that Pynne takes the rap. But then something changed. Trumble must have told Rankin that Pynne knew too much and couldn't be trusted. He didn't just need to be framed, he needed to be taken out, too. This was presented to Rankin as a new development, although it was probably Trumble's plan all along—to set up Rankin as the *real* fall guy."

"So Rankin did all this without knowing that he was setting *himself* up," Luke said. "That must've been kind of like working for the devil."

"Yes, exactly," Hunter said. "To Rankin, leaving the Psalms verses behind seemed like some twisted message on Trumble's part. But he didn't realize that in the process of doing so, he was setting himself up. That he was making himself the Psalmist.

"That was the truly brilliant part of Trumble's plan," she went on. "That he made sure there were key pieces of evidence left behind to implicate Rankin—including the Bible in the bed stand at the house where Rankin was staying, opened to the Book of Psalms. And records of wire transfers on Rankin's computers, making it appear that *he* had master-minded an embezzling scheme against Trumble's organization."

"Creating the appearance of a motive. And identifying Rankin as the Psalmist."

"Yes. And once the media picks a tag like that . . ."

Luke turned his eyes out the window. Hunter looked, too, at the long shadow of the church, and beyond the bluff, sunlight glittering across the bay.

"I can see how that would be a problem," he said.

"It is." Hunter felt her eyes moisten with frustration. "Crowe knows what really happened, but he won't move forward with it. He thinks it's too hard to prove. He's having enough trouble with the racketeering case against Trumble. I don't know if it's because of Sheila Patterson, who was a Bureau informant who got killed. Or troubles with evidence. But for whatever reason, he's barely talking to me anymore."

Hunter looked at Sneakers, sleeping peacefully on the rug beside his tiny reindeer toy, facing the wall, his chest slowly lifting up and down, up and down.

"And what about the prosecutors in these other jurisdictions?" Luke said. "The other murders?"

"They seem to be buying into the story that Rankin and Moss were the killers. Virginia has closed its case now that Rankin's dead. I'm afraid the other two will probably follow suit."

"So, another problem."

"Yeah. There's this widespread feeling, with Rankin and Moss now both dead, what's the point of keeping the case open?"

Luke winced. "Just a little matter of the truth?"

"Yes," Hunter said, "that little matter. My boss told me to do what I think is right. I'm now officially reinstated. So, in a sense, it's up to me." She watched a heron rising from the edge of the parking lot and flap through the shade toward the bay, and she felt the drag of all the forces working against her. "I just have this feeling that Trumble's in jail waiting for me now. Maybe thinking that I'm the last impediment to his freedom. Waiting for me to finally let it go. To give up the case. To save him."

"Well," Luke said. "You know what my response would be to that?"

"What?"

"Don't do it. Ever." He gave her an affirming look, and Hunter began to smile, realizing that was what she'd wanted to hear. Maybe it was why she'd come here. "I'm reminded of what someone else said once about the truth," Luke added. "Someone rather famous."

Hunter watched his steady blue eyes. She took a guess. "You mean how it'll set you free?"

"Yes, that's it."

She glanced out at the shade across the parking lot and the tall marsh grasses waving in the distance and felt something new guiding her, something she might not have recognized two or three months ago. She stood.

"Thanks," she said. "I think I just needed someone to tell me that."

Luke and Sneakers arrived at the cottage a few minutes past six-thirty. Seeing Charlotte's BMW parked in the drive made him feel like a little boy. "She's home!" he said to Sneakers.

It was still light out, but the air had turned cooler with evening shadows. Charlotte was at the stove, making dinner, listening to something modern-sounding—Holst, Luke guessed, or maybe Golijov, the composer she'd been telling him about. Sneakers immediately ran to greet her.

"How was the trip?"

Leaning in over Sneakers, he just managed to plant a kiss on Charlotte's mouth.

"Very productive. Did my men behave while I was gone?"

"What do you say, Sneaks, did we behave?"

The dog was already on his side, his tail thumping the floor.

Charlotte crouched and asked in a baby voice, "How's my little boy-child today? Did you miss me? You *did*? Well, I missed you more."

She looked at Luke and raised her eyebrows, as if it was his turn. Then straightened.

"Something's on your mind."

"Yeah." He had been wondering if he should share Amy Hunter's problem with Charlotte. Now, seeing her concerned eyes, he recognized that of course he would. Charlotte would have an idea. Who knows? If nothing else worked out, maybe she'd decide to write the story herself. Charlotte still had the ability to surprise him, to lead them into unexpected directions like a sudden wind that picks up seeds and carries them to new life.

HUNTER DRANK SEVERAL glasses of red wine, sitting barefoot on her back porch. She watched the sky darken around the marina, working out a new plan in her head.

Later, deep in the night, she heard voices across the water, through screen windows and open patio doors, the sounds that always came with warmer weather—drunken bursts of laughter, uninhibited crescendos of conversation.

She dozed for a while with the window open, waking to a cool silence and feeling Winston breathing against her arm. Wondering if Luke was awake. Remembering what he'd told her that afternoon.

But then she began to hear a different voice, this one in her head: The strange intonations of August Trumble on the day they had finally caught up with him. Trumble's voice as disorienting to her as his appearance—a slightly high pitch, sprinkled with odd, lilting words and inflections that seemed to belong to some earlier time in history.

She blinked in the darkness, wide-awake, recalling their brief exchange once again. A conversation heard by only two people.

What time do you have?

Time? Twelve forty-seven.

Really? No, Trumble said. *I don't believe that's right. I daresay it's much later than that.*

Then she had turned away and stepped outside the car, deciding not to engage with August Trumble again. Because something about the man wasn't right. Something she couldn't explain and didn't want to think about. The way he had spoken to her felt like a summons, sent from the recesses of some ancient, unrequited yearning, from the subterranean places he dwelled, dreaming his dark dreams of redemption, places Trumble would never really be able to leave despite his efforts to live in the open, to be one of us. Sometimes, your curiosity lets you go through those doorways; sometimes, your instincts tell you to stay on this side, knowing the door may close behind you and never open again.

Trumble wasn't finished, though. He had spoken to her one more time, saying, *I've got one thirty-eight or seven.*

Those were the words Hunter couldn't get out of her head now. The peculiar, distinct way he pronounced them—the second part, *or seven,* more drawn-out than the first, like a recording that had been slowed down.

One thirty-eight or seven.

Only now, in the darkness, she heard it differently: Without the *or.*

One thirty-eight. Seven.

138:7.

"Shit!" She clicked on the nightstand lamp and threw back her bedspread. "Sorry," she said to Winston, who was now covered to his head. "I have to look this up."

As Hunter paged through the Book of Psalms, Winston sat and watched her.

And then he purred, for reasons that only Winston understood.

Acknowledgments

Thanks to Laura Gross for your support, enthusiasm, and many suggestions along the way.

And to Emily Krump, whose editorial guidance was invaluable and helped to shape several of the characters in this book/series.

I am also grateful to Joseph Gamble, commander of the homicide unit of the Maryland State Police, who answered my many questions about murder investigations and provided the Chesapeake Bay "fog" comparison for cases without an ID or a suspect.

About the Author

James Lilliefors is the author of the geopolitical thriller novels *The Leviathan Effect* and *Viral*. A journalist and novelist who grew up near Washington DC, Lilliefors is also the author of three nonfiction books. He writes the Bowers and Hunter series for Witness. For more information go to www.jameslilliefors.com.

Visit www.AuthorTracker.com for exclusive information on your favorite HarperCollins authors.